The Cabalist's Daughter

A Novel of Practical Messianic Redemption

by **Yori Yanover**

Dearest Yossi & Brooke, A huge mazal tov on your new sweetie. This may be a good time to read up on the cosmic connection between fathers and their daughters... All the best [signature] 10/24/08

Ben Yehuda Press
Teaneck, New Jersey

THE CABALIST'S DAUGHTER. ©2008 Yori Yanover. All rights reserved. No part of this book may be used or reproduced in any manner whatsoever without written permission except in the case of brief quotations embodied in critical articles and reviews.

Published by Ben Yehuda Press
430 Kensington Road
Teaneck, NJ 07666
http://www.BenYehudaPress.com

Ben Yehuda Press books may be purchased for educational, business or sales promotional use. For information, please contact: Special Markets, Ben Yehuda Press, 430 Kensington Road, Teaneck, NJ 07666. markets@BenYehudaPress.com.

Cover illustration: Maljuk/istockphoto. helicopter & rabbi elements: Salome Worch

This is a work of fiction and any resemblance between the characters and persons living or dead is purely coincidental.

paper
ISBN13 978-0-9789980-9-7
ISBN 0-9789980-9-X

Library of Congress Cataloging-in-Publication Data

Yanover, Yori.
The cabalist's daughter : a novel of practical messianic redemption / by Yori Yanover. -- 1st ed.
p. cm.
ISBN 978-0-9789980-9-7
1. Cabala--Fiction. I. Title.
PS3625.A686C33 2008
813'.6--dc22

2008030528

1st edition
08 09 10 / 10 9 8 7 6 5 4 3 2 1

To my friend and teacher,
Rabbi Hershy Worch,
from whom I've stolen so much...

The people of a small Jewish town were concerned that if the Messiah were to come upon them suddenly, he'd find them unwashed and in their weekday clothes. So they hired Berel to sit a mile out of town and be the messianic announcer.

His cousin Shmerel finds him sitting on the road. "What's up?" Shmerel asks.

"I'm the official messianic announcer," Berel answers.

"Ah.... So, how much does it pay?" Shmerel asks admiringly.

"I'll tell you," Berel confides. "The pay is not great, but for job security, you can't beat it!"

— old Jewish folktale

Forward

THE CABALIST'S HANDBOOK OF PRACTICAL MESSIANIC REDEMPTION devotes a great deal of space and persuasive effort to clarify that God is not Satan's enemy; rather, Satan is an aspect of God, a very Dark Aspect—indeed, the darkest God Himself could imagine.

One of the HANDBOOK's earliest entries states:

> There is no war between God and Samael*. Know that even when it appears as if the Angel of the Dark is defying the will of the Cosmic King, he is entirely without freedom and is only carrying out God's mission.
>
> This will explain why the poor Devil is so full of venom these days: He loyally fulfills his Master's bidding and receives only bad publicity for his efforts. Some scholars suggest the Prince of Darkness is way too enthusiastic in the pursuit of his foul duties. It's one thing to spread misery around because you have to; it's quite another to enjoy it so much.
>
> It comes down to the basic cosmic need that drives humans and supernaturals alike: the need to be acknowledged. Considering the trouble Lucifer regularly endures merely for carrying out God's nastier designs, he feels entitled to some appreciation. The lack of it has always been his secret pain.
>
> And you thought Satan was scary and dark and smelly. Not at all! Satan is a fuzzy chick trotting down a marsh path under a cloudless, blue sky.

---

* The name comes from the same Hebrew root as *semol*, or "left side." In Aramaic, this quality of the Divine is referred to as *sitra achra*, the "other side." Samael is Satan's angelic name.

Book 1

The beginning of the end

1.

The end-run of an ancient plot against God required the services of an innocent-looking black Cadillac at the far end of Springfield Boulevard in Queens. Countless Jews and gentiles who loved God very much had together woven this plot over the ages.

The car belonged to the revered master cabalist* of Brooklyn, a gift from one of his wealthy supporters. The master served as spiritual leader for hundreds of thousands of devotees, adherents to the centuries-old Cosmic Wisdom** movement. Throughout his career, the old mystic showed a remarkable ability to liberate rich people from the guilt which comes from owning obscene amounts of money—without making anyone insufferably self-congratulatory in the process.

The cabalist succeeded where 16th century theologian John Calvin had failed: The rabbi's lesson to the rich was that God expected them to work *harder* than everyone else. All Calvin did was convince a bunch of rich fools that they were God's favorites.

The car arrived at the entrance to Montefiore Cemetery. The chauffeur, Lionel Abulafia, an ancient Jewish man in a well-worn knee-length coat and a tattered, black, wide-brimmed fedora, maneuvered elegantly between the bright orange gates. At over 110 years of age, Abulafia was the best driver in America for the simple reason that if you do anything for more

---

* Cabala is an ancient tradition of Jewish mysticism. A cabalist is an adept of this discipline.

** Cosmic wisdom fills up the universe in boundless amounts, but it is useless without a proper home, much as water is useless without a vessel to contain it. The Cosmic Wisdom Movement seeks to connect to that universal wisdom.

than one hundred years, you get really good at it.

At the movement's headquarters he was considered too much of a loose cannon for official employment. The master's secretaries were in charge of ushering in visitors, filing correspondence, and writing down the cabalist's teachings; Abulafia made sure the master never forgot that he was the master. If a jester was required, Abulafia played for laughs; if more somber input was called for, Abulafia provided that, too. Outside the master's innermost circle—a select group of no more than four men at any given time—the rest of the world saw Lionel Abulafia as an ancient wreck of a man, slave to his own drinking and smoking—the final and weakest link in a long chain of great masters of the past. The role fit Lionel like an old glove.

The car climbed up the gravel path and turned onto a narrow asphalt road where it glided between long, crowded rows of tombstones. When it reached the far north-east corner, it stopped.

A bit on the smelly side after a night of vodka and schmoozing with some of his old-timer buddies from the Orthodox Jewish community of Brooklyn's Crown Heights, the chauffeur nonetheless maintained a pleasant disposition. He pushed his own door open instantly, and hurried around to the passenger's side to open that door with equal haste.

"Come out, young man, he ain't staying dead forever, you know," Abulafia told his ninety-year-old passenger.

The old cabalist of Brooklyn was a stout and burly man. He exited the car, holding onto his black felt fedora, one even wider than Abulafia's, to keep it from flying. Even at his advanced age, he was a magnificent sight to behold, with a long, white beard that split and spread like a cloud over his shiny, spotless, black silk coat.

The cabalist arrived at the burial site reserved for dignitaries from the Cosmic Wisdom movement. Entering the enclosed area, he passed swiftly by the grave of his late wife. During her lifetime, his wife had been a great source of comfort to him. Her father, however, continued to maintain a vital role even *after* his death. Accordingly, the old rabbi made his way straight to the mausoleum of the late mystic of Brooklyn, the cabalist's esteemed father-in-law.

"Will the master require a cup of tea?" Abulafia asked, matching paces with the old cabalist, who was a generation younger than himself.

"Lionel, if you call me 'master' one more time, I swear I'll slap you," the cabalist threatened. "Since my wife's been gone, you're the only one who still talks to me like a normal human being. When *you're* gone…"

4

"Don't worry, old friend, my great-great-grandpa asked God to keep his last male heir alive until messiah comes..."

"Yes, I know," the cabalist said. "I would have loved to have met that great-great-grandpa of yours."

"I'm told that he looked a lot like me, but with a better suit."

The mausoleum was a square stone structure. A dark and narrow enclosed corridor along one side held two wooden doors; one which led to the foot of the grave, the other to its head. The corridor was paved with a thick layer of pebbles covered with ancient puddles of frozen wax—remnants of the thousands who had passed through with lit candles during the course of the last four decades. The wide clearing around the grave was also covered with pebbles, to prevent the rain from turning the place into a swamp. On top of this pebble floor, at the foot of the grave, stood a small wooden shack, built just for the cabalist, with an elongated Plexiglas window overlooking his father-in-law's resting place.

Abulalfia was seized with a deep sense of foreboding. "You sensing what I'm sensing?" Lionel Abulafia asked the old master.

"What do you think, Lionel, I'm wearing this costume for Purim*?" the cabalist of Brooklyn countered. "I know."

"If we leave right now we can make it to the afternoon prayer *before* nightfall for a change..."

"And then what? It will still be waiting here for me the next time... and the time after that. I have no choice."

"Sure you do, you're just spoiling for a fight."

"Lionel, I don't stand a chance today, even *you* know that."

Abulafia sighed, eyeing the shrubbery suspiciously. The Menace was around here, everywhere, taking its time, getting ready to leap—and there was nothing he, Lionel Abulafia, scion of great magicians and holy chanters, could do about it. "I'm not happy about this, you should know," he informed the old cabalist.

"I'll try to be quick," the master promised. He entered the dark corridor, stopped, knocked on the shack's door and waited.

"Go inside already, go inside," Abulafia urged quietly, hoping that the mystic's grave would offer the master protection against the ultimate evil aspect of the Creator, which was by now a palpable presence all around them. A few birds had already fallen, dead as stones, onto the muddy earth—a sure sign of spiritual poison.

---

* A Jewish carnival holiday.

Before entering, the cabalist paused for a few seconds and awaited permission from the Great Beyond. Satisfied that he had received it, the cabalist turned the doorknob, pushed open the door and walked into the small, wooden enclosure.

"With all your showbiz mannerisms and the knocking and the waiting, we'll end up *schlepping* you back on a stretcher, you old fool," Abulafia murmured, not daring to speak this aloud. There was a limit to what even *he* could say to the great man.

The wooden structure was cooled by an air-conditioner, even though this was still early March. The cabalist was known for his penchant for cool environments, so three of his young followers had preceded him to the cemetery in an old Chrysler station-wagon equipped with an electric generator to power the cooling unit.

According to THE CABALIST'S HANDBOOK OF PRACTICAL MESSIANIC REDEMPTION, death is tailored to each individual and is experienced very differently by different people. One of the biggest influences on the quality of a person's death is the extent to which the person valued the corporeal stuff in life:

> *If you are attached to your house and your car and your CD changer and your hat collection, you will miss them a lot once your existence is condensed to a purely spiritual environment. If your body—and the many lovely things it does for you—receives much of your attention, then not having a body will be a serious blow after death; one from which you might never recover. But if you pay less attention to your body and lead a life richer in thoughts and ideas, you might hardly notice dying and, in some cases, might even continue a conversation begun prior to your demise.*

The old cabalist and his father-in-law had never interrupted their discussions on account of the latter's departure; they merely moved the conversation from the parlor to the cemetery. Lionel Abulafia was invited on rare occasions into the discussion of the two cabalists, but those brushes with death pained Abulafia. Although his scholarship was more than sufficient to keep up with the two masters, his appetite for drinking and smoking—and occasionally jumping in the sack—colored his view so that Abulafia found the afterlife mostly depressing.

He now hastily brought the master a giant brown Bloomingdale's shopping bag bursting with thousands of paper notes scrawled with names and requests. The cabalist received the bag with a solemn expression and placed it next to a large candle on a wooden shelf beneath the window. He lit the large candle, said a short blessing and began his work.

Returning to the car, Abulafia opened the trunk, took out his portable Toshiba and went back to his seat. He positioned the computer against the wheel, and had just settled in to write when the car phone rang. He picked it up. It was the master's chief secretary, Rabbi Leo Graneck, calling from the office.

"What is it, Leo?"

"Is he inside already?"

"Who wants to know?"

"I have Yossel Diamant out in the hallway, wanting to consult him about a new venture…"

"God damn it, Leo, don't the man got enough money already?"

"He *gives*, Lionel…"

"I know, I know, he gives. You want I should call the master back to bless Diamant's new gold mine in Perth, Australia?"

"How did *you* know?"

"I'm gifted, and you're a schmuck. Stop kissing his rich ass and tell him to sit and wait like everybody else."

"I can't talk to him like that."

"Why? You're afraid he'll go seek another master?"

"Worse things have happened. Somebody around here needs to think about the bottom line."

"So, Mister Bottom Line, you're telling me I should yank the master out of the shack to take care of Yossel Diamant?"

"You know very well I can't make such a suggestion."

"Then stop wasting my time, Leo. Go learn Torah with him. Keep him happy. I'll bring the master back in the evening, God willing." He hung up with an impatient sneer and scanned the bushes again. A great weight settled on his heart. This was a day for bad things. The master argued that there were no bad things in the world; only good things and bitter things. Lionel Abulafia thought the master had to get out more.

A dozen rows away stood the children's plot. Lionel Abulafia was familiar with it because his own daughter (born and expired in the same year early in the 20th century) was buried there. When they buried the baby, an acquaintance, also long gone, had told him you never get over the pain of

7

losing your child. It goes against the promises of the universe as we know it; shattering our trust in our Father in Heaven. Abulafia searched his heart for the ancient pain and discovered it right where he had left it, in a soft fold of cotton pads and essence of clove. The baby had been teething and running a high fever, which was how Death had fooled them that time. You've got to hand it to the old bastard: He *is* inventive.

Somewhere in the children's plot a young woman knelt before a patch of grass. The child who would be buried there was not yet born, but the sorrow generating from that spot was deep and cried out to be acknowledged.

The kneeling woman, Danielle Herzog, was short and bulky. Her hair was cropped in a manner that suggested haste and lack of interest rather than fashion. The underside of her chubby thighs drew in the fabric of her maroon dress, nearly exposing her stocky hindquarters. However, Danielle Herzog was so completely humbled that nobody passing by could possibly have the heart to scorn her. Any such witness would quickly avert his face and leave.

Lionel Abulafia was aware of the young woman and strained to hear what she was mumbling. He knew that it was somehow connected to the plot that would unfold that afternoon; he just wished that she would enunciate.

He got out of the car and moved silently between row after row of old graves. The dead did not mind. For some, it constituted all the attention they had received in decades. He stopped two rows away and turned his right ear, the better one, toward Danielle. He shut out all the other sounds nearby, which was a risky thing to do with lurking evil stalking his master.

He could hear her now: *"Violets are blue, Roses grow wild. The murderous parent will kill the child…"*

Danielle's age hovered around thirty, but she chanted in a five-year-old's singsong voice. Abulafia reckoned that she had been singing for hours, maybe days. He could recognize a prophecy when he heard one, and this prophecy chilled him to the bone.

This was Abulafia's first encounter with his spiritual doppelgänger, though he had long been aware of their shared spiritual kinship. Just as Danielle began to sense his nearby presence, Abulafia sped away. Danielle assumed she was imagining again, and continued her chant. Abulafia could do many such tricks. Vanishing was a simple one, and so useful.

Abulafia returned to the car to busy himself with work. He had no doubt that terrible things were at hand and there was still much to do.

It was close to three o'clock in the afternoon. The old cabalist stared out at his father-in-law's grave. It was surrounded by a cement wall about three feet high with the eastern wall serving for a tombstone. Piled on the grave were hundreds of pieces of paper, many of them scorched. The devotees customarily set fire to the accumulated notes every few months in order to make room for new ones.

For nearly three hours, the cabalist stood and examined carefully each note from the bag before him. Only thin cloth shoes separated his old feet from the wood floor beneath him. He had spent the previous day standing for hours on end at the Cosmic Wisdom world headquarters, shaking hands with thousands of men, women and children who had come for his blessing. He knew many of them by name (and remembered unerringly their every previous encounter). Those public events were the occasion for once-barren women to introduce their healthy babies, for the formerly ill to display their newfound health, and for the previously destitute to share with the cabalist their new wealth—all the result of his miraculous blessings. This would have been an exhausting exercise for a man half the master's age; and he was even more uncomfortable due to circulation problems in one leg and eye surgery the elderly gentleman had undergone only two weeks before.

The cemetery closed its gates to the public at 5 p.m. The sun had not yet set, but it offered little comfort. A frosty wind blew among the desolate graves, causing the naked tree branches to tremble. It disturbed little piles of dusty dead leaves, leaving behind the chalky aroma of icy mulch. The cabalist continued to manage his paper notes. Lionel Abulafia continued to immortalize the ephemera left by his august ancestors in his ever-burgeoning work, THE CABALIST'S HANDBOOK OF PRACTICAL MESSIANIC REDEMPTION. The three young devotees in their ancient Chrysler debated concerning the exact moment to connect the electric lights to the generator should the master decide to stay on after dark.

But Abulafia, who walked over to the shack every half hour or so to eavesdrop, knew the cabalist would be ready to depart from the encounter with his beloved father-in-law shortly after sunset. Accordingly, at 5:45 p.m., Abulafia replaced the car phone receiver, locked the Toshiba in the trunk and took up his position at the mausoleum, right outside the wooden shack.

By 6 p.m., the cabalist had gone over all the notes in the shopping bag. Some had been replaced in the bag after examination, others, shredded and scattered over the grave.

The brain stroke occurred just as the old man set foot outside the shack. Of all the master's devoted followers, Lionel Abulafia alone was chosen to witness the cabalist's collapse. Their gaze met. Abulafia saw the master's wide blue eyes fill with urgency, fear, warning and finally, acceptance.

God damn, it's starting, Lionel Abulafia thought. He said a silent farewell to the universe as he had known it.

Abulafia braced the collapsing body with his own arms, chest and stomach, all the while shouting to the three young men in the car. It was a nightmarish moment; seconds stretched into hours, sounds lost their distinction, light failed to reflect tangible reality, and space contracted all the way back to the original cosmic egg.

"So, *this* is how you planned it, Master?" the old man wailed, rocking back and forth with the beloved body in his embrace. Oily tears ran down his wrinkled face as he removed his threadbare coat and wrapped it around the master's shoulders. He slowly eased himself to the ground, careful to support the weighty body. His arms hugged the old man tightly.

Lionel Abulafia, a century old but still no friend of the angel of death, closed his eyes and began to recite the book of Psalms from memory. It was what one did while waiting for an ambulance. More than anything, he longed for a shot of booze and a cigarette.

2.

According to THE CABALIST'S HANDBOOK OF PRACTICAL MESSIANIC REDEMPTION, *the Spiritual Continuum of Everything* was formed on the second day of Creation:

> *It was a sad day, without question the saddest day in the history of the cosmos. On that day, the Creator, heretofore a single, unified and uninterrupted entity, gave birth to the possibility of two-ness.*
>
> *Duality was a terrible experience for the Creator. It brought about suspicion, uncertainty, misunderstanding, and self-centeredness. It tore right through the heart of God's simplicity. God could hardly bear it. For the billions upon billions of years which constituted the second day of Creation, God was searching for a good word He could say about the number Two, but none occurred to Him.*
>
> *God concluded that there was nothing good about Duality, other than the fact that it was all just a variant of Singularity. But even He didn't trust this concept completely.*

Only a mere eon or so later, God discovered the emanation of the possibility of measuring stuff. Of course this concept couldn't exist as long as one was the only known number, but the idea took on a life of its own as soon as two came into being.

Like all things in the cosmos, as soon as it was possible to measure, measuring became the rage, and the Spiritual Continuum of Everything was already roaring with life. Except, of course, on the second day it had only one thing to measure: God/No God. Which explains why, as the second day was entering its billionth eon and God stumbled into the Spiritual Continuum of Everything, He was not very impressed, to say the least.

God's mood changed only at the end of the Second Day, when He set out to create the Third Day. He was delighted with the concept of three-ness, because it held the promise of mitigation, of selection, and of conciliation. It also gave birth to the notion of Many, which God found particularly cheerful.

Once He had created the concept of Three-and-Up, God had much more fun with the Spiritual Continuum of Everything. God saw the continuum as an expression of His constant desire to put things in perspective, a desire which forced an unintended result of Creation: the fact that everything in the cosmos was either to the right or to the left of everything else on the Continuum.

The further to the left things stood, the more they reflected God's penchant for making lists and setting up boundaries and judging.

The further to the right things were, the more open and available and merciful God's perceived qualities became.

So, for instance, Italian dictator Benito Mussolini (1883–1945) was more than a mile to the right of German mass-butcher Adolph Hitler (1889-1945), but only two and a half yards to the left of American film producer Cecil B. De Mille (1881-1959), known for his spectacular epics, The Ten Commandments *and* The Greatest Show on Earth.

Biblical tough guy, King Nebuchadnezzar (630-562 BCE), was surprisingly stationed a mere foot to the left of Hollywood bombshell Jayne Mansfield (1933-1967 CE).

And the thirty-ninth president of the United States, James Earl Carter Jr., was situated precisely one millimeter to the left of his own dinner jacket.

It can be safely stated that the Spiritual Continuum of Everything represented the first time God's dark side pulled a fast one on Him. It seduced the Creator with three-ness and all the delightful potential it bore for relationships between people and beaches and trees and race cars and watercress sandwiches—to the point where God had forgotten that Three was merely a very voluptuous Two.

The Creator understood that the Continuum represented His exile from Himself. He also acknowledged the Continuum as a creation of His Dark Aspect. This probably coincided with the moment that His Dark Aspect murmured sweetly, "Please fasten your seat belts, dinner will be served shortly. Thank you for flying Air Satan..."

Despite some popular notions that may suggest otherwise, Samael's place on the Spiritual Continuum of Everything is not directly opposite that of God's. His spot is precisely at the mid-point of that ever-expanding ethereal line. He is situated between the two most frightened men who ever lived: To Samael's left stands Eduard Bene (1884-1948), who lost his country Czechoslovakia to the Nazis in 1938, and to Samael's right stands Jan Masaryk (1886-1948), who lost his country Czechoslovakia to the Communists in 1948.

3.

The codification of THE CABALIST'S HANDBOOK OF PRACTICAL MESSIANIC REDEMPTION was begun in 13th century Spain, by Rabbi Abraham Abulafia, dean of the Spanish school of practical cabalism. All earlier entries were passed orally to successive generations. None until Rabbi Abraham had the *chutzpah*—some say madness—to put this work into writing. The book was intended strictly for the personal use of its author, who engaged in black magic in an effort to bring messianic redemption to earth.

On the eve of Rosh Hashanah, 5047 (1276 c.e.), Rabbi Abraham Abulafia finally declared *himself* messiah, and set out to do war with Pope Gregory X in Rome.

Gregory X, obsessed with promoting Christian dominion over the Holy Land, had collected large sums in France and England for his private crusade. In 1274, the Council of Lyons, under Gregory's pressure, provided that one-tenth of all benefices accruing to all churches in the course of six years would be set aside. The tithe was successfully collected, and preparations were made in France and England for the expedition which was never carried out.

Regarding the true purpose of Reb Abraham's mission, evil tongues suggested the messianic publicity was merely a ruse. They believed that cardinals from the peace party in Rome had paid Reb Abraham Abulafia a staggering sum to off the pope. It was a job—nothing more, nothing less.

The pope was greatly disturbed by Abraham Abulafia's threat upon his life—no matter *who* had financed the self-declared messiah's trip from Spain to Italy—and ordered him arrested. The arrest was to be followed by the customary burning at the stake.

The crafty cabalist evaded the papal posse until nightfall on the eve of

Rosh Hashanah. He managed to set up camp with a dozen of his followers outside the gates of Rome. They prayed into the night, fed the fire, and read psalms.

During the night, Abraham Abulafia assumed the form of an eagle and flew into Pope Gregory's chambers. The eagle pecked out the 80-year-old pope's eyes and ate his heart and liver as well. The pope was found dead the next morning, his body a gruesome mass of torn flesh. Whether or not you believe the story about the eagle, the death of the pope on Rosh Hashanah is an historic fact.

Of all the pretenders to the messianic throne, Rabbi Abraham Abulafia reached nearest the prize. His book, THE CABALIST'S HANDBOOK OF PRACTICAL MESSIANIC REDEMPTION, continues to be written by his heirs. In it, his son describes the great cabalist's triumphant reappearance outside the gates of Rome as news spread of the Pope's demise:

> Papa was never a shy man, but now, having slain the little dragon, he was truly beside himself with jubilation. He jumped many feet in the air and performed numerous cartwheels, juggling nine knives and a meat hook simultaneously, all in accordance with his teachings on the proper manner of great celebration.
>
> Alas, in his great ecstasy, he spotted only too late the arrow loosed at him from the bow of a lone, hooded Franciscan monk, who calmly blew on his fingers and whispered: 'Asta la vista, baby.'
>
> I hurried to Papa's side and concluded that the arrow had entered his chest, mysteriously slashing both the heart and the liver, an impossible feat considering the angle from which it had been shot. I held Papa's head in my lap and watched helplessly as the blood trickled out of his mouth. Before he passed to the Garden of Eden, Papa assured me the lucky shooter was none other than the archangel Samael, avenging the pope's assassination.

From a much later entry scrawled in the margin:

> The Dark Aspect was finally forced to concede that Gregory X was not his best protégé. Still, this ambitious pope is revered as a saint in Rome. His feast is celebrated on February 16th. Get it? February 16th is the day that everybody dumps their empty heart-shaped candy boxes in the trash...

4.

Rabbi Abulafia's CABALIST'S HANDBOOK OF PRACTICAL MESSIANIC RE-DEMPTION never made it into print in the conventional sense. The last living Abulafia, Lionel, although not very well respected by contemporary scholars, nonetheless managed to remain alive for well over a century, devoting his life to working on the handbook.

Many doubted Lionel's competence with magic, a force his great ancestor Rabbi Abraham had once been able to tame. Most of Lionel's days were spent mooching cigarettes and small change from folks on Grand Street, on the Lower East Side of Manhattan. Several local synagogues each paid him two dollars a day to show up for *minyan**. On a good day, Lionel Abulafia collected ten dollars for his trouble.

Now and then Lionel would be overcome with a sense of guilt, the origins of which even *he* wasn't sure about, and he would sit at his ancient Toshiba laptop, to continue typing up several centuries' worth of scribbled notes in his exalted family's files. For the record, it is unclear how much of THE CABALIST'S HANDBOOK OF PRACTICAL MESSIANIC REDEMPTION is true to the ancient manuscripts and notes, and how much reflects Lionel Abulafia's own carefree commentary. Contemporary cabalists, however, tend to trust the digitized copy, arguing that the "Bill Haley incident" had taught Lionel an unforgettable lesson.

Sometime in the mid-sixties, Lionel tried to impress some floozy he had picked up at a bar in Chinatown with a CABALIST'S HANDBOOK pyrotechnical trick. Once lured into his dank and impossibly crammed study, the drunk Miss Mitzi Hoffman saw to her amazement how each letter Lionel punched out on his elderly Remington typewriter (no Toshiba laptops back then) would squeeze up from under the key to ignite in a bright, golden flame and hover in the air for a minute or so. Subsequent typed letters rose to be joined together with the others in suspended fiery paragraphs.

"Now behold this," Lionel told Mitzi. Sucking the contents of a bottle of Bud without interrupting his staccato typing, he punched in the lyrics for *Rock Around the Clock***:

---

* The prayer quorum. A minimum of ten is required to recite certain prayers.
** Written in 1953 by Max C. Freedman and James Myers, recorded by Bill Haley and the Comets on April 12, 1954, and, in the opinion of many, turned popular music into an uninhibited, raucous, joyous, delightful noise.

One, two, three o'clock, four o'clock rock / Five, six ,seven o'clock, eight o'clock rock / Nine, ten, eleven o'clock, twelve o'clock rock / We're gonna' rock around the clock tonight.

The words floated above them, flickering. An instant later, the rogue stanza collected itself into great balls of fire which smacked Lionel Abulafia in the face and singed his shaggy white beard. Mitzi Hoffman fled in panic, but not before lifting Lionel's wallet and the remains of his sixpack. The poor scion himself spent the rest of that weekend in the emergency room of Gouverneur Hospital.

Thus, most scholars are fairly convinced that the existing version of Rabbi Abulafia's CABALIST'S HANDBOOK OF PRACTICAL MESSIANIC REDEMPTION is a faithful copy—at least since the mid-sixties.

5.

Of course, the old cabalist master had known well in advance about his coming stroke. Shortly before his collapse at the cemetery, he had made a flamboyant last-ditch effort to force God's hand and usher in the redeemer.

The old cabalist was convinced beyond the shadow of a doubt that these were messianic times, which, to him, meant that people everywhere were soon to be lifted from the quagmire of the Human Condition, and that the Jewish nation would be restored to its Biblical glory.

In the modern era, the title Cabalist Master, or simply, Master, refers to one who teaches methods of connecting to the transcendental. A small region in Belarus spawned a dynasty of cabalist masters who arrived in the United States in the 1940's. The last of the line was known as the Great Master of Brooklyn, or simply, Our Master. The organization he headed was known as the Cosmic Wisdom movement.

The grand master's great achievement was the resurrection of faithful Jewish life after the European holocaust of 1939-1945. He sent thousands of his followers to settle around the globe, seeding new Jewish enclaves and reviving old ones. Like their master, they were aggressive and uninhibited about reaching out to the millions of Jews who survived the Nazis.

One of the old master's favorite sayings was that we must learn from everyone, even from the Gestapo. Just as those murderers were relentless in pursuit of their victims, so should *his* disciples attempt to embrace every last Jew.

One evening after prayers, precisely eleven months before his stroke, the cabalist announced that he wished to speak to his followers. A minor storm ensued, with officials rushing to assemble the devout and connect the loudspeaker system. Several thousand men, most of them in black suits and hats and sporting wild, bushy beards, gathered in the great hall. Thousands more viewed the live broadcast via satellite.

Before his followers settled down, the master burst out in a painful moan, which grew into a scream. Flowing from the old man on the dais was an anguish that threatened to drown his listeners.

It is difficult to convey in words the spastic quality of the master's cry. There was some crackling hoarseness to it, and there were strains of red-hot ire, but mostly it was like a stream of molten lava cutting through an iceberg.

"If now is, supposedly, the time of redemption, why aren't we redeemed?" the master hollered. The thousands of his followers in the huge hall and the thousands listening at home were thoroughly familiar with the cabalist's writings about the coming redemption. Nothing he had previously expressed on the subject sounded even remotely like this.

"Can it be imagined," the master demanded, "that wherever ten Jewish men are assembled in prayer they would not be crying to high heaven, *insisting* that God send down the messiah *immediately?*

"Is it possible that groups of Jews are getting together and they're not even mildly upset because the messiah has not arrived tonight, nor yet tomorrow, nor the day after?

"Isn't it clear that if a single group of ten Jewish men anywhere on God's great earth were to beg for a redeemer with even the *pretense* of sincerity —salvation would have *long been with us?*" He cried and pounded the table with his fists.

His audience sat in silent shock. No one dared turn his eyes away from the master on the dais.

"You are nothing but a bunch of *fakers!*" The master accused his listeners. "Book learning, lip serving, mammon worshipping, chicken munching, good for nothing heaps of human waste, who don't care diddly if this world is saved from its state of perpetual misery or *not!*" Again, he pounded the dais.

"And if you are all fakers, what does that make *me?*" he yelled. "I'm no better than you, I'm a fraud! A 'has been!' Washed out, finished! I'm a *joke!*"

The silence that followed was so intense, several hundred of the assembled men fell asleep out of sheer fear. Others became permanently wide awake. Touched by a truth of such cosmic dimension, their lives were suddenly imbued with a new sense of purpose. This is how the first Messianic Crazies, the scourge of the Cosmic-Wisdomnik movement, were created.

"Look at us, we're so *pitiful!*" The master roared, examining the thousands of anxious faces in his audience. Their obedient silence was driving him to the brink of real anger, not the kind that is useful as as an educational tool, but the kind doctors warn you about at the end of an electrocardiogram test. Why was everybody so subservient, for crying out loud? Had he raised a flock of useless sheep? When had he ever taught that staring silently and waiting for Master's rebuke to end was a quality to be cultivated? He sighed in anguish. "We're all still in exile," he told them in a voice dripping with resignation. "Worst of all, even in our spiritual work we are remote, abandoned, lost!"

Then he charged them to do something constructive to bring the messiah.

"What a shame," he concluded. "We're going to be just another failure on the list..."

The movement was nearly destroyed as a result of this dramatic appearance. Some followers were convinced the master had declared himself messiah, and was ready to redeem the world. Others agreed that the master was the messiah, but didn't necessarily think the best strategy was to grab humanity by the lapel and scream this message into its face.

And the master himself, what did he have to say on the matter of his being God's messenger of redemption? Not much, really. He was preparing himself for the worst part of his life, to be followed by his demise.

Following his stroke at his father-in-law's grave site, the master became aphasic. This meant that although he understood most of what was being said to him, he could not express meaningful responses.

For instance, when one of his secretaries, Leo Graneck, handed him an unwashed cup of wine for a blessing on Friday night, the Cabalist could only hum in disapproval and knock the silver cup down on the floor. In accordance with his tradition, the master refused to make a blessing over a cup that had not been rinsed first. Graneck, the very image of a patient, selfless devotee, bent down and picked up the cup. This scene repeated itself five times, until Lionel Abulafia sneered, "You forgot to wash the *becher*, Leo."

For two years, the master watched helplessly as his disciples waged war with one another over the right to interpret his instructions. Every minute of every agonizing day, uncontrollable neurons fired pain messages throughout his entire nervous system. Nearly as painful, the master was forced to endure the transformation of his faithful followers into idiotic, abandoned children.

Curiously, none of his followers dared pray that the master find shelter in the arms of death. Many of them believed he was much more than human; and who wishes for the death of a beloved demigod? More likely, they still needed him too much to permit him to die.

Some were mature enough to understand that the time had come to be on their own without the cabalist's protection. Nevertheless, they found themselves drawn into political strife by those of their brethren in the throes of a cultish phenomenon: The worse the situation, the better they felt.

The faithful fought over the privilege of pushing the master around in his wheelchair so they could display him to the adoring crowds. Mercifully, those parades were kept short; the master's stiff body would begin to slide down in his wheelchair almost immediately, and the great man often ended up sprawled helplessly on the floor, unable to get up—much less redeem humanity from its woes.

He longed to be in the midst of his people; to absorb the sight of their faces glowing in meditation; to feel the soft kisses of their flowing prayer shawls; to take in their fragrance, fresh from the ritual bath. But his political cadre opted instead to display him from an opera box high above the crowd, an object of adulation.

They quoted things they swore they'd heard him say. They tortured him in the ways that small children torture their sleepy parents on a Saturday morning. However, these children had the advantage of being able to manipulate daddy's body.

Medical tests showed that the master understood everything, every little bit of his private hell. Now he was a god in diapers, a speechless prophet.

One time, against his doctor's orders, the master begged for something that tasted like it was prepared *by* humans, *for* humans; but Leo Graneck denied those appeals. So, taking advantage of one of the sessions when he was on display, the master pointed at a plate of sponge cake perched on a table below. Graneck signaled frantically behind the master's back for the faithful to ignore the request, but Abulafia, who happened to be down among the wooden benches, grabbed the plate and ran up to serve the old man. To Granek's horror, the master proceeded with great gusto to devour every last piece of soft, lemony sponge cake. In all, the master consumed thirteen pieces, which sprouted a lengthy debate among his more scholarly followers as to whether this was an allusion to Maimonides' thirteen principles of faith, or to the age when a Jewish boy takes on the yoke of commandments. Few were ready to accept that the old man simply felt like eating a lot of cake.

The master lived as a puppet for two years, and when his dignity was all gone, he encountered a second, massive stroke, and became a vegetable. Medical tests showed that, too.

The newspapers made much out of the fact that the master had no heir. His wife, who had passed away roughly six years earlier, was barren, and no effort had been made to groom a proper successor. The master was the seventh in a line of cabalists that originated in the 18th century—and it seemed that there would not be an eighth. The newspapers wondered if the master's teaching about the imminence of the messiah was an indication that he believed that there would be no need for an heir.

They thought he was naïve.

6.

THE CABALIST'S HANDBOOK OF PRACTICAL MESSIANIC REDEMPTION asks:

Why would God wish on any of his creatures such pain as the master endured?

There are many views on this aspect of Divine Will. Some scholars suggest Creation is the handiwork of a sadistic celestial child, who delights in pulling the wings off butterflies and babies from their mothers' bosoms. Soon, they surmise, God's mother will come into the room and smack Him, and thus bring an end to all our suffering.

Others teach that God comes from a parallel universe where manure is the most precious commodity. Our enterprising God created this universe to produce enough manure to make Him fabulously wealthy in His dimension. This view has found its most profound expression in the television industry. The only problem with this view is that it's hard to imagine the need for such staggering amounts of manure such as our world produces and it casts a troubling shadow upon any Entity who desires even more of it.

Other traditions describe God as a lazy dreamer, for whom our reality is but an afternoon nap. Refreshed, He will wake up to take His tea and biscuits by the living room bay window. Soon He will recline and dream the same dream

Of course, the true purpose of Creation has nothing whatsoever to do with Mankind. Instead, Creation was conceived purely as a way for God to shake off His ambivalence about the quality of Judgment in Himself.

In other words, like most of us, God was only too happy to be the cosmic Mister Nice Guy, but He wasn't quite sure what to do with the harsher aspects of being the limitless Divine. So He made a universe in which His Nice Guy attributes would be limited by His Mr. Tough Guy persona.

A later version of the handbook's account of Creation, which most researchers associate with early 19th century notions of classicism, if not outright paganism, goes something like this:

One day (a meaningless expression, since this is supposed to have occurred before Time was created), God became aware that there was something wrong with His perception of Himself as a wholesome, righteous and kindly beneficent Entity. It turned out there were forces lurking within Him which were neither noble nor delightful.

Accordingly, God appointed a fact-finding commission that was composed of Himself. The commission issued a report which upset God very much. It turned out that His worst suspicions were true and He was, regrettably, a much more complex all-encompassing Entity than even He had dared to imagine.

God decided to take Himself to court, where He accused Himself of the highest possible crime: treason against God. The Judge, God, found the defendant, God, guilty as charged. He sentenced Himself to billions upon billions of years of hard labor, in a specially created environment in which He would not fill the entire space, as was previously His custom.

In that miraculous place, God would no longer be an uninterrupted blast of goodness and light. Shackles of Darkness would be placed upon Him, defining God the way a contour line defines an object.

Now the CABALIST'S HANDBOOK gets to the exciting part:

In preparation for His prison sentence, God decided to trick Himself by baking the ultimate hacksaw cake. The instrument imbued by God with the awesome power to put a stop to His own shenanigans was the spirit of the messiah. This fail-safe measure was set in place to provide relief in the event that God's presence ever became so diminished that He Himself would be unable to halt the undoing of creation.

A much later passage illustrates the above point:

In 1941, nobody knew where God had gone, and all the angels were so worried. Behind the Holy Screen a voice broke out every night, as our Matriarch Rachel cried over her slaughtered children. Who can forget those days when the universe was altered?

But even though everything seemed terrible and the planet was going Auschwitz and it looked as if God might decide at last to break out of His self-imposed prison cell, He was overcome by regrets.

Imagine: Millions of the very men, women and children who believed He was the nicest supernatural Entity that ever existed, were marched into small enclosures where little pellets that soon made them stop breathing were dropped into their midst. Even that was not terrible enough to bring Him to His senses and inspire Him to stop history.

It may be hard to believe, but since Creation, God has become quite the sentimentalist. He likes His prison cell, He is infatuated with His fellow inmates, all creatures of His divine imagination, and He enjoys the small jobs He does around the facility.

He has grown accustomed to the head counts and the lockups, the unannounced cell searches, the sudden brawls in the mess hall, the smuggled contraband, the aimless hour He spends each day out in the open air courtyard.

Put a stop to His own sentence? Why, He no longer even bothers to show up for His parole hearings…

7.

THE CABALIST'S HANDBOOK OF PRACTICAL MESSIANIC REDEMPTION describes the first attempt to incarnate the spirit of the messiah nearly four thousand years ago, during the days of the Cult of Sodom.

Sodom was part of a four-city, fifty-two-year experiment in perfecting Evil. Humanity was preoccupied back then with the total holocaust that had taken place some two hundred years before: the Deluge.

Disappointed by the moral failures of most humans, as well as those of many animals, the Creator decided to chuck most of the earth's flora and fauna and start again almost from scratch.

He poured scalding rains onto the face of the planet and released steaming, boiling brooks from below, until the highest mountain was covered with hot water. Only one family of humans, and the several species of animals that they managed to preserve, miraculously survived. Everything else was turned into a planetary soup, encompassing billions of tons of emulsified organic matter.

It's no wonder that the generations that sprang from that family of holocaust survivors devoted much of their time to ensuring that never again would such a thing take place. They didn't quite trust God's promises that He was through with trying to destroy the world. His track record was tainted for eternity.

They were particularly annoyed when He pointed to the rainbow—a perfectly natural phenomenon resulting from light passing through the prism of water droplets in the air after a rain—and suggested this was a sign that He no longer intended to kill everybody should they piss Him off again.

DEITY ONCE AGAIN TREATS HUMANITY LIKE CHILDREN screamed the newspaper headlines of the day, although the newspapers which would have borne them had not yet been invented. Humanity had lost patience for divine shtick.

Incidentally, a few short years after the deluge, humanity organized a massive hunt, intending to trap and kill God. It may have been the most dangerous moment in human history. By nature reclusive, God nevertheless responded by going on the offensive, disabling mankind's innate talent of knowing intuitively the needs and intentions of fellow human beings.

It was a cruel thing to do and, as a species, we have never quite recovered. It could be said that insanity was born at that construction site in the city of Babylon, where the God-hunters erected a giant tower from which to launch their expedition.

At the moment God altered us, one workman turned to his friend on the scaffolding, half a mile up in the air, and asked him to pass a tool.

"Give me a saw," he said, enunciating flawlessly. At that time, everyone spoke only Hebrew, the Holy Tongue.

But the other fellow showed obvious signs of incomprehension; he was hearing the Portuguese version: "Dê-me uma serra." So the first man repeated the request more loudly, thinking it was the fierce wind that impeded communication.

Eager to please, but without a clue as to what his friend wanted, the other man looked about, said something friendly, like: "È questo di che cosa avete bisogno?" He then picked up a hammer.

"I want a saw, you dumb ass, what's the matter with you?" People sounded, for the first time in human history, like foreigners to one another. Finally, the first guy became so irate, he took the hammer and drove it through the other guy's skull.

The construction of the tower (and eventually the whole hunting expedition) was called off, but mankind may never recover from the cultural and psychological beating God inflicted that day. It has come to be known as The Day God Invented Languages.

From that day on, the world was cursed with seventy different languages, which *later degenerated into numerous dialects and untold pidgin tongues. Predictably, the more languages we had, the less we understood each other.*

8.

At this point, the handbook becomes cagey, engaging in double-talk and metaphor, improbable allegory and barely-passable rhyme. This chapter of THE CABALIST'S HANDBOOK OF PRACTICAL MESSIANIC REDEMPTION has inspired volumes of lively debate among scholars and remains the most obscure of all the chapters in a collection whose style is generally clear.

The earliest entries were authored by Noah's youngest son, Shem, one of the finest gentlemen who ever lived. Of course, they were oral. By the time the handbook tradition was committed to paper centuries later, it was festooned with accumulated commentary.

Admired by both his older brothers, Shem became the moral authority of the post-deluge world. That didn't mean very many people listened to him, but people felt nice knowing that he was around, doing his righteous thing.

Quiet Shem was not the type to rebuke or persecute folks; instead, he retreated to a small house on a low mountaintop, which years later came to be known as Temple Mount, in the heart of Jerusalem. Young men and women seeking schooling in the divine arts flocked to him. These included our grandfather Abraham, his son, Isaac, and Isaac's son, Jacob. But there were stretches of many years during which no one knocked on Shem's door, and the old man had to go downtown to the marketplace to get his news.

Shem was deeply interested in the affairs of men, kings, empires, and armies. For one thing, most of the people around him were relatives; he was the forefather of all the Semites. Also, he had it on the Highest Authority that everything that happens on earth is mirrored in heaven, and vice versa.

One of Shem's earliest recorded teachings expressed this idea. More a mantra than a lesson, more a tongue twister than a mantra (because his disciples were told to repeat it at an ever increasing speed), it went like this:

"You want a good god; be good. You want a good god; be good. You want a good god; be good."

And so on.

Shem's own view of his role in the world was dramatically different from his popular image as The Really Nice Man From Jerusalem. He worked hard to maintain his benign reputation, which was so convincing, that God Himself fell for it. Shem needed this harmless disguise because he was plotting the most potent conspiracy ever attempted against God.

He made this decision upon hearing the news about the Tower of Babylon. Like all other humans, he, too, experienced The Day God Invented Languages, but unlike the rest of humanity, Shem was able to deduce from the experience the inevitability of a world impounded by Evil.

Shem reasoned: The deluge may have been a planetary catastrophe—all life perished, save for the dwellers of Daddy's ark—but the deluge was, nevertheless an expression of God's optimism regarding humanity. Sure, He had to scrap most of it and start from scratch with one special man and his family, but in this instance God could be compared to a silversmith, who uses fire to remove the impurities from his metal. Fire, water, same thing.

But Shem understood The Day God Invented Languages as much worse than the deluge, even though not nearly as many people perished. That day indicated God's decision to downgrade humanity, and, necessarily, limit His expectations for its future.

The morning after he'd sensed the news about the collapse of the Tower of Babylon, the 100-year-old Shem rushed downstairs to the cave underneath his house. It was there that God had concealed the Foundation Rock around which the earth rotated; this was one of those locations on earth where the boundaries between our world and the higher ones are obscured.

There were two rocks, really; one was a massive thing, darker than the moonless sky, and it hovered above a much smaller, spherical thing, which was known as the Base Ball.

The Rock was known for the hum it generated once a day, at the moment just before dawn, when people easily mistake green for blue. That was the moment evil magicians used to elicit from God approval for their schemes. That was also the moment when, if you kept your head very close to the humming rock, you could think things which God Himself could not hear.

It was part of the arrangement God had to concede to when He negotiated His prison term with God. It was a fine thing to create a place where Evil could thrive, God argued with the convicted God, waiting for His sentencing, but what's the use of all this free roaming Evil, if God knows all about it?

So, on the day after the plans for the Tower were cancelled, one moment before dawn, Shem stuck his face close to the humming rock and he thought, "The holy Bastard might never let us out of His historical narrative, I must do something!"

Then the moment was over. Shem had to go back upstairs and wait patiently while a couple of tourists from the Greek islands offered to him a handkerchief, a rose and a poem, and asked to be told about the Meaning of Life.

"Life is like a river," Shem told them with closed eyes, his head swarming with concealment thoughts produced to keep God in the dark.

The two Greeks, a shapely man and woman of few garments, were stunned by the depth of the idea. They repeated it several times, debated its ramifications and posed a follow-up question.

"Great Master, when the great Master says that life is like a river, what exactly does the great Master mean?"

Shem stared at them through his half-closed lids, sighed and said, "So it's not like a river..."

And so on.

When he had the house to himself again the old man started counting the minutes until just before dawn. He then rushed down into the cave and picked up where he'd left off. Shem thought, "He created the spirit of messiah as a backup tool, in case the world was swept up in unmitigated judgment, but I'm starting to suspect He's never going to use it. Steps must be taken."

At that point, a divine question intruded upon Shem's thoughts, "Shem, My son, what are you thinking?"

Shem had prepared himself for the possibility of getting caught at the other end of a subversive thought. He countered by staring at the small sphere rotating below the much bigger one. He answered quickly, in his most innocent internal voice, "I'm thinking of the Base Ball, Lord."

And so he continued to compose his plot, one man, one thought, every twenty-four hours, for five hundred years. Nothing was committed to paper, naturally, and the ideas themselves were codified in the most elaborate manner, so that no celestial being, all the way to the top, could comprehend it.

In his manuscript of THE CABALIST'S HANDBOOK OF PRACTICAL MESSIANIC REDEMPTION, Lionel Abulafia recorded the entire wealth of Shem's plot as it had been brought down, one extremely cautious generation to the next. Multitudes of men and women had been brought into the plot over the generations, all with their own task, each armed with his or her own unique language and narrative. And the plot? Reach behind God's back and activate the messiah option; redeem humanity and put an end to what the plotters would call, The History of our Suffering.

Shem is also credited with borrowing God's secret of rising above time. In this way, agents of his plot were not bound by time, and could influence events taking place well before or after their own time. This was how our grandmother Leah went back in time to change her male fetus into a girl, to appease her sister, Rachel. But very few know about the night the founder of the Cosmic Wisdom movement, the Really Old Master, went back to the Sardinian birthplace of Napoleon Bonaparte, to the night of his emerging from the womb, to curse the baby with a vulnerability to cold weather—which would later turn the tide of the warrior's 1812 Russian campaign.

With all his gifts, Shem was a realist. He did not expect to succeed all at once. He was well aware of God's watchful Dark Aspect, and knew it would take sustained effort to outsmart that quality of the Creator. So his plot called for hundreds, if not thousands, of messianic pretenders, each one a spiritual kamikaze, ready to draw the wrath of the Dark Aspect. To the uninitiated, these contenders appeared to be failures, often bringing down many followers with them as they fell. Some stood out more than others. One particularly promising young man from Galilee fooled the Romans into capturing him; ultimately his captors embraced many of the improbable things he taught them. But each one of those failed messiahs was a gallant champion in the grand and ancient scheme to release God from captivity.

Noah's wife hadn't raised a fool.

9.

THE CABALIST'S HANDBOOK OF PRACTICAL MESSIANIC REDEMPTION states that:

Biblical Abraham, the forefather of the Jews both spiritually and biologically, was not endowed with the privilege of fathering the very Jew who would lead the nation and with it the entire human race to their final redemption. The quality of the messiah would not come down to the world through Abraham, the man of boundless kindness and generosity. Instead, it sprang from the loins of his greedy and conniving nephew, Lot.

The name Lot is derived from the substance lot (myrrh), a dark resin, tar-like in consistency but rather aromatic, which is extracted from the mastic tree. A kind of miracle occurs when a chunk of the lot paste is thrown into boiling water and mixed with olive oil: The process yields a wonderfully perfumed ointment with legendary healing powers.

As Abraham embarked on the journey away from his Mesopotamian birthplace, his redheaded nephew Lot tagged along. What was it about the perfectly good and utterly humble Abraham which could possibly appeal to his avaricious young nephew? Abraham had been called upon by God to go into the desert and seek the land of Canaan, which God promised to Abraham's children. But who had promised anything to Lot?

10.

Two hundred years after the failed Tower attempt, the descendants of the God-hunters of Babylon founded the cult of Sodom, Gomorrah, Adma and

Tzvoyim, four cities on the shores of the great, sweet water lake which would later become the Dead Sea. Rather than catch and kill God, like the original holocaust survivors, they attempted to rush the redemption of the world, and this way resolve the problems inherent in the Human Condition.

The Sodom cult's argument went: Why wait thousands of years for God to reach His conclusion about the success or failure of His experiment, The World? Everybody knew that redemption would only come in a generation that was all good, or all bad. Why not be as perfectly bad as possible, and force Him to close shop early, so we could all go back home to Him?

Thus, Goodness was outlawed in all four cities. Mercy became a crime, Charity was punishable by death and Friendship was a sin for which you could be flogged in the city square.

Of all the places in the world God could have chosen for the first incarnation of the spirit of the messiah—the one He had created before even creating light, or day and night—He picked the evil city of Sodom. That was the place where even heterosexuality, the very promulgation of the race, was frowned upon, unless it was with your neighbor's wife; preferably while your neighbor was watching, bound up in a chaise longue nearby.

The spirit of the messiah came to life as Pleitat, eldest daughter of Lot, who was the nephew of our Grandfather Abraham. Lot was building a nice practice as advocate and judge in the halls of justice in Sodom, and Pleitat was married off to one of the city's richest men. She lived a sheltered life, and would have followed in her father's footsteps to a position of great influence, if not for the rumors that started to spread.

A shepherd girl came forward to testify before a special tribunal of city elders, that Pleitat had found her dying of disease and hunger, too weak to crawl out of her shack even to relieve herself. Seeing her in such a state, the rich girl gave her water and returned that same day with some bread and figs. Figs!

Later, before the same committee of inquiry, another voice was heard. A beggar accused Pleitat of regularly sneaking him food, and offering him shelter for the night in her husband's stables.

That original incarnation of the messiah was no match for the great Darkness which God had invented on the first day of Creation. Mind you, that Darkness harbored the full might of God's suspicions about Himself, so It was unimaginably powerful. It's no wonder, then, that in an open duel with so much concentrated evil, in the dark heart of Evilville itself, the death of the first messiah was a foregone conclusion. Pleitat, Lot's daughter who dared perform two recorded acts of goodness in Sodom, was executed. Her sentimentality was an affront to the teachings of her cult nation.

This is how the messiah died the first time. It was the last attempt to redeem the world in such an overt, unsuspecting manner. All future efforts would be launched

27

furtively, utilizing misinformation and flummery to fool the Darkness.

The CABALIST'S HANDBOOK goes on to explain that all past attempts to redeem the world ended in failure due to humanity's essential goodness. As long as most people were basically decent, the Darkness remained condensed and its power split among a few nations and their appointed archangels. The smaller the Darkness was, the smarter it was.

But as soon as all the evil parts of the Darkness unite and it begins to grow, the HANDBOOK promises, it will grow more feeble-minded, and become helplessly lost in the quagmire of world politics. This is when a good plot to liberate the world has a chance of fooling the old Beast.

11.

THE CABALIST'S HANDBOOK OF PRACTICAL MESSIANIC REDEMPTION records:

God sent two angels to Sodom that last evening, and Lot, who grew up around his holy uncle, Abraham, was the only one who recognized that certain something you always see in a supernatural being. It could be the wings, or the single leg with the calf's hoof you can glimpse when they hover about; something usually gives them away if you really focus. So Lot rushed over to meet them, because he'd learned from Abraham that you wouldn't gain anything by pissing off the celestials. He prostrated himself on the ground before those two creatures and begged them to grace his home with their presence.

Mind you, it took more than a little bit of courage to show this kind of hospitality in a town that only recently had executed his own daughter for far less noticeable acts of kindness. But we have it on good authority that Lot was acting not out of courage but out of a healthy sense of self preservation. He did the math and was certain those two winged creatures (no one else saw the wings, of course) could hurt him worse than the entire court of Sodom.

The two angels finally gave in and entered his house. Lot was a renowned amateur chef—Canaanites went crazy for Mesopotamian cuisine—and he made them a feast: baked matzos, roast lamb, crispy lettuce and they all had a really good meal.

Why the flat bread and the lamb? Lot remembered that it was the night of the Passover seder. What, you ask? How could it be the night of the Passover seder if the Exodus from Egypt would not take place for another 400 years? It's a good question.

The qualities of each of the Jewish holidays existed since the Creation of the world, and were celebrated by the stars, the moon, the animals, and the rest of creation—along with some special people who were plugged into the cosmic mysteries—well before most other people got around to celebrating them. Lot, of course, had picked up the habits of the holidays from Abraham.

So, they had a wonderful Passover feast which lasted late into the night.

Sometime later, the men of the city, old and young, rich and poor, surrounded the house and began urging Lot to send out the two cute fellas he was harboring, so the mob outside could show them "a real good time."

Lot confronted the mob, "Please, boys, this is like the worst time to pursue that Let's Get All Wicked thing. Trust me, you really don't want to mess with these people."

When the mob refused to heed his sage advice, and got even rowdier—not a small feat for a Sodomite mob—Lot said to them, "Tell you what, I got these two daughters, certified virgins, never touched by a man before, good grades, too, one of them plays piano, the other paints. I'll send them out to you, but lay off my guests."

Again, the shrewd old guy acted on calculation. His daughters' value might plummet, they might even die, but Lot was prepared to pay this price to save his own life.

The maneuver didn't go over well with the Sodomites. They pushed uncomfortably close to Lot, who stood outside with his back braced up against the door. They called Lot a traitor, and threatened to come for him after they were finished with his guests; you get the idea. They pushed so hard, they nearly broke down the door. At the last minute, the two angels pulled Lot inside. They then conjured some mild smiting, blinding all the people outside. The mob continued their now slapstick attempts to break into the house.

Lot's reward was that the angels gave him and his family a warning about the plans for the four cult cities. They told him to get out of Sodom immediately, seek the high ground and not look back.

Like the man said: As long as you don't Sodomy, you can sodo everybody else.

12.

The HANDBOOK relates that:

God rained brimstone and fire on the four cities of the cult of Sodom, toppling buildings, people, animals and plants in a kind of local rerun of the dreaded Deluge. Lot and his remaining two daughters were rescued while the rest of the entire region literally went up in smoke.

Lot went up to the mountain, with his two daughters, and the three of them found refuge in a cave. As far as they were concerned, the world had been destroyed yet again. The plotters were prepared to go to great lengths to save God from Himself.

This was the time when God's trump card, His messiah panic button, was needed desperately.

This time Lot's daughters knew they couldn't use the direct approach. Since the execution of their elder sister, Pleitat, it had become clear that the messiah could only be evoked in roundabout ways, through forgetfulness, if not sheer unconsciousness. So they went about redeeming the soul of their doomed messiah-sister through a drunken liaison with their father.

The question all scholars of the ages have failed to answer is where did those two crafty girls find an alcoholic beverage in a deserted cave overlooking the burning Jordan Valley? Is it possible that they brought it with them from the condemned city? Doesn't seem likely. Is a jug of wine really the first thing a person would grab upon her escape from a rain of molten lava?

Here's what happened: There was an old man waiting for the three refugees inside the cave. He hid himself behind a wall, in the dark, lest the girls, upon finding him, ask questions regarding his strange garb which included a fedora and a long black coat. The bottle he handed the two girls contained 180 proof Stolichnaya, the finest thing Mankind has ever done with a potato.

Naturally, this caused dozens, if not hundreds, of temporal inconsistencies, not the least of which was the fact that the potato would not be introduced into that part of the world for several millennia. Nevertheless, it was done, through the good services of the grand master, who, incidentally, was not at all aware at the time of his involvement in a temporal paradox. All he did was pick up a bottle of vodka, pour himself a hefty portion, turn to the ladies' section of his synagogue, and raise his glass with an exuberant "L'Chayim!"

At the time, this act was considered to be yet another inexplicable action of the master's. All masters did stuff like that, and all their followers knew they were mystically fixing the broken parts of the cosmos with their strange behavior. Otherwise, how would you explain a master gesturing, "L'Chayim," to a group of strange women?

When you do stuff behind God's back, you sometimes leave footsteps all over the place. And the only way to avoid being tracked down is to make things as fantastic as possible. Any halfway decent magician will tell you, it's not how well you perform the sleight of hand, it's how good you are at keeping your audience's attention elsewhere.

So the daughters of Lot each slept with their father on two consecutive nights. The results of this incestuous grace were the births of two nations: One called Moab, which loosely translates as "I did it with my Daddy," the other Ammon, which is a derivative of "I did it with my own."

30

And the plot to instate a viable messiah was on its way, hidden even from God Himself, as per His own design.

Deception, incest and forgetfulness are the keys to our ancient effort to fool God into redeeming the world. They are also the keys to our ongoing discussion with Evil, God's expression of His nasty side. You'd expect the account of the origin of our redeemer to start with a perfect union between loving parents under a shooting star of approval, visible to wise kings everywhere. Not so. Our redeemer came from a town whose name is synonymous with buggery, from an inebriated mating of father and daughter.

On the Spiritual Continuum of Everything, incest rests between a pair of soiled girl's panties and twenty-eight miles of silent and humid darkness.

13.

Rabbi Mordechai Gutkind was an extremely effective emissary for his master. He made friends for the Cosmic Wisdom movement in the halls of Washington, DC. He hobnobbed with billionaires, knew personally every president from Nixon on, and was respected and feared both inside and outside the grand master's movement.

One Hanukkah, in the late 1970s, Gutkind persuaded the president of the United States to participate in a public menorah lighting ceremony outside the White House on the fourth day of the holiday. President Jimmy Carter feared the symbolism inherent in a half-lit menorah. He was a fundamentalist Christian whose religious theory assigned to God only the light work, leavinge Satan firmly in charge of the dark deeds. So, he requested that all eight lights be lit, despite the Jewish law which indicated that only four lights were to be lit that night.

The master's emissary acquiesced, albeit reluctantly, knowing that the president was entangled at the time in a struggle to the death against both the Ayatollah Khomeini, who was holding hundreds of Americans hostage in revolutionary Iran, and Massachusetts Senator Teddy Kennedy, who was threatening to steal the Democratic party's presidential nomination. But when the emissary arrived in the master's chamber to submit his report later that night, he received the tongue lashing of his life.

"I'm so disappointed in you, Motke," the master said and began to cry. "Of all days, how could you be afraid of a president on *Hanukkah*—the holiday of standing up to the empire—of all days? Why didn't you hold your own? What kind of Jew *are* you, my child?"

Whenever he told this story, Motke Gutkind burst into tears. It illustrated

31

the master's harshness in a way that few had ever experienced. Observers were utterly convinced that Gutkind possessed enormous personal strength to tolerate such an unadulterated rebuke from the great man. But when it came to the internal debate over the messianic message of the master cabalist, Gutkind's turned out to be a reluctant, even regressive, voice.

In interviews with the Jewish press, Gutkind was coy. When a reporter asked him if he had a valise under his bed, referring to tales of past cabalist sages who kept a suitcase packed in readiness to leave should the redeemer arrive, Gutkind answered that he *would* have, if he only knew what to pack. This was meant to illustrate that restraint, not unbound exuberance, was the proper attitude for the master's followers. But his subtle intents were drowned in the torrent of messianic fervor that gushed out of his fellow Cosmic Wisdomniks, especially the younger ones. In comparison, Gutkind and his colleagues at the helm of the movement appeared hostile to the very idea of redemption. What did they, paper pushers and bean counters, know about the ecstasy of deliverance?

Motke Gutkind was painfully aware that Leo Graneck and other leaders fanned the flames against him. When Gutkind went to visit the ailing master, his car tires were often slashed by messianic hooligans. People ignored him on the streets of Crown Heights even though, in many cases, he was the man who signed their paychecks.

Lionel Abulafia advised him to fight back by launching a counter campaign, which would adopt the master's message of striving for divine brilliance but in measured, sane ways. "How do you bring the messiah, anyway, Mot'l," the ancient sage said. "when the whole thing is a caprice of God's—*He* decides to bring messiah, whether we're ready or not. Just tell those bastards to pray, eat kosher and be nice to each other. Whether it helps bring the messiah or not, it's still a good way to live..."

But before Gutkind got around to hiring a copywriter and a designer for the campaign Abulafia had proposed, the master passed away. Instead of preaching commonplace goodness, Gutkind launched a relentless campaign to oust the messianists from every position of power they held within the movement. He was tough and thorough in weeding out the offensive messengers.

It seems that he was not quick enough to determine the tone of the first assembly of the Cosmic Wisdomniks' worldwide emissaries following the master's death. That gathering featured more than a thousand rabbis who insisted on displaying in their group photograph a huge banner with the slogan: Long Live Our Master, Our Teacher And Our Leader, King Messiah Forever And Eternally.

Five years later, not one such emissary would dare wave the offending banner.

Motke Gutkind may not have known how to pack a suitcase, but he could certainly pack a punch.

14.

As we near the moment of the old master's death, it is of paramount importance that we discuss the realities of human cloning.

A few months before the stroke, the American Society for Reproductive Medicine declared that human cloning by artificial embryo splitting was an entirely ethical procedure for increasing the number of implantable human blastocysts* used in certain infertility treatments.

However, embryo splitting can produce only a limited number of copies, as the early embryo can be separated only a limited number of times. Furthermore, the procedure is incapable of producing a "clone" of an adult.

Nuclear transfer, the other method for producing cloned humans, does not suffer from either of these limitations.

Nuclear transfer (or more specifically "somatic cell nuclear transfer") is a conceptually simple procedure. The nucleus is removed from an egg, and a donor cell nucleus is inserted into that same egg via micro injection or electrofusion**. The egg is thus "fertilized," and the result is a zygote. This reconstituted zygote has the potential to divide into a blastocyst; if implanted in a womb, it can develop into a child genetically identical to the nuclear donor.

As early as 1992, cloning expert Professor Albert Vishinsky said that he would consider leaving the US, where cloning experiments were banned, if he could find another country where he could carry out the initial animal research.

The *Times of London* reported his statement that he would only use the technology on men unable to father children because they could not produce viable sperm. Professor Vishinsky was one of several eminent scientists

---

* The modified early embryos, typically having the form of a hollow fluid-filled rounded cavity, bounded by a single layer of cells, characteristic of placental mammals.

** Induction of cell fusion of living protoplasts by electrical stimulation.

who argued that human cloning was a way of helping infertile couples who could not have their own biological children by the established techniques of in vitro fertilization (IVF).

Ian Wilmut, one of the scientists at the Roslin Institute near Edinburgh who cloned Dolly the sheep in the late 1990's, told a Commons committee in London that the technical hurdles were not insurmountable and that it might be possible to clone humans, although he repeatedly emphasized his opposition to this on ethical grounds.

The cloning technique pioneered by the Roslin Institute involved the removal of the nucleus of an adult sheep cell—containing the animal's genetic blueprint—and its implantation into an unfertilized egg.

In 1998, and then in 2004, Ian Wilmut was charged by the British Ministry of Health with the illegal production of human clones. It was revealed during the investigation that at least 500 healthy human children in Asia, Europe and the Americas are the young clones of their adult parents.

15.

Two years to the day after his stroke, the old cabalist ended the raging brouhaha among his faithful when he endured a second, more massive stroke. This time, all communication with him ceased. He lay comatose on the eighth floor of Beth Israel Medical Center on the east side of New York.

Despite his advanced age, his devotees were still not ready to let their master go. They kept a vigil in his hospital room at all hours of the day and night. They believed that as long as there was even one Jew sitting at the master's side reciting psalms, the angel of death couldn't grab him. That's how frightened they were to embark on the next phase in their lives.

One night the vigil was entrusted to Yankel Birenbaum, a yeshiva student whose rich father owned a large biotechnical company named Comprehensive Cell Knowledge. Yankel left his post in the master's room to grab a smoke a few minutes before dawn.

As soon as Yankel left the room, the master was spirited away. He was ninety-two, for crying out loud, not at all a bad age to go.

When Yankel Birenbaum returned, only three minutes later, he was filled with a sudden sense of dread. The room was suffused with the multicolored graphics of loss as every piece of medical machinery displayed its own unique variation on the flatline.

A medical storm erupted. Green and white robes performed a crazed dance of crisis around the aged corpse which stubbornly refused to come back to life.

Eighteen-year-old Yankel Birenbaum bore on his young shoulders the undeniable responsibility for this fresh tragedy. Frozen, he witnessed the futile turbulence that ripped through his dead master's hospital room.

One by one, the doctors, each an expert in his or her own field, surrendered to the inevitable.

Yankel held on to his smoldering unfiltered cigarette, permitting the advancing flame to lick his index and middle fingers. By the time he sensed the pain, the burning end had eaten deeply into the flesh. He dropped the consumed butt on the linoleum floor and stared uncomprehendingly at his blistered skin. Half mad with guilt and sadness, the young man whispered the line from Psalms (137:5), *"If I forget thee, O Jerusalem, let me forget my right hand."* He received an odd kind of satisfaction from repeating this verse.

Birenbaum refused medical treatment. A few days later, gangrene set in on his right hand, which finally had to be amputated at the wrist. This too was a great source of comfort to the guilt-ridden acolyte.

16.

Yankel Birenbaum turned out to be a remarkably resourceful young man, considering what he accomplished in the frenzied moments following the master's demise, especially in light of his terrible physical injury and his even more debilitating guilt and shame.

While the master's body was transported to be ritually cleansed and prepared for burial, Birenbaum collected his bedclothes from the gurney. Each object that brushed against Yankel's burnt hand sent a ripple of agony shooting through his body, but he was quite beyond those petty concerns. With the bundle of bedclothes tucked away inside his backpack, Yankel rushed downstairs, cut through the burgeoning crowd of grief-stricken followers, and ran outside to the street.

At 11:00 p.m. he entered a small, windowless lab room in the Department of Biological Sciences at Columbia University, where three anxious scientists had gathered. Led by Professor Albert Vishinsky, the scientists were working on projects coordinated by the university and financed by

Comprehensive Cell Knowledge, the biotechnology company owned in part by Yankel's father. That year CCK had made international headlines with the first published scientific account of cloned human embryos. Despite the news splash, the report was not terribly encouraging. CCK's most successful embryo attained just six cells before it stopped dividing; another reached only four cells.

The Columbia-CCK experiments were widely judged inconsequential, and not a likely target for investors. Only insiders knew that the disappointing numbers were forged. The true results were the stuff of science fiction: Fully grown skin tissue and a variety of body parts had been cloned, and the only thing keeping CCK's ambitious team from developing a complete child was management's hesitation. A cloned child, they knew, would evoke public shock and indignation. Not a good business plan.

The ample collection of skin and hair cells plucked from the master's bedclothes provided the group of conspirators with just the right cause célèbre to move ahead with their work.

The previous year, the US House of Representatives had passed the Human Cloning Prohibition Act by a crushing hundred-vote margin. The resulting ban on the creation of cloned human embryos for reproductive or therapeutic purposes imposed a punishment of up to ten years in prison and a million-dollar fine. Politics and religion had united to gain the upper hand in their war with science. But Mr. Birenbaum the elder was banking on his trump card: genetic material from one of the most popular religious figures in America. If the great master cabalist was revived through CCK's forbidden technology, would anyone dare condemn the scientist who made it possible?

In the debate preceding the House vote, the anti-cloning faction had warned against the "industrial exploitation of human life," conjuring images of clone plantations where human beings would be manufactured and then rended for their body parts. The House majority whip at the time, a Texan, decried the "monstrous science that lacks any reasonable consideration for the sanctity of human life." But would the same horror be inspired by a clone of a man who had promised to redeem the world? How's *that* for a modern-day resurrection?

The door to the lab was locked round the clock; surveillance cameras monitored all motion outside and inside; non-essential support personnel—guards, custodians, service technicians—were replaced frequently.

A dozen test tubes, each holding one human egg retrieved just hours before from student donors, were positioned under microscope lenses, their images shimmering on a bank of video monitors. The eggs' chromosomes were removed, and the scientists moved briskly and efficiently from one tube to the next, fusing what remained of the egg with a skin cell belonging to the dead master. If the procedure succeeded, the result would be a cloned human embryo.

"It's going great," Professor Vishinsky told Yankel Birenbaum the following week. Yankel's hand had already been amputated, but his flushed face showed not a trace of the agony which by rights should have been tormenting him to the point of madness. All that claimed his concern were the painstaking procedures underway. Dr. Vishinsky, a quiet, small man with long hair and granny glasses, had just positioned a small plastic dish on a microscope platform. At the bottom of the dish, under millimeters of liquid, red culture, were millions of fibroblasts, living skin cells taken from the master's pillowcase and sheets.

"They're now in G1, the rest phase that cells enter before preparing to divide again," the scientist explained. "This is the best stage for cloning."

Yankel peered through the microscope at the tiny cells. Unmistakably visible inside each nestled a nucleus containing a full copy of the master's 46 chromosomes. With this freight of authentic DNA, each cell had all the genetic information necessary to build a cloned human embryo.

"It's a bitch, working with only a dozen eggs," Vishinsky said. "It's totally different than animals." In a cow-cloning experiment conducted the year before, Vishinsky's team went through two thousand eggs each day. Cow eggs were shipped from slaughterhouses, while human eggs had to be obtained from live young women, all of whom were paid to undergo two weeks of hormone injections and a painful surgical procedure.

It cost CCK $25,000 for each test tube containing one of the master's embryos, making the final cost of the chosen embryo $300,000.

At five days of development, a human embryo is smaller than a grain of sand. It is a perfectly round ball with a fluid-filled core. Huddled against one wall of its interior is a group of cells known as the inner cell mass. The outside of the ball is destined to become the placenta and associated membranes; the inner cell mass is what forms a baby. But after only five days of development, no cell's fate is yet determined—it's impossible to tell which cells will become blood or muscle, skin or brain, gut or liver. All that's present is the simple raw material from which the more than two

37

hundred cell types in a human body will eventually be constructed.

At last, the embryo was implanted—and $50,000 paid to the surrogate mother. Then came the truly tense part: Would the $350,000 baby survive? Would a legitimate pregnancy ensue?

After six weeks, Professor Vishinsky was ecstatic. Everything was going well. This was the kind of success that scientists are trained to treat with suspicion—you just don't get a human baby from a skin cell on the first try and scientists are trained not to expect miracles. But test after test produced only positive results.

An ultrasound test was performed, utilizing high-frequency sound waves to create pictures of the fetus on a computer screen. This is the most commonly used test in pregnancy. It can verify a due date, check the overall health of the fetus and its development, measure the amniotic fluid, check the condition of the placenta, and determine the sex of the baby.

That final part came out all wrong. At an overall cost just shy of half a million dollars, the master's clone was a girl.

17.

Was this a special miracle created just for this occasion? Scientific study seems to indicate otherwise.

The American Society for Reproductive Medicine sponsored an experiment in the late 1990's, in which one hundred male rats were cloned under identical conditions. Of these, only thirty-five samples yielded viable products. Those were not considered satisfactory results for a program intended to follow a large group of clones through their life stages.

Researchers prepared to scrap this attempt and start again with a larger population, hoping for a yield of at least one hundred viable clones.

A young intern suggested that the embryos be allowed to come to full term in order to check their reproductive organs. She argued that cloned individuals might be sterile, like mules, the offspring of a horse and a donkey which lacks the capacity to reproduce itself. Her supervisors thought this was a stupid idea, since everybody knew that clones were precise replicas of the *entire* original specimen.

But with time on their hands and an intern who didn't cost them anything extra, they figured: what would be the harm in checking thirty-five tiny little rat privates?

The results gave some researchers pause: Two of the clones turned out to be female.

A year later, the same team designed a test with 150 male and 150 female donor rats. The female rats generated only female rat clones. But the males generated three female clones out of eighty-five viable births.

This rate of one hundred percent female from female, and only ninety-seven percent male from male (the remaining three per cent being female from male) is now considered the standard in small mammal cloning.

Incidentally, no official data is available on the *Änderungsgeschwindigkeit*, or rate of change from male to female in larger mammal cloning, specifically in humans. But anecdotal data suggests that the rate rises in proportion to the increased age of the male donor. In male donors above age seventy-five, the resultant clone is equally likely to be of either sex.

She was born in a den that was converted into a birthing room, by a midwife so adept at her métier, she didn't need to slap the baby around to make sure she had all her vitals in perfect order. She was born at dawn, just as the sun peeked behind the horizon; there was no shooting star, no barnyard animals, definitely no wise men—the room was women only.

She gave a good cry on her own, and then sank into the comfort of her receiving blanket. No announcements were made. Only a handful of men and women were to know. Secrecy was of the essence.

Shhhhh...

Her mother nursed her a few days, and then left for the city without ever asking for money. Throughout the nine months of gestation, the young woman frequently referred to her experience as a time of quiet retreat. Indeed, afterwards she was refreshed, even exuberant, once again ready to take on the world. Years later, when stories about her amazing child filtered back to her, she wasn't the least bit surprised.

18.

As soon as the grand master of Brooklyn died, he found himself standing in a pool of his own tears, under a willow tree between heaven and earth. In that place, where an endless, muddy horizon surrounded him beneath a silvery moon, the Dark Aspect of God attempted to eliminate him.

Nobody, not even the archangel of violence and pain, knew for certain whether the old cabalist was the messiah or not. Certainly, dying in the middle of his mission put a serious crimp in that notion. After all, how could a dead messiah breathe new life into the rest of Humanity?

But Samael had been fed plenty of surprise crow by the Boss before, so he didn't take anything for granted, not even the death of the old cabalist. According to THE CABALIST'S HANDBOOK OF PRACTICAL MESSIANIC REDEMPTION, Samael still smarted from his encounters with several other elderly Jewish men considered dead and gone.

Our grandfather Jacob bested the Beast. Upon his death, Jacob's celestial nemesis planned to taunt him a little, maybe ask how the great patriarch felt about his children going into slavery in Egypt in a couple of years. You see, Jacob was supposed to just lie there, dead as a doornail, and helplessly accept the taunt, as millions had before him.

But Jacob never died, as it turned out. When Samael readied himself to spew his well-articulated venom at what he believed to be Jacob's lifeless body, Jacob sat up, dripping Egyptian embalming fluids, and smacked the red one right in the kisser.

A few centuries later, King David showed Samael that there was a literal aspect to the popular chant, "David, King of Israel, is alive and real." As the messenger of nastiness crouched over David's grave, singing a haunting tune of hatred to the killer of Goliath, David's arm tore out of the earth and grabbed Samael by the neck, dragging him down under. Angels don't normally choke in fear, but this one did. For a century or so he couldn't stop shivering. Even petty demons took great pleasure in sneaking up behind his back and yelling, "Hey, look, it's King David!" —causing the poor archangel to hop and scream in fear like a schoolgirl.

Several others continued to function in body despite the fact that their spirits have long since left them. In all these cases, the physicality had been processed out of these bodies by their righteous owners long before their nominal "deaths." Much as those who labor to refine their personalities in an attempt to reduce their attachment to things material, these few men completed that part of their earthly task early, and so, naturally, had the opportunity to transform the rest of themselves.

Samael walked around the master in endless circles, trying to assess the status of his mortality. The master stared at him with glaring scorn. Finally, the master yelled at him, "Go away! What are *you* looking for?"

The vile one stopped in his tracks. "I can't tell if you're alive or not..."

"What's it to *you*?" the master asked. He was still very agitated from his recent passing. Normally, his manner was extremely polite.

"I can't figure you out..." The archangel and drew closer. "I think I'll take a taste and find out..."

"Are you ready to risk it?" The master challenged him. "I tell you, in the mood I'm in, I'd tear you to pieces and bring History to an end right here and now..."

"You wouldn't dare... Not without permission from Him..."

"How do you know I *don't* have permission from Him?" The master was a superb poker player.

The staring contest ended in a draw, which meant that the master won this round. Since that time, Samael would visit and try to destroy the master. Of course, he could only do that if the master was still alive, which had yet to be corroborated one way or the other.

If he tried to kill the old man and it turned out that he was already dead—even Samael himself wasn't sure what would happen next.

So Samael shrewdly resolved to continue his patient work. He would continue quietly to utterly decimate any possibility of redemption. By any messiah at *all*. And he would come back to kill *this* one at the moment that his plot to destroy the Jewish nation hit its conclusion.

He gave it twenty years at the outside, give or take a year.

19.

According to one of the latest entries in THE CABALIST'S HANDBOOK OF PRACTICAL MESSIANIC REDEMPTION, despite his vow to stay away from the grand master, Samael nevertheless could not contain his curiosity. Every once in a while he would pop in or send a demon scout to check on the ancient man, just to be on the safe side. The HANDBOOK adds:

> In this context it is crucial to mention that the last grand master's spot on the Spiritual Continuum of Everything was directly to the left of Abigail, King David's wife. And Abigail was one spot to the left of our Grandmother Leah. This, as it turns out, was an incredibly powerful combination. Both women were blessed with the talent for relentless loyalty, and both knew the secret of sweetening harsh decrees.
>
> Whenever Samael tried to sneak up on the master, either Leah or Abigail would cast a veil of teardrops that ran down from the willow tree and touched the pool at the master's feet.
>
> They were able to maneuver tears so skillfully because Leah had spent seven years of her life crying for fear she would not merit to marry our grandfather Jacob. It seemed she would be forced to settle instead for his coarse brother Esau—

until her sister Rachel fixed her up with Jacob. Abigail also cried for seven years, fearing that she would not merit to marry King David. Abigail was already married—to a mean, rich, old man, Nabal the Carmelite. In the most considerate act of her husband's wretched life, he keeled over just in time for her to unite with the charismatic new king. But until Nabal exited, Abigail for sure had done her share of crying...

Those two important and effective women made it their business to defend the grand master.

On one day of each year, the grand master was particularly vulnerable to Samael's attacks. This occurred annually on the fifth of the Hebrew month of Tevet, corresponding initially to the date, January 6, 1987. It was on this date that a federal court had awarded to the the Cosmic Wisdom movement ownership of the exceptional library of the long-departed sixth master. By gaining control of the books, the movement effectively removed them from the possession of that master's surviving grandson. Although rumor had it that the grandson planned to sell the rare and valuable collection, that did not whitewash the incident.

So, like clockwork on the fifth of Tevet, whole armies of angels took up their posts at the willow tree perimeter. When Samael and his host of demons attacked, as they did without fail each year, the supernatural sparks flew every which way and the entire muddy plain was ignited by white electric fire dancing around black electric fire. If by chance, the master sustained some injuries, the archangel Rafael was soon on hand to heal him. Each time, the cabalist recuperated before Samael could see that his nemesis was very much alive.

20.

Adopted children develop a wide range of strategies concerning their biological roots. These run the gamut from utter indifference, to obsessive exploration which may overtake their adolescent years and mark their entire lives. According to THE CABALIST'S HANDBOOK OF PRACTICAL MESSIANIC REDEMPTION, adopted children are especially motivated to seek their unique place on earth. These children are living allegories for the very concept of a soul coming to this world with a mission.

The question of Nechama Gutkind's roots elicited so much ambivalence in the grown ups around her that she learned to develop quiet ways of detecting information without asking questions. People loved talking to her, and she became masterful at maneuvering conversations to the outer edge of the taboo subject. She patiently collected the bits of knowledge and pieced together a mosaic of her origins.

A fleeting comment from Nechama's mother, Leah, about the hectic preparation for her arrival as a baby less than a week old, was a signal to the five-year-old that Leah was not her biological parent.

A seventh birthday card from her brother, Berel, saying how much he anticipated and expected her success in the future, betrayed his awareness that she was somehow unusual.

Her father Mordechai's insistence, when Nechama was ten, that he alone teach Nechama from the works of the Master of Brooklyn—suggested some mysterious connection to the bearded old man on the book's jacket.

Her existence was no secret. People knew that the Gutkinds had adopted a baby girl late in life and were raising her as their own. But until her twelfth birthday, she was home-schooled by her mother, Leah. This meant that much of her knowledge of human society was strictly theoretical. Nechama was a loner who felt perfectly comfortable, and even happy, in her solitude; her social skills had been developed purely based on her relationships with two Jews in their mid-sixties and a multitude of grown up house guests.

So though she wasn't exactly being raised as a family secret, she wasn't that well-known outside her house.

Secrets were a bad thing, Nechama knew intuitively. Secrets were the reason people drank too much, ate too much and loved too much. Secrets were the greatest source of human pain, to the point where one had to ask if anyone could afford to harbor them. But in an environment so imbued with secrets—the Scranton, Pennsylvania, home of Rabbi Mordechai Gutkind, leader of the Cosmic Wisdom movement—Nechama couldn't confront her loved ones directly about the circumstances of her birth—until she was strong enough to face their reaction.

When she turned twelve she felt strong enough.

One early morning, Rabbi Mordechai Gutkind pulled his prehistoric Oldsmobile into a parking space in front of his house. He had spent several days fund raising among the wealthy Jews of northern Pennsylvania (alas, the number of movement supporters had dropped following the demise of the charismatic master). He spotted his daughter waiting for him outside in the peaceful drizzle.

The small, two-story house on Rochester Street in Keyser Valley served both as the Gutkinds' private home and as the Cosmic Wisdom House for suburban Scranton. Nechama's room was in the attic, a choice which bespoke the haphazard manner in which she had been added to the family. Looking at her through his car windshield, Rabbi Gutkind wondered if perhaps they should have given her a different room.

He sighed. Secrets were an imperfect thing. Lies were even worse. You could hope against hope to keep a secret down, but a lie had a way of taking on a life of its own. Pretty soon, he knew, he'd have to make fast and furious choices between secrets, lies, and even truths.

Leaning against a parked car on a dreadfully late Sunday night (or pitifully early Monday morning), Nechama felt no malice towards her father, although he had avoided her studiously for several weeks now. She understood why she was being pushed around, her neatly penned messages lost, promised return calls never made, appointments canceled at the last minute. She was only twelve, but her innate talent for character judgment was fully developed. She knew ambivalence when she spotted it; she knew shame, and she knew fear.

Her daddy was afraid.

Despite appearances, despite its phenomenal growth, despite its enormous political weight in Moscow, Beijing and Washington, the Cosmic Wisdom movement had still not recovered from the crisis of losing its mystical shepherd. Without that great, righteous man to point out the right direction, the last thing the movement's leaders needed was to unveil the secret of Nechama's birth. Normally, Rabbi Gutkind might opt to quash a source of danger to his movement, maybe discredit it, maybe take legal steps to impoverish the dangerous person or persons at the root of the problem. But how does one quash one's own daughter?

At times, Nechama felt she understood her dad better than many Cosmic Wisdomniks did. In her view, the Secretary General of the Cosmic Wisdom movement was the most authentic Jew she had ever met. And she always understood his toughness as completely consistent with his holy values.

But even at her tender age she knew that her father's enormous resources of strength might be called upon if the identity of the master's biochemical descendant became dangerous to the movement. For all the right reasons Gutkind would not hesitate to do whatever was deemed necessary.

And she knew that he was petrified by the full meaning of that commitment.

"Good morning, Daddy, how have you been?" She rushed over as soon as the old rabbi had opened his car door. Gutkind stared at her.

"I'm sorry I had to stalk you like this, I didn't have any other choice. You've been avoiding me like you owe me money...."

44

"Well, my child, let's start this right, shall we?" Gutkind quickly regained his composure. "Have you had breakfast?"

"Not really," she said. "It's a little early...."

"Not if you skipped dinner and lunch, like me, it isn't early. Can I ask your mother to add a plate to the breakfast table? I believe she's up already...."

"I graciously accept."

"Don't 'gracious' me, little rascal," Gutkind smiled, "I know you're planning to wring me out and hang me up to dry...."

"Funny you should be using dirty laundry imagery," Nechama retorted, "it's just what I had in mind, too...."

"Weisenheimer...."

They ate in the kitchen. The rabbi and Nechama helped cut the three-day-old challah and mix a dozen eggs for an enormous serving of French toast.

The Gutkinds had three grown sons. The eldest, now in his forties, shared his father's responsibilities representing the movement in Washington, DC. The other two were emissaries, running Cosmic Wisdom centers, one in Europe, the other in the Far East.

"Wonderful breakfast, Leah'leh," Motke complemented his wife, a thin woman with sharp, bird-like features.

"You want more?" Leah asked. "Nechama?"

"I'm stuffed, Mom," she said. "And your husband and I must stay alert for our conversation...."

"She's smooth," Leah Gutkind said to her husband.

"I discovered a man named Yankel Birenbaum," their twelve-year-old cut to the chase. "He's a Cosmic Wisdomnik and his family owns a bio-research company. I also spoke to Dr. Vishinsky, the biologist. I know about the cloning."

Gutkind examined her with a clear, unrepentant look. "I know you know," he said. "You're a very dangerous girl, Nechama'leh. Every organization is afraid of people like you. Because you're skilled at getting all the facts; but we're never sure you know and understand the context."

"The context seems obvious. A frightened young man, who believes he's just let the master die, takes a desperate step to undo the damage. He approaches a renowned biologist with the cabalist master's DNA and pays him to produce a clone. A real heir."

"And you're sure this is how it happened?" Gutkind asked.

"Vishinsky sounded very convincing. I'm confident that the technology exists. The only limits appear to be ethical, and, of course, legal."

"Did you check how many successful human clonings have been achieved to date?" Gutkind inquired quietly.

"That we know of?" She began. "Rumors abound. Some say about ten, some say as many as five hundred."

"Do you know how many attempts to clone humans have taken place to date?" Gutkind pressed patiently.

"Oh, I'd say more than a thousand. But the popular view definitely counts Vishinsky among the successful few."

"You say a *thousand*?" Motke Gutkind rebutted. "Try *more than ten thousand!* Thank God, mankind is nowhere near developing the technology to create assembly-line human drones. Some say it would be a nightmare, others suggest there are good things that may come out of it. I say, thank God it isn't here yet.

"So some biologist from Columbia University, financed by an hysterical rich kid from Brooklyn, told you he succeeded in creating a human being out of cells from the master of blessed memory."

"You don't believe it?" she asked tersely.

"I was told that story more than twelve years ago. What shall I tell you? I believe they tried. I also believe a nice Jewish woman—your biological mother—became pregnant after they tried. In itself, her pregnancy was a very good thing. When Vishinsky came to me with the news that there was a brand new Jewish baby about to be born with no one to raise it, I right away asked Leah if she was ready for the job. Your three brothers had been out of the house many years by then, but Leah was eager to once again embrace the precious cycle of diapers, skinned knees, and birthday parties."

"So, you took me in, but you didn't believe that I was a replica of the master?"

"Nechama'leh, Nechama'leh, Nechama'leh... When you tell me that you understand what it means, this term, a master, any master, not just *the* Master, then maybe we could discuss how to replicate it. Maybe we could bottle it, too...."

"Then why did you take in the child?" she pressed on.

"Because a Jewish baby needed a home. What did you expect us to do?"

"Well, I'm sure there were thousands of Jewish and non-Jewish couples out there who would have given their right arm to adopt a baby."

Gutkind fell silent for a long moment. His wife got up to collect the breakfast dishes. When Nechama rose to help, Leah gestured her back into her seat. She noted how nervous her adoptive mother was and figured Leah needed to do something with her hands.

"More orange juice, anyone?" Mrs. Gutkind broke the silence a minute later. Father and daughter nodded yes.

"Nechama, I'm going to say something to you now which I might regret. I'll be saying it with a heavy heart," Gutkind opened. "Because I don't really know if you know enough to understand me, and because, taken out of context, what I'm about to say may not sound so good. But I trust that you know the Cosmic Wisdom movement well enough to believe our motives are pure."

"In the large scheme of things I believe they are, yes," she agreed.

"Oh, I think we're doing a heck of a job on the small scale, too," her father refused to concede to Nechama's reluctant generalization.

"You were going to explain why you didn't offer the baby to anyone else," Nechama said quietly.

"Sooner or later, word was going to come out about you," Gutkind proceeded. "Unfortunately, misguided people have a tendency towards vulgarity. How soon would it be, I thought, before this child found herself the subject of adoration by thousands, if not millions, of people?"

"Would that have been so bad?" Nechama blurted out.

Rabbi Gutkind stopped dead in his tracks. He opted, predictably, for the patient, methodical and roundabout response.

"We had a patriarch named Jacob," he began. "His son, Joseph, happened to be the ruler of all of ancient Egypt, second only to the Pharaoh himself. When it came time for Jacob to die—he was already 147 years old—he pleaded with Joseph not to let him be buried in Egypt. 'Swear to me,' he said to his son, 'that you'll bury me in my forefathers' grave site in Hebron,' which was then in Canaan."

"I'm familiar with the story, Dad," she said curtly. When her father brought up a Biblical tale, it was usually his way of making people play on his turf.

"Why did Jacob insist that he not be buried in Egypt? Why did his son swear to take his body back to Canaan? Because he was nostalgic? Because he wanted to be near his own dead parents? His dead wife? Yes, partly. But more importantly, he didn't want the Egyptians to turn him

47

into a god after he died.

"Jacob was a great holy man, a great master, if you will. When he first came to Egypt, everyone saw the water of the Nile rise above the riverbanks to lick his feet. He was obviously a great, great soul. Human instinct, left to its own devices, would have made Jacob into another Ra or another Isis in no time.

"We saw how a master, our own beloved master," his voice trembled, as it did whenever he mentioned his revered mentor, "was unfortunately turned by some vulgar individuals into a god in his own lifetime and even more so after his passing. I would not permit that baby to become another, forgive me, baby Jesus in the manger.

"I do not believe that you are in any way an offspring of the master. I have never believed it. The whole notion is ludicrous. Utter nonsense. So what? You think the average Joe out there would care? People are so desperate to believe in something. All they would have needed was the wisp of a rumor to deprive you of your childhood, deprive you of a life. You would have become a little Buddha, like those Tibetan children who are the so-called reincarnations of the dead Dalai Lamas.

"So, your mother and I raised you in complete anonymity. You were ours. That is all anybody needed to know."

"What kind of baby was I?" she asked, realizing all of a sudden that this was her very first conversation with her father about her early years.

"A lovely, absolutely wonderful girl," Gutkind assured her with a warm smile, and hurriedly drove home another point. "Which makes the cloning story that much more improbable, don't you think? The least you'd expect from a clone is that it would be the same sex as its parent."

"Actually, there have been reports of an occasional inconsistency in the sexual profile from donor to clone," Nechama commented.

"You read *your* reports, I'll read mine," Gutkind responded dryly. "If you ask *me*, I'd expect a cloned offspring to resemble the parent in every way, but I'm not a scientist. Are *you* a scientist?"

She didn't answer. Instead, she pressed on with her next question. "Why did you name me 'Nechama?'"

"What difference does it make? We wanted to shelter you, not advertise your existence."

"But Nechama is a derivation of the old master's name."

"It's a common enough name," Gutkind stood his ground.

"Nonsense," she argued. "Nechama absolutely comes from Menachem, the master's name. And both names mean comfort and comforter, respectively, which are euphemistic references to the redeemer."

"My goodness, Leah, would you listen to this girl's vocabulary?" Gutkind couldn't suppress his fatherly pride. "And they say the Cosmic Wisdom home-schooling curriculum neglects secular studies. This child's English is better than some senators'."

"Our curriculum definitely neglects secular studies," his wife retorted authoritatively, as the home-schooling parent. "This one just happens to be a voracious reader."

"Why didn't you name me 'Ruthie,' or 'Esther?'" Nechama proceeded, stopping the discussion from degenerating into the area of the movement's education policies—although she, too, possessed strong views on the issue. "You couldn't give up on the notion in your own heart, could you?"

"Nechama also happens to be your mother's paternal grandmother's name," Gutkind commented quietly.

Minutes later, as Nechama climbed the stairs to her little bedroom, the kitchen door opened and Leah Gutkind came running after her. The child stopped and waited for her midway up the stairs.

"No matter what you hear, sweetie, we know that you're a good and righteous person..." her mother said, spreading her arms to embrace her.

"Am I the scion of the master?" Nechama asked bluntly, hoping to take advantage of Leah's sudden vulnerability.

"You know," Leah Gutkind answered in a dreamy voice, "one time, when you were three, I caught sight of you standing in the vestibule, your wavy, golden-red hair parted in the middle and falling over your back, your sweet, chubby cheeks, your open—but I mean completely open—countenance... You wore this adorable, old-fashioned sailor's suit, with a black-striped collar... You're staring up at me and I'm thinking, why is this image so familiar?"

"The master's picture as a three-year-old!" Nechama cried out. You couldn't open an online biography of the old master and not run into that image, sooner or later.

"Yes, that very famous photograph of him as a little boy, before they sheared his hair. I have to say, at that moment I couldn't tell you apart from that photograph."

"Did you take my picture then? Do you still have it?" Nechama asked heatedly.

"No," Leah Gutkind suddenly withdrew, snapping out of the emotional moment. The front door opened and Rabbi Mordechai Gutkind emerged, carrying several packages of educational leaflets, and stood silently beneath them under the entrance light.

"No pictures," Leah said. "We could never take pictures. No pictures…" Without meeting Nehchama's gaze, Leah turned and descended back to the kitchen.

21.

The blossoming twelve-year-old Nechama was such a voracious reader of both secular and sacred books that Leah Gutkind felt no longer qualified to be her teacher. Because of the heavy restrictions on Nechama's public interactions, Leah and Mordechai decided to secure a tutor to come to the house. At least that's the official Gutkind family version of the story.

In reality, Lionel Abulafia simply arrived one morning, stinking of cigarettes and frozen near to death from a night of riding on the back seat of a motorcycle driven by his housekeeper, a huge African woman. Abulafia banged on the Gutkinds' door one morning, demanding to be admitted. He wasn't rude about it, just very impatient.

Leah Gutkind let him in. She had known of him, and had seen him many times in Crown Heights, but this was her first personal exchange with the master's ancient confidant. She thought he looked awful, his clothes all torn, and his head bare, his hat having been lost back on the highway. He looked a mess, and the large, dark-skinned woman standing beside him, wearing a German army helmet, looked downright menacing.

"Leah, right?" Abulafia inquired. "We're here to discuss your little girl. You know me. This is my house lady, Victoria Martin. "

On the Spiritual Continuum of Everything, Victoria Martin was positioned between the Queen of Diamonds and the cherry tree one over from the cherry tree cut down by young George Washington (1732-1799). It is considered by most to be one of the luckiest spots in the universe.

Leah tensed up. She reached for the phone, to enlist her husband's support.

"Relax," said Abulafia, "we're friends. It's just that we been riding the damned bike so many hours, we could use something warm to drink."

This was the first time in Leah Gutkind's many years as housewife and hostess that she'd been too overwhelmed by the appearance of a guest to offer him a cup of coffee or tea. She apologized profusely, then hurried into the kitchen and put a kettle on the stove while calling Mordechai.

"It's Lionel Abulafia, Mot'l," she whispered. "He's here with a huge African woman, says he wants to take care of Nechama'leh's education..."

"An African woman?" Her husband wasn't sure he'd heard right.

"His housekeeper, I think. They rode up here on her motorcycle..."

Motke Gutkind tried not to laugh, realizing his wife was genuinely distraught, but the effort to remain serious was enormous. "You know Purim is many weeks from now," he finally couldn't help himself.

"Yes, I know, it sounds funny," she consented. "What am I supposed to do with them?"

"Give them something to eat, something to drink..."

"I'm doing it as we speak."

"Then call Nechama down, introduce her."

"You're not serious..."

"Very serious. Lionel is probably the finest teacher we could find for her. And if he decided to show up a little crazy, he probably had a good reason."

The clown show put on by Abulafia and Victoria Martin was an act of self-preservation. Call it warding off the evil eye, if you will. The wily cabalist was aware of the multitude of forces already loose in the world, seeking out Nechama Gutkind's scent. Those forces were likely to overlook any possible threat posed by an old man in tatters and a giant black woman crowded together on top of a decrepit motorcycle. Nechama witnessed the entire arrival scene from her attic window. Abulafia's peculiar entrance was Nechama's first lesson.

22.

The seven years that ensued introduced Nechama to a world of intellectual and spiritual treasures. Of course, her mentors had an exceptional pupil on their hands. From infancy, Nechama had been able to judge situations by their aroma, by scents that were impossible for others to discern. Few grown ups ever understood her special gift. It wasn't that she had a superior sense of smell—she couldn't track people by sniffing their handkerchiefs, and she could not smell any farther than anyone else. But she could *read* smells better than a blood hound on a clear Alabama summer night.

There was a smell to fear and a smell to lust and a smell to shame and a smell to forgery and a smell to cruelty and a smell to love.

She could examine the smells and dissect them, hold them up against the light, finger them and detect unusual textures inside. To her, smell had substance and layers of common and uncommon ingredients. Abulafia's instruction meshed well with Nechama's gifts.

His teaching method regarded the student as a newborn babe. Abulafia and Victoria closely duplicated for Nechama the learning environment in which a young baby discovers new smells and colors. The Talmudic lesson on the rules of carrying objects in and out of a house on the Sabbath was presented to Nechama in such a way as to be bodily absorbed by her.

Nechama learned to assimilate intellectual material not as ideas, but as fragrances and bursts of light and sound. She learned how to gauge the height of a tree with her eyes closed by sniffing the aroma of the top most leaves. She learned that one could meet people no longer among the living by falling down on the ground and crying until they responded. She learned how to detect mercy inside judgment and cruelty inside beauty.

She and her two mentors spent many days at a time out in the wilderness. Abulafia shared with her the secrets of Shem's plot to hasten redemption. Victoria taught her how to turn the forest into her kitchen, her living room, and, should the need arise, her bedroom.

The older Nechama grew, the longer their excursions lasted. In a cave halfway between Scranton and Binghamton, NY, the three of them would gather around a small bonfire, chest deep in the sand, for two or three days at a time, taking turns feeding the flame with the energy of their minds.

On one such morning, a visitor entered the cave. Lionel Abulafia should have sensed her from a great distance, but he had been so sleep deprived, his soul could not awaken his body even as the threat grew nearer. Victoria, too, should have noticed the unexpected arrival, but she was out in the woods, miles away, picking berries for a pie.

Nechama alone sensed their uninvited guest, but what she perceived was a presence so meek and nonthreatening, she saw no reason for fear. It was a mistake.

"Over here, watch your step," said the guest to nobody in particular. She was a short and firmly packed woman in her late forties. Her soft voice echoed through the cave.

Nechama was buried in the sand up to her neck and her eyes were closed, but even without her sight she was certain the woman was alone. This was confusing at first, as Danielle Herzog—last encountered in Montefiore Cemetery on the day the cabalist had his stroke—was engaged in constant chatter with *someone.*

"There, have a seat. I'll share this comfy rock with you." Danielle Herzog seated herself with a great sigh. "Whew," she exclaimed, "that was quite a climb... No, dear, I didn't think it was my role to warn you, how was *I* to know? I saw this place in my head, of course I did, but I had no idea the climb would be quite so *steep...*"

Nechama watched the woman carefully through squinted eyes—but she saw no one with her. The visitor's clothes, pink pajamas and matching bedroom slippers, were covered in fresh mud and grass. This woman had left home in a hurry.

"Hi there," said Danielle Herzog, clearly addressing Nechama. "You're going to die a violent death, and everyone will be sorry and they'll cry for days, but you'll stay dead."

Nechama was awestruck. Every fiber in Nechama's body received the unwavering truth rooted in Danielle Herzog's prophecy. Nechama's certitude sprang not only from her well-formed sense of reality, but also from the complete absence of personal interest which radiated from the prophetess regarding the content of her prophecy. Danielle's scent was not evil in the least. She was neither gladdened nor saddened by the prospect of Nechama's death. She simply couldn't have cared less.

This bloodlessness made Nechama wonder. Perhaps Danielle Herzog's prophecy leaked from God's Darker Aspect? But the truth is: Prophecy is prophecy. It emanates from whomever is doing the emanating, and if a nearby mind doesn't immediately discard it as nonsense—which is how sane people react ninety-nine times out of a hundred—it is received.

"I could take care of you now—it's one of my options," Danielle said. She moved toward Nechama and drew a short knife from her belt.

This challenge Nechama was better able to sustain. She smailed and said, "Have you done this before?"

"Kill something? No...," the woman admitted. Her voice turned fainter as some of her self assurance left her.

"It's not easy, killing things," Nechama advised. "They tend to scream a lot and bleed all over the place."

"I suppose..." The woman stopped dead in her tracks.

"Are you feeling an urge to hurt me?" Nechama was curious.

"Urge?" Danielle Herzog tasted the unfamiliar word in her mouth. She never had urges. She always *knew* what had to be done—and did it. From birth she had been a perfect tool employed by the universe.

"Rita has urges all the time, I suppose," Danielle expounded. "Wants things. Right, Rita?"

"Where is your friend?" Nechama asked.

"Right here."

"I don't see her."

"Rita gets that a lot," Danielle Herzog confided. "She's extremely shy. Life and death are not that different, you know." Danielle's eyes grew unfocused and she raised her knife hand again.

"Put down that weapon, girl, and walk away."

Victoria Martin's voice projected from the cave's entrance. She'd sensed danger and had rushed through the brush with a speed surprising for a person of her generous dimensions. Now she suppressed her chest's crazed need to heave for air, in order to appear more menacing to the intruder.

Without warning, Danielle leaped at Victoria, her knife tearing the flesh above Victoria's heart. Even as the strange creature in filthy pajamas flew at her Victoria knew she had to take the blow. She concentrated on damage control, presenting for stabbing the area above the heart rather than the heart itself. Further, Victoria used the energy of her flying attacker to fling Danielle from the cave, where the prophetess mercifully let go of the knife.

By the time Danielle landed on the rocky ground, Victoria had launched a counter-attack. She picked up the short knife. Cupping Danielle's close-cropped head with one hand, she brought down the knife to decapitate her. At that moment, Lionel Abulafia opened his eyes. (In his defense, he had gone without sleep for two weeks. He was due a serious snooze).

He screamed, "Victoria! Kill her, and I die too!"

The dark skinned woman froze. Her master knew just the right words to stem her adrenaline storm.

"She's a vicious little thing," Victoria warned, still poised for the kill.

"She's harmless," said Nechama. "Can't you see? She's completely blameless."

Victoria turned Danielle's head around to stare into her eyes. There was no venom there, no hatred, only open, bottomless curiosity.

"Every day that you and the old man don't have sex, the universe cries,"

Danielle informed her in a cheerful voice.

"Come again?"

"You and the old guy belong together. He can make you climax seventy times in one night."

It should be noted that Victoria Martin had not blushed in several decades. Only an extraordinary embarrassment would render her blushing noticeable at all, yet both Nechama and Lionel witnessed her face turn a fiery crimson.

Victoria let Danielle Herzog go, but shadowed her retreat to a bus stop on the highway. For one thing, Victoria wanted to make quite sure that Danielle left, and for another, she needed to regain the composure seriously rattled by the idea of seventy climaxes with Lionel.

Later, once her head mind had cleared, Victoria asked, "What did you mean when you said if I killed that chick you'd die?"

"I seen her before," Lionel Abulafia said. "Whenever she turns up, bad things happen."

"That's not what you *said*," Victoria insisted.

"She's on my spot," he finally confessed.

"On the *Continuum?*"

"Yes."

"Why, that makes no sense! It defies the very principle..."

"You're telling *me?*"

"What does it mean?"

"Search me. All I know is she and I have the identical spiritual makeup and she was out there the day the master had his stroke."

"Get out of here!"

"It's true."

Nechama and her two teachers remained in the forest for longer and longer stretches. In their eighth year together, they left the cave only to celebrate the high holidays.

By the time Nechama turned twenty, she knew everything Lionel and Victoria could teach her, and was ready to move on. At twenty years of age, one becomes accountable before the Celestial Court. The time had come for Nechama to connect to a Higher Authority.

23.

Before sunrise on Nechama Gutkind's twentieth birthday, she lost the will to leave her bed. Curled up in a fetal position, her eyes squeezed shut, she still could not keep the tears from streaming down her cheeks.

Her tears were shed for everything that was wrong with the world: for hungry children and abandoned puppies and cancer patients and ugly divorces and frightened men in orange jumpsuits on death row.

All teenagers cry sooner or later when they cross the divide between what they've been taught about the world and what it is really like. But Nechama was unlike all other teenagers: Her crying was completely devoid of self-pity. Her sadness consisted of pure empathy.

Nechama had been taught about the brutal realities of life. Lionel and Victoria certainly did not shy away from discussions about the harshness of God's judgements. And her father, Rabbi Motke Gutkind, was a devout Jew who saw all of life as a gift from the Creator, the sweet and the bitter parts alike. If Nechama's parents ever strayed from unflinching acceptance of the misery of the Human Condition, it was to instruct their daughter that God required reality to be this painful so that He could, eventually, deliver mankind from it.

So from an early age Nechama had been familiar with the belief that human suffering was the expression of a Divine Will. But sad as this notion is, it was not the reason for her incessant tears.

Leah Gutkind looked nothing like her daughter. She was hard and brittle where Nechama was soft and curved. The girl had red hair that fell over her creamy-white shoulders. Leah wore a short, tight black wig so faithfully that even Nechama had not seen her mother's hair in years. Leah ran a tight ship at the Cosmic Wisdom center—a permanent "all-business" expression was etched on her face—except when it came to her youngest child. Now she embraced her daughter and wouldn't let go even as Nechama's tears invaded her starched house-dress and rolled down her back.

When half an hour had passed and Nechama was still as effusively tearful as before, Leah took her by the hand and helped her to stand. The young woman followed her mother down the stairs and out to the small backyard. The yard held a patch of grass, a slab of cement and a couple of gnarled oak trees. Leah led her daughter to the ancient tire swing which hung by a rope from one of the branches. Nechama sat and began to rock herself back and forth until the tire took to the air.

The fresh morning air seemed to soothe Nechama. Her mother remained on the grass lawn beside the swinging tire, and watched as Nechama calmed down. When she seemed more herself, Leah asked, "Why so much crying?"

Nechama answered, "Because it needs doing."

In the Gutkind household, this was the best possible answer. And yet, it was the one that hurt the most. From the time Leah first took the child into her arms, she had dreaded the prospect of her daughter's twentieth birthday. Like most parents, Leah knew she would only have her miraculous child for a short while. Unlike other parents, however, she understood that once Nechama reached adulthood, she would forfeit forever any special claim she had to her lovely girl. Leah shivered.

This, too, was part of the Human Condition: that the gentlest, sweetest children are picked to go out into the world and roam the countryside, challenging the status quo. Leah's was merely the most excellent child who ever lived.

24.

So Nechama Gutkind was already graced with the capacity for weeping over the imprisonment of God and the seemingly eternal darkening of His light. Still, her awareness of sorrow had yet to extend beyond the bittersweet region of crying in the privacy of her parents' home. She had yet to venture into the open, where torrents of human sadness awaited her more explicit attention.

Her first effort to get to the next level was a complete flop.

When her mother was satisfied that Nechama had regained her composure, Leah left her in the backyard and returned to her magnificently busy life. Being the wife of the most important living Cosmic-Wisdomnik, her home was open to dozens of guests during the week, and hundreds on the Sabbath. Leah Gutkind managed all the myriad logistical operations which terminated on Friday nights with Rabbi Gutkind's looking really spiffy and benign at the head of their crowded dinner table. The amount of attention she could devote to her mournful child was necessarily limited.

Eventually, Nechama slowed the arc of the tire swing. The time for crying was past, of this she was certain, but the pain of sadness in her abdomen was still palpable.

She jumped to the grass. By trial and error she discovered that when she moved in a certain direction, the pain subsided a bit, while moving in other directions caused the pain to redouble. So she began to march, very slowly, to the drumbeat of her own pain. It was as if a tunnel of lesser anguish was carved out for her inside a mountain of intense emotional suffering. This tunnel led outside, to the streets of the Keyser Valley suburb west of Scranton. Nechama crossed the railroad tracks and picked her way along the path of least resistance to downtown Scranton.

Tink's Entertainment Complex was not a place designed to make religious girls feel comfortable. In the evening and well into the night, the block-wide building pulsated with loud music, crowded dancing and a lot of drinking. At this hour of the morning the last of its patrons were leaving, most of them obviously still in tune with the relentless beat inside their own heads rather than with the sounds of the brightening city streets.

Several prostitutes hung around the club's two exits, waiting for their last customers before calling it a night. They looked almost tearfully tired. Having removed their clothes so many times since sunset, most of them were barely covered at all. Exposed breasts and pelvises were now offered to customers—absent all coquettish affectation.

Her pain delivered Nechama into the midst of these semi-naked women. Untroubled by their utter alien-ness, she was only cognizant of having reached the spot where she was no longer bombarded by pain. For the first time that morning, she was free of the terrible pressure that had collected in her stomach and under her breasts. Standing clad in her flannel nightgown, she bathed in painlessness as if it were a brook of cool water. She stood among the women oblivious to the touch of their skin as it brushed against hers, oblivious to the odors of cheap perfume and heavy perspiration. All she wanted was for the pain to stay away.

A tall, black man in a long, cream sheepskin coat and huge, white Stetson hat floated in on a haze of alcohol. He was half asleep and the other half, mad. He greeted the women in a familiar fashion and clapped his hands a couple of times to call them to order. Grumbling, but essentially docile and cooperative, they set out to follow him to their living quarters a few blocks away. Then he spotted the newcomer.

"What have we here?" he asked. He grabbed Nechama's chin and stared into her blue eyes. "You working without permission from Sam Smith, girl?" He brought her tear-streaked face close to his slim, clean-shaven one. A hot burst of alcohol breath accompanied his inquiry.

The crudeness of his blunt domination cut through Nechama's short-lived state of relief like a butcher's cleaver. She bent forward helplessly and clutched her stomach. She couldn't open her eyes, couldn't move; the pain was back.

Bestial and virile to a great extreme, the man was also weak and vulnerable. His desire to possess her tore right through the young woman's defenses. She found herself afraid—but was certain that he was basically harmless against her. The problem lay in the fact that she was not quite sure what to do. She feared the depth of his need and wondered about its effect on the planet all around her. What if there were others like him—hordes of men and women overcome by brutal, relentless, and eternally unrequited needs? What would happen to her if she were to experience all of those people's needs, all at once?

She desperately wanted her teachers to help her make sense out of the wretchedness. But this time she was on her own.

This was her roughest encounter to date with her spiritual nature, and simply crying profusely would not do the trick. Her body rebelled. She projected an enormous gush of semi-digested food directly onto Sam Smith's stereotypical white leather boots. He cursed and raised his hand to slap her when another hot stream of the stuff hit his face and chest.

Nechama wished only to remain bent over the pool of her own vomit until she collapsed, deaf at last to the world's begging. But the oncoming fist was thwarted by her eight years' worth of highly uncommon schooling. Nechama moved swiftly to avoid her attacker, who lost his balance and splashed into the pool of vomit at her feet.

There was much laughter, mostly the guarded kind. No one wanted to raise the violent man's ire, but everyone was so happy to see him fall.

"Bitch, I'll cut you!" Smith cried and a switchblade appeared in his right hand. Not one to wallow in self pity, he rose quickly from the moist concrete and towered over the offending young woman, eager to remove his shame with one slash to her pretty face.

Desperate to get away from this horrible place, Nechama turned again just as her attacker was going for her with a vengeance. She was two steps away by now and the raging man almost collapsed into the sick again.

He was no match for her. She could have avoided his crude attacks until he collapsed from sheer exhaustion, but she didn't have to. Her father stopped his car nearby and rushed out to collect her. The pimp retreated, recognizing that the bearded, black and white-clad Jew was way more trouble than he had bargained for.

"It's okay, baby, it's okay," Gutkind whispered and kissed her head. He pulled her from the receding reality of aching sexuality back into the safety and familiarity of the family Oldsmobile. Once she was deposited in the back seat, they took off.

"Your mom called me at the airport. She said you had disappeared. I canceled my flight and went looking for you." He stared at her image in his rear view mirror.

"How did you know where to find me?" Nechama was hoarse.

"Easy, I looked for misery at its loudest. I figured it had to be downtown, somewhere, and I started with the nightclubs."

"Nightclubs cause misery?"

"No, sweetie, no places are evil, only human actions are. And those can cause plenty of unhappiness. You were standing in a spot where misery was practically percolating."

She smiled. "My pain vanished when I got there."

Rabbi Gutkind slowed down, then brought the car to a stop on the side of the road. "You followed your *pain* there?"

"Something like that. If I went anywhere else, I doubled over."

"Oh, God..." His heart sank. "It begins."

25.

According to THE CABALIST'S HANDBOOK OF PRACTICAL MESSIANIC REDEMPTION, God had sent forth countless messianic prophesies:

> *According to the prophets: God would one day be hailed as King over all the earth. Also, one could count on the fact that there would be wide recognition that He is one and His name is one. Every nation would be commanded to go on an annual autumn pilgrimage to Jerusalem during the Feast of Tabernacles year after year to worship the King of the Universe.*

Samael, who was no fool, was well aware of these prophecies. And yet he spent years hell-bent (so to speak) on his campaign against Jerusalem. This begs the question: didn't God's least favorite emanation know his plans were futile?

The simplest answer is: It was in his job description. The Left Side was in charge of destroying the Jews, and so followed orders like a loyal soldier.

Also, over the years God had inspired more than 100,000 bona-fide prophets. If Samael were to take every blasted prophecy seriously, he might as well have closed up shop and concentrated on his real passion, creating crossword puzzles for the *New York Times*.

Of course, God's Dark Aspect was a proverbial optimist. One doesn't survive so many divine kicks in the ass and continue to wreak evil with such zeal unless one possesses oodles upon oodles of hope.

26.

Many spiritually sensitive persons understood that during the Cuban missile crisis of October, 1962, the outbreak of nuclear war had been prevented by a higher power. Left to their own devices, the Russian and American leaders were clearly beyond the point of no return. Either side would have been unable to reverse an attack even if it were due to purely "local" circumstances: Rogue ambition, mental fatigue, nervousness, or panic.

Few, however, realized that this conspicuous divine intervention was not the work of God. It was the Prince of Darkness who moved in Cuba. It required a valiant struggle to prevent the two halves of the modern Roman Empire from destroying each other, but Samael knew he would need both of them for the final battle on Jerusalem.

In 2002, Pakistan prepared a nuclear attack against India. At the last minute, Nawaz Sharif, the Pakistani prime minister at the time, received a visit from a tawny-haired European gentleman, with burning eyes and a black homburg hat. The man cooled down the situation with a generous donation to Sharif's favorite Swiss bank account.

North Korea refined enough plutonium for at least one atomic bomb. The fiery-eyed man backed Kim Jong-il of Korea in bankrolling a group of Russian criminals who had access to radioactive materials. The North Koreans would henceforth follow their persuasive visitor's instructions religiously.

Not only did the same Russian syndicate steal and deliver ten atomic bombs from former Soviet republics to Iran, it also smuggled plutonium, uranium, cesium, and other dangerous isotopes to the Iranians.

The ability to launch a nuclear holocaust was once the exclusive privilege of a handful of major powers. American leaders feared that any country with some industrial base and enough fear of its neighbors was well on its way to owning a few bombs, "just in case." How soon before terrorist groups gained hold of such weapons?

On the strength of their anxiety, the Americans launched a campaign of conquest against several rogue nations, including Afghanistan and Iraq.

The fiery visitor in the old fashioned homburg planned to use all these lovely nuclear devices in the final battle on Jerusalem.

Samael timed the first outburst of the Third World War to coincide with the Muslim holy month of Ramadan. It was well known among European conquerors that attacking Muslims on their holy month was something to be avoided, seeing as how this tactic pissed them off even worse than usual. As soon as the last meal of the last night following the last day of Ramadan was consumed, you could burn down their cities and blow up their infrastructure and kill and maim their women and children and they didn't seem to mind nearly as much.

In order to set off an all-out war between the Jews and the rest of the world, it would help if the Jews were considered to have violated Ramadan.

The pieces for the attack had been in place for some time. Samael's twenty-year project, begun with the demise of the cabalist master, was nearly complete. A world without hope, Samael's guiding aspiration from the moment that the spirit of messiah had been created, was at last within reach.

Would God be upset? Samael no longer thought so: Millions of God's supposedly chosen people had walked into gas chambers and not a tear was shed up in heaven. When the Jews who survived the annihilation attempted to create a safe homeland, Samael made it his personal business not only to endanger Israel, but to alienate her from all the other countries. Some countries were pushovers; some were a little more difficult to persuade. But Samael was nothing if not persistent.

So maybe it *was* possible for a really clever and powerful archangel to kill the messiah when God wasn't looking.

27.

At 8:45 a.m. New York time, a squadron of F-16 fighters left Israeli airspace on its way to the Saudi oil fields on the western coast of the Persian Gulf. NATO units stationed in the northern part of the peninsula rose up to intercept. It was soon discovered that one of the Israeli planes was carrying a nuclear device.

In the panic that ensued, no one paid attention to Israel's firm protest completely repudiating responsibility. The "nightmare scenario" was taking shape right before the eyes of the world. What was the point of listening the official statement of denial from Tel Aviv?

Samael had been working on this particular trick since Israel first acquired nuclear capability in 1958. It was beautifully simple: Get a group of Air Force colonels to paint Israeli insignia on some Egyptian F-16's. The bomb: from Pakistan. The pilots: from Syria.

At 5:45 p.m. local time, a nuclear device was dropped on Saudi Arabia. The Midyan oil field erupted in a tower of light. The blaze reached 40 miles above the earth and immediately took out all the communications satellites over the region.

On the Spiritual Continuum of Everything, the fraudulent "Jewish bomb" stood between the Damascus blood libel of 1840, when a Jewish barber was tortured until he confessed to the ritual murder of a Catholic monk; and the Manhattan Project, born of a 1939 letter from Jewish scientists Albert Einstein and Leo Szilard who warned President Roosevelt about Germany's development of an atomic weapon. The letter was delivered to the president by Jewish economist and banker Alexander Sachs. The project itself involved many Jews in key positions, including J. Robert Oppenheimer, David Bohm, Rudolf Peierls, Felix Bloch, Leo Szilard, Eugene Wigner, James Franck, Otto Frisch and Edward Teller. Among the key gentiles working on the project were Niels Bohr, Enrico Fermi, James Chadwick, Emilio Segre, and Klaus Fuchs. One writer dubbed the world saving endeavor, "The Big Bar-Mitzvah."

28.

WWIII began one day before Nechama Gutkind's twentieth birthday, which means that the last year in the history of the world began one day too soon. The symmetry is undeniable, seeing as the world was *created* one day too soon: God's very desire to create a world began to stir on the Sabbath day just *before* the first day of Creation. But who am I to imply that Heaven is populated by petty bureaucrats?

29.

It was dawn again, one day later, and Nechama Gutkind had turned twenty. The house was quiet. The pale, early morning light danced green and blue around Nechama. A sheaf of red hair peeked out and over the pillow in an aimless wavelet.

She heard a child crying. That is to say she didn't exactly hear it, but she knew it, in a plain and matter-of-fact sort of way. A child in mortal danger was summoning Nechama to help.

One moment Nechama lay paralyzed under her covers and the next she walked barefoot in flowered pajamas through the streets, following the child's cry which resonated inside her head.

We humans are hardwired to lose our capacity for tranquility as soon as we hear the cry of a child, just as birds are hardwired to regurgitate their food into the open beaks of their screaming young'uns. There are some among us who find it easy enough to turn their back on a screaming baby and continue to sleep with not a worry in the world. We call such people sociopaths.

The child's cry served as a beacon for Nechama, the same way the intermittent pain in her guts had served her as a guide the day before. And like the pain, the crying subsided the closer Nechama drew to its source. Except, this time, she was afraid that the crying was weaker because the child's life was being extinguished.

In that moment, her tears dried up forever. She never cried again. It was as if the universe had permitted her to shed a lifetime of tears in one day. From that day forward, she was completely available to receive other people's pain.

Even from several blocks away, Nechama could smell the fear radiating from the child's parents. They were older than Nechama would have expected. Their fear was layered with past sorrows. The mother's fear was hot and peppery, sizzling with pungent bursts of panic. The man's was more subdued, with the enduring odor of perspiration after a strenuous exercise, and just the barest whiff of ammonia.

Minutes later, Nechama reached their house and knocked on the door.

The child's mother appeared. Her eyes were red and her face was awash with sweat and tears. She looked roughly forty, her lean body wrapped in a man's striped pajama shirt over white tennis shorts. Her hand on the doorknob shook uncontrollably.

"What?" The woman's voice was so badly cracked, Nechama saw the question fall to the floor in exhausted crumbs as it left her mouth. Everything about this woman was weary.

"I don't know," Nechama said. "I've never done anything like this before…"

"Like *what*?" The woman turned, ready to slam the door in the strange girl's face and rush back to her sick child.

"Save your boy's life…" Nechama uttered the first words that entered her head.

"Who is it?" The father came running from inside the house in a soiled T-shirt and running shorts. He was well into his sixties, his thinning, receding hair surrendering to gray, his wrinkled skin a witness to the ravages of time. The boy was created to bridge the twenty-year gap between his parents, as if parenthood was an island in time's stream. Nechama saw the poor man ensnared deep inside the mental trap reserved for those tangled within the mathematics of loss. His poor mind was aflame in plan words: emergency room, funeral, doctor, procreate again, bury, heal, recover, die— Nechama didn't exactly hear the storm that ravaged his consciousness, but she could tell it was there, the way it drizzles in the city when faraway regions are visited by a hurricane.

"Who *are* you?" The woman sounded shrill, her mental faculties clogged with fear and suspicion.

"What's going on, hon'?" Her husband asked again and put his arm around her waist.

"I live nearby… Your pain—it woke me up, I think… Or maybe I was up already, but your pain brought me here… I'm not sure…"

"*What?*" The boy's mother understood none of this internal musing. Nechama instantly knew that this was the last time she would permit herself a moment's hesitation.

"May I see your boy?" She requested. Her voice, usually cheerful and high, sounded dreamy. She had entered a trance.

The mother would not step aside, but Nechama was by now so convinced that only she could save the faint soul inside the house, she didn't really notice anything else. She barged in, following the burgeoning odor of piss and vomit.

The child's father tried to grab her by the collar, but Nechama slipped away. He attempted a headlock, but by the time he brought his left hand to complete the circle around her neck, the young woman had slipped from his hold. The older man almost fell back and flailed his arms in an attempt to regain his balance. His wife hurried to support him with both her hands when they heard their child's door being slammed shut, followed by the tumbling of the lock.

They expressed their rage, banging on the door from the outside and screaming helpless obscenities at the madwoman inside the room with their boy. But Nechama had a great deal to accomplish in a short time.

On the bed in a storybook nursery painted blue with fluffy, white clouds, lay a thin and terribly frail ten-year-old boy. His lips were pale blue. He gasped desperately for each breath. Fists clenched and face twisted, his entire body was an extension of his tortured lungs.

Hovering above the suffering child was a hazy entity, mostly white, with sudden streaks of rainbow colors which burst along its surface. It was the boy's soul, Nechama knew, or, rather, it was the link between the boy's body and his soul. In the forest cave Nechama had learned to observe the tangible elements of the human psyche, through which the Divine interacted with the mortal. But she had never seen them so separated. She suspected that she was witnessing the moment that a soul departs its host.

Outside, the child's parents began to ram the door with the dining room table, scraping the wood floor in their fury, banging the front end into what looked to be just a hollow, pressboard door. They rammed the door fruitlessly, until the effort exhausted them.

"Call the cops," the boy's mother urged. Her husband flew into the kitchen and grabbed the wall unit.

"Help, our house has been invaded by a crazy woman. She's locked herself in with our son and she's killing him!" the father screamed when the operator answered.

His wife pressed her ear to the boy's door, terrified.

"Please leave us alone," Nechama cried from inside the room. "I promise you, everything will be okay."

"Let me *in!*" the mother begged and rattled the doorknob.

"Later. I must be alone with him, I have to see what's wrong," Nechama cried back.

The rattling and banging continued.

Nechama resolved to ignore the distractions and addressed the entity floating above the sick child: "Why are you leaving this body?"

"You *see* me?" The entity sounded shocked.

"I want you to get back inside," Nechama ordered.

"I can't," the child's soul-link said. "He's totally sick inside, I'm going any minute now, for good, meeting my Maker, submitting a report—you must know the drill."

"What's he got?" Nechama insisted.

"How should *I* know? He can't breathe. He barely has any lungs in there. Born this way. They sold me a bill of goods upstairs, you know, sending me down here. And to think I was actually getting excited about playing ball again, and swimming. Fat chance... That little thing just lies in bed all day, fighting for air... If I'm lucky, I'll never have to come back down to earth again. I tell you, I've been sick on some incarnations, but I don't ever want to feel sickness like this again." The sparkly thing shivered.

"Get back inside," Nechama ordered.

"He's going to die," the little cloud argued. "I can't go back in there. I won't! I won't! I won't!"

"You can't possibly be this mean," Nechama said in rebuke. She approached the child on the bed. His chest rose and fell with enormous effort, but his breathing grew faint.

"He's already dead," said the cloud. "In another few minutes, this shallow heaving will stop."

"What am I going to do?" Nechama despaired.

"You're asking *me?* You're the faith healer..."

"I'm not a faith healer, I just heard the cry."

"Listen, Missy, you're able to see me, which means you're not a fake," the cloud suggested. "Why don't you put your hands on his body, or something? That's what you people *do*, isn't it?"

It was a good suggestion. The Prophet Elisha did this sort of thing. He laid himself over the dead body of a child and breathed life into him, and he was revived. How tough could it be?

The notion of climbing on the dying boy made her gag. But her own pain, shooting with increasing frequency, was a signal from the universe that this was precisely what was required. She noticed that her pain was taking on strong empathetic features now, centering in her own lungs. She struggled for breath. She never expected that faith healing would be this brutal.

With great hesitation, Nechama finally placed her hands on the child's chest. She sensed a very discouraging chill deep within him. The boy's pale flesh clung to the little bit of warmth that emanated from her fingertips. This gave her an idea. She looked around the room until she discovered a bottle of medicinal alcohol. She knew she'd get terribly sick from it for sure, but it had to be done.

"Drink *L'Chayim* with me!" Nechama roared—aping her father's behavior from his Hasidic get-togethers. She filled up a Dixie cup with the liquid and emptied the contents straight down her throat. Drinking proved difficult while gasping for air with empathy pains. She wished she could learn how to make her own pain go away once she had received its message. The message this time, of course, had been that if she didn't heal this little human, she too would die. She made a mental note to ask Abulafia next time they met if there was an off-switch for the pain-o-gram.

The boy's father yelled: "We called the cops, bitch! If you touch my boy you'll get the gas chamber!"

Nechama smiled, filled a second cup and drank another swig, than a third and a fourth. "*L'Chayim*," she cried. The little cloud answered back, completely mystified, "*L'Chayim...*"

Nechama felt the warmth climbing up from her stomach to the rest of her system. She emptied a fifth cup and, completely inebriated and with her brain drenched and pickled in medicinal spirits, turned to the bed and fell over the little boy. She met his bluish mouth with her full, red lips.

Heat rose from her. Rivulets of heat shot through the little body under her, repairing stunted tissues, releasing pressure, expanding lung surface area.

"It's working!" The soul emanation giggled. "You're really doing it! You should go on television, Miss, honest..."

"Get back inside already, little fool," Nechama slurred the command and laughed.

"Yes, Ma'am," the entity saluted in a cloudy sort of way and hopped back into the body beneath Nechama.

Once she sensed that the boy was whole again, Nechama felt free to leave. She staggered to the door and opened it. The father was there, his face distorted in anguish and hatred. She saw his fist coming at her and could have evaded it with ease, but a quiet voice inside her suggested that balance in the universe required her to accept this blow. She quickly assessed the situation. She needed her nose whole because so much of her spiritual prowess depended on her sense of smell, so she moved to let his fist land just under her left eye. The smack knocked her to her knees half way across the room.

"Bitch! Bitch! Bitch!" The man hollered, celebrating his bitterness.

"Marv," his wife cried from their son's room, "Marv come here, Marv, she healed him!"

Nechama crawled to the living room wall and leaned against it. Her attacker disappeared through his son's doorway. Although her head was pounding, Nechama relished the sweet sounds of delight she heard from the room. She was pretty sure she heard the boy's voice, too. He sounded stunningly normal...

When the cops arrived, they discovered a perfectly healthy child sleeping peacefully in his bed. His parents were crying their hearts out, with an empty bottle of medicinal alcohol on the floor between them.

"Freaks," said one of the cops in disgust. "I'm charging them with making a false 911 call."

Nechama made her way back home and into bed and slept for twenty hours straight. She missed her own birthday party and woke up with a massive hangover. That was the day that the first welt appeared on her left leg. Her momma wanted to put some ointment on it, but the girl refused. She'd been trained to regard everything that happened to her body as a message to be contemplated and deciphered.

When she couldn't figure out why she should be punished by the universe for saving a life, she called up the old sage from the Lower East Side. Abulafia wasn't home, but Victoria Martin took the call.

"Child," Victoria told the girl, "you know it's time."

Nechama didn't respond immediately. She was too busy looking around her room, saying goodbye to books and toys and the view from her little window and trying to fight the rising feeling of panic.

"The welt's not going away," Nechama stated as calmly as she could.

"It won't," Victoria said, after a quiet pause. "And there will be more. Every time you do something new to heal the world's wounds, you'll get a new one—on that same leg."

"Look at the lame girl…" Nechama said quietly.

"Resentful?" Victoria asked, but this time her voice was not transmitted over the phone line, but inside the girl's mind.

"Yes." This method of communication did not allow for complicated phrases. There was little room for subtlety in mind-to-mind communication.

"Don't be," was the best advice Victoria came up with.

"Fine," said Nechama.

"Lesions are power."

"How?"

"Means you're right."

"Funny."

"Yes, funny." And on the phone, Victoria added, "God bless you, child."

So Nechama pulled her covers up around her shoulders and fell asleep again, and didn't cry at all. In her dreams she didn't see puppies, or seascapes, or chocolate cakes. She only dreamed messages from the universe: obscure, insistent, even alien. Like the big lady said, it was time.

30.

It took the evil genius of Samael to come up with a Jewish doomsday set-up. For half a century, the average world citizen had expected the United States and the Soviet Union to "push the button." The very imagery belonged to a world in which state executives launched holocausts from the comfort of their offices—pressing a handy, usually red, device conveniently located on their desks.

The nuclear scenario later evolved to embrace the new rulers of the planet: terrorists and the rogue states that harbored them. The culture now anticipated the destruction of millions at the hands of a small band of heavily motivated madmen. But what good was *that* premise to an archangel looking to focus humanity's hatred on the Jews?

The news that Saudi Arabia lost two thirds of its oil reserves came at

8:47 a.m., with three minutes to spare before the opening of the largest stock exchange on the planet. Because the New York Exchange had acquired several other international exchanges, whatever happened on Wall Street happened everywhere, at once. By 9 a.m., the price of a barrel of oil rose to $253. By 9:15 a.m., the price of a gallon of gasoline at the pump reached seventeen dollars.

World War III might have been avoided if top oil company executives had taken more than three minutes to evaluate the new situation, and more than fifteen minutes before sending out instructions to their regional offices.

Samael, a great student of human history, had every reason to expect the oilmen to function exactly as they did. He'd been there in Sarajevo, on June 28, 1914, when a crazed Serb patriot assassinated the crown prince of Austria-Hungary. The regicide was a terrible thing, made worse because every country in 1914 Europe saw it as its opportunity for a power play. In the hours following the Sarajevo assassination the future was still bright—millions had not yet perished, mustard gas had not yet been released into the atmosphere, the tank had not yet been invented.

Likewise, a world crisis could have been postponed if the world pumps had not been set to reflect the bottomless greed of oil executives. But Samael knew the good old boys from Houston couldn't help themselves. They liked money too much and they owned a hose that kept on pouring money. Upon learning that they were down to seventy-five years of uninterrupted pumping, instead of 125, they had to more than triple the rate of streaming money. The math was seductively simple.

Samael was all about simple math.

Here's another point Samael didn't overlook: Israel, with half its land a desert, and with a goodly 200-250 days of cloudless sky, was a world pioneer in exploiting solar power. Beginning in the 1960's, Israelis installed solar panels to provide hot water in most homes. In the twenty-first century, Israeli high-tech companies taught the world about operating cars and running electric grids that suckled on pure sun rays. It was not *their* fault that the world could not be bothered to pay proper attention. The Danes were equally frustrated with the world's lack of regard for their wind power technology. Here they were, running an entire country for free, just because their land was flat and the ocean winds plentiful. But no one noticed.

When the oil wells went up in flames, the news channels were quick to show that in Israel and Denmark the pumps didn't waver. No one thought less of the Danes, but the Israelis would not be forgiven. There you go, making the rest of us pay seventeen dollars a gallon (then nineteen, then twenty-one, to stabilize at twenty-three dollars for a gallon of regular gas anywhere in the United States)—while you rely on your precious solar energy? Unforgivable.

Some talking head on the news channels mentioned "well poisoning." It was a brilliant allusion to the darkest period in the relationship between Jews and European gentiles, save for the Holocaust and the pogroms of 1648-49. Jews poisoned wells, everybody knew it. Water wells yesterday, oil wells today. It was the old excuse for hate crimes, resurrected.

How quickly Israelis became "Jews" again, in the public consciousness. At last, after decades of official suppression, everyone could blame the Jews again for a multitude of ills, without fear of reprisal. The bombed-out wells made it all possible.

31.

It was late night in New York City and Lionel Abulafia was teaching a class in the cloistered study hall in the basement of his tenement building on East Broadway. The room was crowded beyond belief; most of the students were not even human. There were two or three lawyers from SoHo, a filmmaker from Tribeca, a few learned housewives from the Upper West Side, and a gentile professor of Talmudic Studies from Columbia University. Besides this select group, which made it possible for Lionel Abulafia to pay his bills, all his other listeners were good and evil heavenly hosts.

It's easy to understand why angels sought Abulafia's teachings. Angels recognize good material and are trained to identify and retrieve spiritual treasures—they carry them to the higher realms in the folds of their pristine robes when their earthly missions are completed.

Demons are a different story. As it turns out, modern civil rights legislation altered many of the rules of conduct in the spirit world. Fiends, trolls, imps and gargoyles demanded equal access to spiritual resources and won several key lawsuits in the *Really* Supreme Court. The upshot was that Lionel Abulafia was obliged to admit into his night class one angel of destruction for every classical angel of divine goodness.

One inauspicious outcome of the new rules was the odd, often intolerable mixture of odors in the little study hall: The tantalizing fragrance of fresh goats' milk and dripping date honey from the angels of heaven mingled with the stink of sulfuric acid, swamp gas and raw sewage which seeped from the children of hell. This was one of the reasons why the humans in the class were told to swallow Dramamine tablets an hour before and an hour after each class. Another reason for the medication was the stormy fights that often erupted between good and evil in Lionel Abulafia's place. On occasion, these seismic battles would transport the entire basement through time and space—with the inevitable side effects.

Samael wanted very much to enroll in the old cabalist's nightly class, if only to keep up with what spiritually gifted mortals were thinking these days. He decided against it because he was afraid to become beholden to Abulafia. Whenever we learn something new from someone, he or she becomes our master. Samael would not want to be obliged to spare the old man when the rest of the Jews were terminated.

Lionel Abulafia sat behind his ancient little reading stand, which he occasionally grabbed and brought down to lean against his chest, causing the three or four open volumes lying on top to slide under his beard. Despite his thirteen decades, he retained a springy quality, the result of his frequent experiments with levitation. Nicotine and alcohol also helped.

Tonight, he chose to wear the traditional cabalist master's garb of long black robe, flowing fringed *tzitzis* and a tie-less white shirt, buttoned up to his Adam's apple. Other nights he wore dungarees, Hawaiian shirts, corduroy jackets with leather elbow padding and even an old fashioned, full-body, gray bathing suit with red vertical stripes. He'd been told the stripes made him look slimmer.

Lionel Abulafia's biggest vice was food. His housekeeper and companion, Victoria Martin, herself a woman of great girth, was a graduate of a famous French Culinary Institute and the winner of several cooking championships. Since Victoria's arrival in his life, sometime in the nineteen-seventies (her salary paid by Medicaid), Lionel Abulafia moved up from chunky to chubby. It didn't impede his experiments with levitation, but it did cost him a fortune in new clothes.

It was also, necessarily, a sign of his connection to the sin of Eden, which was all about eating forbidden fruits. How appropriate, then, that his lesson tonight was on the truth behind the Biblical account of Creation.

"Everybody knows that in the beginning God didn't create the heaven or the earth," Lionel Abulafia repeated several times, until he was sure he had his students' attention. You had to resort to tricks like these when conducting classes into the wee hours.

"Before heaven and earth, He created the Spirit of God, after which He made the heaven, which was made up of your basic void, darkness and the deep. Then He sent the Spirit of God sailing upon the face of the waters. Everybody still with me?"

Lionel Abulafia counted on the fingers of his right hand, "One: the Spirit of God; Two: Heaven; then Two point one: Void, darkness, and the deep.

"The Spirit of God was, really, the spirit of the messiah. A kind of trump card, if you ask me. God is about to play a high stakes game of Poker with Himself, for everything—*really, really* everything. The game's going badly, people and forces all over the place are doing things they're not supposed to, and God is losing the farm. But then, at the darkest moment, God pulls out the card He's been hiding up His sleeve. He dumps it on the green velvet, it's got the picture of the messiah on it, God wins the pot, redeems the whole bloody world, everybody's kissing girls in Times Square and—curtain."

Lionel Abulafia raised his eyes to scan his pack of students from under his thick, white brows. "I see an old acquaintance is back. Sheila Markowitz, nice to see you again, how's your little Ben?"

"He's doing fine, Rabbi, I sent him to the accelerated studies program at NYU, he's very happy there."

"NYU? How old is the poor boy? He's not even eighteen."

"He's sixteen, and I felt he required more rigor in his study program. You disagree?" Sheila Markowitz, tall and pencil-thin, was the author of two books of short Jewish fiction, and an old acquaintance of Lionel Abulafia, as well as of the late cabalist of Brooklyn. Her son, Ben Markowitz, was a thoroughly frightened young person, who whiled away his hours of lonely terror in his dorm room on the Bowery, in the East Village, taking apart and cleaning his weapons collection, in preparation for the day when he would take down with him as many of his fellow students as he could, in a river of blood and fire.

"The mind is a terrible thing to waste," the future mass murderer's mother said, a little less sure of herself.

Lionel Abulafia closed his eyes and counted to thirty. He was giving Sheila Markowitz a secret gift of charity.

According to THE CABALIST'S HANDBOOK OF PRACTICAL MESSIANIC REDEMPTION:

You cannot possibly give away money in secret. Someone always knows; if you won't tell your wife, then your accountant, your bank manager—someone is bound to find out that you've done this fabulous bit of giving, oh how wonderfully generous of you.

But if someone tells you something really stupid and you're just aching to answer them in such a way that they'd regret the day they were born—but you keep your mouth shut instead—that's a true secret gift of charity! Because only you and God know you've given it.

"I think you should visit the boy more often, take him to lunch, catch a movie," he advised.

"I'll try to make time," she promised.

Lionel Abulafia shook off his feeling of dread and pushed on: "God planned several uses for the spirit of the messiah. He set an enormous battle in motion which rages on between His tendency to give, and His desire to hold back. Like I said, He expected that the messiah would arrive at the last minute, just as everyone despaired of the world's chances to survive the ordeal of its own existence. But as we see from history, every time the messiah shows up, ready to accept the challenge, God destroys him. Each opportunity is too soon for God, as if things down here haven't gone apocalyptic enough for Him.

"You think *you're* afraid of the end of the world, children?" Lionel Abulafia leaned forward, grabbing the far corner of his bookstand. "I got news for you, God is more afraid of it than the rest of us put together. God loves our world and He's going to make it last a long time. You think God wants to go back to the way things used to be before Time—A lone, perfect Entity with no one to talk to but Himself? You *kidding* me?"

The phone rang in the back room and Abulafia heard his housekeeper, Victoria Martin, answering in a subdued voice. But he already knew she would soon be popping her broad face with the unfashionable afro into the study hall. When she did, he knew it was about their "other" student. Victoria rarely expressed affection toward any human being, and when she did, it was usually Nechama Gutkind.

"Her," Victoria commented mentally.

Abulafia closed his eyes. "Yes?" he transmitted.

"Bus," Nechama took over her part of the conversation.

"Problem?" Abulafia grew tense.

"Hookers," Nechama said, wanting to share her new direction with her mentors.

"Yes?"

"Unfinished biz."

The ancient man understood, although he was not necessarily happy about it. Nechama was refusing to leave town before she helped the colorful group of semi-clad young women in Scranton's red light district. In Abulafia's view it signified that she was unable to accept failure and move on—not recommended behavior for proto-messianic figures attempting to challenge the status quo. Sometimes the status quo challenged back: it wasn't something to get hung up on.

"Leave," he transmitted with a uniquely brusque tone he had never before used on Nechama. He expected her consciousness to be a bit rattled.

Instead, he distinctly sensed her smile.

"What?" he inquired, with growing trepidation, "What?"

"I'll fix it!" she declared resolutely; but what "it" was, he did not know.

Abulafia opened his eyes to face the crammed rows of his multi-existential students, but the rest of his lesson was not nearly as inspired as before. He fleetingly considered returning the evening's tuition, and then felt a wave of gratitude for the fact that it was Victoria who managed his finances.

At the Scranton bus stop, Nechama Gutkind hailed a taxi and rode down to the adult entertainment center where she'd been assailed by the depth of depravity of a pimp. The women were still there, in better shape than when she had last seen them, this being the earlier part of the night.

Nechama approached each woman the same way: She placed both her hands on the woman's head and forced her to stare directly into her own blue eyes. To each she said, quietly but with exceptional clarity: "Now is a very good time to leave."

Clever girl, it was the first time she one-upped the universe. She figured if it was time for her to leave, the cunning universe was bound to set up spiritual reality so that the quality of Leaving would gain dominion over every other quality in her immediate vicinity. In effect, Nechama had become a vortex of escape, drawing everyone nearby, permeating them with the desire to get the hell away.

The prostitutes outside the Tink complex did not have to work up their courage to leave, nor did they have to come to terms with who they really wanted to be and how they made their living. Instead, Nechama just opened an irresistible door and they all went through it.

The sidewalk outside Tink's entertainment center had not looked emptier at night in forty years. When Sam Smith showed up, colored sheepskin, Stetson and all, he flew into a raging paranoia as soon as he was hit with the waves of escape lust which were pouring out of the young, redheaded girl.

Never in his life had he harbored an inclination to leave anywhere. His whole being was about *staying* and *maintaining* territory. The only sense of escape that he knew was the terrified kind, like when the enemy comes crashing through the door.

He turned and ran for his life, deprived for the moment of the ability and will to reason.

Nechama hailed another taxi and arrived at the station just before her bus pulled away. She found an empty seat in the back and collapsed luxuriously on the dark naugahyde. Her great sense of well-being was partly due to liberating all those young women, and partly because she, too, had caught a good dose of "escape fever."

The driver of Nechama's bus had never before experienced such a rush of exhilaration at the moment of departure. He felt as if he'd been born to negotiate buses out of their parking bays and was deeply grateful for the gift of being allowed to do this for a living.

32.

Throughout that year, there were occasional news reports about a mysterious young woman roaming the countryside performing miracles and generally challenging the status quo.

Popular culture named her The Girl.

One day, The Girl got off a truck in the center of Aspen, Colorado. The driver was a small man from Georgia named Nathan Carter, who knew all the Shakespearean tragedies by heart, and insisted that the girl take a hundred dollars from him before they parted company.

"*You, you, ay, you!*" he declared with a huge smile spread across his beefy face, "*We have done our course; there's money for your pains: / I pray you, turn the key and keep our counsel...*"

"Othello?" Nechama guessed correctly, not so much because the line was so readily recognizable, but because Carter was doing an obvious African accent. He was delighted nevertheless, and wouldn't hear of taking back the hundred dollars.

Knowing his gesture was honest and free from hidden intentions, Nechama took his money.

Carter sped away, sticking his balding head out the window, yelling at the top of his lungs, *"For let the gods so speed me as I love, The name of honor more than I fear death!**"

Further down the street, a pair of guitar and banjo players were strumming enthusiastically as they belted out a Phil Ochs tune:

...*An assault upon the order, the changing of the guard / Chosen for a challenge that is hopelessly hard...*

A relatively recent addition to THE CABALIST'S HANDBOOK OF PRACTICAL MESSIANIC REDEMPTION points out that :

> *Much of America's Left-wing revolutionary lore suckles on the cultural nipples of Christianity. This is why the permanent face of America's social revolution is that of an adolescent, much like Jesus himself, who combined stunning moral simplicity with a gift for throwing grand tantrums.*

For that reason it was difficult for Nechama as "The Girl" to escape the familiar mold of teenage rebellion, too easily attributed to raging hormones rather than a yearning for Truth and Justice. But how different was she, really, from other youth heroes?

Nechama listened to the boy and girl team for a moment, then decided that Nathan Carter's money had been in her possession long enough. She placed the hundred dollar bill in the banjo case.

"Thank you very much, Ma'am, you have an excellent taste in counter-cult'ral music," yelled the boy singer.

"Have fun," said The Girl with a pleasant smile.

As she walked away, Nechama felt a new welt form on her left leg. She still held onto the hope that these lesions were due to a rash, but they only got worse with each passing day.

Every time she did something nice for anyone, a new bump would pop up on her leg. When she had the opportunity to actually save a life—help a man re-discover his worth; convince a woman to back down from a rooftop—more severe lacerations would appear, trickling blood and oozing puss, and they refused to heal.

Following visits to six or seven different dermatologists across America, Nechama had come to understand that modern medicine could not help

---

* Julius Caesar, Act 1, Scene 2

78

her, nor even determine the cause of her lesions. In the meantime, she had become expert at nursing her bizarre wounds.

Nechama sometimes asked herself whether it was worth it, destroying herself to redeem others. And every time the answer was the same. These things needed doing. She came to accept it.

Eventually, painful welts would appear every day, whether The Girl's actions were common or exceptional. As Nechama's mythical existence expanded, the feeling of hope generated by her goodness radiated outwards, and so the universe resorted to its traditional way of balancing out the splendid light which glowed from messianic figures of great charisma: It endowed Nechama with physical suffering in order to tame her wild beauty.

At a motel on Yampa Avenue in downtown Aspen, the plump, dark-haired woman behind the desk predictably fell in love with The Girl on sight. Nechama was offered a room for the night in exchange for cleaning work. Apparently, the regular housekeeping staff had walked off in considerable hurry.

Nechama smiled gratefully and was already on her way to claim her room and jump into the shower, when she became aware of the reason for the flight of the motel staff. She saw the two bellhops.

Short and hunched over, they were both equipped with abnormally long arms that hung limply alongside their bodies, and reached their knees. They wore red tuxedos, stiff visor hats, dark glasses and red bow ties. One approached The Girl curiously, craning his dog face to check her out.

"Excuse me," The Girl said in near-whisper to the woman behind the desk, "are you in some kind of trouble?" and she rolled her eyes in the direction of the bellhops.

Maria Advanta, the motel owner, was alarmed. "You can see them? I thought I was the only one who could see them. Everybody been sayin' I'm crazy."

"Of *course* I see them. Ugly things they are."

"They're a menace, dear, a menace. They arrived last week with this New York businessman, but I don't think he knew they were with him. Then things started breaking—lightbulbs exploded, milk spilled out of the fridge, the ice in the machines melted. A couple days ago it got much worse. People felt something trying to push them down the stairs. One guest almost drowned in the pool."

"Where's your husband, Maria?" The Girl read the woman's name off her breast pocket.

"He's away on a fishing trip."

"Does he fool around often?" The Girl asked kindly. The past few months had taught Nechama that no demon ever enters a domain uninvited.

Maria was clearly taken aback at being approached so blatantly by a woman easily twenty years her junior. But at the same time, The Girl's voice was so completely free of judgment, Maria didn't take offense.

"I don't know... Lately he's been gone more than he's been here," she began sobbing.

"Look, if you want these two things to leave, I'll need your help."

The grotesque creature retreated and, a moment later, Nechama heard the sound of a plate glass window being smashed behind her back. The bellhops had driven a chair through it. Nechama knew the situation would grow more volatile now, as the creatures sensed a threat.

"What do you want me to do?" The woman spoke through tears. She reached blindly for the box of tissues on the counter.

"I want you not to succumb to despair. Or anger or depression."

"I know it's hard, but feelings like these give life to these monsters," said The Girl, who had learned not to be intimidated by anybody. It did not matter whether they were rich and powerful or poor and meek.

"And if I can't stop being sad, you won't help me?" asked Maria, newly frightened, now.

"Oh, I'll chase these nuisances away regardless. I can't imagine they'll let me sleep in peace, now that they know I'm aware of their presence. All I'm saying is, if you accept your sadness, you can work your way through it and be happy again. And if you're happy, they won't come back."

"What should I do?" The poor woman was beside herself.

"You have cash?"

The woman's face turned hostile instantaneously and she pulled back. "Are you gonna scam me now, Missy? 'Cause I'll tell you, this hen don't get plucked too easy."

"Oh, relax, woman, I just want you to go hire that fine couple of singers playing not two blocks from here. And I want you to print out a batch of invitations right on this here fine computer. I want you to invite the whole town to a barbecue at your fine motel. Then I'll ask you to kindly go pick up some meat and corn and taters and anything else folks up here likes to eat. By then I surmise you'll be so happy, them two creatures won't dare cross your path again."

Maria agreed. She didn't necessarily trust The Girl, but at least she wasn't telling Maria to go see a shrink, like her friends were suggesting.

"What's a spice you could live with if I made the whole place absolutely reek of it?" The Girl asked.

Maria smiled, gaining confidence—or was it hope?—that her new acquaintance might actually be able to help. "I suppose cinnamon wouldn't be too bad," she said.

"Fine, cinnamon it is. Can you bring me a giant family-size jar of it?"

Nechama knew that magic was not confined to any specific potion or item. In fact, any substance at all could become a potent agent of the mind that controlled it. She also knew that minor demons, as well as commonplace gremlins and imps, were not aware of this fact. Netherworld creatures were incurably superstitious, a fact that was both surprising and useful. It was one of the gifts of the universe, Nechama was certain of it, and she offered a silent, heartfelt blessing of thanks.

Nechama opened the large jar Maria had brought from the kitchen. By now the two bellhops were in a fit of rage, one smashing furniture, the other riding on a light fixture to tear it down. They looked a lot like a rock band after a concert, only not as old. Every once in a while, one of the varmints would muster the courage to approach Nechama with bared teeth, but would invariably lose nerve and retreat to a safe distance.

Maria Advanta watched in awe as The Girl snapped into action. She was lovely in her onslaught, like a magnificent bird of paradise bearing down on a swarm of insects. She closed her eyes and began to hum a lively melody, interspersed with the the biblical verse (Psalms 63:3) traditionally used by apprenticing prophets searching for divine inspiration: "I have envisioned You in the holiness... to see Your might and glory... my soul thirsts for You... my body craves You...."

Humming pleasantly a tune which enables mortals to glance the Throne of Heaven and other numinous furniture, Nechama poured a generous hill of cinnamon into the palm of her right hand and blew it in the direction of the crazed bellhops. The reddish powder became a puffy cloud that ballooned ever larger, threatening to envelop the two creatures. The Girl's tune became louder and more ecstatic, as she laughed and puffed inexorable red clouds at the demons, over and over again.

The miserable bellhops attempted to resist. When they tried to attack Nechama, they were swept back against the reception area's broken window. The jagged glass shredded their red tuxedos. After several attempts to overcome their attacker, they gave up. Acting in tandem, they each spat a putrid black glob out on the rug, and escaped to the yard outside. The red clouds pursued them until, spewing a string of antiquated Babylonian curses, they leapt over the rear gate and fled into the Colorado slopes.

Back inside, on the rug, the black globs settled and began to pulsate as if they had life in them. The globs turned brown, then yellow, then cream, then white. When they were completely white, they split open like egg shells to reveal piles upon piles of green cash in hundred dollar bills.

Maria rushed out immediately to hire the boy and girl singing team, her face wet with tears of joy. She also hired a great mariachi band from a local club, just in case the boy and girl got tired. She bought a mountain of barbecue meats and then ordered the local Kinko's to print out a thousand cinnamon-red leaflets inviting the whole town to come and celebrate.

"What was that mesmerizing tune you sang?" Maria Advanta asked The Girl later that evening, after both of them had cleaned up and had a chance to sip a few beers, waiting for the party to start.

Nechama smiled. "There are so many wonderful tunes..." she said, and her voice trailed into silence. Her left leg felt as if it were on fire from fresh welts, and she closed her eyes to keep the tears of pain inside. She had mastered the technique of turning a painful sensation into a feeling of comfort, but it took a lot of concentration.

THE CABALIST'S HANDBOOK OF PRACTICAL MESSIANIC REDEMPTION recommends the following practice: Using the terrible horseradish root (*Armoracia rusticana*), one is advised to cut a small piece and chew it until it is no longer bitter, but rather becomes a sweet and flavorful fiber.

One thing is for sure: The only way to turn a piece of foul tasting horseradish root sweet is to taste every bit of the bitterness lurking inside it. Any fragment that isn't processed with salivary enzymes will remain bitter.

The exile which God imposed on the Jews—and on Himself—is a lot like the horseradish root. We have to taste its terror in its entirety, to be able to sweeten every aspect of the Human Condition. But sweeten it we will, it's all only a matter of time.

Not surprisingly, on the Spiritual Continuum of Everything the horseradish root stands between a frosted Italian Cassata made of strawberry and pistachio ice cream; and the cathartic diner scene from the film Five Easy Pieces *(directed by Bob Rafelson in 1970) in which classical pianist-turned-oil rigger Robert Dupea (Jack Nicholson) confronts his waitress (Lorna Thayer) who stubbornly refuses to serve him a plain omelet, a cup of coffee and a side order of wheat toast, because in her restaurant there are No Substitutions. She tells him "I don't make the rules" once too often, and the young Nicholson suggests," Okay, I'll make it as easy for you as I can. I'd like an omelet, plain, and a chicken salad sandwich on wheat toast, no mayonnaise, no butter, no lettuce. And a cup of coffee." To this his waitress responds: "A number two, chicken sal' san', hold the butter, the lettuce and the mayonnaise. And a cup of coffee. Anything else?" And Nicholson pours it on: "Yeah. Now all you have to do is hold the chicken, bring me the toast, give me a check for the chicken salad sandwich, and you haven't broken any rules." The flabbergasted waitress says, "You want me to hold the chicken, huh?" And our hero Jack brings home the sweet punch line: "I want you to hold it between your knees," and on that note, he sweeps the contents of his table to the floor.*

Just before the world reaches a critical mass of entropy and despair, we, the Jews, hope to be able to pull a righteous, Jack Nicholson sweep across the lunch table of history. No more meaningless rules and standard practices that trample the spirit. We will no longer stomach communist and capitalist and liberal and conservative menus that assault men's appetite. Let us deliver our glorious comeback to thirty-five hundred years of No Substitutions!

Outside the HANDBOOK, Jewish history continued to taste like fresh horseradish. An international coalition was amassing on Israel's borders, with soldiers of every member country of the United Nations on hand to punish the Jews for their most serious act against humanity, the attack on the Saudi oil fields.

A *New York Times* reporter discovered several encampments on the Jordanian and Egyptian side of Israel's border. As terrorist groups added their number to the world community's efforts, distinctions seemed to blur. Their arms and camouflage fatigues were Coalition issue. After all, they were all fighting for the same cause, weren't they?

Jewish pundits continued to argue that the Iranians, the North Koreans, the Pakistanis and the Syrians, were equally capable of carrying out the oil well bombing mission, and on top of that, were also committed to annihilating the Jews. But those voices were relegated to the trash bin, along with the conspiracy theory blokes who still claimed the Trade Towers were felled on 9/11 by the US government.

33.

Running Fox was feeling bored, so he picked up a hitchhiking woman in his truck, even though his insurance man always warned him against it. The woman had red hair and was pale skinned, but she was unlike all the other white people Running Fox had ever met. And just to prove to himself that she really was different, Running Fox decided to give the woman a test.

"Can you see the line that runs between the sky water and the earth water?" Now, all the other white people, and many of his own brown people, had no idea what Running Fox meant by his strange question. But this woman didn't skip a beat.

"Are you trying to see if I'm crazy?"

Running Fox had to admit that she was right, and also that, clearly, she was not crazy. Only crazy people were able to see the line between the two waters, and they had no trouble admitting it.

"One time I saw it," Running Fox told the woman. "You believe that?"

"Sure," she said. "I seen the carving on your boot."

This time Running Fox was very impressed, because the woman paid attention to his left boot, which rested on his right thigh when he was driving, and she could read his special carvings.

"How come you never married?" Nechama asked him. This meant she understood the moon sign of longing on his boot.

"I'm afraid of marriage," Running Fox admitted. This was the first time he had ever dared to put this notion into words.

"No money?" The woman read the jackrabbit poverty sign on his boot. Things were very bad in the Navajo settlement where Running Fox regularly parked his truck. No work, no money, government food and government liquor, people living to age forty and then dropping, people shooting themselves in the mouth at twenty. This young woman, clearly, knew all about it.

"Where you going?" Running Fox asked.

"I'm coming with you, Bro," Nechama said. "Will you accept my help?"

That night, Running Fox called a meeting of all the people. Only about fifty showed, but everybody thought it was a very good start. The woman spoke right away. She asked the people how long it would take them to put together twenty thousand dollars. The people laughed and wanted to know why she needed so much money. The woman told them she needed it to make them rich. The people wanted to know what she meant by rich. The woman said she meant they'd never again have to worry about money. They could get up in the morning and just go fishing and hunting and not worry about paying the electric bills or the phone bills or the Internet bills. The people said that sounded fine, but they couldn't trust a complete stranger with this much money. Would she mind if Running Fox held on to the cash? The woman agreed easily.

The people sold their jewelry and emptied their savings accounts to come up with the money, because they believed in the woman. And the woman and Running Fox drove down to a company in Flagstaff, where they bought many crates of solar power and wind power equipment. A man from the company came back with them to instruct them on the working of the equipment, because the woman asked him to come. It didn't hurt that she also promised him the people's gratitude and many good meals in return for his help.

In two weeks, everybody in town had free power. They had more power than they needed. They began to offer nearby towns the chance to pay a lot less for their power than what the big company charged for it; what did *they* care? They got it for free!

The Gas, Electric Light and Power Company was very upset. They sent messengers to warn the people that getting their own power from the sun and the wind was dangerous. The messengers showed them brochures with case studies of communities that thought they could use renewable energy for free, but went bankrupt because no one knew how to maintain the equipment, since they were amateurs, just like the Navajo.

But the woman spoke up to the messengers from the Gas, Electric Light and Power Company and told them not to worry, the people would figure out a way of repairing the equipment when the time came. She also reminded the people that they had solar *and* wind power. That gave them *two* sources between which to alternate if the need arose. The people thought that the woman made more sense than the Gas, Electric Light and Power Company officials.

A few of the young men made marriage offers to her, but the red-haired woman did not accept any of them, although she was very nice about it. She told her admirers that she was too young to marry, that she was still just a girl. So the townspeople took to calling her The Girl instead of The Woman.

None of the men who had proposed marriage to The Girl felt rejected at all. Instead, they were made to feel powerful and desirous, and every last one of them found himself another wife inside a month. Each new family produced a baby that year.

34.

One night, three men from the Gas, Electric Light and Power Company waited for the girl outside the bar that Running Fox had opened with his savings. Nechama was a little tipsy and didn't see them at first, and when she did, it was too late. They looked almost identical, broad and muscular, and their skulls were shaved. They worked silently and efficiently. Two of them grabbed her by her arms and the third lifted her feet off the ground. They threw her in the trunk of a brand new, white Cadillac SUV and took off into the desert. They rode for a long time. The night was pitch dark and moonless. The Girl was hoping they would chat during the ride, so she could pick up some helpful information about them, like if they were humans or demons, but they remained silent.

The ride ended at the edge of a canyon. The three men ringed the trunk and popped it open. Once again they grabbed her by her limbs and threw her on the dry earth. They hit without anger; picking a target above or below her neck, they smacked, accurately, harshly, competently and repeatedly. She understood that they'd been hired to administer a certain amount of punishment, and so she waited until it was all meted out. It was painful but tolerable. Also, her tormentors knew how to keep her conscious throughout her ordeal. They valued their violence too much to let her miss any of it.

The blows began to travel downward to her abdomen. Blood streaked from every exposed part of her face and body; she began to groan as the blows fell on her internal organs; her breathing became spastic; she'd been receiving the beating for a full thirty minutes.

On the thirty-first minute, two of the men pinned her down by her bruised shoulders and the third one tore off her dress. She closed her eyes, hoping to pass out and return when they were done, but no such luck.

Desperately, she aimed a feeble kick at the man pulling at her undergarments. She didn't think her blow had connected, but the man began to scream.

"She *burned* me!"

The Girl's eyes opened in wide surprise to see the flesh coming off his arm. The other two assailants dropped their hold and rushed to help their injured friend.

Looking down, she saw her bare legs weeping with open sores. The open lacerations on her left leg emitted a toxin so harsh, it burned a man's flesh off his arm. Who knew...?

When one of the men pulled out the revolver that had been tucked in his belt, The Girl had anticipated his move. It was time to destroy the evidence. When the tip of the bullet had almost reached her chest, her physical being skipped a beat, electrons and subatomic particles halting their reappearance until it passed through and was buried in the ground. She re-manifested an instant later, seeming dead to the naked eye. The men left.

After some moments, The Girl sat up and considered her options. She opted to stand up on her own, despite the shooting pains. She put on her dress again, as best she could, and then walked through the night back to the reservation. She arrived in her little hut after sunrise, but the settlement was still in the throes of sleep. Everybody on the reservation had taken to sleeping late as part of their new, relaxed lifestyle.

The next day, The Girl woke up, and tenderly examined her injuries. She decided she'd live. Calling one last general meeting, she told everyone what had happened and made it clear that the Gas, Electric Light and Power Company would never leave them alone. She told them to get together with all the other reservations and keep watch over the solar panels, windmills, battery cells, and wires. They had to take up arms and protect their assets.

The people thought she made sense. They had no trouble imagining the Gas, Electric Light and Power Company being antagonistic to their endeavors. They promised to be vigilant.

The people had a lot to protect now. They could go fishing and hunting without worry, run their microwave ovens and use the Internet for free. They kept telling anyone who passed through their small and prosperous settlement about The Girl, and all the good things she taught them.

When the people had enough fishing and hunting and free power to make them feel human again, they decided to continue to organize more projects together. This they had learned from The Girl. Now, all five thousand residents showed up at town meetings. They decided they wanted nicer homes, clean paved streets, and safe playgrounds. Soon they discovered that they had the power to do just about anything they dreamed up. Then they understood that The Girl didn't really liberate them from relying on costly power. The real gift The Girl gave this Navajo town (and the many other Navajo towns who copied them), was liberation from the mean old ways in which they used to look at themselves.

One morning The Girl baked a stack of tortillas which she put in her little backpack and took to the road. Everybody on the reservation was sorry, but they had known since the start that she had never meant to stay.

35.

A couple of months after Nechama Gutkind had performed her first miracle, healing an asthmatic child in Scranton, Pennsylvania, Pope Innocent XV began to sense the change in the air. He looked outside his window, the famous one, overlooking St. Peter's Square, sniffed the moist wind, checked the color of the sky and sat down to make a few phone calls. Afterwards, he wrote some notes and underlined a few names in the papal phone book. He then ordered his staff to prepare a full dossier on the Jewish child whose aroma so intrigued him.

Later that evening, his personal secretary, the young Jesuit Brother Marcello, furnished him with more details than any other clandestine agency possessed. The dossier included the young woman's name, her allegiance to a proto-messianic, Hasidic Jewish movement, and several pages of reports filed by American Church officials of various ranks and political biases, describing public miracles performed by her.

The pope sighed in obvious discomfort. This one Jewish woman was more dangerous than any ten suicide bombers—a lot more dangerous.

None of the ancient empires of antiquity had stamina equal to Rome's. Egypt, Assyria, Babylon, Persia and Greece may all today maintain some connection to their ancient origins, but they have long since turned into third-rate powers, their imperial drive spent, their glorious past the stuff of tourism.

Only Rome, which began its quest for domination more than 2500 years ago, continued to rule, and would remain the ruler of the planet until the arrival of the messiah.

What was the secret to Rome's survival? Above all, it was the empire's cultural flexibility: Rome had the ability to not only tolerate competing cultures, but ingest them beyond recognition.

The Pope politely asked the sleepy receptionist to connect him with the president of the United States. After she had verified the source of the call, the poor woman, a devout Catholic, experienced severe difficulty speaking.

"Holy Father, please forgive me, I'll connect His Eminence immediately."

"Very good, child," the pope said and leaned back in his plush armchair.

Only the day before he had visited the storage room new pontiffs are shown when they assume office. He touched the gold *menorah** which had once stood in the Jewish Temple, scanned the inventory of sacred utensils once used by the Jewish High Priest in slaughtering and carving animal sacrifices. The thought of giving back any of these splendid objects, should the Jewish messiah demand them, was repugnant to the leader of one billion believers. This is why it was imperative that he alert the American president.

Another key element of Rome's unprecedented endurance was geographic elasticity. The empire's center had been moved to Madrid, to Vienna, to London and, finally, to Washington, DC. Despite those continuous changes, the citizens of the empire remained deeply conscious of its existence: It could be relied upon in times of stress and it was the best guarantee against the barbarism that lay outside the empire's walls.

Rome was the key to postponing the world's redemption. As long as Rome continued to wield power, history was forced to continue upon its familiar path. When Rome was finally toppled, the world could embark on a new epoch.

This is why the messiah had to arise in modern-time Rome, the United States, as close to the seat of power as possible. When the time came, it would be the messiah's first job to topple Rome.

"Mr. President," Pope Innocent XV said into his receiver, "our culture is experiencing a menacing turn…"

The American head of state, Pete Clark, an energetic Generation X'er in his third year in office, fidgeted in his Air Force One seat. If the old

---

*   Seven-branched candelabra

man wanted to gripe some more about rock song lyrics and Hollywood nudity, he, the president, despite being one-quarter Catholic, planned to fake a bad connection and hang up.

"Your very office is in danger, Mr. President," the Pope continued. "You must begin a nation-wide search for a young Jewish woman by the name of Gutkind. She may be passing as a hitchhiking hippie in Nevada, or a simpleton farm girl in Colorado, or some other clever disguise. You must capture her."

"With all due respect, your Eminence," the president said, "how dangerous *is* this woman?"

Pope Innocent XV was not a very patient man. He didn't mince words with the Caesar: "If you don't catch her, Mr. President, she will destroy us both."

After the conversation had ended, the Pope called up his security chief, a beefy Swiss lad, and instructed him to post additional guards outside "The Room." Innocent XV was not known for his sentimentality, and yet it broke his heart to consider the possibility of—sometime soon—having to hide the magnificent Temple vessels and utensils somewhere outside the Vatican.

A few days later, the president of the United States called a meeting of his internal security advisers and found out they had already known something about The Girl. They didn't think she was a grave security risk, but if the chief gave the word, they also didn't think it would be difficult to eliminate her.

"The funny thing is," an FBI official suggested, "she's become such an urban myth, we could terminate her physically and she'd still be 'out there,' roaming the countryside."

"That's quite all right," said the president, "as long as *we* know better."

Shows you how much politicians know about the power of folklore: zip.

President Peter Yuma Clark's spot on the Spiritual Continuum of Everything was right beside a team of 150 attorneys who perished in a plane crash near the resort island of Aruba, on October 5, 1999. Terrorism was faulted, but the real culprit in that tragedy was the fact that the universe had reached a moment in its development when it had to unload 150 lawyers or burst at the seams.

90

36.

The most important legal case in America was about to begin. The federal courtroom in Washington, DC filled up to capacity the moment the doors opened, at precisely 9 a.m. The front end of the room was already crawling with government prosecutors and defense attorneys. The importance of this case was evidenced by the fact it pushed headlines about World War III right off the top half of the front pages of *The New York Times* and *The Washington Post*.

The Most Important Federal Court Case Today involved a government sting operation. Fourteen FBI agents had lured a group of elderly citizens into growing marijuana in their back yards, first for personal consumption and later for profit.

The defendants, twenty-eight men and women ages fifty-eight to seventy-five, were looking at twenty-five years in prison each. The fact that not one of them had displayed any interest in growing illegal plants *before* their government had seduced them did not alter the severity of their crime in the least.

Law Enforcement Through Show Trials dominated the way the US justice system preferred to conduct business. Classic police work, involving interrogation of witnesses, analysis of evidence, and forensic investigation was expensive and, worse, unpredictable. A citizenry conditioned by watching trillions of television hours did not tolerate dead-end investigations. It was no wonder career prosecutors on the state and federal levels preferred the sting operations.

Sting operations yielded effective Deterrence, albeit occasionally at the expense of Justice. For a sting to work satisfactorily, government agents initiated and often financed and even conducted the crime. The defendant was needed primarily during the second phase: sentencing.

The group of jump suited elders in stainless steel hand and leg chains was herded, waddling like a colony of oversized penguins, into the courtroom. Each defendant was released and assigned a seat. Their attorneys, fifty-two altogether, hovered with serious expressions on their polished faces, conveying the enormous significance of the event. It was the largest sting operation in US history that did not involve terrorists or mobsters.

Twenty minutes into the scheduled time for the court proceedings Judge Ernest Escobedo was still locked up in his chambers. His secretary, Evangelista Gomez, had buzzed him twice already. Gomez was concerned: All she knew was that some redheaded woman had asked to be seen urgently just before the trial. Against all precedence, Miss Gomez was ordered to admit her.

Miss Gomez tried to eavesdrop through the intercom, but all she could hear was silence, and the occasional rustling of clothes. What were those two doing in there? she wondered.

Had she been able to spy on her employer, Evangelista would have seen him in a state of hypnotic trance, leaning back in his luxurious swivel chair, eyes closed, a slight trickle of drool staining the stiff collar of his crisp, white shirt.

"Lovely," Nechama thought at the drifting judge.

"Love...ly." In his mind, Judge Escobedo and the pretty young women were walking into a bubbly brook on his estate in Maryland. It was a perfect summer day. Barefoot, their soles found luxurious purchase in the soft mud.

"You know, Judge, I've looked into your mind for some time," the young woman said. "You're a decent man."

"Decent..." Escobedo echoed.

"You're fair, you give folks a second chance, and you basically *like* people."

"Like... people..."

"You know what's missing?" Her blue eyes turned the color of steel.

"Missing?" He was confused. What could possibly be missing?

"You don't hate Evil," The Girl stated plainly. "It's not your fault, it's just not part of your personality. Every day you pass judgment on criminals, but you sleep soundly at night despite all the suffering you witness during the day."

"I'm sorry..." The judge's forehead wrinkled in his effort to understand.

"I want to bless you," said The Girl. "Each time you hear about the agony of another human being, it will get you right here." She touched his stomach. He retreated, but it was too late. "If you hear a second and a third horror story in one day, I bless you that your whole being become consumed with pity. I don't wish for you to mete out more severe sentences, only truly righteous ones—and when you do, you will recover from your

92

pains of empathy—until the next time."

Holding his balding head between her palms, she whispered: *"May God bless you and guard you... May God light His face unto you and forgive you... May God raise His face to you and give you peace..."*

Back in the courtroom, refreshed from his nap, the Judge turned his gaze to one of the grandmothers before him. Her pain and fear bore through him like a hot poker. He turned his face away from the old woman and doubled over, clutching his abdomen. What in God's name had the red-headed woman done to him?

He found that he could feel everybody's pain. Some was manageable—anxious prosecutors riddled by envy and fear of failure, that sort of thing. But each time he encountered the offended dignity of the old people whose freedom was threatened because of an invented crime, he gagged.

Eager to put a stop to the charade, Escobedo discovered that he was physically unable to pronounce the very words which would rescue him from the most embarrassing day in his professional life. The mere thought, "recusal," burnt the inside of his throat and would have probably caused him permanent damage if he had dared to express it.

Like a marathon runner seeing the finish line, he knew the agony would go away as soon as he dismissed the case. To make sure he would recover completely and speedily, Escobedo added a stern paragraph admonishing law enforcement agencies for neglecting their true mission: "Stop this foolishness. Address real crime. Act like men and women of law."

When Judge Escobedo was asked to describe the girl for an artist's sketch, he found that the results fell short of the luminous subject. His secretary agreed, although she was no more successful in describing her.

Escobedo decided to stop at his church for a short while before going home. The judge was a deeply religious man, involved in his parish and on close terms with his local priest.

On his way out of his chambers, he snuck a glance at himself in the mirror. He looked fabulous! His hair seemed fuller than usual—even less balding! And he appeared more resolute, more purposeful. He looked like the kind of person he used to admire as a young man. Strange, he mused, to be in top physical shape on the very day your career goes in the toilet.

Father Cullen was in his office on the ground floor of Our Lady of

Sorrow. The priest stood up when Escobedo entered. "What a surprise, Ernest. The day you had!"

"You're not kidding," said the judge. He shared with his priest all the details he could reconstruct from memory.

Cullen was impressed. "The blessing she gave you, that's from Numbers 6, verses 24 through 26. It's called the Priestly Blessing. The Jewish Temple priests used to recite that twice a day. Powerful stuff. Are you sure she recited it in English?"

"Father," Escobedo shook his head, "I'm not sure of anything, ."

"Well, you've had a spiritual awakening, Ernest, judging by your brave assault on government thuggery."

The judge looked up in anguish. "It wasn't me, Father. I was a puppet, acting only to stop my personal pain."

"Well, then, go change your decision. I'm sure the government would be happy to round up the defendants again."

"There's double jeopardy attached." The judge whispered, "All I wanted was for the pain to go away."

"You have acquired a true blessing."

"Blessing? In my current state, injustice makes me double over in pain. Violence on the news makes me throw up. I've become totally sensitized and I fear I'll go mad if this continues much longer."

His priest examined him with a curious smile. "You may now be the only sane man among us."

"Thank you, father, for the gift of your philosophical distance," the judge said bitterly.

"I'm sorry, Ernest," said his priest. "I never said being moral meant not feeling pain. I suspect the opposite is true."

When Judge Escobedo had left, Father Cullen got up from his desk and entered the sanctuary. Looking up at the golden crucifix, he said with a smile, "I'll bet she's Jewish, like you."

That evening, Judge Escobedo's story dominated the television channels even though it was not a slow news night.

There had been skirmishes during the afternoon between Israeli border patrols and coalition forces, according to the NBC anchorwoman in Gaza. Those forces, formerly known as terror organizations, ignited the world's imagination with their daring raids into the heart of the Jewish bastion.

Interestingly, on the Spiritual Continuum of Everything, the Secretary General of the terrorist organization, Hezbollah, Sheik Hassan Nasral-

94

lah, stood immediately to the left of the great prophet Mohammad (570-632). To Nasrallah's own left stood the beautiful Miss Lorena Hickok (1893-1968), First Lady Eleanor Roosevelt's lesbian lover, who exchanged some 3,500 fairly lascivious letters with her over a period of thirty years.

37.

The Department of Homeland Security agencies were in an uproar following the collapsed drug sting. Their attention was focused not on Judge Escobedo, whose career would shortly thereafter enter its decline phase, but on the testimony of his secretary regarding the young, redheaded woman.

"I reviewed the video surveillance files," said Kate Collinwood, assistant to NSA Chairman General Nathaniel Kane, during a video conference that included second-tier representatives from sixteen different DHS apparatuses. "No young woman fitting the description entered the court building, no young woman approached the judge's door. *Nada*."

"Somebody got to the files," a man on the CIA screen suggested.

"Not likely," said Collinwood. "The system is clean, the files are continuous. I have no explanation."

The DHS coordinator asked if the sketch artist had come up with anything.

"I have something," said Kane's assistant and switched her screen control to show an unremarkable portrait of a young woman. It was as if the judge's secretary had lifted the image from a Sears Catalog.

All sixteen screens in sixteen offices remained silent for a full minute. A rough estimate would put the cost of that minute of silence at $75,000.

"Well, we all know what needs to be done," said General Kane, breaking the silence. "Go back to your people in the field and send them out to dig up anything that can be found on a young woman, Caucasian, age twenty, give or take, red hair, with ties to subversive organizations."

"Sir," Colonel Amelia Lopes said from New York City, "We know who she is."

All eyes in all sixteen offices were on her, as she continued, "We've been receiving chatter about a mysterious figure known as The Girl. She's very big with Catholic parishes in the Southwest, where they're making her into a saint. I just completed a year of service in Arizona, and she's becoming huge down there."

"What does she do, exactly?" the General wanted to know.

"Hard to say," Lopes responded. "I suppose there's a real person somewhere in there, but all the real details are obscured by myth."

"What does she do?"

"She challenges the status quo, basically," was the best answer Lopes could come up with. "Very Jesus-like."

"Oh, crap, it's the Gutkind woman," General Kane spat, "I want her terminated. I don't care how many laws you have to break, this is a presidential priority. She is a most dangerous individual."

"I believe you're right, sir," Lopes agreed.

"We'll meet again by the end of the week, and all of you will be able to tell me something," Kane ordered before he turned off all sixteen screens.

He didn't need this, in the middle of a world war. He clicked to the *Washington Post* website and observed the headlines in disgust. Who would have expected the Jews to attack the oil wells? There was no scenario for this, it was seat-of-your-pants stuff, beginning to end.

Kane was aware of the possibility that the burning wells were part of a plot to embarrass Israel in the world's public opinion. But the president readily accepted the view that the Jews were responsible, and seemed content to drive US foreign policy in that direction. It was the first time General Kane, a familiar figure in several administrations, had ever heard the notion of putting an end to the Jewish state tossed around the cabinet table. He did not think it was a good idea, even if it *was* the president himself doing the tossing.

38.

One of the more notorious rumors cultivated about The Girl had to do with the struggle of the International Longshore & Warehouse Union.

In a stunning move, the Container Carrier Council, representing thirty major steamship lines, announced that it would begin using non-union labor to work its ships. The union, seeing its membership reduced at that time from some eleven thousand to as few as seven thousand, offered the company a concessions package that translated into a fifty percent reduction in labor costs. The council of major carriers sensed it had a once-in-a-lifetime opportunity to bring down one of the country's last truly independent labor organizations and rejected the deal.

Longshoremen load and unload cargo ships. They climb on top of containers to release latches. They crawl down into ship hulls to lash cargo so it can be lifted by giant cranes. They operate the cranes, they drive heavy lifts, they track and inspect shipments and they control truck traffic to and from the docks.

The major carriers were under pressure from global corporations to lower labor costs. More funds were needed for securing cargo carriers from random terrorist attacks and for ransom payments regularly issued to terror concerns worldwide.

Dock workers' wages in 2005, at the Southern California ports of Long Beach, Los Angeles, San Diego and Port Hueneme, reached an average of $105,000 annually, with foremen receiving an average of $180,000.

In comparison, dock workers in Charleston, SC, where the Union had been broken, earned an average annual salary of $40,000, doing the same work as their West Coast counterparts.

In Long Beach harbor, one thousand riot-equipped police were deployed one night to protect twenty non-union workers who were hired to load the freighter *Beatrice*.

Around midnight, some eight hundred workers left their union hall and marched to the terminal entrance, where they stood in a picket line, shouting slogans, and shaking their fists at the "scabs." The cops unleashed dogs at the protesters. Several workers were injured, but the dogs were held off by protesters brandishing their banners. Workers threw rocks at the cops and the police drove their vehicles into the picket line. Other riot cops crouched not far behind, firing smoke grenades at the protesters. During the protesters' retreat, a police car ran over a group of them, injuring several.

Union Vice President Kenneth Jones, bewildered by the workers' militancy, tried to create a buffer between them and the police. He was clubbed in the face by a cop and hauled off to jail.

This so unsettled Ken Jones, a patriotic American and part of the great middle class, that he hung himself in his cell that night.

The day after the riots, the district attorney opted to go to a grand jury and managed to obtain an indictment of forty-five protesters. He told the press that his plan for them was "Jail, jail, and more jail."

In addition, the Container Carrier Council (which had started the whole mess by bringing in the non-union workers in the first place) sued the union, its president and the rest of the accused members for fifteen million dollars in financial losses allegedly resulting from their picketing and other disturbances. The union offered to settle out of court without admitting guilt, but the company refused the offer. It looked like the end for one of the country's finest and most democratic labor unions.

On an early Tuesday morning in late January, a young, redheaded woman in denim overalls and a gray T-shirt walked into the ILWU hall in Long Beach, Southern California. She entered her name and union i.d. on the "shape-up" list of members looking to work that day, and then went to the refreshment table, dropped a quarter in the plate and poured herself a cup of coffee.

Normally, four or five hundred men and women hung around for the first shift shape-up call. Due to recent events, there were only about two dozen there, more for the company of their fellows than out of an actual hope to find work. The thirty or so CCC companies had united in an effort to impose a virtual lockout on all West Coast harbors. Officially, the CCC denied responsibility for shutting down port operations, blaming shipping delays on unionized workers.

The redhead walked around the large, well-lit hall, eavesdropping on conversations, getting into the rap here and there. A half-hour went by, then she went upstairs to the office of Local 119 president, Louis Harris.

Harris, a forty-five-year veteran longshoreman, was set to clear out of his office. To avoid corruption, ILWU leaders could only be elected to a maximum of two one-year terms, after which they returned to their former jobs on the docks. Harris was due for his retirement soon, except that now, with the pending lawsuits, he was worried that his grandchildren might be visiting him in prison for the holidays. There was also the threat that those suits, should they linger indefinitely, would drain the union's pension fund.

Tall and athletic, Lou Harris certainly did not look sixty-four, and the sight of a gorgeous redhead entering his office made him feel and act like a twenty-year-old. "What can I do for you, young lady?" he asked, standing up to greet her, a broad, friendly smile on his deeply suntanned face.

"I got an idea," said The Girl and sat down on the canvas sofa across from the local president's desk. The rest of that morning encounter belongs among the great myths of the labor movement in the United States.

"We can't fight them," was the next thing The Girl said. In some of the tales she was described as being bundled in an oversized denim jacket and oil-smeared dungarees. In others she had on tight black pants and a pink tank top. In some she was in a dazzling miniskirt, with a pointy black brassiere. In our version, we're going with denim overalls and a gray T-shirt.

"We're not trying to fight them," said Harris, who was taking an immediate liking to this lovely creature who had entered his space uninvited. "We'll be happy just to survive."

"We can't do that when the other side wants us dead," said The Girl. "They want us dead, Lou."

Harris sighed. She was right. All his life he'd been walking around with the disturbing feeling that all this was just too good to be true. He knew how other longshoremen lived elsewhere in the world. He knew that in places like Liverpool and Bremen, Marseille and Lisbon there were no longer any unionized dock workers. Even in North America they were down to a few thousand. The ILWU story really had been too good to be true. The global economy had a way of grinding the working man, cutting him down and chewing him up. In the past they were just as nasty, but they didn't own all the means of communication, and they didn't own all the politicians. Now they owned everything and everyone, and if you didn't play by their rules they starved you to death.

"But we can go above their heads," said The Girl, after he had finished telling her all that.

"Whose heads? The shippers? Were you listening to me a minute ago? The government is on their side, that means cops and U.S. attorneys and federal grand juries..."

"As long as we're the old ILWU, you're right. But what if we disappear? What if we become, say, Marine Terminal Services Incorporated, and what if we work outside the CCC, go directly to the manufacturers and offer them a better deal?"

"That's just silly," said Harris, already starting to listen intently. The young person on his sofa had an intriguing idea.

"They want to bust the union? Heck, let's bust the CCC!" The Girl said, putting the idea into appropriate slogan language.

Then she cautioned: "But we can't be overt about it, Lou, or the jig is up. We need to figure how much less than the big shippers we can charge, then quietly go and buy us a few carriers, everything very quietly, everything through proxy. We'll own the ships, we'll run the loading and unloading, we'll give the end-clients a bargain they can't refuse. What say, Lou, you wanna bust the CCC?"

She was magnificent that rainy January Tuesday morning in Long Beach, California. And she was absolutely radiant a couple of days later, in snowy

Chicago, when the ILWU leadership secretly purchased several operating carriers which were each already on their way to a West Coast harbor. Then the end-clients, all of them Chicago-based traders, received surprise visits from their new service providers. And liked what they had to offer: Get your goods on time—no strike-related delays, guaranteed—and pay only sixty percent of normal shipping costs. Refuse that kind of an offer and be prepared to be fired by your shareholders at their next meeting.

Was The Girl really sporting a Wonder Woman outfit, complete with red cape and bare, muscular thighs, when she negotiated the purchase of ten ocean-worthy carriers in Chicago? Or was she in a killer business suit, crisp white shirt unbuttoned down to her navel? Who knows? Once myths take shape, what's the point of verifying every detail?

Nevertheless, there was a reality to the story. Newcomer shipping conglomerate MTSI appeared on the scene, seemingly out of nowhere, to undercut the major international shippers. It took the new arrival a scant six months to triple its holdings, and to drive out of business ten of the thirty companies that comprised the CCC cartel.

The chief reason MTSI was able to offer ridiculously low-priced contracts to world corporations was its remarkable success in dealing with its work force. Speculations abounded, some tying the MTSI to the Mob, others hinting at profit-sharing deals with the union. Only much later did industrious *Post* reporter Danielle Herzog discover that MTSI was, in effect, just another name for the ILWU. But by then the company was making so much money and owned so many politicians, no one really cared.

According to THE CABALIST'S HANDBOOK OF PRACTICAL MESSIANIC REDEMPTION, the power of prophecy was taken away from responsible grown-ups around the time of the destruction of the First Temple. Biblical Ezra is considered one of the very last prophets who managed to lead a normal life, get married, hold a steady job, etc. In our time, prophecy is readily available only to small children, to the severely deaf, and to the insane—those whom we rarely take seriously.

Danielle Herzog was one such insane prophet. Information which was only available to others through hard and tenacious labor, came to Ms. Herzog seemingly through the ether. She just knew things.

Danielle Herzog had no idea why she ended up on a Jet Blue flight from New York to Chicago. She left the condo that morning in the company of Rita, her life-long companion, and Maurice, her loyal fact checker. She planned to stop by the *Post* building downtown to pitch a few stories to her editor, and thought it would be best if Maurice came along. Rita, of course, almost always came along everywhere.

Rita had first appeared in Herzog's life when the latter was five, and had been keeping her company along with many other creatures of the mind ever since. By now Danielle was so used to their presence, even the scary ones, that she only took her psychotropic medication before important interviews. Other times she was perfectly content to be surrounded by a menagerie of beings who seemed to tell the future quite nicely, but were decidedly errant about many aspects of the present.

Suddenly, Alex showed up out of nowhere, and said they had to ride out to LaGuardia. Why? He wouldn't say. But he got the four of them on the plane and there they were now, inside the Meridian Hotel and there was a girl she had to pay attention to, wheeling and dealing with some beefy men. It took Maurice half a minute to figure out the plot here. It took Danielle six weeks to sell her scoop to the *Post*.

So the media became aware of The Girl. But folks didn't need the media to tell them about the mysterious redhead roaming the countryside in search of adventure and good deeds. They had been waiting for her for centuries.

After her meeting in Chicago on behalf of the union, The Girl waited with her cohorts for the elevator to take them down to the restaurant of the Meridian Hotel. Eager for a good lunch, the Longshoremen piled into the elevator car leaving The Girl on the twelfth floor to wait for the next one.

Danielle Herzog walked up very close to The Girl. Nechama was surprised, but she recognized the bearer of horrible news from the cave. It seemed so long ago, but it had only been a year.

"Violets are blue, Roses grow wild, The murderous parent will kill the child..." Danielle Herzog chanted directly into Nechama's face.

"What does it mean?" Nechama asked.

"Search me," said Danielle. "This song came into my head."

"Oh."

"What do *you* think it means?" the bizarre woman asked innocently.

"I don't know," Nechama admitted. "It sounds menacing, though."

"I suppose," Danielle agreed. "Give me some money," she blurted.

"How much do you need?"

"I don't know. You got a hundred?"

"Sure. Here."

Standing alone on the twelfth floor before the bank of elevators, The Girl watched the hefty figure disappear in the hallway. She had no doubt they'd meet again. She was hoping, though, that the line about the parent killing the child was not directed at her personally.

"My mom was a test tube and my dad was a petrie dish," she said and smiled broadly. Then she grimaced as another welt appeared on her left leg, right on schedule.

A slender businessman carrying an expensive looking attaché case in one hand and a calf-length, camel hair coat over his arm, glided down the hall in brilliantly-polished black shoes, and stood next to The Girl. They entered the newly-arrived elevator together.

Even before the doors closed, she smelled danger. Most people would have lost precious milliseconds trying to determine the source of the threat, thus sealing their doom. But The Girl had the ability to trust herself without question; this was part of her prophetic talent.

THE CABALIST'S HANDBOOK OF PRACTICAL MESSIANIC REDEMPTION informs us:

> Imagination is the part of our brain which blocks us from the waves upon waves of prophecy permeating the cosmos. Imagination was given to us by our Creator as a survival tool. Sure, we did some wonderful things with it later on, but originally, our imagination was supposed to help us complete our stories.
>
> Walking through the woods you notice something fly by really fast. You haven't enough information to decide whether it's time to flee or fight. What do you do? Oh, it's already being done for you, it's automatic, bundled into your Homo Sapiens package. Your brain takes whatever you did grasp from that dangerous-seeming flying thing, compares it to other flying things stored in the system and issues a conclusion: It's just a harmless little sparrow, continue with the berry picking; or, it's a freaking pterodactyl, hide, man, hide!
>
> It doesn't really matter, for survival's sake, whether your brain forms a true analysis of what's going on. What matters is that it provide you with enough warning before you're eaten. Too many strong warnings, however, can drive you into paranoia, which is exhausting.
>
> Eternally concocting stories, the brain is a relatively useless tool when it comes to perceiving reality as it is, not as it should be. Imagination, preconceived notions, prejudices, wishes, ideology, morality, nostalgia, and memories, all conspire to warp the power of perception into an impenetrable web of lies.
>
> A prophet is simply someone who has rid himself of these sticky, unreal notions,

and is unflinchingly prepared to see God's universe exactly as it is.

In God's universe that morning, the businessman with his expensive looking attaché case and amazingly well-polished shoes was an assassin sent to kill Nechama. His scent was pungent, laced with layers of ammonia and carbolic acid. He came from an evil place—The Girl had no doubt. But while the rest of us would be faced with the option to either fight or flee, The Girl had numerous other options at her disposal.

She could un-be.

She could pray her surroundings into suspension.

She could generate unreasonable fear in her attacker.

Mind you, these fancy talents were nothing more than capabilities all of us possess and use in our everyday life, except The Girl's utilization of them was intense and complete. We've all disappeared in a crowd, we've experienced time stretch during an emergency, we've found ways of intimidating people who, all things considered, should have intimidated *us*.

The Girl chose to become someone else. She collected her flowing red hair into a severe bun, hunched her shoulders, expanded her right eye to twice the size of her left and permitted a globule of drool to dribble down her chin.

The well-dressed assassin immediately lost focus. The transformation was so thorough, he forgot the fact that only a moment ago he had identified his target with complete certainty. His target, for all intents and purposes, was now gone. He didn't need the headache of offing the wrong person in the middle of a posh Chicago hotel, thank you very much. When the elevator doors opened again, he let the ugly female out ahead of him and contemplated his excuses.

When he was gone, The Girl shook loose her lovely red hair and wiped her face. Her eye shrank back to size slowly. It was a tricky thing with the eye.

Fair question: Why was The Girl able to avoid the demonic assassin in Chicago, but earlier she had surrendered to a severe beating in the Arizona desert? And why was she subject to the blows from those three men, but not their bullet?

The answer has to do with Nechama Gutkind's classical mystical education. Her mentors had transmitted a brand of magical conjuring that the Abulafia clan had wielded for so many centuries, but it exacted a price.

According to THE CABALIST'S HANDBOOK OF PRACTICAL MESSIANIC REDEMPTION:

Moses was the first prophet to ask Heaven to execute a man. The target was an Egyptian policeman who beat a Hebrew slave. Moses found this intolerable.

Uttering the explicit, seventy-two-letter name of the Creator to bring down Heavenly wrath is not an automatic process. When the execution is Divine, then the process is more courtroom drama than a lynching, and all of the defendant's prior and future acts must be taken into consideration. Moses had to look back and forth: into the man's past, to see if there were any mitigating influences, good or evil, and into the future, to take into account the possibility that one of his descendants would wind up doing something great, like save the Jews or invent a blender that doesn't drip all over the counter top.

Likewise, whenever anyone elicits Divine help, he himself is judged, including all his past and future failures. This is why mystics are reluctant to overuse their powers: Who wants Divine scrutiny on their ass every Monday and Thursday?

The Girl joined her union buddies at the hotel bar, ready to toss back a few beers. It was a very good day.

It isn't easy to become an American Labor folk hero. So many start out with such promise only to end up in the Leavenworth penitentiary. But The Girl will forever remain an untainted heroine of the US Labor movement, because she busted the bosses, and because she moved on afterwards, pure of heart and mind, instead of staying on to become a boss herself.

39.

While The Girl spent her days making trouble for the powers that be in Chicago, her nights and Sabbaths had been spent at the Cosmic Wisdom House of Evanston, IL, run by Rabbi Yitzchok Marcus. The rabbi was a young and robust man, who at first mistook Nechama for a hitchhiker seeking spiritual nourishment. During supper his wife took him aside and whispered The Girl's identity in his ear. Marcus was delighted. But Nechama would have received the warmest kind of welcome no matter who her parents were.

Back in the nineteen-fifties, the late cabalist had been chastised for exposing his flock to the temptations of the secular world with his policy of opening outposts for those who wished to explore their connection with Judaism. The general trend among fervently pious Jews at that time was to shield themselves and their children from the outside world. But this fervently pious Jew was not afraid; rather, he was excited by the challenges posed by the secular world, and he urged his people to labor on its behalf.

At the master's behest, more than three thousand Cosmic Wisdom Houses sprang into existence, from Shanghai to New York and from Anchorage to Cape Town. In the United States alone there were more than one thousand such institutions.

A side-benefit of this ambitious project was that twenty-year-old Nechama Gutkind had at her disposal an extensive network of shelters. If the government was wondering how The Girl could be so effective at galvanizing communities around the US without ever charging a meal in a restaurant, the answer was: She didn't need to.

For instance, when The Girl was changing the landscape in Aspen, Colorado, Nechama kept the Sabbath at the Cosmic Wisdom House on Robinson Road. The rabbi gave her a room and set up Shabbat candles for her on Friday afternoon.

Throughout her one-year run across America, Nechama was similarly assisted, whisked away to safety, hidden and otherwise cared for in the ubiquitous Cosmic Wisdom Houses. Some of the Cosmic Wisdomnik folks who helped her were friends and associates of her father. Many were not. A few were even his ideological enemies: the dispute invariably rested on the issue of the late master's messianic status—Reb Gutkind was a minimalist on this count—others in the movement thought he came up short in the faith department. But not one of Gutkind's opponents would *dream* of rejecting Nechama, or any Jew, for that matter, over such political trivialities.

During her travels, when Nechama Gutkind sensed adulation in the hearts of complete strangers, she would become alarmed.

In El Paso, Texas, a trucker dropped Nechama off on the outskirts of town in front of a local church where a crowd was leaving mass. Somebody pointed and yelled, "There she *is!*" Only then did Nechama realize that the church was called "The Girl of Great Compassion." Emblazoned on the building was a mural based on the sketch from the courtroom in DC. It was stupefying.

For one thing, her admirers could rob her of her intuition. Abulafia and Victoria both had warned her about this: When you start playing for the crowd, you lose your inner voice. It doesn't happen right away, but one morning the smell of the street outside is just that: No more clues, or hints, or premonitions. *Finito.* The universe severs its special connection with you.

She was most immediately concerned for her "followers," mainly women, who pressed toward her, their eyes brimming with love. Suddenly, she knew what to do.

"Hold my hands," Nechama said. Many had to settle for holding on to others who, in turn, held onto her. She waited quietly, until everyone in front of the church was connected to her in some way.

"Your feelings for me are wonderful," she said very quietly. Everyone had to strain to be able to hear her. This was good, because it kept their minds from wandering. This was her first experience in creating an intimate connection with many people at once.

"Your emotions fill me up. They are so genuine and sincere. But they don't belong to me. They belong to your friends, your husbands and wives, your children, your parents. I thank you for your love—but I'm not really a part of your lives. I bless you now that all your sweet emotions find their rightful places with your families and friends. And maybe the occasional stranger." She giggled. "You're a very nice crowd," she added.

She gently removed herself from the circle and hailed another passing truck. She chased after it, her leg burning, until it stopped to admit her, eventually dropping her off not two blocks from the El Paso Cosmic Wisdom Center.

The people she left behind remained standing together, as if in a dream. They basked in each other's warmest emotions and chose not to let go of the circle for a long time. When an hour had gone by, one of them suggested that they create another circle the next time they met.

The newly founded shrine of The Girl had just invented its first and most popular ritual.

40.

The first attempt to assassinate The Girl was followed by more of the same, and would invariably occur whenever she scored another victory against the status quo.

After the Aspen motel episode, the Prince of Darkness was somewhat concerned because that event suggested The Girl easily matched powers with run-of-the-mill demons, indicating that she had received schooling in the occult arts.

After the failed Chicago attempt on The Girl's life, the P of D decided to kill her personally, which meant he was now *extremely* concerned. He usually preferred to delegate evil assignments to lesser minions. When people see you get your own hands dirty they tend to think you might not be such a big shot after all. But the deed had to be done properly; he had an unforgiving schedule to keep until the final destruction of Jerusalem.

He picked the time and place carefully, crossing The Girl's path at dawn, when she was standing on the shoulder of US Route 508 outside West Orange, NJ. Samael conjured a black BMW Schnitzer and slid to a stop right next to the lovely hitchhiker.

Nechama became aware of the foul stench of sulfur and excrement; the most potent she'd ever encountered. She backed off, but felt certain that she could not flee this creature. So she stopped and faced the half beast/half BMW owner that advanced upon her.

Samael possessed little curiosity about this child. He had no interest in striking a conversation. He did not care to make it look like an accident. He intended to murder her in the most direct and effective manner, then vanish, and to hell with the witnesses.

As historic events began to approach their natural conclusion, he bothered less and less with covering his tracks. This explained why world violence had become so crude. There was simply no time left for baroque cruelty.

The Dark Aspect of God simply unsheathed his black claws and attacked with a vicious growl, grabbing Nechama with one hand and bringing down his other hand to slash her throat.

Nothing happened. He didn't grab her, he didn't touch her throat. He had missed her completely while she stood right beside him, watching calmly.

He tried again; each time he'd aim just to the right or to the left of her. It was very frustrating.

Motorists on the highway slowed down to get a good view of the strange little fellow in a homburg hat, dancing madly around the lovely young redhead. This created a traffic jam that lasted two days and was recorded by the New Jersey Department of Transportation as the heaviest traffic interruption not caused by accident or weather. It was a new statistic, created especially to record this traffic incident.

Remember Nechama's caution regarding appealing to the Heavenly court because of the risk of encouraging a jaundiced examination of her own files? Remember that both her mentors emphatically trained her concerning excessive use of the Heavenly appeal? Well, in Nechama's case, both Lionel Abulafia and Victoria Martin were wrong.

According to THE CABALIST'S HANDBOOK OF PRACTICAL MESSIANIC REDEMPTION, Samael was unable to touch The Girl, much less hurt her, because she was a perfect sphere, spiritually speaking.

When Evil tries to hurt us, it always looks over the surface of our spiritual geometry, in search of a flaw inside which it can deposit some of its protoplasm. Evil has to get into us in order to hurt us; we must cooperate, we must create the opening, and we also have to accept it inside us. But The Girl had no such opening. She was a graceful, perfect whole, neither causing nor inviting harm at all.

Only one other person in recorded history had been such a sphere, our teacher Moses. He was so perfect that when it came time for Moses to die, on his birthday at the age of 120, God had no idea how to kill him. And Moses, all too aware of his advantage, was reluctant to cooperate.

He even tried to negotiate a compromise. "Look, God," he said, "since we both know You can't kill me, why not just let me live on as a simpleton. I'll give up my rank, Your precious history can continue, uninterrupted, just leave me be."

It's not that Moses was so hooked on life: Something bigger was at stake. God wanted Moses, his finest creation, to die in the wilderness and not set foot in the holy land. This was because God knew all too well that, with Moses watching over them, the Jews would never give Him a reason to mess with them. And if Moses built the Temple, it would stay built.

Then Moses said, "At least let me live on as a raven, or a donkey," just so he could get into the holy land. But God was well aware of the power of divinely inspired ravens and donkeys to influence events, and there was no way He would grant Moses his wish.

God finally simply asked Moses to accept his death. It was a request Moses was unable to refuse. God kissed him gratefully on the lips and received the great man's soul.

The angel of death was powerless against Moses, only God could claim his soul. Moses' system completely fused the great man's physical and spiritual aspects, and his only weakness was that he was born of a sexual liaison. At the instant a man and a woman achieve orgasm, they're neurologically incapable of including God in their thoughts. So that moment of no-God was a chink in Moses' armor. Though sealed before the angel of death, God Himself could reach through it to grab Moses' soul.

But The Girl had no vulnerabilities, having been conceived without a sexual liaison. Perfectly perfect, she won't even have to agree when God politely notifies her that her life on this plane is through.

Samael was shocked. In his darkest dreams—and even his light dreams were pretty darn dark—he had not imagined a foe like The Girl. She could ruin everything. What was an evil archangel to do?

He knew what had to be done. Only one quality could overcome The Girl's kind of indefatigable goodness.

Betrayal.

41.

When The Girl *did* appeal for Heavenly help, she usually had to pick an advocate to present her case. Over her year of wandering, she became extremely adept at this, and knew every available soul with the requisite spiritual brains and brawn, and how they could be roused.

Nine times out of ten, she would call on our mother Rachel. According to THE CABALIST'S HANDBOOK OF PRACTICAL MESSIANIC REDEMPTION, a second pair of sisters was also involved in the messiah project.

Of great service were Rachel and Leah, the daughters of Laban, a great evil magician who was Grandfather Jacob's uncle.

Mother Leah's province was the past. She was the only one among the matriarchs with the ability to travel freely as far back as the first day of Creation and mess with history. Whenever you read about characters moving up and down the timeline in unexpected ways, it is Leah's doing.

Mother Rachel presided over the future. She had the ability to go thousands of years forward, find herself a nice, shady spot on the side of the road and just sit and wait patiently for everybody else to catch up with her. She was the one who informed Grandfather Jacob about how the Temple would be destroyed and how his children (her children too) would be dispersed around the globe for many centuries.

Of course she didn't mention a globe per se, because, unlike herself, Grandfather Jacob was accustomed to the construct of a flat Earth. So she revealed to him instead that their children would be cast to the four corners of the Earth. He got the point, regardless, and cried bitterly. He hadn't figured on History lasting so many thousands of years. He thought, in five hundred years, max, God would enact some serious redemption. In some way he felt cheated, and told his children so. In retaliation, God revoked his power to prophesy.

Leah was destined to give birth to Judah, the paternal grandfather of the messiah (Moab, Lot's older bastard child, was the maternal great grandfather). So the two sisters, Rachel and Leah, decided to cheat the Dark Aspect of God and draw its attention away from Leah. They made him focus on Rachel instead. And in order to fool the old Dragon, they had to fool Grandfather Jacob, too.

Rachel was as beautiful as the first drop of fresh milk that hops merrily out of a jug into your mouth at dawn. She was sassy and brilliant. She danced like a happy lamb and kissed like a shameless Ashtoret priestess. Is it any wonder Jacob fell head over heels for her? The moment he first saw her at the well in Haran, where she came to water her flock, he grabbed her and planted such a kiss on her lips, History did a double-take. Whole commissions of heavenly hosts were sent down to investigate whether this really was Jacob, son of Isaac, the great holy man in whom were merged both his grandfather's unlimited mercy and his father's unstoppable might.

Rachel played it up so smoothly, she even warned Jacob that there was a plot to fool him into taking Leah for a wife instead of her, Rachel. She suggested they decide on a password, which only he and Rachel would know, so that, naked in the darkness of their wedding bed, he could test and see if he had really gotten the wife he had bargained for.

Then she revealed the password to her sister. Rachel hid under their wedding bed and cried out passionately, while her sister and Jacob were copulating, so Jacob was sure the whole time that he was with his beloved Rachel.

Faked orgasms are not a recent discovery, that's for sure.

By the time Grandfather Jacob woke up the next day and realized he'd been fooled, it was too late. His marriage to Leah was consummated.

Rachel hadn't even begun protecting her sister and her sister's offspring. She continued to attract Samael's attention the way a lightening rod attracts the wrath of the elements. She played coyly with Jacob after he married her, too; she pretended to be a spoiled child, completely trusting that her man's infatuation with her would suffice to keep her out of trouble. One night she even rented Jacob out to her sister so she could sleep with him, in return for a fresh bunch of mandrakes.

Both her children, Joseph and Benjamin, continued for the longest time to be considered the proper lineage for the messiah, while the real scion of the redemptive line was Leah's son, Judah. Leah said his name was a derivative of toda (gratitude). She was thankful to God for giving her a fourth son; and to her sister Rachel, the most devoted and conniving sibling who ever plotted the birth of the world's redeemer.

With all of Rachel's efforts on behalf of redemption, you may well ask: What did Leah accomplish? With Leah's ability to change the past, how come she didn't go back and change terrible things like pogroms and holocausts and exile?

Whoever told you she didn't?

110

42.

Numbers are a devious component in every tradition, but inside THE CABALIST'S HANDBOOK OF PRACTICAL MESSIANIC REDEMPTION they practically cheat little old ladies out of their social security checks. Most notable among those is the number 130, composed in Hebrew numerology of the letters *kof* (the equivalent of one hundred) and *lamed* (the equivalent of thirty). Together they make the word *kal*, which means light (as in "not heavy").

The HANDBOOK relates:

After Cain murdered his brother Abel in the field, Adam, the father of both these men, sank into a deep depression for 130 years. During this entire period, the father of all mankind sat in the shallow part of a river and masturbated.

It was not life and joyful creativity which was associated with this self-gratification; instead the act was accompanied by sadness and a faint memory of death. Poor Adam was experiencing the first human grief, the stuff of parental nightmares: one son a killer, one son dead, wait till The New York Post gets a hold of this one...

So, what's he supposed to do? He sits in the freaking river playing with himself. What would you do in his place? True, 130 years is a bit over the top, but when you live 970 years, devoting 130 of them to any hobby is still within reason.

But Adam's sperm didn't get wasted: It turned into the troubles which have been nagging mankind ever since. Put that in your Pandora's box and smoke it!

So the origins of the number 130 are linked with mindless sexuality, the bestial kind, the joyless version. Next we find it in connection with Grandfather Jacob. He'd been fooled into marrying Grandmother Leah, and he worked his ass off for seven years for her, too, in addition to another seven years for Rachel, his true love. He loved Rachel so much, the years seemed like days to him, like hours. And when he was done, he yelled out to Laban, his crooked father-in-law, "My days are fulfilled, you lying bastard, give me my wife, so I can mate with her!"

Just like that. The esteemed patriarch, on his wedding day, behaved like a sex-starved maniac. Eleventh Century sage Rabbi Shlomo Yitzhaki (Rashi, 1040-1105), the sweetest Bible teacher that ever lived, is aghast at Jacob's exuberance. "How can he talk like that? The lightest of the lightest among men wouldn't dare speak this way!" Light, remember, is kal, which amounts to 130.

The man is sixty-four years old already, argues Rashi, he wants to get moving with giving birth to his twelve children who will comprise the twelve tribes of Israel. He wants to get on with the work of bringing the messiah. It's holy baby-making time.

But even Jacob doesn't know all the mysteries of the number 130. He doesn't know that his smart second wife and his tearful first wife have conspired to bring him to this state of lightness, to strip him of all mental and social inhibitions, to get him back to where Adam was when his sorrow was replaced by an irresistible yearning to grab his manhood and fall back in the shallow part of the river.

You can't be obvious any more when it comes to bringing the messiah. Samael is everywhere. You try and conceive the perfect baby, you try immaculate conceptions and virgin births and the Prince of Darkness will be all over you in a second, after which it won't matter all the nice stuff your baby will be teaching—it will turn into rivers of blood. Oh, no, if you want a messiah baby, you con Samael into believing a horny old man wants to be with his delicious new wife. Shrewdest girl that ever lived, that Rachel.

Next time we meet this number, 130, it's when the first real redeemer is born. Gosh, was that a coup. Yochebed, wife of Amram, was 130 years old when she gave birth to the boy who eventually took the Israelites out of bondage forever. The trouble that went into fooling the Dragon: First Yochebed and Amram got divorced. Then they got together again. And all Samael could see were two elderly Jews embracing outdoors, under an apple tree. The thought of redeemer-birth didn't even cross his dark mind.

And Moses, he was truly the one. If God had played it straight with Moses, we'd never have gone into exile. But God doesn't play fair, you know that already. He, in His sacred wisdom, pulled stunts on Moses that would have caused an Alabama sheriff hunting for New York motorists to blush. But we digress.

There's only one place in Scripture where the true meaning of the number 130 is revealed. It seems a safe place and seemingly outside the realm of negotiable history. It is Psalm 130:

Out of the depths I cry to you, God. Please hear my voice, please let your ears be attuned with the sound of my begging. If You, God, should start recording our iniquities, who will stand a chance? But there is forgiveness inside You, remember, it's Your capacity to forgive which makes us fear You the most*.

I wait for God, my soul waits, I dream of the day when I'll finally hear Him. My soul waits for God worse than the night watchmen wait for the dayshift. The best thing for Israel is to hope God will eventually come around, because only God knows where He's hidden His ample storehouses of mercy and redemption. Then, you'll see, He will redeem Israel from all their iniquities.

At this point the handbook's author gets a bit teary-eyed and declares he is going to get himself a nice flask of vodka and be back shortly to finish

---

* Because if You don't forgive—and decide instead to destroy us for our unmentionable behavior—we would experience considerable relief; but if You forgive us and keep us around, we'll *never* stop having to deal with You.

the entry, but, as is to be expected, he never does.

43.

According to THE CABALIST'S HANDBOOK OF PRACTICAL MESSIANIC REDEMPTION, deception, incest and forgetfulness are keys to the ancient effort to fool God into redeeming the world. Yet, the man least capable of promoting these values was, actually, the bravest man who ever lived. This was Judah, the fourth son of our grandfather Jacob.

Judah was the bravest not so much because of his performance in war - his brothers Simon and Levi made a far feistier fighting machine together. Why, one time the two of them slaughtered an entire city because the mayor's son had sex with their sister.

Judah was the bravest because he was always prepared to accept responsibility for his actions. This, more than any other quality, prepared him for the role of king of the Israelites. Oh, and the fact that his mother, Leah, said so....

Both of Judah's elder sons, Er and Onan[**], were enthusiastic worshippers in the cult of On. God was in a rage over the two men. They each in turn married the same woman, Tamar, and God killed them both on account of the masturbation thing.

Ritual masturbation was an old Egyptian tradition, which spread like wildfire throughout the Near East around the 1500's BCE. On (Power) was the Original Being, and his First Act was to ejaculate into his own hand, then drink his semen. This was the first pleasure ever experienced by any entity, according to the ancient Egyptians. On decided to bring into existence other entities with whom he could have Pleasure. The Temples of On celebrated and preserved the ritual of Divine Sexuality. Outside the Temple doors were statues of On as a male goat. Inside the Temple, On was depicted as a large, naked man holding his erect penis in one hand, in the original act of masturbation which created the world.

Now, normally God doesn't go around killing any guy He catches masturbating because, let's face it, this could spell the end of mankind. But God had a thing for Tamar. She was the daughter of the exulted Shem, son of Noah, one of the original survivors of the Deluge holocaust. God had great plans for this woman who, just between you and me, was an hermaphrodite. She was also the most sexually dexterous and aggressive person in recorded history. Use your imagination, for crying out loud.

[**] The names mean "seed spiller" and "self-gratifier." Did that Judah have a knack for names or what?

So God is irate at the fact that both these slouches, Er and Onan, are in bed with this incredibly delicious and mysterious hunk of a woman, and the best they can do is self-gratify, to use polite language. And Judah—Judah has a third son, who is still not of age, but, between you and me, Judah isn't so enthusiastic at the prospect of marrying the little guy off to this man-eater, Tamar. Two sons down is more than enough by his account.

He tells Tamar to wait, and she waits. And waits. And waits. Now, she knows she's supposed to start a messianic lineage, and God knows she's involved, somehow, in the messiah thing, although God is trying to keep out of it—He figures, the less He knows, the better.

One day Judah, who by now is a widower, is going up to Timna, not far from Gaza, to shear his sheep. Tamar hears this and she takes off her widow's garments, puts on a seductive veil, a sassy pushup bra, maybe, a short skirt, high heels, and takes up a post by the road to Timna.

You would think that all this sex appeal, plus the hidden identity thing with the veil and whatnot, would drive Judah bats, but it didn't. This was because Father Judah was pure intellect. He would never have dreamt of having sex with a whore on the highway, not because it wasn't nice, but because what would be the point?

It was touch and go there, for a while, and in heaven they all trembled in their poopiks*, because they knew it was time to conceive the messiah, and if Judah had to wait until it made sense to do it, the world would be doomed. It never makes sense to procreate. We all die. More people only means less food. We procreate because God imbued all creatures with desire, and so we're all chasing some kind of tail, which is better than sitting at home watching television all day.

But Judah, the son of Jacob, was so intensely invested in intellectual and moral pursuits that he was incapable of producing the kind of life force that was required to conceive the messiah. This is why he produced such weaklings as Er and Onan. A special messenger had to be sent to pour a bucket of cosmic lust on the poor man's head.

In a bizarre turn of cross-temporal events, this messenger was, once again, a certain grand master from Brooklyn wearing a black fedora, who sneaked up on Judah and grabbed him by his thighs, setting his manhood aflame. This was the only way to work up enough fizz in Judah's loins to bring down the soul of the messiah. He had to crave penetration, he had to go mad with the need to hump somebody right then and there. No crap about fulfilling the holy commandment of procreation was going to do this job.

In his own temporal reality the grand master was seen grabbing the face of

---

* The Yiddish word means, literally, "navel." The idea that one shouldn't take on excessively ambitious challenges is expressed as "Don't jump higher than your own poopik."

his closest disciple, Reb Motke Gutkind, and planting a hot, lip-smacking kiss on his mouth. Who knew?

Drenched in sudden, unexplained desire, Judah spotted the harlot on the highway and was helplessly drawn to her. He had never heard himself say the kind of vulgar stuff he said to her next: "Let me do it to you, baby, hubba, hubba hubba, let's get it on, sister." The poor man was on fire, for the first time in his life.

Tamar had a hard time hiding her huge smile behind the veil. But she stuck to the script and asked to be paid in advance. He told her he was a wealthy sheep grower, which he was, and that he'd gladly send her a lamb or any other sweet little thing as soon as he was done. So she asked for a collateral. He asked what she had in mind and she said his phylacteries would do nicely. (The text merely says that Tamar asked for his ring, staff, and sash. But as any child could tell you, if Judah was out walking on the highway, could it be that he was not wearing his phylacteries? Impossible!)

Now you begin to understand how much lust drove this man's actions. He was overcome. Without hesitation, he tore off his phylacteries, and with the same motion was already undoing his pants. She accepted the deposit and invited him in.

Later, Judah sent a friend to Timna with payment for the harlot on the highway, but there was no such person to be found. The friend came back and told Judah the locals had never seen whores at that particular intersection. Strange thing. Obviously, Judah had to make himself new phylacteries, or shell out a good eight hundred to a thousand dollars for a decent off-the-shelf pair.

A few months later, word got out that Tamar, daughter of the holy Shem, was pregnant with a bastard child. In those days Shem was high priest of a small mountain outpost later to be named Jerusalem. Poor Tamar. When you're a slut and your daddy is a man of God, you burn—the old fashioned way—with molten lead poured down your throat.

She was hauled before a court comprised of Isaac, Jacob and Judah. This was some high court, considering two of the judges were aspects of God himself, and the third was father of all the Jews. No matter how aggressive Tamar was, this court made her knees buckle.

When Tamar realized it was her moment of truth, she produced her father-in-law's phylacteries and said, "These belong to the man who knocked me up."

And Judah recognized his old phylacteries.

Now, most other men in his situation would have kept their mouths shut, especially in the presence of the two most august human beings on the entire planet. But Judah was the bravest man who ever lived, so he admitted his responsibility and accepted as his own the twins that were later born to Tamar. Some say he moved in with Tamar and had the best sex you can imagine for the rest of his life.

The stage was set to bring down the spirit of the messiah in a conniving, roundabout way, because the frontal approach only gets him killed.

In a few generations, Ruth, the descendant of the incestuous sex between Lot and his daughters (the younger daughter deserves credit, too, because her night with daddy served as a subterfuge), would marry Boaz, the descendant of the incestuous sex between Judah and his daughter-in-law. And their grandchild would be our redeemer.

Mission accomplished.

Not really...

44.

More than ten months after she had left her Scranton home Nechama continued to seriously threaten the status quo.

As usual, The Girl was not aware of why and where her internal pain compass was leading her, only that she needed to get to a candy store in Hoboken, NJ.

She was in bed, in the guest room of the Cosmic Wisdom House in nearby West Orange, when the pain started. She didn't even try to fight it—it couldn't be done. Instead, she sat up in bed, washed her hands in the small bowl the rabbi's wife had provided for her, then changed the dressings on her left leg. By now, that leg was so riddled with sores, crusted and fresh, it was a big job to keep it infection-free. She dabbed every open sore with a cotton pad drenched in alcohol, then covered the leg, from calf to upper thigh, with a length of gauze.

Her night table clock read 10:45 p.m., in large red numbers. The house was silent. She hated more than anything what she had to do next: going to her hosts' bedroom door and asking for a lift.

Rabbi Mendy Kasowitz, a short man with a huge, salt and pepper beard and a sweet disposition, had to gather all his internal strength and love for all the Jews, near and far, to retain his civility.

"Go back to bed, I'll take you wherever you want to go in the morning," he said. This young woman seemed strange enough when she had appeared on his doorstep out of nowhere, asking for a meal and a bed. He recalled feeling a special sense of gratification at being able to grant her both. Now she wanted more.

Kasowitz didn't really understand why, when she repeated her request, he could not refuse her, even when it turned out she had no idea where she wanted to be driven. She assured him that she would know when they got there.

"Are you upset with me?" she asked sheepishly as they swept east on US 280. "Turn right here, get off the highway," she added and he followed.

"I was very upset before, when you woke me up," he recalled honestly, because it made no sense not to be honest when addressing this young woman. "Now I'm fine," he added. He realized he was better than fine; he was filled with a sense of purpose the likes of which he had not felt in a long while.

The life of a Cosmic Wisdom rabbi offers few opportunities for true meditation and spiritual growth. For the most part, the job entails chasing after the members of your town who have the bucks. It's a business; fish for 50 or more Sabbath guests don't just fly into the pot. It isn't that you forget to tend to your own spiritual needs, you just kind of never get around to it. Soon enough, your prayers become fast and economical, you abandon the practice of meditation before prayer, even learning sessions are more preparations before lectures than what used to be study for study's sake. Your attention span grows shorter and shorter—most evenings you're more likely to turn on the Internet than open a holy book.

You tell yourself that, like any community leader worth his salt, your life belongs to others. But the pursuits you've abandoned leave behind them a trickle of shame you cannot ignore. Somewhere inside the secret compartments of your heart is a deep yearning to get your life back. Even a sabbatical would be nice.

Now, all of a sudden, Mendy Kasowitz's life felt like it was his own again, at least for the duration of the drive from West Orange to downtown Hoboken. When he parked across the street from a candy store, its window bright with garish neon signs depicting beer and palm trees, it was just starting to drizzle.

Kasowitz said, with a huge smile, "You're Motke Gutkind's daughter, aren't you?"

Nechama smiled back.

"Give me a *brocha**," he asked.

"What do you need?"

"I know I should say *moshiach***," he said, and a bit of her smile was now spreading on his own face.

"You want *moshiach* now?" She paraphrased a hugely popular, if somewhat

---

*   A blessing
** Messiah

vulgar, Cosmic Wisdom tune.

"Yes," he said vehemently, "I really do."

"You're ready to abandon everything, take the wife and the kids and follow him to Israel?"

He had to think. "I want my congregation to come along, too," he said.

"It won't be an easy job, talking them into it," she cautioned, "even when *moshiach* comes…"

"It's not an easy job making them go to *shachris**."

She laughed and his face lit up, reflecting a new, inner light that hadn't been there before. "You've really earned it, Reb Mendle," she told him. "I bless you that you'll see *moshiach* in your lifetime."

"*This* lifetime, right?"

"Mende'le," she rebuked him coyly, "I'm not a demon, you don't have to peg me down with word definitions, I don't do double talk…"

"I'm sorry," he cried, fearful that his crassness might dispel the magic of this moment.

"Thank you for the ride," she said when she noticed the neon candy store sign and realized that she had reached her intended destination. "Go tend to your flock, get them ready, tell them it's really happening."

Rabbi Mendy Kasowitz drove away wondering why he believed Nechama with such a passion.

More disturbing was Nechama Gutkind's own puzzlement over the blessing she'd just given the fine, generous gentleman.

How did I know all that? she asked, and there wasn't a soul in the world who could tell her.

45.

There she was in Hoboken, New Jersey. It was a town of Asian immigrants, poor and middle-class blacks, Neuvo Yuppies dispossessed from terrorist-scared Manhattan, and old-time Irish and Italian families too poor to flee when the fleeing was good. This uneasy combination provided for the kind of public life that typically emerges near the nation's great concentrations of toxic waste. On the other hand, since it wasn't deemed by most terrorists to be worth the effort of bombing, at least it was a quiet

---

*   The morning prayer

little stinker.

It was well after dark when Nechama came out of the rain into the National Flag Candy Store on Fourth and Jackson. A few middle-aged men, physically out of shape but otherwise pleasantly civil, stood in line before the lottery counter. As each man reached the young Yemeni person operating the lottery machine, they handed him their betting slips and money—some a few dollars, some several twenty-dollar bills—and received in return their printout tickets for the night's drawing.

Prior to 1964, lotteries had been banned in every state except New Hampshire. A mere few decades later, every state boasted legalized state-run lotteries. Across the country, administrative costs for lotteries rose faster than the cost of any other form of revenue collection.

In the more recent year for which figures were available, the American people wagered 134.5 billion dollars on lotteries. Of this sum, state governments received a fraction as their share: 24.9 billion dollars. Lotteries contributed only 1.7 percent of state government revenues, yet the popular view persisted that these lotteries were a major contributor to public education and other useful projects. Even out of the relatively small lottery revenues diverted to the states, more than half were actually used to take care of the shortfall in the states' budgets, in direct violation of the states' own gambling laws.

Rather than improve state economies, lotteries simply transferred wealth from the many to the few, from the poor to the middle and wealthy classes. As an economic force, lotteries played a regressive role, with ticket sales reducing all other retail purchases. Folks with limited or fixed incomes couldn't buy lottery tickets *and* all the other stuff they needed, so they settled for tickets. Lottery ticket sales were highest in neighborhoods with the lowest income levels and the highest proportion of minority residents. The poor played the lottery more than any other income group, and they spent a larger portion of their income doing so.

Tonight's jackpot would not be exceptionally large, so general interest in the drawing was moderate. Clearly, everyone in the store was a regular.

Nechama shook the rainwater out of her long, wavy, red hair, and struck a conversation with the last man in line.

"How much are you planning to spend?" she asked.

The man turned around to examine the young woman with suspicion. A former garment worker who used to supervise textile production in a nearby plant, he was laid off when his shop was transferred to some village in Central Asia. "Did my ex-wife send you?" he demanded. "Because if she did, you better tell the goddamn bitch I'm sending her my child-support checks every month, and I get to do whatever I goddamn please with the rest!"

Nechama laughed. "I was just making conversation," she assured him.

The man was charmed back to civility. "You a gambling woman?" he inquired.

"I never felt drawn to it, to tell you the truth," she said. "How much money do you need to win?"

He didn't know how to answer that question. "I guess the more the better," he finally said. Something about this young woman made him feel completely comfortable and terribly ill at ease at the same time.

"Well, how much money is at stake here?" Nechama asked.

"Wait, I'm not sure," he said and turned to the swarthy youth behind the counter. "Hey, Mohammed, how big is the jackpot tonight?"

"Six million," said the young man.

"Do you need six million dollars?" Nechama asked in the kind of polite demeanor that forced many people to tell her only the truth, sometimes even against their better judgment.

"I don't need that much," he confessed. "I owe on the credit cards about twenty-five thousand dollars. Just been through an expensive divorce, as you probably figured out from what I said about the child support. I have a son. I'd like to send him to a better school."

"Is there a specific money figure you could settle for that would make you happy?" She egged him on.

"Well, I don't know about happy," he said, "takes more than money to be happy, you know. But with two hundred thousand dollars, I could get by nicely."

"Two hundred thousand? Final figure?" she asked, smiling.

"Wait, wait," he became serious all of a sudden, as if she were some leprechaun sitting on a pot of gold and ready to dole out the wealth. "Make that half a mil. Half a million dollars will be a very satisfactory amount, thank you very much."

"How about the rest of you?" she asked the other men in line, who'd been eavesdropping on her exchange. Everyone agreed that half a million dollars would be a fine sum of money to win, no question about it.

Nechama asked to look at their lottery tickets. She examined them carefully, held one or two up against the light, then returned all the tickets to their rightful owners, thanked them for their time and patience and walked back out into the rain.

Nechama had to find a safe dry spot where she could change the bandages on her left leg. She found lately that she was most comfortable if she took the opportunity to check her dressings every few hours. Her beautiful leg was quite a mess and she found it easiest to tend to it by pretending that it belonged to someone else. So far, she had been very lucky in escaping infection.

She left an almost tangible silence behind her in the candy store. Each of the men in line played over the previous few minutes in his head and mulled over the bizarre sensations evoked by the exchange. But more than anything else, all the men were astonished at how the five hundred thousand dollar figure resonated as the exact amount of money each required to escape his personal rut. So much so, that by the 11 o'clock lottery drawing they were more focused on their recollections of the captivating young woman than they were on the fact that no one had won anything. Even those among them who were out fifty or more dollars weren't nearly as depressed as usual.

The next drawing day, the regulars at the National Flag store were not surprised in the least to discover The Girl waiting for them by the glass doors, her hood pulled over her red hair, only partially protecting her from the constant drizzle.

"I've got an idea!" she announced, as soon as all of them had arrived. They remembered her from the previous night. "Let's assume that only one or two tickets purchased anywhere for tonight's drawing are going to win the jackpot," she began.

"Even fewer than that," someone mumbled. The most recent drawing yielded no big winners, and so the current evening's pot was worth twelve million dollars.

"Let me ask, then, if all you need to win is *one* lucky ticket, why do you guys spend so much money?"

They laughed and told her she didn't understand; they couldn't quite come up to the counter and ask to purchase the night's winning ticket, could they? It was a matter of chance.

"It makes sense that way," one of the men said. Everyone nodded and mumbled their agreement.

"I know that it seems a matter of chance," The Girl reasoned, "but if you trust the odds you may as well give up before you start. Let's assume for the moment that something else is at work instead of chance. Let's say that if you *are* meant to purchase the winning ticket—you will. It doesn't matter how many you buy. Only one will win, and if you are the one meant to receive it, you will.

"So here's my idea," continued The Girl. "Tonight, buy only one ticket for all of you. That'll cost two dollars. You will pool the rest of the money that you would have spent on bum tickets, and invest in shares of *future* winnings. You want a greater portion of the prize money? Invest more. Keep track of how much each participant puts in. Those who invest more will have a greater share in the winnings. Whether you were planning to spend a lot on the lottery, or a little, you get to put that money in. And... you pool all your luck on the single ticket you buy."

"But what if the ticket loses?" Asked one of the men. Those gathered around seemed comfortable to have him do the talking.

"Well, what did you do the *last* time you lost?" The Girl asked.

"You mean every single time in the past ten years?" Ed asked and everybody laughed.

"Exactly," said The Girl. "Except this time, whenever you don't win, your bank account gets bigger. Now, all you folks will need to do is to sign a binding contract with one another, pick a trustworthy treasurer to keep clear records, and start earning interest on your 'losses.'"

Yes, it made perfect sense. Add to this the fact that the fledgling investment group won that night's consolation prize—forty-five thousand dollars—the one presented to players who guess five out of the six numbers, and you'll understand how The Girl's lottery, or *anti-lottery*, scheme took off to become, in a mere few weeks, the way folks began buying lottery tickets all across the Garden State.

In one month, the New Jersey Lottery sank sharply into default. Its daily intake had shrunk to under two million dollars, while its prize output remained largely the same as before. The collapse of the New Jersey lottery happened so quickly because, with an upkeep so steep, what with state-of-the-art monitoring systems, expensive promotions and huge staff, even a short-term decline in revenues was enough to bring it down.

Soon the novel gamble spread to neighboring states. Betting operations, formerly cash cows for politicians, were fast becoming liabilities.

46.

The lottery cooperative caught the eye of the night editor at the *New York Post*, who thought it was a pretty nifty story. He ran it in the Metro pages:

MYSTERIOUS WOMAN GRANTS LOTTERY WISHES
Hoboken Winners Claim They Were Organized In Original Lottery Group By Homeless Girl.

Now file this in your "It's a small world" directory: the lottery story, accompanied by a photograph that was reasonable likeness of Nechama Gutkind, was published under a Danielle Herzog byline.

Danielle Herzog sensed the story when she was over in Trenton, NJ, consuming a free cocktail and observing a slick promotion of the new feature of the New Jersey Lottery, the Dance of Millions. The idea was that everyone and their friends, wives, and kids, could come, free of charge, to these great gazebos that were installed in malls across the state. People were treated to dinner and drinks and given the opportunity to dance on a touch-sensitive floor. The bettor's dancing feet would leave a logarithmic trace on the floor, which would be computed to provide him with a unique lottery ticket, or tickets—as many as were wanted. If that didn't guarantee a lucky draw, heaven knew what would.

Ms. Herzog got the gist of the scheme halfway through the presentation. She collected the printed material and photographs from the press table and left the auditorium. "Let's go home," she said, seemingly to no one in particular. A very lonely and confused woman, she had long since lost the capacity to discern whether she was alone or in the company of others.

"I'm dying for a nice onion soup with lots of melted cheese on top," said Rita, Danielle's imaginary companion. Ms. Herzog nodded in agreement. But rushing out of the auditorium, she overheard a conversation in an elevator that grabbed her reporter's ears.

Two men spoke in hushed tones about some trouble facing the lottery operation in Hoboken, on account of this strange young woman. If the trend continued, they feared bad things would befall their business.

"We just *have* to go to Hoboken," said Maurice, her imaginary researcher and fact-checker. "If we're lucky, we'll get a good description of the woman and she might still be in the area."

"I'll settle for any detail at all," said her imaginary friend Alex who grabbed her bag in readiness. But Danielle knew better than to count on him. Somehow, whenever Alex carried their stuff, it turned up in Lost & Found departments all around the metro area.

The ride on the high speed train from Trenton up to Hoboken took a full forty minutes on account of sharpshooting. The train sustained some damage, and the Feds on board made everyone wait while they chased after the shooters. But when Ms. Herzog finally arrived, there was no mistaking the National Flag Candy Store on Jackson Street. A great crowd surrounded the small storefront. A large banner proclaimed that, yes, this is where you could join the lottery cooperative, and advertised that twelve members had already won a significant amount of money.

Many of the customers were perfectly willing to speak to the reporter, but none of them, as it turned out, had ever seen The Girl. The only one who had was the Yemenite Mohammed. Danielle, typically unrestrained in her pursuit, clarified for him how easy it would be to call an Immigration and Naturalization official, who would surely ship him back to the Arab peninsula in no time. Reluctantly, he handed over a photograph recently taken with an old, disposable Kodak. It was a picture of The Girl on her second visit to his store.

Nechama was capable of distorting the image she projected to digital cameras. She could mess with the gaps between pixels and generalize pictures beyond specific recognition. However, she was powerless before celluloid film, which involved a simple chemical reaction to her reflected light.

And so, for the first time since her birth, Nechama Gutkind's somewhat blurred image had been captured. It would soon be endlessly duplicated.

Although Danielle Herzog filed the first recorded story about The Girl, she did not recognize her from their two previous encounters. This is because each encounter had been a unique prophetic episode, with its own Divine source and machination.

For Danielle there existed no personal, intellectual subtext to connect her disparate prophetic experiences. Except for those times when she was committed to a facility for treatment—following some uncontrollable incident or other—and some doctor in a strange town administered psychotropic substances, Danielle Herzog had no means of differentiating her experiences. They were all mind images to her.

There was a good reason why Danielle Herzog had stuck with the *New York Post* all these years, even though competing news organizations would have killed to have a reporter of her gifts on their payroll. After she'd worked one week for another news outfit, she was shipped off to Bellevue Acute Care Hospital for three weeks—but after *years* at the *Post*, no one there thought she was particularly strange.

47.

One of the copies of The Girl's picture ended up in the possession of Ben Markowitz, the youngest participant in the Special Accelerated Study Program at New York University. Normally, one had to have earned a Master's degree in some field to qualify. But in Ben's case, with his unusually high IQ and his equally unusually aggressive mother, nominally renowned author Sheila Markowitz, the prerequisites were waived.

Students at the Special Accelerated Study Program were randomly schooled in an endless string of disciplines and areas of interest. A student like young Ben would attain an expertise in Egyptian burial ceremonies on Monday, master 19th century Hungarian literature on Tuesday, and assist in open heart surgery on Wednesday.

The expectation was that indulging in absolutely everything would produce scholars with a new and exciting perspective on the culture. The jury was out on the success of this very prestigious program. As to Ben Markowitz's progress: He was clearly turning into a homicidal maniac, certain to endanger his own life and the lives of others in the near future.

His mentor in the program entered a specific warning to that effect in Ben's file. It was his responsibility to protect the program from future litigation, should the young man actually perpetrate a mass murder on school property.

Ben's life began to unravel shortly after a visit from two government security types in dark shades and ear-pieces, who knocked on the youth's dorm door on the Bowery. They pushed him aside and examined the room, pulling open desk drawers and rifling through bookshelves.

"Lots of knives and guns," one of them remarked.

"What do *you* want?" Ben asked, speechless with anger since their whirlwind arrival.

"Nuffing," said one of them, a burly, brown giant with a blank expression.

"We're here to secure the parameter," said the other gorilla, flashing an NSA badge. "All clear," he announced towards the living room, and a young woman in a khaki canvas skirt and a white cotton blouse came in, carrying an attaché case.

"Hi, Ben," she said, "my name is Kate Collinwood, I'm—"

"Assistant to the President's National Security Adviser, General Nathaniel Kane," Ben Markowitz completed her title for her. "You probably already know that I'm astonishingly smart," he added.

"Very impressive," she said. Ben looked victoriously at the two gorillas.

"You brought your guards, there are probably two more in the limo, that means you're concerned about what I might do to you," Ben analyzed. "It also means you've had me followed, you know about the gun club, you know about my academic program, you know about the learning enhancement drugs."

He closed his eyes for a fraction of a second, then opened them and proceeded patiently: "You need something from me... There's a war going on, but you have better people for that... So it's the war at home, but you're NSA, not FBI, so you're looking for a gifted operative for... let me see... It's not an assassination, I wouldn't be much good there, so it's surveillance. You're looking for someone even your people cannot trace... Who would that be? Some crazy terrorist Arab? How would I find him, what do I know about Arabs that you don't? Some Jew illegally purchasing technology for Israel? Again, I'm the wrong guy... But it has to be somebody totally elusive... What do you have in there?" He pointed at Collinwood's attaché case. "It's a picture, has to be, of this person. Go ahead, dig it out, lady, you know you want to."

Silently, Kate opened her case and took out the only known picture of Nechama Gutkind.

Ben Markowitz took the picture with feigned disinterest. His academic experience had always been lousy with security types, looking to recruit his IQ. He didn't hate them, he feared them, knowing what they were able to do to him if so ordered. So he picked up the picture nonchalantly and his life changed—completely.

A new, irrefutable internal voice told him that the young woman in the photograph was the one with whom he had been destined to live out his life. She was so young and so very fresh and luscious and bright; how could there be any doubt?

"Who is she?" His mouth was dry.

126

"We don't know," Collinwood admitted. "We're asking smart people like you to help us find her."

"What has she done?"

"Nothing. We're not looking to arrest her," Kate assured him. Smart or not, the Ben Markowitzes of the world were never adept at hiding gushing hormones, and Kate was not about to lose him over this minor point.

"What are you going to do to her?" he asked.

Kate had to think fast. Deception came easily to her, but whatever she said had to withstand the scrutiny of two hundred IQ points.

"We believe she'd do very well in a biosphere, based on some anecdotal testimony we've received. We want to offer her a spot."

She certainly caught Ben's attention with that one. "I didn't know anyone was launching a new biosphere," he said. "Who's doing it?"

"Can't tell you," she said.

"Civilian or military?"

"What do *you* think?"

He accepted that. "Can I apply?" he asked.

"I don't make those decisions, Ben..."

"You won't find a better candidate," he pleaded.

Outside Columbine, her internal voice quipped. Her outside voice told Ben: "Bring me some information and I'll see what I can do."

Later, Ben Markowitz scanned and enlarged the captivating image to poster size, then hung it on his wall and spent as many hours staring at the young woman as he did cleaning his gun collection.

Kate Collinwood met with eleven young men that day in the New York City area, each in the two hundred IQ range. She observed with interest as most of them fell head over heel for the mystery woman. Only one reacted differently, flying into a rage storm because she looked so much like his sister. Kate didn't mind that approach either. She needed information fast.

48.

With the first part of our story nearing its end, we leave our modern, proto-messianic Nechama Gutkind ready to pounce on History and make it nibble the kibbles out of the palm of her hand. We need to examine the conclusion of Shem's original plot, both out of reverence to the many men and women (mostly women) who labored to bring it to fruition, and as a lesson to all the messianic plotters out there, who are still fantasying about final, decisive arm wrestling matches with God.

So let us return to THE CABALIST'S HANDBOOK OF PRACTICAL MESSIANIC REDEMPTION.

Lot's daughters and Judah's daughter-in-law seeded the birth of the perfect messianic child, the magnificent King David, great grandchild of both Judah and Lot.

David was a red-haired, blue-eyed devil, who romanced all the women and danced with God Himself into the morning hours. He messed up more times than any of his subjects, and would then turn around and fix his mess. He taught the world about fixing messes.

King David inspired in others a passionate urge to fix their own messes. Seeing how he would scrub his soul as if he was laundering his shirt in the river, one was dazzled by the brilliant whiteness of his cleansed soul. His passion was perfect, his friendship was sweeter than the love of a woman, and even his lust was selfless.

So God accepted David as the redeemer of the world, accepted his bloodline after him as the future redeemers of the world. Then He played His own trick hand, which He had hidden all those eons with no one noticing, not even Himself.

He gave David an heir who understood the world. Really understood everything—how the cosmos rotated, and what was electricity, and what happens when a little kitten falls in love, and what happens when an unstoppable force runs into an immovable object, and how much pi truly is, and why do angels dislike hiding under beds but monsters love it, and how to make a woman climax with a poem, and why are feathers built just that way, and how many times a man can go into the same river.

And the game was lost. Because the wise son of the most compassionate man who ever lived was bound to destroy—in the most lavish and grandiose way—everything his father had succeeded in building.

God doesn't play fair. We're tired of telling you this.

49.

According to THE CABALIST'S HANDBOOK OF PRACTICAL MESSIANIC REDEMPTION,

Salvation is an improbable idea by definition. Only when History itself denies the very possibility of Deliverance, may the process begin.

In the early years of his reign, the twelve-year-old King Solomon was imitat-

ing the manner of other kings, getting drunk, screwing by the haremload, and sleeping late. Heck, if smoking, snorting and shooting were available around 800 BCE, he'd have done all that, too, for sure.

His mother, Bat Sheba, who had been only nine years old when she gave birth to Solomon, tied him up and whipped him, to get him back on the straight and narrow.

"Everyone knows that your father, David, was a righteous man," she told him, "so when you misbehave, they'll blame me."

(Take that, Oedipus, and that…)

Disaster finally struck on the night Solomon celebrated the inauguration of God's new Temple. Solomon chose that same night to wed the Pharaoh's daughter. Imagine, just when his nation celebrates the housewarming of the dwelling place of the Creator Himself, the king is shagging a new shiksa!

To add insult to injury, we're told that the sounds of joy that poured out of the wedding celebration drowned out the sounds of joy at the Temple ceremony.

Are you paying attention? We're talking about our most perfect messiah, whose very name, Shlomo, was a derivative of Shalom—a word meaning both peace and perfection. At the same moment in which David's son took his best shot against history and for redemption, he also sowed the very seeds of our destruction.

The archangel Samael was summoned into a closed session with God Himself—not even his two top rivals, Michael and Gabriel were invited. And God, peeved beyond belief, handed His Dark Aspect a branch of a gourd bush and ordered him to go to this boot-shaped peninsula in Southern Europe and stick the branch wherever he, Samael, felt like, and fly away.

So Samael hid the branch under his red robe and flew to the delta of one of the major rivers on that oddly shaped landmass, and stuck the branch in the water. Immediately, sand began to collect around that branch, until a new field rose out of the water, ready to be inhabited by human beings. And the name of that place would be Roma, which means "up-high," as in ruling over the world, as in oppressing everyone and everything that isn't similarly up high, as in impaling and hanging and burning and raping and pillaging and sending into exile all of God's children.

On their wedding night, Solomon's new Egyptian bride worked up some trickery. She hung over his bed a canopy that looked like the night sky, with a perfectly realistic moon sailing across the dark-blue heavens. As a result, the inebriated Solomon was fooled into oversleeping and thus caused the first sacrifice in the new House of God to be delayed until everybody in all the worlds was exasperated, God included.

NEW KING OF ETERNAL PEACE PISSING OFF RULER OF UNIVERSE.

At that point, with the world holding its breath, the frightened people turned to the Queen Mother for help and she bound and whipped the boy king to get him back in spiritual shape.

You miserable sonova bitch, Bat Sheba screamed while lashing her boy. After all the care I put into you, this is how you repay me? Don't you know, I sacrificed my first husband just to give birth to you! I had sex with your father when you were in your third trimester, to guarantee you a smooth delivery! I had your half brother Adonijah offed just to clear the path to the throne for you—and this is how you repay me?"

What could young King Solomon say to his mom between lashes? That redeeming the world couldn't possibly happen just by building temples and bringing animal sacrifices? That the very notion of achieving perfection was enough to drive any sane man to drinking and whoring? That the only real thing he could hold on to with a reasonable expectation of comfort was his manhood?

That he was scared out of his mind of redeeming anyone or anything?

Bat Sheba intervened, and her exuberant lashing saved us from Solomon's rebellion in the nick of time. But nothing could stop the process of corruption.

King Solomon's condemnation by our rabbis was thorough, because they, too, apparently, reached the same conclusion: It was all Solomon's fault. In a heated discussion over the fate of several kings who would not merit an afterlife, the sages insisted on adding Solomon to the list.

Imagine that, the perfect messiah sunk so far as to inherit eternal damnation!

His father, King David, came down to plead for his son, but to no avail. Finally God himself came to Solomon's defense, essentially telling the sages there was no substitute for Solomon's spiritual grandeur. Solomon, according to God in this debate, had pushed the holy envelope as far as it could possibly stretch; but all the same, Solomon was pure of heart and mind and his actions were condoned by heaven.

This the sages accepted, and agreed that they had misunderstood Solomon. They decided that God loved Solomon so much, He let him break all boundaries.

The rabbinical establishment, like Mother Bat Sheba, employed a stern hand, wishing to extinguish the rebelliousness, even at the expense of losing the rebellious son. But his true Father intervened, released Solomon, took away his mother's whip, kissed away his wounds and restored him to his throne.

We have all tasted the rods of History on our backs; we're black and blue and red from the beatings. When it is time for God to kiss our wounds, you will see that all the beatings, even all the killings, all the millions upon millions of slashed and burnt and gassed corpses—they were worth it. You'll see.

BOOK II

The Final Two Days

50.

The tip came from NYPD narcs: Some drug dealer traded the information for a lighter sentence. A suicide bombing would occur in the Crown Heights section of Brooklyn. The dealer didn't know the exact time, but he knew it would happen near the big synagogue on Eastern Parkway. He also knew the bomber would be disguised as a Hasid.

Two Thorough Response Units for Special Targets were dispatched to the area early Sunday morning. Checkpoints blocked nearby subway exits and access roads within a five-block radius. Local private security organizations, Hasidic and Haitian, had been informed and were also patrolling the sidewalks. Still, it was difficult to avert suicide bombings, even *with* advance notice. The fact is, a man who's not afraid to die is hard to stop, except with a bullet. On the other hand, no suicide bomber ever acts alone. Any one bomber is situated at the top of an elaborate support pyramid, like a fighter pilot, and any member of his team is stoppable. It takes regular police work: Knock on a door, grab the suspect, beat the stuffing out of him or her until they squeal, then go pick up the next suspect. Somebody in law enforcement was, no doubt, already busy with that part of the procedure; but for the THRUSTs, the immediate mission was to prevent detonation of the human bomb.

The most effective component of the current heightened DHS, Department of Homeland Security, action was the new Thorough Response Units for Special Targets, a belated post-9/11 invention, reflecting the political realities of a new era.

Federal and state lawmakers had learned the hard way that cooperation between the different HS agencies was meaningless, unless it took place in the field, at the investigation level.

Endowed with the capacity to gather intelligence, carry out complex anti-terrorism tasks, and execute emergency powers of prosecution, the

131

THRUSTs quickly became the standard model for security teams in the 21st Century.

They enjoyed investigative liberties rooted in the new legal doctrine of the Roaming Martial Law, developed in response to global terrorism, which declared that any terrorist-induced conflict zone was a legal bubble, inside which the Bill of Rights, Geneva Convention and any other commonly accepted restraint were temporarily suspended. Starting as early as 2002, at various interrogation centers in and out of the US, this flexible approach proved exceptionally useful in dealing with an enemy hell-bent on destroying the world's democracies. Needless to say, RML was one of the more popular security measures passed by both houses of Congress.

The standard size of a THRUST team was six members, including the chief, a linguist, a systems analyst, and a medic—all law school graduates who underwent an additional two-year training in police work and military combat. With state-of-the-art surveillance and combat equipment, the THRUSTs could be deposited in the middle of a terrorist desert camp or outside a terrorist cell's apartment building, and become fully operational in under one minute. In addition to fighting, they were also equipped to run banking operations, drug production, printing and publication and a myriad other unexpected and highly useful functions.

A THRUST was capable of remaining active for months on end without outside support.

The parkway in front of the synagogue was scarred by blackened craters and littered with burnt vehicles—souvenirs of previous attempts on the synagogue by determined Muslims. It was a war zone.

Jonah Simpson, tall, broad-shouldered and muscular, with bouncy, black curls and large, capable hands, drove one of the two black THRUST vans, doing four miles an hour around the block where the synagogue and world headquarters of the Cosmic Wisdom movement stood. Like the Cosmic Wisdomniks, he too was Jewish, but that's where the similarities ended. The Hasidim were devout; Simpson was strictly ham and Swiss.

Jonah respected the Hasidim well enough, but his team members were family: Lieutenant David Hammonton headed the crew; Jerry Osmond was their medic; Jay Hollander supervised communications, Penny Brown was their linguist; Ted Blum, their master marksman; Dawn Brockowitz, resident systems analyst, and Jonah Simpson took care of Investigation for the team.

Still, his three years on the job with THRUST had taught Jonah to appreciate the kind of organization inherent in thousands of years of tradition; professionally speaking, it made him proud of his Jewish tradition.

Surveying the area, Jonah noticed a young man in a black fedora and long black raincoat jaywalking across Eastern Parkway. Something about the guy rang false.

"Team alert," Simpson said urgently into the comm/link, "stop the guy in the hat and coat who just crossed the parkway—"

"Which *one?*" Penny Brown asked from the back of the van. Penny was a sweet looking blond in round spectacles who knew twenty different ways of killing a man with her bare hands. With even greater urgency, she countered, "They're *all* wearing black hats and coats, for Chrissake!"

"The one with the wedding band on his finger!" Jonah cried out, suddenly realizing why the man had triggered his mental alarm. Hasidic men didn't wear jewelry.

He leaned out his driver's side window, took aim and blew the suspect's head off with a whistling lob from his M203 grenade launcher. The headless target balanced on one leg in mid-stride for a stunned eternity, then collapsed with a rambling thud that echoed throughout the parkway. His black raincoat flew open, revealing a wide explosives belt. An instant later, two team members swarmed on the target and the explosives were secured.

"Good call, Simpson," Lieutenant David Hammonton yelled into the comm/link. "Look around for Number Two!"

This was standard operating procedure: Suicide bombers attacked in short, successive intervals, so that a second explosion targeted those rushing to save the victims of the first one, and so on.

"This is a CRP, clear the sidewalk!" The public address system on the other THRUST van blasted the announcement. The locals, well trained in Civilian Response Procedure, emptied the street at once, leaving only security ops and bad guys in the field.

Absent an immediately visible second target, Hammonton and the chief of the other THRUST team initiated a standard procedure alert, taking it for granted that the bomber's partner got cold feet and fled.

Hammonton got on the comm/link with the choppers. "There's a wet one roaming near Kingston and Eastern Parkway," he advised. "CRP was declared, target a Hasidic man or woman in a big overcoat." He went back to the side of the van, where Penny Brown and Dawn Brokowitz had broken out a thermos of hot black coffee.

"I just hope this don't mean open season on Hasidim," Penny joked.

"That's the purpose of the CRP," Hammonton was only too happy to recite his most favorite topic. "A disciplined civil society is the key to success in our war on terrorism."

It meant that the Hasidim of Crown Heights, as well as their Haitian neighbors, who were hated by fundamentalist Muslims almost as much as the Jews, would stay indoors for the next hour, until the emergency was lifted. It was a nuisance that America had learned to live with: Those who adjusted better lived longer.

An ambulance arrived at the curb, where Jerry was packing the pieces of the bomber into a body bag. Simpson's choice to hit the bomber with a grenade was by-the-book. Even an off-target grenade takes the suspect down; it causes pain, often stunning its victim, denying him the clarity of mind to trigger his load.

Just then, sniping began from the rooftops on the other side of Eastern Parkway. "God damn it! Get inside, everybody!" Hammonton yelled out and got into position behind the machine gun. "Hollander, can you get us an image?"

Jay Hollander brought up the live satellite image of the five boroughs and zoomed in until the roof across the street filled his screen. The rest of the team received the same image on their eyepieces.

"I see one, middle of the block, behind the Nike sign, and at least two others, all pros," said Ted Blum, Hammonton's sniper. "Hard to lock on them from down here, though."

"There are at least five sources up there, three active" said Hollander. "We can just take out the whole roof and be done with it…"

"Penny, infra the top floor apartments for signs of life," Hammonton requested.

Brown scanned the fifth floor with an infra-red detector, looking for heat signs. She spotted a stove in every apartment, pilot lights burning in each, but nothing more. "Looks vacant," she reported in a moment. This was to be expected. When the sniping began, top floor tenants knew to flee.

"Take the blessed thing out," Hammonton ordered.

Jonah Simpson and Jay Hollander came out of the van on the sheltered side. Jonah shouldered a bazooka, the end of which he leaned against the van's rooftop. Jay loaded it up and tapped his shoulder. Jonah aimed just under the huge portrait of a blue-striped white pair of sneakers. He squeezed the trigger and the sign, along with a few small, flailing human figures, was blown away into the gray morning sky.

"Give our boy a medal," said Jerry Osmond, back from doing his medic's duty.

"Give our boy a day off," Jonah rebutted. When he felt Jay's tap again, he squeezed the trigger again, lifting the remaining half of the roof off the building...

"Not freaking likely," said Hammonton. "But I'll give you the afternoon, if nothing else comes up. Nice work, Simpson. Meeting and exceeding expectations once again."

51.

A couple of years earlier, Jonah Simpson had uncharacteristically disappointed his superiors.

In the far reaches of mosque-dotted Atlantic Avenue, in West Brooklyn, way off the grid, when a man forgets to put out his lights before going to sleep, his neighbors do it for him. It saves kerosene and prevents fire, which might spread to everybody else's property.

So when Izmir the carpet seller came back from the neighborhood café late one night and saw the light in Mustafa's first floor bakery window, he thought nothing of pushing in the door to get to the lamp over the bread oven.

He found Mustafa sprawled on his back; but instead of being in a hashish stupor, he was dead. Above him stood a muscular, young Caucasian in black fatigues. When Izmir's eyes became accustomed to the lamp's dim yellow glow, he let out a scream.

Mustafa's chest cavity had been slashed open, and the white man stood over the flayed carcass holding Mustafa's heart in his fist.

When Izmir turned to flee, the THRUST soldier swiftly pocketed the heart and rushed to block the small Arab's escape. Izmir ran into a hand of iron which tightened around his throat. His vision blurred.

"Please don't kill me..." he hissed desperately through the tight hold on his trachea.

The man seemed to sympathize. "No screaming," he said. Izmir shook his head vigorously. The man with Mustafa's heart in his pocket smiled benevolently, turned Izmir around and whacked him on the back of his head. Izmir collapsed.

Jonah Simpson remained deep in thought for another couple of minutes, then removed a zip-lock baggie from his coat pocket and brought out the now cold and silent human heart from his other pocket. Sealing the heart, he spoke into a small microphone adhesive strip that looked like a band-aid attached to his Adam's apple.

"Simpson here. I've got it, where do you want me to bring it?"

His tiny earpiece spoke in a tinny, woman's voice: "The Iranians are where you left them two days ago, Jonah, in the Coney Island apartment. The Russians are looking for them, but they're laying low. Perhaps you should also cut off an ear or two for good measure..."

"They'll just have to trust me," Simpson said, without a smile.

The THRUST culture offers several versions of what happened next to Jonah Simpson, but one thing is clear: The heart Jonah removed from the chest of the Iranian operative never made it into the waiting hands of Rashid's enemies. Instead, Jonah was found a week later, wandering around the Brooklyn Navy Yards, dazed and starving, and entirely incapable of relaying to his superiors a single event from the previous week.

They kept him under observation for a month at a hospital in McGuire Air Force Base in New Jersey. He was then sent to a recuperation camp in Mexico for another month. Once released, he was able to resume his former duties.

You'd be amazed how many THRUST members end up with this type of overhaul. But Jonah was not a simple rank-and-file THRUST operative. His superiors had been grooming him for major black operations, and his failure to deliver the heart attracted much attention among the anti-terrorism brass.

His disappearance remained a mystery, even to Jonah himself.

52.

WWIII had been underway for nearly a year. Although hostilities centered in the Mideast, the average New Yorker still had a one in ten thousand chance of becoming involved in a bombing or sniping incident, according to the latest government statistics. These were bad odds compared with most other US cities, save for Los Angeles (one in nine thousand).

Conversely, Las Vegas was the safest spot on Earth. Visitors to Sin City were promised zero bombing and sniping incidents for the duration of their stay. This was possible due to the uncompromising security measures the city fathers (or godfathers) imposed on everyone desiring entry.

All personal belongings, down to the arriving passenger's last stitch of clothing, were to be left in Locker City, a forty-by-forty-block fenced facility adjoining Las Vegas' McCarran International Airport. After stripping and undergoing a full body scan, arriving passengers were given an assortment of disposable undergarments and linen suits in a variety of fashionable prints, comfortable sandals and a lovely boxed lunch, all at the city's expense.

Las Vegas' hyper-secure system became the butt of many jokes, but visitors to the entertainment Mecca were encouraged by the prospect of not being blown up or shot on their vacation. The city's extremist policy turned out to be cost-effective as well: The price tag on collateral damage incurred from New York's one hundred annual suicide bombings and sniping incidents, amounted to ten billion dollars. Las Vegas' no-nonsense hospitality went for under half a billion per annum.

Of course, places like Cairo (over one thousand bombing and sniping incidents annually), Jerusalem (eight hundred), Tokyo (seven hundred and fifty), Moscow (five hundred), and London (three hundred and fifty), were hardly in a position to quarantine their new arrivals the way Vegas did. Instead, those cities shifted to the Anti-Terrorism Economy. This worked pretty much like the 20th century's War-on-Drugs Economy, with the illegal narcotics trade bankrolling armies of undercover agents, policemen, prosecutors, defense attorneys, judges, corrections officers—and those hired to wash these people's laundry and cook their meals.

The only problem was that with all this excess government activity, the world was fast running out of people who knew how to *make* things. There were still many who could flip a burger and push drinks, but fewer and fewer out there knew how to repair the machines when they stopped making shoes. Nevertheless, in the face of a world rife with terrorism, humanity's diminishing competence remained just something one read about in amusing op-ed articles.

53.

Jonah Simpson opted to spend his free Sunday afternoon standing outside McSorley's Old Ale House with a mug in one hand and a tightly rolled cigarette in the other.

When the dimensional shift occurred, it was both completely unexpected and entirely acceptable. In New York City almost a year into WW3, anything could happen. On the other hand—a dimensional shift?

Jonah leaned back in his black THRUST fatigues against the red brick wall of McSorley's—which happened to be on the ground floor of his apartment building on Fifth Street. One moment he was nursing a lovely German import with a big, frothy head on it, and the next a huge sneeze erupted out of him, beer gushed up his nose, his cigarette flew out of his mouth and he was transported to a realm of haze and darkness which only loosely resembled the block of Fifth Street between Second and Third Avenues.

Perhaps this was how the block used to look when the planet's primordial soup had not yet settled; and mist rose from beneath the soil to water the ancient jungles.

Jonah looked around at the thick tropical vegetation, listened to the bird cries, and followed the clouds of mist rising from the shadowy ground. The place looked dangerous, and Jonah was relieved to discover his sidearm was still in its holster. Still, despite the clear sense of danger, Jonah felt a wave of nostalgia coming over him. How would one *expect* to feel in the place where his species originated?

Jonah Simpson's connection to the family of man was tricky. Orphaned by a subway bomb that took both his parents, he was raised by his mother's sister, Gertrud. Aunt Gerty was not an emotional woman. She took him in because that's what one did, and she gave him what she had to, nothing more. At seventeen, he signed up for the service, and she didn't stop him.

Raised by an aloof aunt and the US military, Jonah's ties to humanity were strictly professional. He felt a sense of belonging, while remaining open to competing offers. That's how he felt about the service, too. Loyalty to the team and the corps was a vital value, but not the *only* value.

Jonah stared at the glass mug in his hand and wondered if he was still required to bring it back to the bar.

His musings were interrupted by the sound of loud, angry screams produced by distinctly male throats. A large gang appeared. Tall and muscular men in black running suits waved handguns and screamed in a mad discharge of excess adrenaline. There had to be at least a hundred of them, and as they passed Jonah they caused a gust of salty, warm wind to hit him in the face. But despite this evidence of their tangible existence, Jonah wasn't completely convinced. The law enforcement operative inside him picked up several suspicious details: For one thing, although they ran at great speed, they passed him quite slowly, more like a frieze of a bunch of menacing ruffians than the real thing. And they looked more like computer-animated images than real warriors on the attack.

Still, protocol had to be followed. He discarded the beer mug and drew his .38 handgun. That's when he discovered that the laws of physics weren't as eager to comply in this place as they were elsewhere. Somehow he continued to hold the mug in both hands, as his *other* hand unholstered his gun. And his *other* other hand started scratching the back of his head in puzzlement.

Behind the screaming gang appeared a young red-haired woman, running for her life, then the screaming troops swept by him again in hot pursuit.

They were running in a circle.

The young woman appeared once more, great strands of fire flying all about her beautiful face, adorning her slim and elongated body, sparkling like sun rays above her generous breasts. This was the moment, during her second lap, that she stole Jonah's heart forever. She took his breath away, too.

He turned pale, then even paler. The event had only lasted a second, but it also stretched over a hundred years. And in some way, Jonah was still embracing and being accosted by that one precious moment when the young girl again passed close to his longing eyes.

"Who are you?" Jonah asked, although there was no way a woman being chased by so many menacing warriors would stop to chat.

The young woman's bright and sweet face appeared on a giant video billboard that hovered high among the treetops, with yellow text spanning the bottom of the image like ticker tape.

"I'm The Girl," she said in flashing yellow words at the bottom of the billboard. The chasing party stopped briefly, looked up at the billboard, then down at their prey, who was still running from them. They were baffled for a moment, but in the end they found a renewed sense of purpose and began screaming and chasing as before.

"You're beautiful," said Jonah.

"Thank you. It's a pleasure to meet you." the ticker tape flickered.

"What's going on?" he wanted to know. She smiled. It was the kind of motivational smile God gives newly hatched planets to set them circling.

"*Life's* going on," the running yellow text told him. "Welcome aboard."

"Welcome aboard?"

"One of my people will contact you shortly," she assured him via the scrolling yellow letters, her blue eyes trained down on him from the billboard.

"Is this like a fund raising thing?" he asked, more perplexed than a zebra at a Highland Gathering.

"Do you have money?" she asked.

"Not really."

"Then it must be something else."

At last they were all gone, the woman and her pursuers. The primordial scenery faded away to reveal once again the solid face of Fifth Street on a drizzly Sunday afternoon in October.

54.

"What was that?" Jonah Simpson asked no one in particular. Looking to his right and left, he quickly realized that the four or five other men loitering outside McSorley's with their frothy beer mugs had not heard the piercing screams which still hung in the moist October air. Even the most jaded New Yorker would be impressed by transportation to a parallel universe, no matter how brief the trip. In other words, those beer guzzling slobs on his side of the street had not seen what he had seen.

Eventually, a fellow witness did emerge from the crowd, but eager as Jonah was to confirm his own experience, he avoided this person, mostly because he smelled really bad. He also had to be at least a hundred years old—past the age when one cared very much if one's trousers were zipped, let alone worried about multi-dimensional transports.

The man wore a black, wide-brimmed hat so badly frayed that strands from the lining hung over his ears. His calf-long, black overcoat was nearly as badly shredded as were his black pants and brown-spotted white shirt.

The man's white, tobacco-stained mustache and beard grew wild. His white sidecurls were wound round his ears, and they were stained yellow. The index finger and thumb of his right hand were dyed a permanent purplish-brown. When he walked over to speak to Jonah, his gravelly voice also reflected his commitment to nicotine.

There was a visual trick involved in the man's appearance. Jonah could not put his finger on it, but it bothered him until he simply got used to it: Standing only half a city block away, the ancient man looked not only disheveled, but particularly short. But when the man was standing right before him, it was the six-foot-three Jonah who had to look up to meet the other's eyes.

Lionel Abulafia knew that the very best way to attain invisibility was to skip a few showers.

When he opened his nearly toothless mouth to speak, a gust of turnip and garlic wind escaped from his very insides, forcing Jonah to turn away. It was as if the nicotine in his lungs had sponged the contents of his gastrointestinal system to create a simulation of the smell in Satan's kitchen.

"You seen her," the old man said flatly. "I could tell you did, then you figured no one else seen anything, so you thought maybe you went crazy. But you seen her."

"More or less," Jonah admitted, turning his face away from the ill wind and pulling back to avoid the man's intensely minimal need for personal space.

"How long you been a soldier?" the man asked.

"I'm not a soldier, I'm in a THRUST."

"Same thing. What do you do there?"

"I do everything anyone else on the team does, plus I'm an investigator." Jonah wasn't sure why he was so forthcoming with information, although these details weren't exactly classified. There were other, darker aspects of his service, of course. He had a great future as a government employee because, unlike many soldiers, he never flinched before a kill. Men like him, after receiving the proper training, could name their own price.

Jonah concluded that his atypical openness with this old man had to do with the confirmation the latter was willing to provide that he, Jonah, hadn't gone mad, and that the unfathomable recent events he had experienced, incomprehensible as they may have appeared, had really taken place.

But the man's face remained blank. He either had no idea what "investigator" meant, or this was his way of getting additional information from Jonah. In a strange way, the old man was behaving as if he and Jonah were old friends, and that it was only a matter of time before the younger man realized it.

"I dig up stories on people, stories we file away for future use. It's like a gossip column, but without a newspaper."

The man's face brightened. "You pick up dirt on people, that explains a lot. What's your name?"

"Jonah Simpson."

"Nice to meet you. I'm Lionel Abulafia, historian and teacher. You seen

The Girl."

"Yeah, I saw the girl... Wait a minute, was this *The* Girl?"

"You're catching on," said Lionel Abulafia to Jonah Simpson. "What else you seen, besides The Girl?"

"There was a bunch of guys—I'm guessing Arabs," Jonah answered. "Anyway, she was running from them."

"Beautiful creature, isn't she?"

"Why were they chasing her?" Jonah demanded.

"You'll find out soon enough," Lionel Abulafia said. "Tell me what else you seen."

"Not much, she ran right around the corner over there, then they all disappeared. Twice."

"That's it?"

"That, and the fact that everything around here became so weird."

"Like a jungle?"

"Yeah, like a jungle. But it was all some sort of trick, otherwise why wouldn't anyone *else* see it?"

The old man sneered. "This your first vision?" he inquired.

"I think so—"

"You're probably wrong. The previous times just wasn't so dramatic is all, so you din' notice. My friend, you entered the *pardes**, which is another way of saying you seen the world as it really is."

"I have no idea what you just said."

Abulafia sighed and patiently tried again, "There's the fabric of *perceived* reality, right?"

Jonah nodded, not entirely sure he was following.

"Then there's the stuff we don't see—it's too small—little crawlers, mites, ticks, lice. Then there's microbes and viruses. But besides the part of the world that gets littler and littler until you don't see it, there's the part that gets less and less tangible, more ethereal, until you can't see *it*, either."

"Like what?" Jonah refused to accept what sounded like sheer mumbo jumbo.

---

* The higher plane, as in *paradiso*, a place of great happiness and bliss. Jewish sources explain this higher state of consciousness as being comprised of the four elements of study: *Pshat* (literal meaning), *Remez* (clue, hint, implication), *Drash* (homilies, the stories behind the story), and *Sod* (secret, the real reasons for everything). This book is an attempt to play all four elements against the middle.

"Like the demon lying on the sidewalk across the street. See?" Abulafia pointed at a rumpled heap leaning against the wall, a heap that appeared to be just another homeless person.

"That's a bum, not a demon," Jonah contended.

"Oh, really?" and Lionel Abulafia quickly took from an inside coat pocket what appeared like a perfume decanter and squeezed its bulb twice under Jonah's nose. A small cloud of sickeningly sweet gas was sprayed into the younger man's nostrils and he was struck by a wave of dizziness that threatened to send him retching.

When the discomfort subsided, Jonah saw the demon. It was a coal-black creature in red swimming trunks, with small bat wings and snazzy, gold-rimmed aviator sunglasses. Asleep, it was hiding from nosy onlookers under the bum getup.

"Wow," was all Jonah was able to express in response.

"There are many ways to enter the *pardes*. Personally, I've catalogued two hundred and eighty. My guess is that for you it was the beer. Drank it too fast, sucked it up your nose—and of course, there's your obvious exhaustion, also a good way to ascend—whatever it was, it got you there."

Then the man in the wild beard dropped the niceties. "We're getting to the real point of our conversation, so pay attention," he said, bearing in on Jonah Simpson, hellish halitosis and all. "I need you to volunteer to save the world."

"I beg your pardon?" Jonah pulled back in renewed alarm.

"It's an emergency and you—I forgot your name . . ."

"Simpson."

"You, Simpson, are the most qualified person available at this moment."

"Listen, old man, we'll make a deal, okay?" Jonah attempted the friendly approach. "I'm going to keep my end of it by pretending you didn't just harass me. You'll do your part by going away. It *could* mean you won't spend the night in jail..."

"You don't have no choice," said the crazy old man.

"I'll give you five bucks!" Jonah promised and reached for his back pocket. But the old man shook his head violently.

"I'll take the money, but I'll still keep bugging you," he assured the younger man.

Jonah's bemused agitation slowly turned into anger bordering on despair. "Why *me?*" he pleaded. "There are so many other nice men out on the street you could irritate—"

"You *seen* her."

"This is nuts," Jonah snapped back into his THRUST persona and barked at the man, "I order you to go away, or I'm cuffing you and throwing your old ass in the can!"

"Does this mean you won't volunteer?"

"Very much so."

"Too bad."

"Yeah, too bad."

"No, it's *really* too bad," said the strange old man. "What happens next is they blow up your house."

55.

"I don't think that's funny," Jonah said to the crazy old man, but Lionel Abulafia ignored him. His intense gaze was now riveted to the counter inside McSorley's.

Jonah followed with his own eyes, requiring a moment to adjust to the dark interior.

He noted a yellow beam of light which appeared suddenly in a doorway behind the counter, then a matching beam of light which suddenly shined in the ceiling above the bartender's head.

Why was the bartender drenched in so much yellow light?

And why were the two light sources locking and moving in tandem across the crowded, dark space—

"Holy crap, it's a scanner bomb*!" Simpson yelled and tapped his shoulder comm/link. "Bomb at McSorley's bar, number five Street between number two and number three Avenues, lode under main counter, scanning bomb device already operational, going in to investigate—"

"No you're not, you fool!"

Jonah's attention was forced back to the old man, who grabbed him by the sleeve.

---

* The scanner bomb is a remarkable example of how destructive technology absorbs everything in its path. The bomb utilizes the operating principle of a bomb scanner to activate its explosive charge. It was invented by a Hamas engineer named Yakub ibn Yusuf Al Mansur, who once stood in an airport line watching his bag going through and suddenly thought, "Hey, I can make this thing blow up!"

"You go in there, you die," the old man warned, still pulling on Jonah's sleeve. "Hold my hand tight," he ordered. "Don't let go of my hand no matter what, or you'll fall and die, and then this world is lost forever, God forbid..."

With that uncompromising, albeit only semi-coherent statement, Jonah's wrist was clamped in a vice of bony fingers.

"What are you doing?" Jonah struggled to release his arm, but, luckily, the bomb was detonated inside the bar before the old man lost his purchase on the younger man's wrist.

Deafened by the explosion, Jonah looked up and saw an entire slab of rooftop flying above his head, then coming down at an incredible speed, filling up the sky. Then he realized that while the chunk of rooftop was coming down, he and Abulafia were going up, tossed by the violent gust of air the explosion was forcing in all directions.

The slabs of metal and stone flying every which way around him were pieces of what used to be his apartment building, but Jonah was still in no condition to understand that he had just lost his home.

In those early moments of the disaster, Jonah's mind still maintained two radically contradictory notions: One, that his building was in ruins, and, two, that he still lived there.

When the idea that he no longer possessed a home sank in, Jonah Simpson would be truly available to become a hero, capable of saving a world to which he was even less connected than before.

The rent on an average one-bedroom apartment in New York City ranged between five to ten thousand dollars a month, depending on the neighborhood. The exception to this rule was a lucky class of rent-controlled apartments, whose monthly fee, for a variety of idiosyncratic reasons, remained frozen near their World War II levels. On the island of Manhattan the tenants of these apartments held the status of demigods, and both men and women actively sought to lavish sexual and other favors upon them. That's because the only way to obtain the lease on a rent-controlled apartment was to inherit it from a parent or a spouse.

Jonah earned the coveted lease through years of indentured servitude to his aunt Gertrude, followed by a nasty two-year legal battle with her landlord. Once past these trials, Jonah was free to relish his new status as one of humanity's favorite sons, a rent-controlled-apartment-dweller, looking forward to long years of paying a measly one hundred and fifty-seven dollars and thirty-two cents in monthly rent in Manhattan. In *Manhattan!*

Abulafia pulled Jonah by the arm again, maneuvering him out of the way of the falling masonry. Still flying upward, the old man drew with his free hand an imaginary circle around himself and Jonah, then closed his eyes and recited in a hoarse whisper:

"And he rode upon a cherub, and did fly: yea, he did fly upon the wings of the wind*... Wind of the wings upon fly did he; yea, cherub upon rode he and"**..."

Jonah stared at him in astonishment, having never before experienced mid-air flight with an old man who whispered anagrammatic incantations. He could see that the chanting was working, since the two of them were defying gravity, hovering above the chaos.

This should have excited and perhaps frightened him, but then Jonah realized—for the first time—that they were flying above the ruins of his rent-controlled apartment. The thought line containing the explosion at the bar below met head-on with Jonah's continued notion of having a place of his own in the city, and at last the latter gave in to the former. Unable to hold on to the fading thought-line, Jonah moaned in great anguish.

"My apartment," he cried, "I've lost my apartment!"

Smoke, screams and bursts of electric sparks erupted as the entire six-story building collapsed, filling up the street instantly with a mountain of debris and bellowing clouds of smoke and dust. Jonah and his ancient benefactor were soon drenched by a kind of dry white mist, made up of tiny, lighter-than-air droplets of disintegrated bricks. But the magically drawn circle that kept them afloat apparently functioned as a protective sphere as well, stopping the dust and smoke at arm's length.

Down below, as often happened following a major bombing incident, anonymous snipers targeted the injured lying in the street, and the Emergency Medical Service and Fire Department workers who rushed to rescue them. Bullets flew from rooftops all around the block, occasionally stopping and flattening a figure down below in mid-run.

Before long, Jonah realized that his own ordeal was far from over, as Abulafia's voice grew weaker and the raging clouds of soot and powder penetrated now and again through their magic bubble.

---

*   Psalms 18:10
**   Smlasp 10:18

The old man's face registered alarm. He raised his voice for a moment, lifting himself and his charge up a few feet; but minutes later he began to cough, as his already brittle smoker's lungs fought off the fine dust of the explosion. Each coughing spasm caused the old man to drop a few feet and he and Simpson became engulfed in thicker dust and smoke.

"Can't you bring us down gently?" Jonah yelled in panic.

Lionel Abulafia didn't stop chanting, but shook his head "no" and gazed downward, both motions costing them a few yards. Just then, a new blast of air, born by a secondary explosion, kicked them way up again. Looking down, Jonah observed that this blast had just ignited the Con Edison gas lines running below the pavement. Going down now, no matter how gently, would mean getting barbecued.

Jonah also figured Abulafia would have taken them sideways if he could, and so concluded that the old man didn't do sideways. For the record, the old man could go any which way when flying alone, but carrying another man by the wrist severely limited his range.

"We're going to die!" Jonah shouted. "Somebody out there, help us!"

It wasn't clear, even to Jonah himself, whether his cry for help was of a religious nature, and if so, of what religion, or what particular kind of help he was expecting. Still, it's important to note that in his time of utter panic, Jonah was able to seek out some power outside himself.

Help arrived swiftly, following the young man's cry. A red and white luxury chopper stopped at their eye level and a side door slid open.

"Lionel, what's shaking?" a cheerful voice sounded from inside, as an elderly gentleman in a shiny black silk coat and a round, wide and tall, light-brown fur hat leaned out to seize both airborne refugees.

Abulafia helped Jonah in first, since the latter would have scarcely been able to keep himself aloft on his own. He followed, and collapsed in the back seat of the flying limo.

"Shimmele Amsterdam, you old scoundrel, what'cha been up to?" the old man gasped. "Meet my friend, Jonah Simpson. He digs up dirt on people for the government, very hush-hush, but, believe it or not, he visited the *pardes* today…"

"Ho, ho, *ho!*" The gentleman in the fur hat seemed impressed.

"I kid you not," Abulafia assured him.

"What's even more amazing, if you ask *me*," their host and rescuer intimated, "is that it looks like he made it out alive."

But Jonah wasn't paying attention to the admiration he was stirring. His pain was too great. "I owned a rent-controlled apartment in the building down there," he lamented. "I was paying 157 dollars a month!"

"Oh, my God, that's terrible," the man in the fur hat rolled his eyes heavenward. "Will the suffering never end?"

"You see?" Abulafia turned to Jonah. "The world is going berserk and only you can help."

"You're a very sick man," Jonah said to the person who had just lifted him to safety from a raging inferno. He looked at his host, who had also just saved him from certain death. Once again, he felt anger and resentment.

"You're probably as sick as he is," Jonah muttered.

"It's possible," agreed Shimmele Amsterdam. "But he's right. If you can travel in and out of the *pardes* unharmed, the world needs you."

"The world owes me a rent-controlled one-bedroom," Jonah replied.

56.

They flew above the Manhattan cityscape, while their host allowed them some time to recover from their trauma.

"Crazy world, eh?" He shrugged his shoulders, opening both his palms in resignation.

"How did you levitate above the fire, anyway?" Jonah asked the man who had saved his life. Like most 21st century Americans, Jonah had run into many mystics who claimed to be able to fly, as well as heal the sick and converse with the dead. But this was the first time Jonah had seen such a trick carried out in a way that didn't involve complex camera angles and a black screen.

Abulafia ignored Simpson's question, but their host in the fur hat was happy to oblige. "Lionel here is scion to a long line of cabalists," he told Jonah. "If he only applied himself, he could be a very rich man today."

Then Amsterdam sighed. "What can you do, it's the way of the world. Idiots like myself make a bundle, while the true geniuses go hungry. Cigarette, Lionel?"

The old man accepted eagerly. At twenty-five dollars a pack, an offered cigarette was nothing to scoff at. "I see the master cabalist business is going pretty good," he commented without malice.

"Can't complain," said Shimmele Amsterdam.

Their host was a self-proclaimed cabalist master. Three years after the passing of the great cabalist of Brooklyn, the last of the Brooklyn line of grand masters, Shimmele, who until then had been a bookkeeper for a Manhattan electronics marketing company, attracted some publicity when he made his debut as the next master.

In media interviews, Amsterdam argued that his flock, a handful of religious Jews residing in various neighborhoods of Brooklyn, were yearning for a righteous man to provide them with spiritual nourishment, a yearning he, Amsterdam, was only too happy to fulfill.

A member of the Cosmic Wisdom movement from birth, Shimmele Amsterdam donned the round fur hat (although the late master himself favored a wide-brimmed fedora), put on a black silk robe and became every bit the new cabalist master.

Having more than one mystical master was not a new thing for the Brooklyn-based movement, which traced its origins to 18th century Belarus. At one point there were as many as thirty-five concurrent Wisdomnik masters, each leading his own faction in different towns across Eastern Europe. Still, Shimmele Amsterdam was a great deal more colorful than many of his holy predecessors.

"I don't know what the people see in me, to tell you the truth," Shimmele Amsterdam confessed. "All my life I could barely get my own wife and children to grace me with a second look. But since becoming the master of the mysterious, the whole world wants a piece of me. I'm just coming from a meeting with the mayor. Very nice woman, by the way. She wants to know what I can do to help alleviate the tensions in the city."

Abulafia cracked a big smile, exposing his very few, and very yellow, front teeth. "What did you tell her?"

"I said, 'Madam Mayor, maybe if we all prayed in earnest, God will listen.'"

The older man burst into a great big laugh, slapping his thighs with joy. "Atta' boy, Shimmele, you wuz born for this!"

"You're not kidding," said the younger mystic, who was well into his 70's.

Lowering his voice and speaking aside to Jonah, Amsterdam added, "Our Mayor is a secret *ba'alas t'shuvah*, you know, a *returnee**—she, her husband,

---

* Returnees or *ba'alei t'shuva* (Heb.: practitioners of repentance) are Jews from non-religious backgrounds who have been excited by Judaism. Originally the term was used by Jewish sources to describe sinners who sought absolution, their children, they're all returnees, every last one of them climbing back up from a life devoid of spirituality."

Lionel Abulafia put out his cigarette and sat up. "Jonah and I seen The Girl today," he told Amsterdam.

"How is she?" Shimmele Amsterdam asked with great interest.

"They're chasing her, same bastards what blew up McSorley's."

"Who is she, really?" Jonah demanded. "And why did the people chasing her blow up my building?"

Shimmele smiled and looked at Abulafia. "He can be trusted?"

"If a two-timing old dog like *you* can be trusted, why not him?" Abulafia muttered.

Amsterdam was only too happy to proceed. "We pretty much believe she's the messiah," he said. "Sooner or later, she's going to redeem humanity. Stands to reason that the *other side* wants her eliminated."

"Very funny," said Jonah.

"Okay, it's funny," Amsterdam responded mildly. "She's *still* the messiah, and she's *still* going to save the world."

"Says Shimmele Amsterdam," Abulafia pointed out, "a certified fool with a dead skunk on his head."

"Since the destruction of the Temple, prophecy has been given to children, to the deaf and to fools," the new master cabalist recited. "I, the fool, say she's it. I say she's coming to redeem the world, and you know I'm right, Lionel. And, by the way, the hat is pure sable."

"Redeem the world from what?" Jonah asked.

"Wait one minute, I have it written down someplace," said the new master cabalist and dug a folded, typewritten page from his silk robe inside pocket. "I expect she would redeem us from…" he declared, clearing his throat, and continued: "*abhorrence, abomination, acrimony, affliction, agony, alienation, anguish, animosity, animus, antagonism, antipathy, anxiety, apprehension, aversion, bitterness, coldness, contempt, despondency, detestation, disaffection, disapproval, discord, disfavor, disgust, disharmony, displeasure, dissension, distaste, distress, distrust, disunity, division, doubt, dubiosity, enmity, ennui, envy, estrangement, execration, fear, fissure, foreboding, fracture, grief, grudge, hate, heartache, horror, hostility, hurt, ignominy, ill-will, jealousy, knocks, loathing, malaise, malevolence, malice, malignance, martyrdom, militancy, misery,*

---

but, as many *t'shuva* industry specialists would attest, there are by far more Jews doing the discovery thing than there are repenting sinners. The economics are obvious.

150

misgiving, odium, pique, prejudice, quarrel, rack, rancor, repugnance, repulsion, revenge, revulsion, rift, rupture, sadness, schism, scorn, scruple, secession, separation, severance, shock, skepticism, spite, spleen, split, strife, suffering, suspicion, torment, torpor, torture, travail, tribulation, venom, wariness, withdrawal, woe, worry, wretchedness, xenophobia, and yoking."

When Amsterdam was finished, he folded up the paper neatly and returned it very carefully to his inside pocket.

Jonah remained silent for a minute, then he said what you, the reader, want to say: "This is just a bunch of words from the Thesaurus!"

A faint grin on his lips, Amsterdam took out the paper once again and unfolded it one more time. He examined the list carefully, then declared, "Yes, some I added from the Thesaurus. Many have been on the list for ages, though. You'll find them in Jewish liturgy going back centuries. Tell him, Lionel."

Jonah raised his head and looked at Abulafia. "You also think she's the messiah? She's going to save us from that list of terrible words?"

Shimmele interrupted. "It's not just the list. There's a Henny Youngman joke: A man tells his doctor, 'It hurts me when I do *this.*' So the doctor says, 'Don't *do* this.' When this little girl will tell *us* not to 'do that,' we'll *listen.*"

Abulafia chuckled; twisting his mouth in what had to pass for a smile. "A female messiah? Perish the thought," he mumbled.

"You're saying she's the messiah, he's saying she's not," Jonah said, addressing both old men. "So, please, explain to me what possible connection does my poor building, with my poor rent-controlled apartment, have to do with The Girl being chased around on some mythical plane? Why did those thugs blow up my house? It makes no sense."

"It makes sense if the whole universe knows you're destined to save her," said Abulafia. "Like it or not, the other side wants you both very dead."

Jonah Simpson wanted to scream in fury, his blood boiled, his temples pounded, adrenaline coursed through his system, and every part of him was forced into unexplainable alert. He felt he was either about to die or climb a mountain.

57.

To Jonah's great surprise, the young warrior found himself capable of returning to the primordial scenery of the *pardes* on his own. This time it was his rage that transported him, but he was beginning to understand the process, and could envision undertaking the trip without the introduction of physical stimulation.

He savored the tingling waves of anticipation. Soon he would see the creature of astonishing beauty he had glimpsed earlier.

He advanced past the thicket and through the mist of sparkling raindrops and zigzagging lightening bolts, to discover a river that ran through a perfect meadow, where deer and antelopes grazed fearlessly and the bright, blue sky stretched to eternity.

The Girl sat on a white rock, quietly reading a book.

Jonah came up to her noiselessly, knowing how fast she could run if she had to. Had she opted to flee, he knew, he might never get another chance to bathe his soul in this vision.

After some time he discovered, as often happens on higher spiritual planes, that the distance between himself and the lovely creature had not diminished, despite his fast pace. He suddenly saw himself moving backwards, across the river, beyond the thicket, to where he had entered the scenery. Obviously, one didn't move in these quarters with one's legs alone. He had to *think* his progress.

"If I were near you I wouldn't as much as make a sound, I wouldn't disturb you in the least," he thought in the direction of the beautiful young woman. "All I want is just to look at you."

"Whatever for?" Nechama asked and put down her book. It took Jonah a moment to realize he had just been swept across the landscape, all the way up to his beloved.

He was speechless, as was to be expected.

"Fine, stare away, stare all you want. Have fun," Nechama said and returned her gaze to the book in her lap.

"I'm paralyzed with unbearable affection for you," Jonah suddenly thought.

She smiled and raised one eyebrow.

What dexterity!

Jonah was flooded with gratitude for being acknowledged by this magnificent woman.

Being noticed by her at all was almost orgasmic. The idea of actually conversing with her was unendurably pleasurable.

"Ever since I laid eyes on you, I can't stop replaying the scene in my head," he said, this time using spoken words. "The chase, those men, your lovely figure dashing through the jungle..."

"You enjoy watching women running from their would-be captors?" she inquired and graced him with a slanted look.

"No, not at all! I'm sorry. I understand your own experience may have been less gratifying."

"Hey, every event is viewed in uniquely different ways by different spectators," she said. "In this instance, yours happens to be more poetic than mine. For me it was a metaphor—a warning of things to come."

"It had the feeling of a stage play," he agreed.

"Something like that."

She sighed and put down her book. Every gesture she made increased her beauty, if that were even possible.

"I've longed to see you up close," Jonah confessed. "I know that this may not be real, but I'm grateful, nevertheless, for this rare moment."

"Oh, gosh, you're making me blush," she said. "So, what can I do for you?"

"Do? Nothing, I told you, I'm just an admirer."

"That's nice," said The Girl, "but you must realize the cosmos has gone to great expense to make our meeting possible, so there must be some practical end to this. Tell me, where are you hanging down below, as we speak here?"

"Down below? Are you suggesting I'm elsewhere *and* visiting you here at the same time?"

"Well, what did you expect, silly boy?" Nechama said and a symphony of silver bells was let loose as she laughed, taking his breath away. He would have loved to stop breathing altogether, so there would be more space in him to absorb those beautiful sounds—he was truly mad with love—but she became alarmed and cried, "Breathe!" so he obeyed.

The Girl explained that, with only a few noted exceptions, visits to the *pardes* did not entail bringing along one's body. And only two of those who had ventured up there with their corporeal parts ever made it back intact. One was Moses, who entered to receive God's teaching. The other was Second Century master, Akiba, preeminent disseminator of Moses' oral teachings.

"So, where have you left your body?" she insisted.

"I suppose my body's in a chopper right now, with two old Jewish guys; one of them claims to be the eighth great master of the Cosmic Wisdom movement, for whatever that's worth; the other has to be a hundred years

153

old if he's a day, and he's some kind of magician. He flew me out of a bombing site."

"Lionel Abulafia," said The Girl. "He's 130 years old."

"I'm not surprised," said Jonah. "I should take it for granted that you know everybody and everything, right?" he added.

She smiled. "That's a good general recommendation for any man with a woman in his life," she said.

Jonah couldn't believe his ears. She was being flirtatious! With him!

"Where are you headed?" Her voice was suddenly deadly serious.

"No idea. I just lost my apartment. I guess I should go back to my unit. I'm in the service, you know..."

"I know," said The Girl. "Promise me you'll come back here to report to me."

"On what?"

"Anything."

"Fine," said Jonah.

"No, no, mister, I said promise me," she insisted. "It means you're making a commitment. It means this will become part of history. It means you're coming back here even—even if it puts your life in jeopardy."

"I will come back here even if it means I die," Jonah vowed.

"Thank you. By the way, what's your name?"

"Jonah Simpson."

"Very nice to meet you, Jonah Simpson, I'm Nechama Gutkind. How do you do?"

Next he opened his eyes in the chopper, with Abulafia's face stuck directly in his.

"You went there again, din' you, fella'?" the cabalist concluded, mercifully pulling back.

"Yes, I did." Jonah saw no point in denying it.

"Seen anything good?"

"Only the most beautiful creature in the world—"

"My word, our boy is in love!" Shimmele Amsterdam announced and applauded with great fanfare.

58.

Gliding in the chopper towards downtown Manhattan, Lionel Abulafia turned to Jonah Simpson and said, "Here is where you come in, my boy."

"It is?" Jonah had just caught the feeblest nap after his most recent *pardes* experience and the old man's raspy voice woke him up.

"Well, isn't it obvious? Somebody has to protect The Girl."

"Protect her? From what?"

"Are you kidding me?" the cabalist roared. "Wake up, man, how long do you think she can continue to roam the countryside like this, suckling honey out of the flowers? There are dark forces out there; she must be protected!"

"I've seen her take very good care of herself," Jonah argued.

"Once, twice, five times, yes. But they'll never give up!"

"While you're on the subject, who exactly are *they?*"

"The anti-Semites, the government..."

"The government?"

"Of *course* the government! You saw what they did to Julius and Ethel Rosenberg!"

"Actually that was quite a bit before my time," Jonah commented.

"I sense great danger, my boy, and I need your help. *She* needs your help."

"He's right, you know," Shimmele Amsterdam joined the discussion, although he continued to stare outside his window at the cityscape flying below.

"With so many righteous and able rabbis around, it's *my* protection she needs?" Jonah asked.

"See, sometimes what's needed is not a bunch of great leaders, but one good, honest follower. We need a foot soldier, Jonah," said Abulafia, "a sentry."

"Have you stopped to think how lonely the poor girl must be out there? If you only provided companionship, you'd be doing a lot for her."

"Isn't this discussion a little premature? We don't even know where she is," Jonah pointed out. He had a very strong feeling he was being set up, although to what end he wasn't yet sure.

"Well, we know she'll turn up some time today or, at the latest, tomorrow," said Lionel Abulafia. "The world is coming to its end, you know."

"It is?" Jonah asked.

"Listen," said Lionel Abulafia, "we have no intention of conning you into service. We couldn't even if we wanted to. Not because you're so smart, like you think, but because of the demands of the job."

"What he means," said Shimmele Amsterdam, "is that there's a chance you'll have to defend her with your body."

"I know exactly what he means," Jonah Simpson conceded, after a long moment of silent reflection. "I'd be honored to take a bullet for her."

The two old Jews exchanged a quick glance and Lionel Abulafia closed his eyes and leaned back silently. Amsterdam let out a sigh of relief.

Later, when recording this moment for THE CABALIST'S HANDBOOK OF PRACTICAL MESSIANIC REDEMPTION, Abulafia wrote:

> Jonah Simpson was recruited in less than one hour to defend the messiah with his life, if it came to that. You think this is a small thing? Go back to your history books and find me another messiah who has ever had a Jonah Simpson at his side.

59.

The red and white limo chopper dropped Jonah Simpson outside the THRUST ready lot downtown. Lionel Abulafia was particularly infuriating with his parting words, "When we meet next you'll be ready for the mission."

The younger man resisted throwing a mild punch in his direction, figuring it would look bad should it be picked up by one of the streetcams. He could imagine the embarrassing headline:

"THRUST OP HITS 130-YEAR-OLD MAN."

A light drizzle began as the chopper lifted off into the fall sky. About twenty black vans stood inside the lot. Most were surrounded by their crews who were either coming off a detail or about to go out on one. In the dim, late afternoon light, the personnel in their black fatigues and shock helmets appeared like a flock of Asian shadow puppets.

Lieutenant Hammonton's van stood vacant. The chief was at an emergency meeting upstairs with the regional THRUST commander, Colonel Amelia Lopes. The rest of the crew had scattered in the general direction of Chinatown in search of dinner. Jonah approached the van, positioning his face before the van door to allow the retina scanner to sweep his right eye. The door opened with a hum as the interior lights came on. Jonah sat down heavily in front of the comm/console and linked up the team.

"This is Jonah, back from a break. Where's the fire?"

"No fire this evening so far, Jonah—other than McSorley's. They blew it up," responded Osmond.

"You telling *me?* It's my building, and I was there."

"Sorry for your loss, man." Osmond sympathized. "Hey, my couch is free."

"Thanks. I may just take you up on that." Jonah felt suddenly grateful for his friend.

"Sure. I'm on Mott Street now picking up Chinese. Can I bring you something?"

"Yes, thanks."

"Anything special?"

"Surprise me."

"Loud and clear."

THRUST team assignments were not designed to be permanent; the initial idea was that variably manned, mission-specific squads could be assembled out of a large set of modular components. But theory was one thing and reality another. Regional commanders quickly discovered that their recruits were happiest when they worked alongside familiar teammates. They also discovered that casualties were lower when team members knew each other well. Not surprisingly, during a "situation," substitute personnel always seemed to get hurt first.

Jonah dropped into the rear seat and dragged a pillow up from the floor. The van had to pass military style inspections every morning, but it was amazing how much junk food was accumulated by six soldiers in twelve hours. The underside of the pillow felt sticky and moist, like the floor of a movie theater at midnight. He dumped it in disgust and rested his head on his left arm instead. With his right, he pulled a cigarette from his breast pocket and stuck it in his mouth. He fumbled for his lighter as the the van door slid open again. He trusted the retina scanner's ability to block unwanted visitors. So when the familiar redhead appeared in his field of vision like Venus rising from her seashell, Jonah almost swallowed his cigarette whole.

"Hot damn! Who are you? How'd you get *in* here?" he blurted, choking on the wet filter.

"*Ve haff our vays,*" Nechama smirked. Jonah noted how her eyes lit up when she smiled. He quickly raised himself in the seat and backed up a bit, to get more of her in view.

"No, seriously, you're not supposed to be in here, it's a government... thing." He knew he'd just lost his train of thought. He couldn't possibly gaze at this young woman and think his own thoughts at the same time. She was too perfect, too—the word "holy" kept offering itself regardless of how many times he rejected it.

A minute passed, maybe more. She was still smiling.

"Holy Hannah, it's *you*! The real you—in the flesh!" He suddenly snapped.

She giggled at his revelation.

"Nechama Gutkind! You really *do* exist!"

The silver bells of her laughter pealed, just the way he'd heard them in the higher realms. What a day he was having!

"Come," she said, putting her hand on his shoulder, "I've got a job for you, very urgent."

"Where? How?" These were not so much questions he was expecting answers to, as sounds he was making while getting in gear. Her touch on his shoulder made him feel strangely calm.

"I'll tell you where and what in a minute. Go get behind the wheel," she ordered.

"I can't just take off," he argued, already strapping himself in the driver's seat.

"Sure you can. Article 2, Part 16 of the RML: 'Any member of a THRUST team is authorized to take action in an emergency, utilizing whatever means are available and necessary. Emergency action is not subject to peer review but may be later evaluated by the appropriate commander.'"

"Nobody uses 2/16, ever," Jonah protested. "It's practically the first thing they tell you in boot camp."

"Urrrrh," The Girl made a game-show buzzer sound. "Wrong answer. The *right* answer is: THRUST gunner Graham Pickfort, who noticed suspicious activity on the tarmac while securing the Detroit Metro Airport. Starlight inspection revealed a dozen or so hostiles about to take action against a group of parked aircraft. Acting *without proper clearance*, Pickfort maneuvered six empty THRUST vans by remote control, lights rolling and sirens blurring. He single-handedly surrounded the enemy and arrested all of them—on his own."

"Okay, but Pickfort was like a regular Sergeant York, and he really couldn't spare a minute, he had to act."

"We cannot either, Soldier," she assured him.

"Where's the fire?" he asked, already rolling the van to the street exit.

"Take Worth to the Manhattan Bridge," she commanded and Jonah Simpson eased out of the lot and turned right. Sirens blaring, they reached the lower-level entrance to the bridge in under a minute, startling the Sunday evening drivers out of their way.

The Manhattan Bridge spans east toward Brooklyn, over the East River. On the lower level, three car lanes are set in the middle—flanked on either side by train tracks. A pedestrian lane and a bike lane flank the train tracks like parentheses. To get to the embedded car lanes, Jonah would have had to fight through the predictable Canal Street traffic congestion.

"Take the bike path, not the middle lane," The Girl ordered.

"Too narrow," Jonah argued. "What's the difference?"

"*That's* the difference," she said, pointing at the front car of the D Train emerging from the Manhattan side, having just left the Grand Street Station on its way east to DeKalb Avenue, Brooklyn.

"Are we after that train?" Jonah asked.

"That's the vibe I'm getting," she confirmed.

"The vibe?"

"Okay, premonition. Works better for you?"

"If you want the train, I can take the middle lanes," he suggested hurriedly. "This is too risky..."

"No time! Get on the bike lane *now!*"

"We'll never make it," Jonah mumbled even as he jumped the curb, gunning his vehicle into the entrance to the bike lane on the south side of the bridge. There was under an inch of space between the van and the railing on either side. Jonah had no choice but to turn the wheel over to the autopilot.

"Blockage on the road in five hundred yards," the van system warned them as the autopilot took over.

THRUST vans are built with village street chases in mind; they're narrow enough to fit through and maneuver around obstacles that would even prove challenging to a motorcycle. But the THRUST van could not fit through the pair of cement anti-tank cones, which someone in Homeland Security had apparently divined to position there. It obviously made *someone* feel safer...

"We're screwed," Jonah yelled and turned to his right to get his companion's response, but her seat was already empty. He whipped his head around just in time to see the backseat door on the left click closed. Looking out of his left side mirror he just caught the whirlwind reflection of The Girl leaping from the van. To his amazement, she didn't land on the pavement but managed to grab hold of the eight-foot-tall wire fence that separated the bike lane from the trains. She scaled the fence, climbed halfway down the other side and waited for the approaching eight-car D train to slow down. When it did, she grabbed the steel railing that connected the fifth and sixth cars and heaved herself onto the train.

On the bike lane, Jonah demonstrated why the New York State spent a fortune on THRUST vehicles. He switched into flight mode and ordered the autopilot to lift above the cement barriers and brought the van into hover mode, keeping pace with the train. Just then, his comm/link came to life.

"Yo, Simpson, what the f—?" asked Jerry Osmond, holding a bag of to-go Hunan plates, and staring at the team's vacant parking spot.

"Sudden hostiles," Jonah informed him. "More details soon..."

"Where *are* you?"

Simpson killed the connection.

On his left, through the windows that ran the length of the train, he could glimpse The Girl running through the aisles towards the front of the train, occasionally bumping into passengers.

Jonah followed her progress, hovering nearby.

She reached the front car and started banging on the motorman's door.

There was no response.

From his position, Jonah could now see the motorman. He was wearing a gray sweater that bore no resemblance to the Metropolitan Transit Authority dark-and-light-blue uniform, and he screamed angrily over his shoulder several times in answer to Nechama's frenzied knocking.

"Holy crap, he's a baddie," Simpson realized, reaching for the loaded RPG launcher under the dashboard. He trained the weapon at the motorman's cabin, knowing that subway trains were programmed to stop dead in their tracks if the helm was damaged. He took the shot. A huge, smoldering hole replaced the nose of the train which came to a sudden, screeching halt. Simpson ignored the sounds of screaming passengers. On first glance, there seemed to be no grave injuries. But *she* had been so close to the front... For one frightening moment he could not see her; much of the first car was engulfed in smoke and flames.

160

Then doubt set in, followed by dread. *If she was wrong then I just blew up a New York City train for nothing...*

But then there was Nechama, climbing out of the wreckage carrying a bulky briefcase. She ran to the fence and motioned for him to catch it, tossing it to him. Determined, Jonah stuck half his body out the driver's side window and managed to grab the thing by one corner, like an airborne wide receiver. Nechama clambered to the top of the fence and waited while Jonah suspended the autopilot to maneuver the van closer. He opened the van's left passenger door and she jumped in.

Flushed and excited, she gave Jonah the bad news, "It's a dirty bomb— we have to dump it in the water—I have no idea when it's set to go..."

THRUST soldiers are conditioned to experience an overriding sense of calm during an emergency. This is accomplished after many weeks of motivational hypnosis, and it's a remarkable phenomenon to behold. In this case, Jonah Simpson took the van above the railing on his right and flew it over the water. He increased hover speed to the maximum thirty knots, bringing the vehicle very quickly to the point where the East River widens into New York Bay. He wanted very much to reach as far beyond Brooklyn into the Atlantic Ocean as he could, but he wasn't sure it was such a good idea.

"Wait until we go past the wider berth and dump the thing," he told his companion. "We'll never make it further out."

"A million people live on either side of that bay!" she said.

"If the load hits bottom before it blows they'll be fine," he told her. "But if it goes while we're in mid air..."

Instead of arguing further, The Girl opened up the briefcase.

The smallest Radiological Dispersal Device combines a stick of dynamite with a package of radioactive material. Depending on its size, an RDD explosion can contaminate areas populated by civilians and harm life and property. Although a dirty bomb is not as destructive as a nuclear bomb, its radiation can disperse within a few blocks or a few miles of the explosion, depending on the amount of explosives used. Glancing at the open case, Jonah Simpson estimated it contained about ten kilos of plastique and ten bricks of radioactive material each wrapped in a thin sheet of lead foil. It was big enough to scare him. He identified the trigger mechanism—a miniature cellphone. This baby was designed to go off by remote control. Simpson had no way of telling if the operator was the recently deceased motorman or one of his controllers, still at large.

"Can you disconnect it?" The Girl asked, bringing the case closer for his review.

Simpson reconnected the autopilot and turned around. "The explosive cake is fused with the detonator," he said, "if we try to dislodge it, I'm pretty sure it'll blow."

"However?" she inquired.

"However, only one radioactive brick is physically connected to the explosive," he pointed. "We could extract nine bricks and dump the case with just the one still attached."

She understood at once. Hastily, she removed the excess bricks and tossed the case out of her window. Jonah reasserted steering control and veered left, towards the Brooklyn Navy Yards. Behind them they heard the explosion and saw a geyser of seawater rise and fall.

The Brooklyn waterfront was a glitzy stretch of luxury high risers but in between the glass towers there were gaping holes, making the east bank look like the smile of a cavity-prone idiot. Those were bombing sites, of which every New York City borough had its share.

Simpson got back on his comm/link. "Found and disposed of RDD on Brooklyn-bound D Train," he reported to his unit.

"Picked up perpetrators?" Jerry Osmond inquired.

"Retired one, presumably receiving his seventy virgins as we speak."

"Duly noted. Your dinner's getting cold, Captain Courageous."

"Heading back," said Jonah and killed the connection again. Then he asked Nechama Gutkind, "How'd you *know* about this? This wasn't just premonition—you headed directly to the source."

"I would tell you if I understood it myself," she said. "I only felt this—sorry, I don't really have a word for it—like a burst of fear, violence, hate and rage. More than anything else, it's rage. But I felt it strongest just before I got out of the van, believe me. Now I'm getting very strong sensations about Atlantic Avenue."

"I'm calling it in, if you don't mind," Jonah told her, as the van touched down on the service road that ran alongside the waterfront.

"Not this one," she said.

He gave her a slanted look, but she was watching the road ahead intently, so he just floored the gas pedal and roared along the water. The windshield wipers weren't much good in the drizzle. He had half a mind to turn on the autopilot again, but autopilots obeyed speed limits and protocols and reported to base. Something told him his next episode with the Gutkind

162

woman should remain private.

THRUST soldiers have premonitions, too.

"I know that neighborhood," he said. "I did a job there once."

The Brooklyn Navy Yards lay south of Brooklyn Heights. Here, more than half a century before, the outcome of the Pacific War was decided by thousands of tireless workers, men and women. The Girl directed Jonah through the front gate at Morton Street. The entire tarmac, dotted by small metal enclosures, was dark and empty. Theirs was the sole vehicle.

"I'm feeling a bit exposed," Jonah said.

"What else?"

"Unsafe? I don't know."

"Anything familiar?" The Girl pressed.

"I know the place, sure."

"That's it?"

"What are you getting at?" He wasn't sure he wanted to know.

"Keep driving, you'll know when we get there."

"Get where?"

"I have no idea, Jonah, I'm looking for a cue from you."

He shrugged his shoulders and continued to drive, more hesitantly and slowly than before. "Should I keep the lights on?"

"What do *you* think?"

"This is getting a little annoying," he told her.

"I'm sorry."

He stopped the vehicle and turned off the beams and leaned back in his seat. He scanned his surroundings in sections, reading an entire limited area, then moving on, until he completed a 360 degree survey.

He opened the driver's side door and landed on the soft asphalt. The drizzle hit his face but he didn't mind. Outside the van he was beginning to perceive—something. He sniffed and closed his eyes.

Fresh sourdough bread.

The aroma permeated the open yard, pungent and aggressive. There was a commercial bakery on Ninth Street, it made wonderful rye and pumpernickel and sourdough, and the aroma...

He knew.

Two years ago he was here, right at the point where he was now standing, except there had been a structure standing here, a prefab. They must have hauled it away since. He had lain there for a week; without food or drink, but not because he wanted to die—he was following strict instructions:

"As long as you don't nourish, I'll stay with you..."

"Damn, it was the old man!" he cried and banged his fist on the side of the THRUST van.

Nechama came out and walked around the hood. "Abulafia?" she asked.

"Yeah, him. He derailed me."

"Derailed?"

"I was supposed to deliver a human heart to an Iranian cell down in Coney Island. I obtained the heart—"

"Obtained?"

"Whatever. It wasn't cut out of the chest of an angel, I assure you."

"Ah."

"I packed it and went outside, then this old man in a lousy hat starts walking next to me, matching his pace to mine. Holy crap, I completely deleted the whole scene from my brain... They worked on me for months and I never tapped that scene..."

"You didn't recognize Abulafia this afternoon."

"No. I'm stunned. I'm supposed to be better than this."

"Lionel Abulafia's got a lot of tricks up those 130-year-old sleeves."

"I suppose..."

"What did he tell you?"

"Oh... Let me see..." Jonah's forehead was wrinkled as he was trying to recall. "He said I had to stop doing this, or I couldn't ever go back."

"Stop doing what?"

"I suppose he meant cutting up people and putting their hearts in Ziploc baggies."

"It might have pushed you over the edge, don't you think?"

"Yes. It *was* kind of creepy walking down Atlantic Avenue with someone's heart in my pocket."

Before Jonah Simpson suffered his battle fatigue episode, he had been approaching the kind of suicidal rampage worthy of Camus, Hemingway, or Bukowski.

His bosses were planning a lucrative career for him in the international assassinations business, performing wet work for the richer and softer Europeans. He was shown his list of targets: Always some kind of Muslim fanatic, always a suspicious and ruthless SOB. who got to where he was by taking out many others just like him. The hours were good. He wouldn't be expected to do more than one kill a month. He would get to open platinum charge accounts, and he had his eye on a Bentley.

Why did it become too much to bear so soon? Why did this magnificent warrior begin to experience doubts almost immediately? Lionel Abulafia thought he knew why: Jonah was already transforming.

The men he was going up against with the THRUSTs were faithful and sincere. They were cruel and vicious as well, to be sure, but those qualities were par for the course in Simpson's world. Nevertheless, each one of his targets impressed him with his capacity for self-sacrifice and courage.

The doubts accumulated. Simpson resented the very idea of his unending assignment.

Lionel Abulafia saw all of this in an instant when he first became aware of Jonah's presence two years ago. The gladiator was breaking down, and in the mystic's view, when a man of Simpson's stature disintegrated, there was no telling what would befall those who happened onto his path. It became crucial to isolate him from his operators and give him an opportunity to consider calmly whether he wanted to continue killing people on command. It was obvious to Abulafia that, sooner or later, Simpson's target would be Nechama Gutkind.

"He brought me down here, to the Navy Yards, and then I realized he wasn't really there."

"What gave it away?"

"I went in through the gate, the way we drove in just now—but he came in through the *fence*."

"He was a figment."

"Yes. But very convincing."

"He stayed with you for seven days?"

"Yes. He taught me…"

"What?"

"About my connections. Man, I remember everything, now! My dad, my mom, my grandparents, the whole family, immigrants, Russia, pogroms, crusades, the whole shebang. And all I had to do to stay connected was not to eat or drink."

"Starvation high," she said.

"Anorexic cheer leaders," he couldn't help himself.

Silver bells. She got the joke. Phew…

"He had to stop you because otherwise you'd be lost to *me*," she said.

"I suppose."

"Are you angry?"

"Yes. But the good kind."

She smiled. Not as wonderful as the silver bells, but also very nice. Then she hugged him.

He grabbed her with such force, she almost activated her sphere thing to block him, but when she realized this was the sweet kind of violence, she relaxed her defenses.

He picked her up and laid her down over the front seat. Moving closer, he put his mouth over hers and their tongues celebrated a long, moist dance together, before he rubbed his face against her very hot cheek.

She wasn't certain if messianic figures did this sort of thing, but she was powerfully attracted to this man. She relaxed into his kiss, and it was a fantastic relief from the sores, and the running, and the miracles, and God.

The power of this kiss brought three new planets into being and created a distinct species of bird in Australia. Seventeen couples around the world who had been thinking of divorce decided to give marriage another try and 36 couples who never should have been together in the first place decided to call it quits. And on the very small, consistently rainy Polynesian island of Huahine, the sun came out from behind the clouds and radiated gently upon the grateful populace for a full 15 minutes.

When they pulled apart from one another, Jonah comm/linked with the team and reported a false alarm, which was acceptable. He went to relieve himself near the fence, then got into the van and started the motor. About to begin the short route back to Manhattan, Jonah looked around for his beautiful passenger and wasn't the least bit surprised to discover she was gone.

"I don't care if she's real or not," he mumbled, mystified. He had half expected that having sex with The Girl would tarnish her glow for him, if only a little. Instead, he had become insanely ravenous for her presence. And the notion that he was the only man alive who had known The Girl in the biblical sense only made his passion burn hotter.

"What's that?" Penny Brown's voice came over the comm/link.

"Oh, nothing, I'm babbling. Too tired to drive—I'm putting this thing on autopilot."

"You deserve it, Boy Wonder," said Jerry Osmond. "Go to sleep, I'll monitor your robot."

It was a righteous 2/16.

60.

"What do you take with your tea? Honey, sugar, artificial sweetener?" asked Section Chief Amelia Lopes. Short, wiry, fit, and not particularly beautiful, Lopes exuded a sense of self-confidence. She was very good at being in charge without ever having to push her authority.

The holstered service gun, which hung against her suspenders as an homage to Elliot Ness, certainly helped make the authoritative thing stick. Amelia Lopes was one of those women who wore her business suit as if no man had ever worn one before.

THRUST Chief Lieutenant David Hammonton wasn't particularly thirsty, but he knew from past experience that his boss needed the tea-puttering to help her concentrate. The cabinet above the little dinette counter in her office held jars of black and green teas from four continents; her little kitchenette featured a display case with at least twenty different highly polished tea vessels, including several whistling kettles which—rumor had it—she could set up to whistle a close approximation of "The Star-Spangled Banner."

It was an unscheduled, late Sunday evening meeting. THRUST Team Chief Hammonton had no intention of failing this early in his tête à tête with the boss.

"I'll take it straight," Hammonton said. *Let the ballbusting begin...*

"Manly choice," she responded with a thin smile. Hammonton wondered which kind of abuse was preferable, the old, boozy, macho way his male bosses used to torment their underlings, or Amelia's more genteel, but no less emasculating, technique.

David Hammonton was as all-American as they came: Tall, and broad-shouldered, with short-cropped, light-brown hair, he sported a square jaw and the self-assured wellbeing of the favorite son of the system. He was well aware of his physical advantages, but also knew that those very attributes could drive some of his colleagues batty. He wasn't sure whether Lopes, herself a shooting star at the agency, liked him or not, but he knew she was resentful of him.

"Sit down, David," Lopes instructed him finally, and they both lounged

167

near the coffee table at the center of the room. The panorama window behind Lopes' back offered a view of Centre Street, from Worth to Chamber. When she first occupied the office, Lopes removed the traditional, enormous mahogany desk and replaced it with a small writing desk and a laptop. This turned the already large space into an intimidatingly huge executive office.

"I have an impossible assignment for your team, David," said Amelia Lopes. "It's the kind of assignment no cop should be given. I wish I had a team of priests working for me, they'd be much better at it, I'm sure."

"Don't tell me—we're going to arrest God," said Hammonton.

Lopes cracked a smile. "Close," she said and placed several stacks of typed paper on his side of the coffee table. "Read these and pass them on to your people. Also—" and she handed him several soft-cover textbooks, "read these: *Tales of the Hasidim*, by Martin Buber. By tomorrow morning I expect you to become well versed in Hasidic history and philosophy, especially the Cosmic Wisdom movement. It's very entertaining."

"What's the assignment?" Hammonton asked, picking up and leafing through the top volume.

"I'm not sure," she admitted. "Let's start with this: A few years ago a major Jewish mystic died in a hospital downtown. According to his thousands of followers, he was the messiah."

"I thought we've already had a messiah," Hammonton said cautiously.

"Not if you're Jewish, you haven't," his boss assured him. "The Jewish faith holds that the messiah will come at the end of History, to redeem the world of its suffering. Jews suspect that Jesus wasn't the real redeemer because, let's face it, human suffering is still raging out there."

"Okay, but you just told me this Jewish man *also* died before redeeming the world," Special Agent Hammonton pointed out.

"Yes, thank God, our world is as far from redemption as can be imagined, so both our jobs are safe," Amelia Lopes laughed. "But this *cabalist* apparently had a daughter or a niece that nobody had heard of while he was alive. He died more than twenty years ago, at the ripe old age of ninety-two, but she appeared on the scene only very recently. Her name is Nechama Gutkind."

"If twenty years ago *he* was ninety-two, how old would *she* be today?"

"Twenty-one."

Hammonton fell silent and just knew his boss was savoring his discomfort. Tough honky David Hammonton having a bad Math moment.

He finally gave up. "How can it be?" he asked.

"We have no idea. We don't have real data, only—" and she paused to tap on the stacks of paper on the coffee table, "a massive accumulation of rumors, which is something I expect you to correct shortly." Her face became very serious. "You must find this alleged successor, David. The assignment comes from the very top."

"The very top?"

"As in the President of the United States. He wants this daughter or niece captured. He wants her out of the way in the most direct and un-compromising manner. Am I being clear enough?"

"Yes, I'm supposed to kill the girl."

"The president believes she is a threat to our national security. Don't ask me to speculate, but you and I both know that a well-trained, highly motivated individual can cause practically unlimited damage. We have no other choice but to eliminate her."

According to the THE CABALIST'S HANDBOOK OF PRACTICAL MESSIANIC REDEMPTION, THRUST Chief Amelia Lopes occupied a unique spot along the Spiritual Continuum of Everything. She stood to the right of Yoko Ono, who in 1969 broke up the Beatles, and to the left of Mikhail Gorbachev, who in 1989 broke up the Soviet Union.

"I'm on it." Hammonton said decisively. His boss favored him with another smile.

"Here's her picture," Lopes said, handing him the final item from her own dossier on The Girl. "It's the closest thing we've got so far to an actual portrait. With hundreds of appearances across the land, you'd think there would be more pictures…"

Hammonton took a short look at the picture.

"Sweet looking girl," he commented. He added the picture to his pile, and was about to stand up, but Lopes motioned with her open palm for him to stay.

"There's more?"

"You're not going to like this assignment at all," she said in a softer tone than before. She was about to intimate the *real* info, the stuff he wouldn't find anywhere in the stacks of paper she'd piled on him.

Hammonton leaned back and stared his boss in the eye. *Let it rain,* he thought.

"Since she appeared on the scene, less than a year ago, this girl has generated nothing but positive chatter in her wake," Lopes said. "She pissed off the Justice Department when she hypnotized a judge to dismiss a sting-based case—"

"That was *her*?"

"But otherwise she doesn't seem to have done anything particularly subversive. She cured a cancer ward in Palo Alto."

"The whole ward?"

Lopes laughed. "She walked in, and said, 'Cancer doesn't make sense': This is direct eyewitness testimony from a senior medical doctor. She said, 'If God lets us live longer now, it shouldn't be just to spend our extra time in illness,' and she cured thirty-two patients."

"How do we know it was *she* who cured them?"

"Of course we don't know, David, that's the beauty of a folk hero. *We* don't know, but the culture knows."

"The culture?"

"On Long Island, one week ago, Massapequa—she grabbed a guy in a bank, took away his suitcase, and gave it to the guard. It had a bomb in it. Big enough to take out the block."

"Wait, if this was in a bank, there should be videos..."

"None. She has the ability to distort digital information. It's been established and verified."

"That's weird..."

"Gets weirder. You've heard about the McDonald chain of fast food restaurants?"

"I believe I've sampled their products, yes..."

"It's going to close down. Sell your shares if you have any."

"I have a coupon for free fries..."

"Use it soon. McDonald's going down. Or, at least, they're about to change their menu radically."

"Because of her?"

"Persistent chatter. You heard about the Cow Rebellion?"

"The what?"

"You spend too much time chasing terrorists, David, you're missing out on all the wacko news..."

"Talk to my boss..."

"Cows in thousands of stalls across America are refusing to go to slaughter."

"Come on..."

"When the stall doors open and the cows are herded into the truck for their one-way trip to the slaughter house, they balk. They attack their owners. They force a confrontation in a most un-cow-like manner. Examination of carcasses revealed adrenaline levels hundreds of times higher than what you'd expect the most docile meat animal on the planet to secrete."

"Ruins the meat, too." Hammonton contributed, then added, "Sounds like bull."

"Maybe," Lopes said. "Follow the McDonald stock, see how it does."

"You got more tidbits?"

"Roughly seventy-five hundred reports, most of them from the continental forty-eight, but some from Europe, India, Chad. Orphans fed, ethnic cleansers stopped in mid-cleansing, collapsing circus tents hovering in the air until the audiences leave, trout colonies replenished, coral reefs revived..."

"Any water to wine miracles?"

"I got the Cleveland water supply purified overnight. I got fifty migrant workers at a slave market in LA sharing one chicken salad sandwich. I got grapevine disease cured in Napa Valley, *that's* almost a wine miracle..."

"She's one intensive little saint..."

"Obviously, not all of these reports are true, and not all the ones that bear resemblance to the truth could possibly be done by one girl."

"So it's a *few* girls?"

"No, much worse, it's the ignited imagination of the culture, David. They want this messianic figure so badly, they'll create her out of thin air if they have to. Have you been to a Shrine of The Girl yet?"

"A what of the what?"

"To date there are three thousand of them: In homes, storefronts, office buildings, church basements. You know what they *do* there?"

"Beats me."

"They form the Circle. Men, women, children, stand in a huge group, hugging each other with their eyes closed. An hour, two hours—*three hours!* That's the service; no texts, no sermons, no hymns, no collection plates. The FBI estimates one hundred thousand attend the service once a day. Perfect strangers hug for hours with their eyes closed, then go to work."

"Freaks?"

"Average Joes."

"And my assignment is to shoot Jesus?"

"More or less."

"And you're okay with it?"

"We're soldiers."

They both remained silent for a few seconds, each contemplating the weight of the Colonel's statement. Finally, Hammonton got up. "I'll try to bring her in unharmed," he promised.

"Those are *not* your orders," Lopes insisted.

"After all of the above, Colonel?"

"The problem with all of the above is that none of the miracle stories are necessarily real; and the shrines will probably continue to thrive with or without this woman. On the other hand, our orders come from a very real source, with the power to enforce them."

"You're right. I hate it," Hammonton said.

"Good boy," his boss said and stood up. Now he could leave.

Downstairs, the black van was waiting to pick him up. David Hammonton took the front passenger seat and dropped the stacks of reading material on the work top between his and the driver's seat. Penny Brown, sitting two rows back, leaned forward to pick up the same volume Hammonton had leafed through upstairs.

"Martin Buber? Haven't read him since high school. Are we going after the Hasidim now?"

"Apparently," the chief confirmed.

"What have they done?"

"Not they. *She.*"

"We're looking for a Hasidic woman?"

"Them's the orders."

"Any pogroms coming up we should know about?"

Hammonton turned around to face his smartass linguist. "You know something," he said, and meant it, "that's not entirely impossible."

61.

"Sir, we're receiving a satellite alert," Jerry Osmond said from his comm/console.

"What is it?" Hammonton asked.

"There's been a sighting of our special target at Montgomery Street and the FDR Drive. What's our special target?"

"That was fast," Hammonton mused and rose stiffly in his seat. "Take us to Montgomery Street by the FDR Drive," he ordered Dawn Brokowitz at the wheel of the black THRUST van. "What else?" he asked his communications man.

"Not a whole lot. Target has been sighted roaming here as of ten minutes ago. Who's the target, boss?"

"She's a myth, a folk hero, a mystery," Hammonton said. "We're supposed to shoot her on sight."

"What's the story?" Jonah had catnapped on the way back from the Navy Yards, while the van was remote-controlled back into the city. It had been an amazingly packed day: He'd taken down a suicide bomber—that seemed like ages ago—then his building exploded, right after he'd tripped like he hadn't tripped since college, and yeah, he met The Girl, both on a mystical plane and up close and real. But it appeared the night was still young.

"Totally top secret," said Hammonton. "If you ask me, it's dirty stuff, and I mean the kind of dirty that can bring down governments."

"No foolin'," said Simpson and leaned back. So, you spend daytime on the side of the angels, night time you give the Devil his due. All in a day's work.

New data began to stream, and Osmond ran it immediately on Hammonton's dashboard screen. The chief almost leaped out of his seat with a hunter's glee. "Oh, mama, I didn't think it would be this easy," he muttered, and instructed his driver, Dawn Brokowitz: "Take us to the East River Park, target's been spotted in real time!"

"That was easy," Jonah muttered.

Brokowitz rode the van downhill on Montgomery to the water, then turned left at the Department of Sanitation pier. She followed the service road under the FDR Drive, which hugged the knee-shaped Lower East Side of Manhattan. It started to rain heavily, the way it sometimes did in New York City after a bombing. Jonah Simpson glanced at the figures on the McSorley explosion which had been stacking on Osmond's console. He grimaced: At least twenty were killed and double that number had been injured.

Four had perished in the subway on the Manhattan bridge. "Could have been a lot worse," Jonah thought, burying his guilty reaction.

There was a commotion on the service road, near the exit ramp to the uptown lanes. An old, homeless man and a young, homeless woman, both wrapped in ancient military raincoats, stood in the middle of the muddy road alongside the highway, next to a supermarket cart loaded with empty soda cans.

It was raining even harder now and the young woman's hair was hanging in heavy, frozen lumps over her shoulders. Her left leg was covered with countless bandages, which by now had become so wet, they were untangling and drooping behind her as she limped along the broken asphalt. Both she and the old man were engaged in a lively discussion, oblivious to both the torrential rain and the danger of oncoming traffic.

Suddenly the woman grabbed the loaded cart's handles and demanded, "Why are you returning those soda cans?"

The old man stared at her in confusion. "I bring them to the store in the morning, I get paid a nickel apiece."

"Not nearly good enough," the young, homeless woman said and put her arm around his shoulder. Pulling him in, to speak directly into his face, she deliberated: "There's like two hundred cans in here? Would that be ten dollars' worth, at a nickel a can? "

"I suppose."

"What if you didn't return them? What if you kept them to yourself?"

"Why? I need the money," the man's confusion grew.

"Yes, but are you making as much money on them as you could?"

"Aren't I?"

"Come with me, I'll show you," the young woman said and tugged him by the shoulder towards the East River park.

The man smiled, exposing an empty mouth, not a tooth in it. "Lead the way," he said.

A local lilith—whose usual gig was lying in ambush for yuppie businessmen who stumbled out of the bars along Water Street late at night— happened to spot the young homeless lady talking to the toothless man. She knew that the lady was a great deal more than she appeared to be. It was obvious from the moment she saw the young woman's eyes.

"Holy Mackerel! The old man will pay a lot for this information," the lilith mumbled and leaped down from the undercarriage of the pedestrian bridge where she had been perching. "Don't let her git kilt before I obtain my recompense..."

The woman continued her efforts to help push her companion's cart on their way into the East River Park. At that moment, Hammonton's dark van appeared from behind the Montgomery underpass wall, its driver obviously aiming to ram full-force into the homeless couple.

"Hit them, God damn it! They're the freaking target!" the THRUST chief shrieked, slapping Dawn Brokowitz's shoulder in fierce delight. Jonah had never seen him this bloodthirsty. Then he looked again at the man and the woman in Brokowitz's cross hairs and his heart leapt to his throat.

"Stop! Stop!" Jonah Simpson screamed.

"Run them over, it's an order!" The chief slammed Jonah back into his seat.

"Mustn't let her git kilt." The lilith moved to intercept. Narrowing her eyes into tiny slits, she flew directly into the van's armored windshield. Brokowitz slammed the breaks and let out a cry of terror, staring in disbelief at the creature from the netherworld on the armored glass, inches from her face.

The lilith pushed her little head against the windshield and exposed her pointy teeth as she scanned the crammed interior. The van swiveled crazily and crashed into the curb, swerved again, hit a fire hydrant, nearly toppled the other way and came to a halt, blocking much of the road. A geyser erupted from the smashed hydrant, and splashed noisily on the cracked and dusty asphalt. Soon, a small lake formed around the van wheels.

The homeless young woman and her much older friend didn't stop to look back, much less interrupt their conversation. They reached the entrance to the park amphitheater and climbed uphill, disappearing into the heavy rain.

"I'll introduce you to the gang," the woman promised, her voice fading in the distance. "The store pays you five cents a can? We'll recycle the cans ourselves and sell finished aluminum sheets at ten bucks a sheet. It only takes fifty cans to make a sheet, Frank, not two hundred, only fifty!"

"No harm done," the lilith hissed after a scant examination of her own body. She was a cute, coquettish thing, barely five feet tall, with impossibly narrow hips and huge, pointy breasts imported directly from the fantasy world of most living American males. Like a panther, she sprang away from the hood of the van, reached the curb effortlessly and continued to leapfrog up Montgomery Street, scaring the stuffing out of the elderly nun who kept watch outside the Mother of Mercy Home for Wayward Women. To everyone but the driver, she had been little more than a blur.

Back at the intersection, the six van passengers filed out of their seats, shaken by the sudden termination of their mission. Brokowitz kept turning her black helmet like a makeshift rosary in her nervous fingers, causing the shiny, black visor to strobe with hellish reflections of the magenta street lights and pinkish, rainy sky. She was entirely unable to convey to her excited passengers, including the Chief, just what it was that had made her

175

slam on her breaks and endanger everyone in the car.

"It was a satanic thing, for sure," she mumbled.

"You know who the homeless girl was?" Jonah Simpson asked Hammonton.

"Sure, I do," said his boss. "It was The Girl—most dangerous person on the DHS current list."

"And we tried to run her over?" Penny Brown was astonished. "It explains why we were stopped so abruptly."

"Yup," Hammonton agreed. "This one won't go down easy...."

62.

Ben Markowitz had been staring at the poster on his wall for six hours, interrupting himself only to turn his attention to his laptop, run a quick search, and return with a confirmation for every single one of his speculations.

The Girl's clothes were no challenge at all. The loose, blue blouse hanging outside the similarly loose denim skirt, hanging at mid-calf, screamed "religious girl." The face was essentially Semitic, despite the red hair and pale skin, so he didn't even bother to check out a Hispanic, Catholic option and went directly with Jewish. It was a religious Jewish girl, probably from somewhere on the East Coast, judging by her hairdo, which was no do at all. There was an austere quality to the way she managed her appearance in general, but, most profoundly, her hair style had to be New Jersey, Western New York, maybe Pennsylvania.

"A Cosmic Wisdomnik," he said finally, because of her attitude. She was wearing all the modest threads, but her expression packed enough immodesty to unsettle a sensitive person—and Ben Markowitz was hyper-sensitive. He had read something online about Cosmic Wisdom girls, what was it?

He reached the web site promoting books on Jewish education, with a segment on Cosmic Wisdom girls: *As a whole, they are taught to think about the Jewish soul... They think seriously about how they treat other people... As a result their sense of self worth is remarkably richer and stronger than other teenage girls...*

He returned his eyes to the poster—it wasn't even a contest, the girl was definitely a Cosmic Wisdomnik.

It fit perfectly the persona that emerged from the 7500 reports on his screen.

Ben was elated, because his discovery virtually guaranteed this young woman was a virgin. Religious girls never fooled around. He would steal her heart with his amazing intellect—he already knew more Talmudic passages by heart than most religious Jewish boys. He would don a skullcap for her, eat kosher—why not? All he liked was pizza, anyway. He had to tell Mom, right away, she had to know!

Just then, his comm/link scanner, which he souped up to follow all DHS events in the vicinity, kicked into life again, with news from the East River Park. There was an accident and the target got away. *Don't envy those poor bastards,* he thought, *ran into an accident and lost their target, how inept can one team of gorillas be...*

"Scanning the park for her," came a comm/link message from a surveillance chopper team. "Stand by..."

Then Ben Markowitz got it. "Oh, my God!" he screamed, "They're trying to kill her!"

Who else would be a female target? And who else would evade a government hit with a crafty accident? It had to be her. "Biosphere my ass," he ranted, picking two 9 mm. Luger pistols out of the locked case and tucking them in his belt. He ran downstairs and opened his yellow sports convertible, which was waiting for him, as usual, right in front. He tapped the hundred percent authentic DHS Parking Permit on his windshield for luck and gunned the enormous engine. "I'm coming for you, baby!" he screeched in the drizzly wind that was hitting his face at seventy-five miles per hour on Houston Street. "Ben's gonna take care of you!"

The fact that he turned west on Houston, rather than east, would only slow him down a little bit. Eventually, he'd hit the West Side Highway and come round the bottom tip of the island and up the FDR Drive to the park. Gives us more time for all the other violent things that are about to happen next....

63.

Victoria Martin, wearing a roomy, green-and-yellow muumuu and a matching African head scarf that made her seem even taller, knocked on the study hall's door. "There's a demon to see you, Master."

Abulafia looked around at his students, a few of whom, particularly the humans, had been nodding off for some time.

"When are you due to sing your song of praise this morning?" he asked

Angel Rachmiel, who sat directly in front of him. The angel, a disciple of Archangel Raphael, had been on a healing mission in Westchester County, and decided to stop by for a lesson before going up the line again. All angels who have completed their missions must participate in the morning choir that exalts God. On regular weekdays, the choir performs for a minimum of one hour—two hours on Sabbaths and holidays—and all day long on Yom Kippur. It's a lovely sight—and sound—to behold, more grandiose than a Busby Berkley marathon at Radio City.

"When's sunrise? Six?" Angel Rachmiel asked.

"Five fifty-seven," a murmur came from the rear benches.

"We're in no hurry," said the angel.

"But I am," Lionel Abulafia said and stood up. "You'll make it upstairs on time for a change…"

The crowd of his many students rose in deference.

"I'll see you all after midnight tomorrow, I hope," Lionel Abulafia told everybody. "Let the demons out first, you don't want them behind you."

When the small room was cleared of mortal and supernatural creatures, and the dense remnants of their lingering odors had subsided a bit, Victoria approached Lionel where he sat in a wingback chair. Gently, she placed her huge palms upon his head. He shut his eyes as she guided him into sleep. His body slowly slipped forward in his chair, and the large woman blocked his fall with her soft stomach. He rested his head there and continued to sleep deeply for the next five minutes. Then he opened his eyes, his expression one of torment, and straightened up in his chair.

Victoria quietly brought Lionel Abulafia a pitcher of water and positioned an empty, blue enamel bowl on the small table next to his chair. He placed his hands over the bowl and Victoria solicitously poured water over them. When the water fell on his skin, Abulafia floated back to the realm of Life from his nightly sojourn in the Kingdom of the Dead. Cool and frothy, the water washed away the ashes he had rolled in through the eternity of his five-minute sleep. He now waited patiently for the brightness of his soul to draw him out of the terror of his extra-corporeal existence. The water soothed the invisible sores, welts and cuts inflicted upon him by mischievous sprites in the dark worlds.

Victoria handed him a clean towel. He adjusted his large, black skullcap after Victoria helped him on with his oversized fringed garment. He blessed Victoria for her ministrations. He blessed his returning soul.

The older he got, it seemed, the deeper the injuries he sustained from his nightly duels with demons. As if he were the only one aging. Of course, that couldn't be true. His demons were aging right along with him, moment by interminable moment. But to Lionel Abulafia, they seemed younger, and always in better shape than himself.

Sitting in his nightly class they remained courteous for the most part, except for the occasional brawl with the agents of Good. But in his dreams they were lethal. He didn't hold it against them. After all, this was their job.

The old master cabalist was the one who taught Abulafia how to recognize demons during the day, even without the aid of consciousness-altering substances. "It's their vacuous stare," he had said. "They have no reason to *be* unless someone invites them to serve as his or her demons. That's when the light returns to their eyes. But between gigs they're without purpose."

Furthermore, according to THE CABALIST'S HANDBOOK OF PRACTICAL MESSIANIC REDEMPTION, demons always live in Apartment 5-B. As crazy as this may sound, it has been established, anecdotally, at least.

Demons are by definition city-folk. Like policemen, emergency room doctors and journalists, demons require the presence of mischief for their very livelihood. They would not survive one day out in nature. Even in the city, they die much faster than normal humans do. Without a victim they grow despondent and wither away.

The master once showed Lionel Abulafia a group of demons seated against a barred storefront on Rivington Street, near Essex, one doorway down from the local methadone clinic. One of the nasty creatures looked up just as the master pointed at him and Abulafia saw for the first time an authentic nightmare vision in broad daylight. It was a scrawny creature, with woolly, matted, brown hair; its face was chiseled in broad strokes, without much detail, like a hastily kneaded clay figurine; and its eyes were distant, empty holes, a pair of dark caverns that ran, in serpentine fashion, down into the skull.

As soon as he realized he'd been detected, the creature attacked, red eyes flashing and talons slashing. Abulafia pulled back but the master was completely fearless. He closed his eyes, spoke a short verse (there are five hundred different verses to protect against demon attacks) and the creature was struck dead by an invisible wall. It fell to the sidewalk and remained lying there, lifeless, until an ambulance came by.

But Abulafia's guest tonight was not a demon. Lionel Abulafia was surprised at his housekeeper's error. He attributed it to the late hour. Anybody in the business as long as she should have been able to tell a demon from a lilith. Perhaps Victoria meant to slight the little creature; this was more in line with the African housekeeper's newfound territoriality where Abulafia was concerned. It might just as well be a result of Victoria's negative disposition regarding all his supernatural visitors. He silently resolved to make another marathon date with Victoria soon.

The small lilith rushed in through the doorway, skirting Victoria's bulk as the housekeeper left the room. The lilith planted herself on Lionel Abulafia's bookstand. She was sassy, juicy and head-turning in her capacity for unabashed sexual vulnerability.

A million years ago, her race mated with humans, producing hideous offspring, coarse and bent over, their noses close to the ground, picking up clues about the world from animal dung and dried up snail tracks. Then most of them were destroyed by our distant ancestors, the first new humans. But since those distant ancestors of ours weren't excessively efficient, thank God, they ended up murdering only the ugly ones, mistaking the lovelier liliths for their own kin.

Big tits and narrow hips were as useful for survival back then as they are today.

"You live in the neighborhood?" Lionel Abulafia asked his guest.

"I get around," she whispered. Liliths don't have a highly evolved larynx. They can't sing at all, despite their reputation as world class temptresses. But late at night, a lilith's whisper is quite alluring.

"What can I do for you?" Lionel Abulafia inquired, and gestured for the small creature to come down from his bookstand and take a seat facing him. The lilith complied.

"I wish to trade knowledge," she offered.

"What do I got that's of any value to you?"

"You fly."

"Don't you also fly?"

"You make me laugh. I hop like a frog, I glide like a squirrel, I flutter like a cockroach. You fly, I seen you. School me in the flying arts."

"That's a tall order. I'm not sure it can be done."

"Why not? You school your uptown students."

"But they're human. They have human souls. You…"

"I have a *soul!*" The pain of a million years of discrimination pulsated in her hoarse cry. "My mother bedded Adam. *Your* Adam. Is that soul

180

enough for you?"

"Yes," said Abulafia with new respect. "You have a soul and I should be able to teach you to fly. Now, what can you trade in exchange for my valuable service?"

"*How* valuable?" Her kind had been swindled out of their birthright by humans, and she expected only the worst from so-called men of God.

"My usual fee is fifty thousand dollars."

"Merely to learn to fly?"

"It's never *merely* learning to fly. We cover a lot of ground before my students can even attempt levitation. It's a fair price."

"My information is *worth* fifty thousand."

"Let's hear it." Lionel Abulafia sat up and straightened the skullcap on his white, scraggly hair. Habitually, he wound his white and yellow side curls tightly around his index finger.

Victoria Martin entered the room and removed the blue enamel laver to replace it with a tray of sugar cookies—her own recipe. The buttery morsels had earned her first prize in six consecutive Annual American Royal International Cookie Competitions (she was begged not to enter a seventh time).

The lilith grabbed two under the large woman's watchful gaze, before Victoria swept from the room with the full water bowl. Leaping back to the top of the bookstand, the lilith continued, her mouth grinding and speaking at the same time: "I spotted her tonight. Here, in the neighborhood."

"Her?"

"*Her.*"

"Oh, my God, she's coming to me," the elderly mystic teacher whispered. His eyes became very moist all of a sudden. "How is she?" he demanded.

"Not good. Bad leg. Maybe crazy, too, I think."

"I expect she might be by now, poor girl. Where did she go?"

"I seen her crossing over to the Park. Methinks she sleeps in the amphitheater, with the bums. Near running water. It's safe, most nights."

Then the tiny lilith raised her pretty head and smiled, exposing two pearly fangs. "I saves her from a car, you know."

"Is that so?"

"You don't believe me?"

"Let's go check her out," Lionel Abulafia said with sudden urgency.

"Have we a deal?" The lilith held firm.

"Sure, sure we do. What's your name?"

"Why?" She froze in mid-act of rising from her seat, with renewed suspicion.

"You don't have to tell me. I was just wondering what I should call you."

"Stick with Lilith for now," she instructed hoarsely. "And don't get any bright ideas."

The two of them emerged from Lionel Abulafia's doorway a few minutes later, he in his black and white street clothes, she as she had entered, in a sort of body-tight black thing that emphasized her chest and hips and made her seem somehow taller and bigger than her actual stature.

Victoria was waiting for them at the front door. She handed Lionel Abulafia his round, tattered, weekday black hat. "Should I wait up?" she asked.

He raised his eyes to meet hers. "She's here, in the park," he said, in uninhibited excitement. "You want to come along, Victoria?"

"If it's all the same to you, I'll wait here," the giant woman said and examined Lionel Abulafia's new companion. "Is it safe to go with this one, though?" she asked, as an afterthought.

"I resent that!" The lilith whispered in protest.

"Go, get some rest, Victoria, you'll have plenty of new people to insult in the morning," said Lionel Abulafia and went out to the hall. The lilith followed.

Victoria shrugged and closed the door behind them. She wanted to enjoy some quietude; she was certain that her skills would be required later that evening.

64.

A sniper had left Lionel Abulafia's study hall with the other students late that night. Snipers first began to appear in America's streets a dozen years earlier. They proliferated to such a degree that most public establishments, such as restaurants, theaters and hotels, commonly advertised the installation of special safety features to protect patrons from being targeted on their way to and from their cars.

The snipers viewed their role in society in a slightly different way than did the suicide and other bombers. The latter saw their acts as educational, terrorizing the populace to the point of a mass rejection of the current state of things. The snipers viewed themselves as human coyotes, thinning the human herd of anyone they found undesirable; if a target looked vulnerable enough to die without much of a hassle, they sprang into action. Our particular sniper considered the task a divine calling.

An entire genre of instructive literature developed on the best way to dress, walk, talk, eat, drink and otherwise behave in public, to avoid the wrath of the snipers. Truth be told, the value of these sniper-aid books was not in providing real, useful information, because the randomness of sniping incidents suggested that such information didn't exist. Sniper-aid books were useful because they gave the populace a sense of control over events. If the sniper got you, it was because of some mistake in your attire, or the way you put out your cigarette in public (imagine that, smoking in the open, right there in the street, it was like she was asking for it), and not because Death was let loose on the public places of America, toppling men, women, and children without distinction.

Why did the sniper attend Lionel Abulafia's class? Was it human? Was it demonic? What need did this messenger of violent expiration have for the teachings of the great master? What was the point of learning the secrets of the universe, only to spend the rest of one's time extinguishing life?

But there you had it, a spiritually inclined, urbane mass-murderer. The sniper walked around the corner of East Broadway and Clinton toward a dark-green Jaguar. Opening the trunk, the sniper took out a briefcase. In the sniper's mind it had long since become the Holy Briefcase, the one whose contents were used in advancing the cause of God.

The sniper stepped into the corner building and ran up the six flights to the rooftop with little difficulty. One thing few people imagined about the coyote snipers: They spent hours upon hours each day keeping in shape. When the moment of truth came, when that one lucky law enforcement person had figured out their location, they either reacted like lightning or went down.

From the rooftop, the sniper observed the small group of humans and super beings still assembled outside Lionel Abulafia's building in the dim, pre-dawn light. The sniper opened the briefcase and in moderate, methodical fashion, assembled the parts of the Panther 308 high-powered rifle that were stored inside.

But the sniper wasn't aiming for these classmates. Across the street, in a dark van, several government agents maintained a surveillance of Lionel Abulafia and his students. They had received a tip regarding a clandestine meeting between the individual known as The Girl and the Lower

East Side holy man. It was time to thin this little herd, the coyote sniper concluded.

Perhaps there *was* some rationale for all the murders committed by all the thousands of snipers on all of America's rooftops. Perhaps the definitive common denominator to all the killings was the victim's momentary foolishness. Perhaps if we went back and analyzed every single case of public execution by high-powered rifle, they were all about a truly merciful thinning of the herd after all. In this case, the surveillance team's faux pas was the choice of a Boar's Head logo for their clandestine van, on the most Jewish block in the Lower East Side.

Metal-piercing bullets tore through the fake van in two speedy clusters of six each and all four agents died almost as one. Did the sniper feel satisfaction at a job well done? Not necessarily. Random snipers were motivated by the idea that they provided a valuable service; they did society a favor by removing its dimmer members from the gene pool.

But not all of them drove Jaguars.

65.

God's malevolent side was not the only mythical creature looking to quash any attempt to bring history to its conclusion. A resident of Brooklyn for several decades now, who flaunted an exotic assortment of flowing robes and scarves, Al Qaedar had the bronzed face of a genuine archangel. Tall and handsome, this creature was capable of uprooting mountains and, on occasion, could even make the sun stop in its track.

Tonight, this powerful entity was sitting at a tiny round table in a juice bar on Fourteenth Street. He sucked on liquefied papaya and coconut and brooded darkly. Ever since the 7th century, when believers had outlawed the drinking of alcohol, his general disposition had taken on a kind of permanent gloom. He was still able to enjoy the rising sweet smoke of fat Lebanese hashish, but nothing compared to the fumes of a good cognac, particularly when the last time you sniffed any was thirteen hundred years ago.

According to THE CABALIST'S HANDBOOK OF PRACTICAL MESSIANIC REDEMPTION:

Al Qaedar began his life as a local desert deity down in the Arabian peninsula. Then, nearly four thousand years ago, Hagar, the Pharaoh's daughter, came to

Grandfather Abraham and Grandmother Sarah seeking their teachings.

At the time, Abraham and Sarah ran a kind of monotheistic revival show, which started back in Mesopotamia and continued to draw huge crowds as they traveled across the Syrian desert, down to Canaan. Wherever they pitched their tent, Abraham and Sarah taught the locals about the discovery of a singular God who ran the universe, and reception was, without exception, excellent. The proceeds were also excellent, and the two became immensely wealthy.

Their tour of Egypt was more successful than all their former engagements put together, especially after God Himself had to step in to force the Pharaoh to keep his hands off Sarah. Grandmother Sarah was the most beautiful woman who ever lived—which was another reason the show was such a hit.

So Hagar, the Pharaoh's daughter, ran away with the circus, so to speak.

"I'm better off as a slave to this couple than as princess of all Egypt," she declared. For that, the universe owed her a debt of gratitude.

And Ishmael, the son she bore Abraham, was the first male child ever to be circumcised on God's command. That's two debts of gratitude.

Nevertheless, when the archangel Al Qaedar was appointed heavenly governor of the Ishmaelites, he voiced grave reservations.

"In the end," he argued, "the Jews will rule and my nation will revert to being slaves."

He and God were in the heavenly sauna at the time. God was still deliberating His notion of Steam. During the creation of the world there was a moment when everything transformed from pure light into substance, and the first tangible element was hot air. Ever since that moment God had a fascination with condensation.

"It's not such a sure thing, you know," God said. "I'll admit I am bound to the Jews with a covenant, but come Apocalypse time, all bets are off."

Bursts of electricity rose out of Al Qaedar in a marvelous interplay of light and reflected light, beams cut into beams, sparks shot into the dark cosmos. He knew he was being sold a bill of goods. Still, when you're the "small-g" god of vast empty deserts, any change in status, however temporary, is a big improvement.

Now here he was, archangel in charge of one fifth of the planet's population, and Apocalypse was suddenly around the corner. He knew he had to move fast, or the new millennium would see him give up his high post, his private choir, all-expenses-paid trips to Mecca, and the virgins, man, oh man, the virgins…

Like all supernatural creatures, Al Qaedar was well aware of the appearance of The Girl a year earlier. Even before news spread regarding her intriguing capabilities, the feisty archangel understood that the future of his people hinged upon her destruction. He ordered dozens of his secret teams to set aside all bombing operations and go looking for The Girl.

After all, he argued, what good would the collapse of the West do, if the new emerging power would end up being not his people, but the Jews, marshaled by this mysterious female?

Still, each time his men attacked, The Girl evaded them. Al Qaedar was sickened by his growing sensation that she was not only a mystical creature, but represented a kind of divine fix which even *he* could not shake loose. Memories of the sauna meeting with the Creator of the universe came back to haunt him. Was he assigned the role of history's patsy? Look at the great Al Qaedar, too impotent to off a little Jewish girl.

He received intelligence from his people in downtown Manhattan the day before. The Girl was presently located on the Lower East Side. That very night she had torpedoed his plan to bring down a considerable portion of the New York metropolitan area with a nuclear device.

This left him in such a rage at his men, that he ordered a suicide bombing raid on Gracie Mansion, the historic uptown residence of New York's mayors—just to watch some humans being mowed down. Now his mood was improved. He sensed that The Girl was still in the downtown neighborhood.

"It's time to kill," he said quietly and stood up. Goodness, what he would have given for a nice glass of Martel.

66.

Sarah, Abraham's beautiful wife, had a fabulous idea, says THE CABALIST'S HANDBOOK OF PRACTICAL MESSIANIC REDEMPTION.

Since she was too old to bear a child (she was in her late seventies at the time), she would hand over Hagar, who had become her maidservant, for Abraham to beget a child. Everybody involved were sophisticated adults and so the deal went through. Hagar became pregnant with what would be Abraham's first-born son.

But as soon as the slave girl bore the master's seed, she began to lord over her mistress. The stuff of soap operas, right in your own family Bible.

So Sarah said to Abraham, "I'm totally upset with you, man of my life. I allowed you my maid, and as soon as the little hussy conceived, she's making like she's the boss and I'm the maid. Is this fair, I ask you?"

Abraham had no doubts as to who was right and who was wrong, who was the wife and who was the maid. He said, "Take your slave girl and do with her as you please." Which Sarah proceeded to do. She became one bitchy boss, who turned Hagar's life into a living hell, until the poor thing fled the revival tent trailer park and disappeared in the desert.

The archangel Al Qaedar found her in the wilderness, crying her eyes out on top of some well. You must understand, he was worried. She represented all his prospects at this point. If she died now, his own career would be cut extremely short. So he came down from heaven, dressed in a flowing black abaya, tinseled in gold, with a long, curved, golden shabariya hanging from his belt.

And he asked, "Hagar, where are you coming from, and where are you going?"

And she said, "I flee from the face of my mistress Sarah."

And the archangel Al Qaedar grabbed the pregnant girl by her shoulders, made her stare directly into his glowing face and said, "Hagar, listen to me. I'm going to ask you to do something really hard, but you will see that the rewards will be immeasurable. I want you to go back to your mistress, and submit to whatever hardship she will put you through."

The girl began a tearful protest, but Al Qaedar would have none of it. He gently covered her mouth with his swarthy hand and continued, "You're going to have a son. And he will become the head of a great and numerous nation. And you will name him Ishmael, which in Hebrew means "God will Listen." Whenever your offspring will cry out the name of God, they will be answered. I have it on the Highest Authority."

Then the archangel expanded a little on the kind of person Hagar's son would be. Basically, he painted a picture of a wild man, feisty, quarrelsome, some unresolved ego issues, but, like Hagar, capable of self-sacrifice. A kind of big-hearted hood.

"In the end," Al Qaedar promised the expecting mother, "there will be a struggle for the eternal domination of the world. Eternal, you hear me? And my money is on your son, Ishmael."

The poor girl was beside herself with glee and fear, awe and anticipation. At last, she accepted her lot and returned to the camp of Abraham and Sarah.

Al Qaedar had accomplished his first mission. For the next few millennia his job would be to follow his initial success to its natural conclusion and hope for a good end run. But the foundation was solid, he and every supernatural creature out there already knew. A mother who was prepared to eat crow for the sake of her child's future promised as bright a start as one could hope for.

67.

Lionel Abulafia and the lilith rolled down the soggy, grassy hill towards the amphitheater's cement stage. A few trash can fires flickered in the thick fog. At least one hundred homeless men and women stood, walked around, sang, preached, or leaned against the stage's enormous orchestra shell. A few slept on the damp concrete.

A small group was sitting in what looked like a grotesque medical center. There were five of them, covered in festering lesions. They were all removing their bandages and replacing them with fresh dressings. It wasn't clear where they could have gotten these large packages of gauze, but most of them were still in the original vacuum packing, and sealed with a red band.

Several supermarket carts were parked nearby, most of them loaded with every conceivable household object, from toaster to desktop computer. One was packed only with soda cans.

The young woman the lilith pointed to was dressing her wounds in a different manner than the others. While the rest of the people first removed all the old, soiled bandages and then replaced them with clean ones, this woman removed her old gauzes one at a time, replacing each bandage and then proceeding to take off the next one.

"Why is she changing them one bandage at a time?" the lilith asked.

"So she can pick up and go without delay if she gets called," Lionel Abulafia said. "She's the genuine article, you know."

"I saw it right away," the lilith confirmed. "She was looking different places with her left and right eyes. Like a chameleon."

Lionel Abulafia gave her a sidelong look. "How did you know that?"

"Everybody knows," she said, and recited what sounded like a children's ditty: "*She'll be looking at the clouds / And her right eye, yeah / Would get dark before her left / Before her left eye, yeah.*"

Lionel Abulafia led his companion along the moist grass. The lilith kept pace with him. "What now?" she asked.

"Now we find out why I was summoned here."

Meanwhile, on stage, an old man in a rain-drenched military coat gave his testimonial under the cover of the orchestra shell. The young woman was tending to her lacerations, half-listening with a satisfied smile on her pretty face. One or two other listeners applauded politely, which caused the old man to burst into tears of gratitude. A few of the people onstage ushered him down, where a makeshift assembly line fed washed soda cans into a machine that turned them into strips of sheet metal. The production area was covered by scraps of wood and metal in lean-to fashion, which for onlookers maintained the appearance of yet another homeless person's dwelling.

"Welcome to the cooperative," an elderly woman in a bright-red wool scarf said to the newcomer and favored him with a big smile. She helped him roll his loaded cart to the washing area. "Get these ready for processing, then go register. You'll need health insurance, I assume? And I want you to look at our housing complex on Rivington Street. As a new member of the cooperative, you're entitled to share a studio apartment. Any questions?"

"Yes, one question, how can you afford all this?"

The elderly woman's smile broadened considerably. "It's The Girl. She showed up here one day and changed our lives. Look," she opened her mouth and the newcomer could see her neat set of pearly teeth. "This mouth was an empty cave, like yours, only a few months ago. But The Girl came and taught the street people how to trade with our metal. We're not rich yet, but we already live like human beings."

Lionel Abulafia and the lilith followed this conversation and many similar ones around the grass lawn and the amphitheater. "Isn't she wonderful?" the old master marveled, his eyes bright with excitement.

"Very unusual," the lilith admitted.

"She certainly is, " Lionel Abulafia said. "You should have met her father. He was without equal."

68.

"Here's how you see voices," Lionel Abulafia began the lessons for his new charge, the lilith. They sat on the grass at the East River Park amphitheater, watching the young homeless woman Nechama Gutkind mingle with her peers. In the meantime, Lionel Abulafia figured he would start the lilith on Spiritual Navigation 101.

"Sound and a sight both begin at the same place, both being the result of Divine Desire. What is Divine Desire?"

The tiny female closed her eyes and rummaged through her heart for the words: "It's anything that happens any time any place."

"Very good, you're way ahead of most of my other students! Next: Our flesh is conditioned to perceive some things as sights, others as sounds. But we can disregard our conditioning. How do we do that?"

With her eyes still shut, the lilith said, "By dropping our protective impulse, our imagination. Imagination changes everything you see into a story, so you can make sense of it."

Lionel Abulafia's voice now attained a sing-song quality, like an incantation, as both he and the lilith were sinking into a colorless, shapeless void. "Hear only the sounds, don't try to make sense out of them. What do you hear?"

"Traffic, here and there..."

"'Traffic' is not a sound, it's an explanation. Hear the *sounds*, not their names."

Now she began to hear horns, roaring engines, flying pebbles, clicking switch boxes, rattling garbage can covers and finally, the screeching of car wheels on rough pavement, followed by furious footsteps.

"What's the color of the screeching object?" Abulafia queried.

"Dark green," the lilith said the first thing that materialized in her mind.

"And the footsteps?"

"Streaks of blue against silver."

"The clanging metal?"

"Dirty copper."

"Do you see the sounds advancing?"

"Yes, they're about four city blocks from here... maybe five... more like ten... Running diagonally through baseball fields and tennis courts. Others are coming across the overpass."

"Now focus on all those very colorful sounds the way you might focus on a stereoscope until the images converge to become three-dimensional. It's the same principle, really..."

"What's a stereoscope, Lionel Abulafia?"

The aged master sighed. Cultural barriers, that's all he had to deal with, day and night. "It's an image viewer, haven't you ever seen one? They used to be very common in my youth..."

"Lionel Abulafia, I perch under bridges..."

"Fine, I understand. Just listen until you can see real-life pictures in your head. I promise you, this is how it works..."

Suddenly, the darkness in her optic center came to life with bright-white on a chalkboard-green grid, displaying the unmistakable advance of many men and women who rushed up the grassy hill behind her back. And just as suddenly, a pall came over the greenish projection and all of it vanished, sights and sounds alike.

"Some bad people are coming, Lionel Abulafia," she squeaked in panic. But when she opened her eyes, Abulafia was already trotting downhill towards the stage.

"Wait *up!*" she rasped and began leapfrogging across the rows of seats.

A team of men and women in dark suits, carrying automatic weapons and complicated communications gear, appeared over the hilltop. They moved quickly, hunched forward and grim faced, and spread in several paths to surround the stage.

Penny Brown scanned the amphitheater stage for anyone with red hair. Her screen revealed two possible targets, one a woman in her sixties, the other much younger.

"I've got her," Brown reported over the comm/link. "Straight ahead, smack in the middle of the stage, the one wrapping those bandages on her leg..."

"Everybody, move, move, move," Chief Hammonton ordered into his mouthpiece and rushed forward. "Circle the stage and wait for a final positive ID. Remember, she evaded us easily the first time. Let's focus."

Jonah Simpson moved more slowly than the rest of his team. He recognized the redhead on stage as his own Nechama. It was hard to believe that the wretched woman on stage was the lovely creature who shared the magic of life with him that very evening. And that this same woman, bandaged leg and all, was the cartoon heroine he had first discovered in a primordial forest on East Fifth Street.

What would be the point in killing her? She was the loveliest creature he had ever laid his eyes on, it made no sense. A national security threat? The Girl?

Lagging behind, Jonah was the only one on his THRUST team to spot the group of several hundred dark figures advancing stealthily through the park trees toward the grass lawn above the amphitheater. Irregulars.

"Intruder alert," he whispered into his comm/link. "We're surrounded, look back—"

The THRUST team stopped dead in its tracks and Hammonton ordered everyone down. The folks on stage had not yet seen either the small group in black fatigues up close or the much larger army of men by the tree line.

But the Irregulars, the new official tag for the former terrorists now fighting alongside Coalition forces, were cognizant of the THRUST's delay and they, too, stopped and hugged the damp ground.

"You know what I think?" Jerry Osmond ventured. "They aren't here to fight us; they're here to make sure we do the job right. Somebody's taken out an insurance policy on this mission."

"How do you know?" whispered Penny Brown.

"I've seen these guys when they actually try to stop somebody—they don't hold back."

Hammonton acknowledged his man's observation, and couldn't help wondering if his own boss, Anita Lopes, had been the one to take out this insurance policy. It was in keeping with her warning regarding the top priority of the mission. Still, it stung.

Jonah Simpson had been trained to notice when he was being approached stealthily from behind by a 130-year-old man, who then planted a gnarled, bony hand over his mouth and toppled him with a kick behind the knees. But, alas, 130 years of experience trump special training.

"Shush," Lionel Abulafia warned him and helped him to a sitting position.

"They're going to kill her," Jonah whispered.

"I told you to shush. Nobody's killing nobody," the ancient man assured him. "You, come with me."

"But there's a whole army back there," Jonah protested, keeping his voice low and his hand over his comm/link.

Abulafia grabbed him by the lapel and brought Jonah's face uncomfortably close. "Listen to me, *schmendrik*," he said slowly and with great emphasis on each word. "God *Himself* can't kill this girl, you got it?"

As they walked away, a kindly looking red-haired gentleman in black fatigues followed them with his glowing gaze. "The old fool," he murmured discontentedly. "But now—bigger fish to fry."

69.

Lionel Abulafia led Jonah Simpson to the northern end of the grass lawn, near the FDR Drive. The rain was now heavy and relentless, but they were both too tired to pay attention to the elements. Jonah was wondering silently just how long he'd continue to put his blind trust in the man holding his hand. Then he reminded himself that, earlier, this man's hand had saved his life.

When they reached the fence separating the park from the highway, Abulafia steered him into some shelter under a beech tree.

"Now I'll teach you one more path into the *pardes*," the shabby cabalist said, and without hesitation inserted a stiff piece of rolled up cardboard into Jonah's nostril. The powder inside the cardboard tore right through

Jonah's brain, painting his soul hot red.

Jonah groaned, and made an urgent mental note to stop the old man next time he tried to shove anything else up his nose. Then he found himself next to Abulafia at the heart of an endless, muddy plateau, gray-brown and sparkling in the light of a murky, silver moon.

An elderly Jew in a black, knee-length coat and a wide fedora stood in the middle of a shallow pool at the center of the plateau, with tears streaming from his eyes. His white beard, which split in two somewhere near the middle, was completely drenched in the tears. A closer look revealed that the pool around the old man was knee-high with those tears. The man had been standing and crying for twenty-one years.

Drip - drop - drip - drop, more tears fell into the pool. Above, the sky was the color of copper. Feathery, hoary clouds passed by and cast frazzled moon shadows.

A weeping willow grew on the bank of the pool of tears. Crowds of black birds were perched there. They were demons who over the years had taken to spending their breaks in this place, examining the endlessly crying Jew with jaundiced eyes. When enough of them were gathered, they often joined together in mock revelry: "*Long live our master, our teacher and our rabbi, King Messiah for ever and eternity...*"

There was no mistaking the old man's identity. He was the late grand master of Brooklyn. Even Jonah Simpson was familiar with his famous countenance, which in some New York neighborhoods was as popular as the cross-legged Buddha, or Jesus on the cross.

The bird-shaped demons were having much fun, slapping their black wings on their foul thighs and rotating on their perched talons around the droopy willow branches like deranged bats. The song they mangled was the same ditty which stirred messianic fervor in thousands of hearts a mere 21 years before.

"Hey, Messiah," the demons yelled out, "*Deiner hoisen is schoin nas, gay schoin arain.*" *Your pants are wet, go inside already.*

"He's arm-wrestling with God, you know," Abulafia explained. "The demons are trying to break his spirit, make him give up."

"Poor man," Jonah said and stepped towards the old mystic in the pool. His companion grabbed him by the wrist again and pulled him back with crushing strength.

"Here you don't do nothing unless I say so, got it?" Abulafia hissed. "Misstep up here, and you won't ever leave."

Jonah froze in his place. "I didn't ask to come here," he whispered in near-panic.

"Why not? It's very different, no?" the older man stated wryly.

He told Jonah that, on occasion, other visitors had been known to come by. In most cases it would be an angel, who whispered something into the crying man's ear. The master always nodded in refusal and the angel would walk away with drooping wings. Other times it was a dreamer, who wandered over as his soul was visiting the higher worlds.

The dreamers never forgot the sight of the crying master, according to Abulafia. By now there were thousands of them, all of whom reported seeing the master in his pool of tears.

Jonah asked why the grand master was subjected to such unseemly conditions. Before the old mystic had a chance to respond, the two of them were treated to a spontaneous floor show, with demons hopping and floating, light beams appearing from nowhere and an invisible band striking a fast, sweeping Hungarian *chardash* dance. It was obvious the local creatures enjoyed this, and looked for the merest excuse to put on a show.

One of the demonic birds shape-shifted to become a tall and massive Jew, in a wide-brimmed black hat, a coat with flying tails and an exuberant, crowd-pleasing disposition. He grabbed a mike and said hoarsely, in a mild Eastern European accent: "Welcome, ladies and gentlemen, to the annual 'We Want Moshiach Now Telethon.' We have an evening packed with entertainment for you, and remember, it's not what you keep in your wallet that counts, it's what you keep in here—" and the demon-turned-Cosmic-Wisdomnik cartoon pounded his chest, "in your Jewish heart, that *really* counts! And now, without further ado, allow me to introduce the one, the only: Messiah!"

The great light beams turned on the ancient man in the pool of tears. He blinked a few times under the harsh illumination, then covered his face and continued to cry.

"Well, maybe he is the messiah and maybe he isn't, but he's spent the last twenty-one years of his death standing here, refusing to go into the Garden of Eden unless God brings redemption to the world..." the demon announced in a heart-broken voice.

"A very dedicated bunch, aren't they?" said Abulafia. "It's all part of the campaign to break him down."

The demon rediscovered his cheerful inflection and continued:

"What devotion, ladies and gentlemen, why the sheer stamina of the

194

man should impress you, not to speak of his righteousness, integrity and, don't let me forget—vision! Please make your checks payable to Friends of Moshiach, and have a grand evening, as we bring on our first number. She was a pop singer, did drugs and hobnobbed with the greats of Rock n' Roll, until she discovered her Jewish roots and now she's back in the fold. Let's give it all up for Rita Coolidge!"

Incidentally, THE CABALIST'S HANDBOOK OF PRACTICAL MESSIANIC RE-DEMPTION states:

> Two-time Grammy winner Rita Coolidge did not have Jewish roots in the conventional sense. She was born in Lafayette, Tennessee, the daughter of a Baptist minister who married the organ player of his church. But Rita was one of the rare souls who have not been reincarnated since the human race was expelled from the Garden of Eden. Her soul was directly related to the soul of our mother Eve. The great R & B musician Leon Russell hinted at that quality when he dedicated his song Delta Lady to her, with the revealing lyrics: Please don't ask how many times I found you / Standing wet and naked in the Garden....
>
> Coolidge indeed hobnobbed with the greats of Rock n' Roll, like Eric Clapton, George Harrison, Joe Cocker, Bob Dylan and Jimi Hendrix, and was even described, in a Times of London article from the mid-eighties, as possessing "the sexiest voice in the world."
>
> The demon who invited her to sing at the grotesque fundraiser on the master's plane was a direct son of Adam. It just so happened that his mother, and the brave lilith's mother, were one and the same.
>
> Yes, it truly is a small netherworld.

70.

The cabalist master's somewhat melodramatic handling of the afterlife has been reported by many. When the master was still alive and in full control of his body, he had declared his determination not to enter heaven until the messiah arrived. He planned to use that ploy as a bargaining chip with God.

Of course, the master was not the first righteous man to try this sort of arm-wrestling with God. But if the reports about his standoff are accurate— and we have no reason to assume they are not—then he managed to go farther than any of his predecessors. A tied score in a struggle with God is nothing to scoff at.

According to some reports, the master's heavenly neighbors were upset by the entire hullabaloo, and a few already complained to the highest authority.

This, too, may have been a first in heaven's history.

What wasn't being reported by the dreamers is the following bit of divine politics:

Two weeks or so before the cabalist master's final stroke, a Jewish doctor in Hebron killed twenty-nine Muslims in the Cave of Machpela, resting place of the Hebrew patriarchs. To date it isn't clear what motivated the bloody event. Perhaps it was the result of the man's exacerbated rage.

Such a massacre had occurred once before, in 1929, when dozens of Torah scholars, along with their wives and children, sixty-seven Jews altogether, were slaughtered and mutilated by an Arab mob.

The problem was that the Muslims who were killed in the cave passed from the earthly plane with the index fingers of their right hands pointing to heaven, to signify the oneness of God. Stunts like these go a long way in heaven.

It turns out that God, who accepts only the purest of thoughts and actions from Jews, is far less critical when it comes to gentiles in general, and the sons of Ishmael in particular.

The very name, *Yishma-El*, "God will listen" in Hebrew, suggests that the sons of Ishmael don't need to be right in order for God to hear their pleas, it's enough that they be very loud.

Only a few minds were aware of the connection between the deaths of the Hebron physician and the grand master. And those that were would not speak about it, not even to God.

But then, nobody except God, and one or two archangels, knew that after a mere two years of an afterlife, the terminally restless soul of that same doctor was reincarnated in the body of baby Ben Markowitz.

71.

Two members of Hammonton's team, Jerry and Dawn, hopped on the stage in their dark fatigues at the same time. They rushed the young homeless woman with the bandaged left leg and expertly disabled her, bracing her arms behind her back. She kicked, she screamed, but she didn't get away.

A dozen supermarket carts were tossed aside, empty soda cans and piles of additional objects that defied identification spilled out and rolled every which way. The stage by now had been cleared of the terrified vagrants, who continued to watch the violence from the nearby bushes. As much as they loved and admired The Girl, they couldn't stand up for her before a team of professional assassins. The newly-learned independence easily disappeared from their minds when old survival habits reasserted themselves.

The rest of the team now circled the homeless woman. A silent game of cat and mouse ensued, in which the woman attempted to find a crack in the wall of her tormentors, and they, in turn, defeated her leaps to freedom.

Hammonton got a message through the comm/link to his boss, Anita Lopes: "The prey is at hand, please instruct."

Back in her office, Lopes scanned the five-minute-old satellite image of the East River Park amphitheater.

Lopes' superior, General James Bixie, was a tall and muscular man with sandy, close-cropped hair and a leathery neck that stuck out of his black THRUST uniform. He pointed at the screen. "What's this little army behind them, in the woods?"

"Irregulars," she said and looked up at him. "I thought *you* called them in."

"Why would I do *that*?"

"In case my guys screwed up."

"Anita, I would never do something like that without proper notification."

"Like hell."

"Well, I didn't. And if neither of *us* invited them, who did?"

"Not sure," said Lopes, "but I don't think it's prudent to proceed without proper reinforcement. They outnumber my team twenty to one, easily."

"If they wanted their own piece of The Girl, they would have moved in a long time ago."

"Maybe they can't," ventured Lopes.

"Explain."

Lopes sighed. "This young woman is not easily killable, Sir. Earlier tonight, my team spotted her and tried to run her over, clean and simple."

"And?"

"Not so clean, not so simple. A creature out of hell jumped on their windshield, the driver lost it and the van was wrecked. Maybe these irregulars have already tried to off her, failed just like us, and expect the government to do the job."

"That's free enterprise for you," Bixie complained. "When push comes to shove, everybody wants Uncle Sam to pull their chestnuts out of the fire..."

Lopes spoke into her comm/link, "David, don't stand down, don't execute. Keep her surrounded, but don't kill, I repeat, do not kill."

"The target is circled, boss," Hammonton informed her.

"Yes, I understand. Also, David, take a look at the tree line behind you—you've got company."

"I know," Hammonton said. "I thought you sent them to keep an eye on us..."

"You trust me so little?" Lopes's voice stopped just short of a full-throttle whine. "For the record, Lieutenant, they're not with us, and we have no idea what they're up to."

When the three hundred or so figures rose from their hiding places around the amphitheater in their black Ninja suits they looked like a dark wave, rolling downhill. The THRUST team onstage froze, and the homeless woman decided this was her chance to flee. But a pair of massive arms grabbed and immobilized her.

The Archangel Al Qaedar, who followed the special government team from a distance, and sported the same dark outfit as the mortals, was troubled by the sudden appearance of Lionel Abulafia right outside the circle of agents. The last thing he needed was direct confrontation with the old man. He kept his face veiled with a spell that he hoped would prove effective.

Ignoring everyone and everything on stage and behind his back, Abulafia concentrated on the lilith. He grabbed the tiny creature by the shoulder and pulled her towards him with great force. "Do you know what I want you to do now?" he demanded.

"Only if you guarantee my life."

"I can do that, but you'll have to tell me your name."

"Lydia Hoffschteter."

He gave her a quizzical look.

"It's a long story..."

"I need your mother's name, too..."

"Lilith."

Al Qaedar saw the Jew reach into his pocket and pull out a book of Psalms, no doubt in order to cast a protective incantation. This was very bad, because the trick to making it to the finals of World Domination was in sticking to some pretense of virtue. Al Qaedar couldn't afford to engage in an open confrontation with a powerful holy man, whose merits outweighed his own. It was time for decisive counteraction.

Al Qaedar spoke the kill command into his own mouthpiece, in such perfect imitation of Hammonton's voice that the Chief himself soon accepted that it was he who had given the order. In an instant, the homeless woman was embraced from the back again, without hope of escape. A blade appeared in the hand of one of the attackers, who grabbed the woman by the hair and slashed her throat.

An instant later the assassins were gone and the woman lay in a shiny pool of blood at center stage.

As Samael and Al Qaedar each hopped into their respective black vans, each caught a glimpse of the other and did a memorable celestial double-take.

"You!" said the Prince of Darkness in disgust.

"You!" The archangel of all Arabs spat contemptuously.

Their vehicles took off in opposite directions, but each celestial creature made an urgent mental note to get the other's files pulled, before the final attack on Jerusalem.

"Get an ambulance," Lionel Abulafia yelled at the homeless men and women who gingerly returned to the scene of the murder.

She had trusted him. He had promised to protect her during the switch. He picked up the body with its lifeblood ebbing away and hugged it in both his arms. Wading in the blood, he sat back on his heels and placed his hands on the wounded throat in an attempt to stanch the bleeding. He squeezed with just the right measure of strength and gentleness. "Such a brave little lilith," he said, and examined the face of the dying Lydia Hoffschteter with outpouring compassion. "Such a brave little lilith..."

Victoria Martin's voice emerged in his head. She was in Lionel Abulafia's living room above his study hall, using two tall white candles to help her focus. She made them rise just an inch above the small coffee table before her, then caused the two flames to separate from their wicks, float in an amusing circle, and return to their rightful place.

She sipped from her cup of hot cinnamon tea. Lionel Abulafia could sense the hot liquid's spiciness in her thoughts and was filled with a longing for a cup of his own. But time was short, the desire for tea would have to wait.

"What?" she asked, curtly.

"Murder," he answered.

"Park?" she checked.

"Park," he confirmed.

"Arabs?" she asked.

"Arabs," he confirmed.

"Government?" she asked.

"Could be. Saw Al Qaedar," he told her.

"Bastard," she hissed.

"With government!"

"New connection."

"Yes."

"Girl hurt?" Victoria asked, worried.

"No! Lilith!"

"?"

"Volunteered."

"Price?"

"Never mind."

"Help?"

"Bleeding."

"I come?" Victoria already knew the answer.

"Please..."

"I come."

Now there was nothing to do but wait; for the ambulance, for his big-boned housekeeper, and for the grace of Heaven. Lionel Abulafia bent his body forward until his chin touched his crotch, and began to beg for the lilith's life. Turning himself into a sphere—with his beginning melting into his midsection in an uninterrupted fashion—Lionel Abulafia was able to connect with the very foundation of the universe.

And as Abulafia was considered to be the crotch of the entire world—his divine, gushing benevolence provided a steady source of universal nourishment—one can only imagine how much life force he radiated.

72.

According to THE CABALIST'S HANDBOOK OF PRACTICAL MESSIANIC REDEMPTION:

The universe was volleyed into existence like a fine net of phosphorous fiber, and well before it reached its outermost stretch, it had already initiated the process of returning to the bosom of its Maker. This was possible because the universal ability to return was created together with the universal ability to spring forth into existence, and both had been there well before the universe itself materialized.

Like a golden boomerang, the universe was flung into the void, which reflected none of its majestic shimmer. Vibrating with exhilaration, the universe turned on its own axis in the course of its outward flight and was already in mid-course back. Out it went and in it went, all at once.

THE CABALIST'S HANDBOOK OF PRACTICAL MESSIANIC REDEMPTION cautions:

The universal ability to spring forth into existence should not be confused with the notion of an ever-expanding universe. Despite the fact that both seem to express a process leading from "smaller" to "larger," this is merely a language-based deception. In reality, the expanding universe is in a process of returning to its original state of nothingness. That is what will occur once the universe is as large as it could possibly become.

So this is how all matter behaves in this universe—it rushes to die while bursting to be born—all at once.

The secret to begging for a life is, therefore, in embracing death.

You have to be very courageous to really, urgently beg for a life. And you have to know that there's a price to pay for every part of your wish that is granted. And you have to know that only by knowing the risks of your wish do you stand a chance of being answered.

Inevitably, when begging for someone's life, an angel comes and asks you how many years from your own life you would like to donate to that person.

But Abulafia could not give away any of his years even if he wanted to—blessed as he was to stay alive until the coming of the messiah. All this meant was that he had to supplicate even harder. This tradition begs the question: When the Grand Master of Brooklyn was dying, why did no one volunteer their years for him? Because no one dared imagine that his illness was terminal. He had assured them that they would see the messiah in his lifetime: as long as they hadn't seen the messiah, how could the master die?

Then how had the master died before the messiah arrived?

Who says he did?

73.

The art of begging God for mercy was first taught to Moses by God himself, says THE CABALIST'S HANDBOOK OF PRACTICAL MESSIANIC REDEMPTION.

> God thought this was a worthwhile subject for a dissertation, so He descended in a cloud, and stood next to Moses, in a huge silence that sucked off all sound everywhere, and announced that He would now show how expert begging for mercy was done, please pay close attention.
>
> The infinitely silent cloud of God passed before Moses and proclaimed, "Adonai, Adonai, merciful and gracious, long suffering, and abundant in goodness and truth, extending mercy to thousands, forgiving iniquity and transgression and sin."
>
> Moses first hesitated, suspecting that those lines may need some editing-down for his crowd of runaway slaves. All he wanted was a good way to say, God, I'm so sorry for the mess I made, please don't kill me, give me a chance to fix it.
>
> But as God displayed signs of brewing impatience, Moses hastened to bow his head toward his crotch. Moses then recited those difficult supplications many times over, until he knew them well enough to teach to his disciples.
>
> Does this mean God is the biggest megalomaniac in the universe? You betcha'. But then, again, when you're big enough to create galaxies and black holes and spiders—the list just goes on and on—you may be entitled to a wee bit of megalomania.

When the emergency medical team first arrived at the scene of the slashing, they attempted to pry the elderly Jewish gentleman loose from his grip on the dead woman's throat. They also tried to do something similar about the enormous black lady at his side. But they soon discovered that whatever bizarre and gruesome act the two were performing was working.

They were a strange threesome. The paramedics hauled the tiny body together with Victoria, who dragged herself alongside on the ground. Lionel Abulafia stayed with them and landed lightly next to them when they were in the ambulance. Victoria and Abulafia continued to guide the female creature into death and then back into life again. By the time the ambulance reached Beth Israel the little lilith registered a pulse.

By that time, the elderly rabbi was crumpled into a near-motionless bundle of misery on the floor. He was mourning the evil that God imposed upon humanity. Like Moses, he accepted the ultimate cosmic truth: To get anything in this world, you have to kiss God's ass.

Victoria Martin found the spot in Lydia Hoffschteter's throat that could be manipulated to make her blood rush through her body at far higher rates than normal mortals could tolerate. The liliths had been formed as a kind of sketchy prototype for Humanity, before God made up His Mind to attach moral and spiritual attributes to the limbs and organs.

Hearts are in charge of generalized feelings, kidneys of morality, noses of anger, and eyes of sexual longing. A human cannot afford to have an oxygen-carrying liquid soar through his system at high velocity, because it could mop away whole segments of personality in its wake. But liliths have their entire spiritual essence well ensconced in their oversized genitalia, so that, at most, the rush of blood Victoria brought on would make a lilith feel unexpected pleasure.

The advantage of maintaining blood pressure of 600/450 is that you get adequate amounts of oxygen to the body, even after a good two-thirds of the patient's blood has been lost. Admittedly, at that rate the body isn't doing anything except remaining alive, but what more could Lionel Abulafia and his able housekeeper ask for, considering the circumstances?

Lionel Abulafia had no idea what blood type liliths had, and was about to confess the fact to the ER physician, Dr. Irena Bogdanov, but then he stopped himself, realizing the last thing he wanted was a blood test for the six thousand-year-old illegitimate daughter of Adam.

Victoria decided to take a chance. "She can receive any blood type," she told the doctor. The great African healer assumed the lilith's sturdy little body would be less finicky than human bodies when it came to blood types. Again, what else could they do?

"Oh-Negative," said the physician without missing a beat and wrote so in the patient's form.

Victoria Martin let go of the lilith's throat for the first time since the attack in the park. The cut remained unhealed, but the blood coursed too quickly through her veins to spill out.

Lionel Abulafia closed his eyes and contacted Victoria Martin. She nodded, aware of the need for utter secrecy, and lowered herself into a blue vinyl chair in the waiting room.

"Yes?"

"She'll live?"

The weariness in her master's thoughts saddened her to the point that she nearly dropped their connection. But she caught herself in time, brought her feelings up gently to a state of quiet joy and responded:

"Much bad."

"Much," he confirmed.

"She'll live. Girl?"

"Ran," he said.

"Saw Al Qaedar?"

"Saw Samael, too," he answered.

"You sleep?" Victoria asked.

"Never mind, get moving, new killings!"

"What?" she groaned mentally in response to the holy man's sudden note of urgency.

"The young man, come, they'll stop him—don't let."

"Where?" She asked.

"Now coming, now they stop him! Don't let!"

"OK, I won't let, I won't let."

The giant woman rose reluctantly from her seat. These were the least coherent marching orders she had ever received from a master, and she could tell you stories about some incoherent masters. But she understood that the old man was just on the panicky side these days, on account of the world coming to an end.

74.

When Jonah Simpson finally came to on the damp and near-frozen ground, he was shivering and his teeth would not stop rattling inside his mouth. Next to him, he expected to find Lionel Abulafia, but the ancient man was long gone.

"I feel sick," Jonah said, to no one in particular. He couldn't stop shaking. The night's damp chill had invaded his body. "I'm homeless," he reminded himself. "Oh, and AWOL from my unit. That's gotta be bad, too."

He meditated on that for a while, then said, "Boy, meeting that girl really changed my life."

Just then Shimmele Amsterdam's red and white limo chopper landed noisily on the open lawn near the Cherry Street entrance to the park and a pool of light appeared where its door opened.

"Come along, boy, time to rock and roll!" Shimmele hollered at him.

He picked up a large, white, flat cardboard box from the seat next to him.

"Kosher pizza!" he cried out in high-pitched singsong. "Come and get it!"

Jonah stood up with great difficulty. He hadn't eaten anything in many hours. The chopper took off as soon as he was seated inside.

"Where are we going?" Jonah asked and bit into his steaming slice of pizza.

"Do you know how I can afford all this?" Amsterdam answered with a question.

"You got rich followers, maybe?" Simpson guessed.

"Forget it, they're a bunch of bums, they don't have this kind of money," Amsterdam said and then told him how he had become so rich.

"It's Yossel 'Moneybags' Diamant. He's the man makes things happen for me."

Since Jonah had not yet become the expert on local Hasidic Jews his commanders wanted him to be, Amsterdam explained: Ten years earlier, the famous Wisdomnik Australian millionaire Yossel Diamant sought to expand into the field of new-age cancer care, as many religious-Jewish patients who had given up on conventional cures were eager to try experimental treatment—provided they could still eat kosher food and keep the Sabbath. As was his usual practice, Diamant looked for an insider to run the recruiting end, and Shimmele's name came up. So as long as God in His wisdom planned to keep cancer's cure to Himself, the new great mystic of Brooklyn collected ten percent on every desperate soul he could talk into going to Diamant's facility on Long Island.

As time went by, Shimmele became a useful messenger for various members of the Cosmic Wisdom movement's leadership. His good connections with the press (everybody loves a clown) couldn't be discounted either. So, all in all, he was worth every penny.

"I want you to meet Leo Graneck, one of the old master's secretaries. He has something I want him to share with you..." Shimmele Amsterdam told Simpson.

"Is this where you're taking me?" Jonah asked.

"If you don't mind..." Amsterdam sat back and wiped the olive oil from his white beard. "God damn all of them," he suddenly cursed, in a completely uncharacteristic manner. Then he smiled and added, "I mean it in a good way..."

Then Amsterdam filled Jonah in on recent Cosmic Wisdom movement history.

Rabbi Leo Graneck, now in the throes of cancer, was popularly considered the premier secretary of the late cabalist master of Brooklyn.

He was an enigma among the master's secretaries, most of whom were devoid of personal ambition and even personal color. Graneck was all charisma and drive and so, after the master's senior secretary died, Graneck naturally assumed a dominant position at the movement's "world headquarters."

Twenty-three years ago, after his master's stroke, Graneck continued to intercept the messages, requests, and questions that were still streaming in for the ailing cabalist. When rumors spread that the old man was suffering from expressive aphasia as a result of his stroke, it became crucial for Graneck to spread the notion that the master was not only alive and well, but in complete possession of his prophetic faculties.

One stormy August day, the Jewish community of Southern Florida asked if they should obey the governor's order to evacuate before the next hurricane arrived—and risk the looting of their property, which is always to be expected during a mass-evacuation. Leo Graneck told them to stay put, no harm would come to them.

"Lo and freaking behold, with minor exceptions, Jewish lives and property were spared in the hurricane," Amsterdam concluded, "which Graneck's circle proclaimed was proof of both the master's power and Graneck's privileged access. Hallelujah, we had ourselves a miracle!"

The happy-go-lucky jester-cabalist closed his eyes in an attempt to relive the events of that summer. He was humming a sweet tune, and then, when he was ready to continue, opened his heavy lids:

"But Motke Gutkind discovered it had all been a mad gamble. The bloody bastard Graneck risked the lives of thousands just to solidify his own power base. The master was running a high fever and definitely in no condition to respond to the inquiry from the Miami folks by the time Graneck came out with his supposed official instruction from the master.

Gutkind went nuts. All he could think about was the next hurricane. What would Graneck do *then*? And when Graneck was exposed as the fraud he was, what would become of the movement?"

Amsterdam smiled sadly. "They put together a *minyan*, a quorum of ten Jews—"

"I know what a *minyan* is," said Simpson.

"Good for you," said Amsterdam sweetly. "Anyway, those were the ten most powerful Wisdomnik rabbis still standing. And together they begged

God to stop Graneck."

"Stop him from doing what?"

"From becoming the next cabalist master, of course."

"They can do that? Make God do things?"

Amsterdam laughed. "They offered Him a bargain," he said. "If He stopped Graneck the monster, they'd let Him crown Shimmele the clown as the eighth master."

Jonah hadn't expected that. "But now you're friends with Granek?" he wondered.

Amsterdam turned up the flame under the chicken soup of sympathy. "He's going to die in a few weeks, despised by his colleagues, forgotten by the new generation of Cosmic Wisdomniks; a man who once rubbed elbows with prime-ministers and millionaires, now a meaningless footnote in the history books. How could I refuse him?"

"And why am I tagging along?"

"Because I haven't seen him in twenty years and, frankly, I'm a little afraid of the old bastard—and you're so young and strong.... You like the pizza?"

75.

For years it was known in the Cosmic Wisdom movement that two of the master's secretaries, Rabbis Leo Graneck and Benzion Keel, both in charge of passing letters and notes of request from the devout to the master, were barely on speaking terms with each other.

According to the THE CABALIST'S HANDBOOK OF PRACTICAL MESSIANIC REDEMPTION, in a previous incarnation, Graneck and Keel had been brothers who lived and plowed their wheat fields on Mount Moriah, a thousand years before anything of a Biblical magnitude had ever taken place there.

One of the brothers was a childless bachelor, the other had a beautiful wife and many lovely children. One night, after the harvest, the childless brother woke up and thought, "My brother has so many mouths to feed, and I have so much; let me give him half my yield." And with that he got up and collected half his bales of wheat and moved them over to his brother's plot.

It so happened that on the same night, the other brother also woke up and thought, "I'm so lucky to have my big family, and my brother has nothing to cheer him. Let me give him half my yield, at least he'll have that to make him happy." And he, too, got up and pushed half his yield over to his brother's plot.

In the morning, the two brothers discovered that they still had the same amount of wheat they had started out with and realized how great their love was for one another. And God said, "On this mountaintop I want to build My sanctuary."

In their latest incarnation, the competition between the two secretaries was at the root of their mutual animosity. Access was the name of the game; their value to individuals and institutions was weighed by the speed and quality of the responses they were able to elicit from the master of Cosmic Wisdom and to dispense to the hundreds of daily inquiries. Both Graneck and Keel were thus completely exposed to public scrutiny.

Many of the folks who chose to go through Graneck did so because of his great scholarship. The master's responses were usually laconic, often just proofing marks on the original note, meant to be studied and deciphered by the addressee. Graneck would spend a long time with some individuals, explaining the master's answers. Keel was not as learned as his competitor, but he possessed a softer, kinder personality, and many preferred pouring their hearts out to him, rather than to the more self-absorbed Graneck.

When representatives of institutions inside the world-wide Cosmic Wisdom movement needed the master's approval for their decisions—which normally touched on the fates of hundreds of people, as well as large budgets—they had to decide which of the secretaries would best represent their case before the master. This required that the secretary be familiar with their activities, understand their special needs, and get the fastest possible response from the master cabalist.

Obviously, the better either secretary performed, the stronger his position became within any given institution. By necessity, the secretary became involved in decision-making in the institutions he advocated for, to the point of a mutual dependence, as the heads of "his" institutions became his circle of supporters inside the movement.

One night, Rabbi Leo Graneck passed through Secretary Keel's office and saw the pile of faxes and letters from the master's followers on his desk.

"How unfortunate that all these requests from good, God-fearing Jews would be delayed needlessly, when an advocate such as I could be giving them a more timely treatment," he thought. "Let me help my colleague and unburden him of this toil." And with that he collected the pile of paper and took it over to his own office.

As it happened, on the same night, Rabbi Benzion Keel passed through Rabbi Graneck's office and saw an equally large pile of papers on his desk.

"How unfortunate that all these good, God-fearing Jews should receive dubious treatment for their requests," he thought. "Let me help my colleague and at the same time offer a deeper, more considerate presentation of their needs before the master." And with that he collected the pile of paper and took it to his office.

In the morning they both discovered that they still had the same number of notes as before on their desks and never spoke to each other again.

And God said, "*Déjà vu* just ain't what it used to be."

76.

"Stay on the open ramp by the synagogue," Shimmele Amsterdam instructed his pilot. "Please wait for us to come back. We may be awhile."

Jonah Simpson, in his black THRUST fatigues, and Shimmele Amsterdam, in his majestic fur hat and satin robe, came out of the limo chopper, not far from the spot where, earlier that day, Jonah had decapitated a suicide bomber. The two men walked across the wide marble plaza, a remnant of the great renovation project that took place there two decades earlier, in preparation for the arrival of the redeemer.

Jonah's comm/link began to hum softly, its red light blinking. He tapped it and his ear piece began to transmit. It was Chief Hammonton. "Simpson, where the bloody hell are you? Did you leave the park grounds in mid-mission?"

Jonah wasn't exactly scared, but he did need to come up with an excuse, fast. "I was following a lead, boss," he said. "Turned out to be nothing."

"Where are you?" Hammonton demanded.

"The big synagogue on Eastern Parkway, we were here this morning."

"How'd you get there?"

"Long story."

"We screwed the pooch tonight, big time," Hammonton told him wearily. "Target got away again. I'm getting sick of this."

Jonah smiled in enormous relief. "We'll get her next time, Boss," he said.

"You got a chopper ride out of here," Hammonton said matter-of-factly.

"You're satelliting me?"

"Sure am. What are you up to, man, another legendary Jonah Simpson AWOL?"

"I told you, I followed a lead—didn't pan out."

"Who's there with you?" Hammonton wasn't letting go.

"A source."

"My screen is showing a chopper and at least two other people. What are you involved in, Simpson?"

"I'll tell you when I get back, promise," said Jonah. Now he was a little more afraid. His commander was imaging him, and you don't train a satellite on someone because you want to make sure they flossed.

"I'll be counting the minutes, soldier," Hammonton cut him off.

Shimmele Amsterdam, studiously ignoring the sudden turn in his companion's demeanor, reached the synagogue intercom button and an armed security guard opened a small window in the armored side door.

"Can I help you?" he inquired in an infuriatingly soft Israeli accent.

"Graneck is waiting for us," said Amsterdam.

"Who?"

"Leo Graneck, used to be the master's secretary?"

"No kidding, that must be the old guy they brought in a wheelchair tonight."

The bearded guard opened the door, satisfied that the two men weren't suicide bombers. "He's down in the bunker, take the stairs, watch your step."

"You coming?" Amsterdam asked. Simpson faltered, and then decided his unit could wait another ten minutes. It may have been a mistake on his part. His ID image and the APB to stop and detain were already being issued. Deserting a THRUST unit in mid-operation was not a minor infraction.

At last they reached the basement bunker, at the bottom of a long and narrow staircase. It was the popular new model most homeowners were installing. The bunker door opened and Amsterdam walked inside, followed by Jonah.

Rabbi Leo Graneck had been an imposing man. His enormous, white beard, bright, blue eyes and roaring laughter blasted charisma. He also knew how to look hurt and vulnerable, which only added to his magnetism.

The years and his illness had not been kind to Graneck, who, Jonah speculated, had to be in his late eighties. His decay had been dramatic and cruel. The boisterous giant became a decrepit, ashen sack of skin and bones. Clumps of thin, white whiskers marked his cheeks, sickly remnants of the lion's mane which had once been his beard. A stained, old, black skullcap drooped from the back of his head. His hospital gown reeked of body fluids, his pajama pants were torn in several places. On his ivory feet he wore ancient leather slippers, easily twice his foot size, which threatened to trip him with each step.

The bunker office was dilapidated, a typical example of the contempt with which the spiritually-driven Cosmic Wisdom folks regarded their worldly surroundings. Half the fluorescent lights were out or flickering, and large water stains on the walls attested to a recent deluge. Luckily, most of the brown and gray stains were concealed by impossibly precarious mountains of newspapers, reaching up to the ceiling among islands of collapsed cardboard boxes.

Graneck had gotten out of his wheelchair to greet his guests, but the effort exhausted him and he was forced to lean on his attendant, a small, middle-aged black man who didn't seem in great health, either.

"Are you in shock?" His high-pitched voice was entirely devoid of the resonant authority that years ago rallied crowds of followers.

"You're not looking well, Rabbi Graneck," Amsterdam said. "I'm sorry."

The elderly man's attendant led him to an armchair. Graneck fell into it and the attendant helped him straighten his posture. At last Graneck pulled his gown together, put his arms on the seat supports and invited his guests to join him.

"Do me a favor, Abdul, go see if you can get us some drinks from upstairs," Leo Graneck asked his attendant and turned to Jonah Simpson. "What will you have?"

"Just water, thank you," said Jonah.

"Water? What kind of a Jew are you?" Graneck joked. "Bring us something stronger than water, Abdul. Can't have a get-together without some righteous drinking."

"You heard the rabbi," said Shimmele Amsterdam and smiled at the black man, who nodded graciously and left the room.

"Much obliged," Graneck said. Jonah was amazed by the confidence the sick man was able to project, once he was sitting down.

"I've already forgiven Shimmele here for what he's done to me," Graneck sneaked one in. "Now he has to forgive me and everything will be fine in time for my funeral..."

"I forgive you," said Amsterdam, "But I doubt Motke Gutkind ever will."

211

"He still says I killed the great master," Graneck cut in and then, in the heavy silence that ensued, leaned back in his executive armchair and stared at his guests in great anticipation.

"You killed the great master," Amsterdam repeated, finally. "You were responsible for his medication. He was taking aspirin every day, for his heart. They suspended the aspirin for his eye surgery, but you were supposed to renew the aspirin after two weeks. You didn't. As a result he had a plaque buildup in the arteries and stroked."

"Even *you* wouldn't suggest I did it intentionally," Graneck retorted.

"I don't know what to suggest, Leo. You had such a love-hate relationship with him."

They paused, staring at each other with mistrust that was decades old.

"You know I see him many nights?" Graneck changed the tone of their exchange.

"In a pool of tears?"

"Yes, in the pool of his own tears."

"A lot of people have had that dream," said Amsterdam. He shot Jonah a meaningful look. Jonah was taken aback. How much did Abulafia and this Shimmele guy share?

"In my dreams he talks to me," Graneck said.

Riveted, Amsterdam relieved Abdul of his tray of drinks without really looking at it or the attendant. He drew closer to Graneck.

"He says, 'Leo, find Shimmele, warn him. He's going to kill my baby.'"

"His *baby*?" Amsterdam puzzled.

"That's what he keeps saying."

"*I'm* going to kill his baby?"

"Not you, Motke Gutkind."

"Leo, what are you *saying*?"

"I'm telling you what he told me. When I got sick, I started having these dreams," Graneck continued. "'Motke Gutkind will kill my baby.' You think I'm making this up?"

"The possibility has crossed my mind."

"Then screw you, Shimmele, I ain't making this up. I don't care what happens to Motke Gutkind, I don't care what happens to anyone, I'm a dead man."

Graneck fell into a burst of coughing and wheezing. Amsterdam handed him a glass which he emptied eagerly.

After he calmed down, Graneck continued: "You know they made a clone of the master after he died."

"Everybody knows that. But Motke's the one who *raised* her, Leo, how can you even imagine that he would try to kill her?"

"To tell you the truth, I wouldn't be surprised," said Graneck, flashing a crooked smile. "I believe Motke Gutkind wouldn't hesitate to do anything he thought was necessary. You know what I mean? I may have been a little dishonest here and there, but for the short knife in the back—ask for Motke."

"Good, you told me. Now we leave," Amsterdam said and stood up, nodding for Simpson to follow. Jonah noted that the man's jovial clownishness had evaporated.

"I want justice, Shimmele!" Graneck's face became distorted as he spat these last words. Then the bile rose in his digestive tract and an acrid-smelling, green liquid began spilling from the corners of his mouth. He was overcome by an explosive coughing fit and motioned frantically for his oxygen bottle.

They wished him a quick recovery, knowing that he was not long for this world, and left.

Jonah Simpson asked, "What now?"

"Isn't it obvious?" Shimmele Amsterdam met Jonah's eyes with a piercing gaze. "We gotta' go stop Motke Gutkind from killing The Girl."

77.

The private red and white chopper touched down on the grass lawn near the Cherry Street entrance of the East River Park, and Jonah emerged, warily probing the dark vegetation for a potential foe. Shimmele waved to his passenger and the aircraft began rising when he saw the black-outfitted figures converging upon his young friend. "Take cover!" Amsterdam screamed, but it was too late. He watched sadly as the first blow to Simpson's midsection made the young man double over.

"Get us out of here, fast," Shimmele ordered his pilot. The last thing he needed was for one of the nasty persons down there to drill a rocket through his flying machine.

Down on the ground, Jonah Simpson was smacked around a few more times—he couldn't tell if it was his own comrades or members of some other team. They worked silently and their faces were covered by regulation ski masks. The blows were not intended to cause internal injury, only maximum pain, which Jonah accepted.

Blindfolded, handcuffed, and bleeding profusely, he was finally hauled into the familiar interior of a THRUST vehicle. He sat with his hands behind his back and focused on drawing a mental map of their route. It was clear they were taking him out of the city, and it had to be the Williamsburg Bridge, because they drove straight onto the familiar, serrated pavement, rather than climb up on a ramp. They proceeded at high speed, which meant the Brooklyn Queens Expressway—they couldn't sustain those speeds on surface streets. They were flying on the highway, that much was certain. But where to? He knew of several nearby interrogation facilities. It would be nice to find out. He had good friends in some of those places... and an equal number of enemies.

As he sank into sleep in his blood-soaked uniform, he realized that he had been poked with a sedative during the struggle. The rough rocking of the van worked its magic on his consciousness. He was transported in a fluffy, white cloud to an old, familiar reality.

It was wintertime in Aunt Gertie's apartment, after nine in the evening. He knew it was past nine, because that's when the heat was turned off and he couldn't stop shivering from the damp chill.

Out the first floor window he could see the schoolyard all covered with snow. Someone else, however, occupied Gertie's favorite armchair. Curious, Jonah glanced over and instantly regretted it. Ensconced in the plush red velvet seat was the disfigured body of Mustafa Rashid with an enormous hole in his chest, where Jonah had dug out the man's heart.

Mr. Carter, Jonah's ninth grade math teacher, sat in his pinstriped suit on the sofa to Jonah's left, shaking his head in disapproval.

"You've disappointed all of us, my boy," he said coldly.

"But sir, I can't do this."

"You can't or you won't?"

Jonah fell silent.

"Too good for this sort of thing, are you?"

"I've reached my limit, Sir."

"What have you done with the heart?"

"Buried it in the Muslim cemetery near the water."

"Whatever for?"

"Out of respect for the dead."

"You botched the operation. We promised the heart to the Iranians. Their cooperation was on the line. Do you realize how many lives were lost because we never received the information they promised in return for the heart?"

"I've failed before."

"But you never left us before."

At some point, old Mr. Carter, who may have been dead and gone for years, for all Jonah knew, was replaced by David Hammonton, who also had a hole in his chest. The Chief tapped his fingers nervously on his bayoneted M-16 rifle.

"Will you come back, Jonah?" The question was nearly a whisper.

"There's nothing to go back to, you know," said the old Jewish man who had now walked into Gertie's living room unnoticed and uninvited. "It's mere scraps of nostalgia which they've conditioned you to hold dear. It's an appeal to your yearning for a home; your desire to find relief in a grand and completely satisfying way; to belong as you've never belonged before. But the Department of Homeland Security can't give you a real home. All they've got for you is more of this," and the old Jew pointed at the dead man in the red chair.

Jonah looked at Abulafia in astonishment. He had just put Jonah's complex internal storm into simple and direct words.

"Neither the old apartment nor the old job truly measure up to your deep longing to go home," Abulafia continued. "What you need is a *real* home."

"But I can't even remember ever having one," Jonah said.

"That would explain your heavy yearning."

At that point, Mustafa Rashid sat up, his liberated innards spilling out of the hole in his body. He said to Simpson, "I swear, you're the most unhappy person I've ever met, and I *torture* people for a living!"

"I'm not so unhappy," Jonah tried to argue, but his own internal voices began trailing off and he woke up. The harbor chill was so intense, his body felt as if it were shrinking. The sensation was debilitating, particularly as he discovered that he was unable to part his lips to open his mouth.

Finally, when he was once again in relative control of his muscles, the first words he said were, "I have to get out of here."

Even he was not so sure if he was referring to escaping from his current imprisonment or from the DHS.

78.

On the hill above the dark and moist grass lawn on Cherry Street, THRUST Chief David Hammonton turned his back on the now deserted amphitheater and returned in disgust to his team and their banged up van. Two dead-tired men and two equally exhausted women in black fatigues looked up and understood the news before Hammonton had a chance to pronounce it.

"If he ain't here by now he ain't coming, boys and girls," spat Jerry Osmond. "Damn the freak, pulling this stunt on us."

"He left Brooklyn an hour ago in a chopper, how long does it take to fly from there to here?" Penny Brown reasoned.

"The bastard's gone missing again," said Dawn Brokowitz and turned on an electric cigarette, setting it to Non-filter Chesterfield. "I say we put a price on his head and wait for somebody to roll the body in."

"David's done it already," said Jerry.

"Will you all shut up, please?" Hammonton yelled at his people, more angry at himself than with them. "He is one of us. I was notified that he would arrive here on a private chopper, and I have no reason to doubt my orders. Am I being clear?"

"Except none of us knows what he's been up to," said Penny.

"The cavalry has arrived," said Dawn and smiled wickedly, pointing at the night sky.

Two black cobras appeared above the water and climbed over the grassy hill, headed directly for the THRUST team.

"I'll betcha' they're coming to arrest the poor bastard," Osmond said. "They're not giving him another chance."

"Poor guy's a freaking hero, what a shame," Hammonton said.

The two choppers now hovered only some 200 feet above the park. There was something terribly menacing about their posture. Hammonton realized it before anyone else did.

"Take cover!" he screamed and got up, his rifle already bursting rapid fire. "Shoot them! Shoot them!"

Neither he nor his team stood a chance against four air-to-ground Hellfire missiles set loose from such a short distance. What used to be Hammonton's team erupted in a giant ball of flames.

The two cobras returned to their base, with their teams of irregulars. Neither of their celestial masters were feeling very generous this late in the game.

79.

After Lydia Hoffschteter saved her life, where could The Girl run?

She sensed the coming switch on the stage of the East River amphitheater, she knew she would be rescued from her assassins, but even as the relief at being saved yet again was spreading through her mind and body, she also felt paralyzed.

During the course of her transformative year, when one chapter was over and this or that group of people had been liberated from whatever shackled their humanity, The Girl would receive a clear sense of where she was needed next. She had grown to trust those feelings. In response, she'd quietly pack her belongings and take to the nearest main road, where inevitably someone stopped and delivered her precisely where she had to be.

But now, Nechama Gutkind had no idea what to do next.

She jumped off the rear of the stage, never looking back at her beloved Abulafia, whose indelible presence she had sensed in every fiber of her body.

She hit the wet and muddy ground and ran and kept running until she reached a red brick wall at the end of the park's path. What was she going to do now? She looked back nervously. The air was cold and thick with drizzling raindrops.

A yellow sports car stopped on the FDR's dangerously narrow service lane and a skinny young man stared at Nechama from behind the wheel.

Ben Markowitz still had the familiar urge to kill someone or something, but now it was competing with his new, undying devotion to the lovely creature from his dorm room poster. He had finally reached the park after some annoying navigation issues, but was then frightened away by the hundreds of dark, armed figures among the trees. Through his high-powered binoculars he witnessed the assassination attempt, and was impressed by the switch that saved his woman's life. When she began running, he was after her with a zest for life and adventure which would have made his shrink proud.

"Hey!" Ben cried at the object of his undying love. "Hey!"

Pencil-thin like his mother, but with none of his mother's aggressiveness, Ben's cumulative experience in communicating with members of the opposite sex was limited. Once, at age fourteen, he tried to do it with a whore at an Eighth Avenue hotel room, and threw up in the middle. He would have killed the unfortunate creature who glimpsed his shame, but she was too fast and he too riddled with remorse. Since then, he only dealt with females during class hours. Saying something clever or charming to a girl in distress in the middle of the night was completely outside his range.

"Hey, you!" Oh, how he wished for better words, but despite his two hundred IQ points, none emerged.

The Girl looked at him and waited for the whiff of his scent that would allow her to judge whether the strange lad was good or bad news. But just then the wind shifted directions and she couldn't sniff him out, so to speak. Scared out of her mind that her assassins would renew their pursuit, she decided to take a chance on the boy. She climbed the fence expertly—thanks to her Scranton, Pennsylvania, childhood training.

Seeing her up close took young Ben's breath away. His mouth was completely dry, his tongue stuck to his palate.

He felt so humiliated: He should have been reciting Shakespearean sonnets and Talmudic passages for her. Instead, he was barely sentient, an animal really, a dirty, irredeemable beast....

Action proved easier than words for the boy genius. Ben Markowitz leaned over and threw the car door open for his betrothed. She sat down and began to thank him, but then two things stopped her in mid-sentence.

One thing was the noseful of information she suddenly received from him, which was all the wrong kind. The youth was a bubbling, boiling cauldron of rage and self pity, not someone she should be hanging around with tonight, of all nights.

The next thing was a beer bottle, with which Ben hit her on the back of the head.

Ben put the bottle down behind The Girl's seat and shifted into Drive. He had to act fast, he'd need the cover of night to bring her into his dorm building. Then, with some meds and maybe a little more beer, he should be at peak performance. He wondered if arranging for a wedding the next morning was too rash a move. He'd have to consult his mother—but that would ruin the surprise... What to do?

A minivan that came speeding up the highway nearly hit him, and the other driver pumped his horn madly. This shook Ben back into a semblance of higher functioning. He leaned over to fill up his head with the young creature's fragrance, then floored the accelerator and climbed up the exit ramp, back to Houston Street.

New York University was founded in 1831 by a prolific Swiss immigrant named Albert Gallatin. He was an ethnologist, a linguist, a diplomat, and a US Secretary of the Treasury. His place on the Spiritual Continuum of Everything was between the Pharaoh Thutmose II, the "pussy-whipped Pharaoh," made to marry his older sister, Maatkare Hatshepsut, who became the first female ruler in recorded history when she took for herself the full title of Pharaoh, in 1502 BCE; and the last bedpan owned by the great Polish astronomer Nicolas Copernicus (1473-1543), whose great work, De Revolutionibus, asserted that the earth rotated on its axis once daily and traveled around the sun once yearly—a ridiculous and dangerous notion in the eyes of his contemporaries. It was a very good bedpan, and Mr. Copernicus never expressed a complaint about it, neither for its outward appearance nor its utility.

80.

Jonah Simpson woke up to realize a set of facts, which he listed in remarkably professional fashion:

His eyes were no longer covered.

His hands were free.

He was still wearing his black THRUST uniform.

He was in a windowless cell with an evenly lit ceiling.

There was a blank metal door, hinges on the outside.

There was perfect silence.

He closed his eyes. If his captors were watching, it was better they think he was still out. As soon as his lids shut, he was transported again.

"My goodness, you're dependable," said The Girl, who was still sitting on her white rock, the book in her lap, the sun dancing about her golden-red tresses. "I've missed you. We should do this more often."

Once again, Jonah Simpson couldn't quite figure out how she was able to speak to him without having to raise her voice at all, when, as far as he was concerned, she was at least a mile away, on the other side of an enormous wheat field. He tried to walk up to her, but discovered once again that there was no movement on that higher plateau.

And so he conceded to a conversation that was conducted from either side of a giant wheat field.

"What did Leo Graneck have to say?" The Girl asked.

"It looks like you need to watch for another attempt on your life."

"Hmmm... there have already been several attempts on my life, but, thank God—"

"Motke Gutkind, your adoptive father."

She was silent for a long time, considering they were both in a place where time did not exist. "Did you believe Graneck?" She was not sure that she wanted the answer.

"I didn't think he was lying. He said he heard it from the old master himself, and whether he did or not—*he* believed he did."

"My, my... That's—unsettling," she commented.

"I found Graneck to be frank and disarmingly vulnerable."

"Appearing frank and disarmingly vulnerable is Graneck's stock-in-trade," said Nechama Gutkind. "But you may be right. My father certainly never hesitated to do the cruel thing, if it meant the good of the movement, which really meant the good of the Jews, or, as he sees it, the good of the world."

"Do you mind if I ask you a very personal question?" Jonah requested.

"It's about the cloning thing, right?" She knew his mind effortlessly.

"How would you be able to tell whether or not you're a clone?"

The Girl giggled. "Wanna' see my barcode?"

Suddenly Jonah was pulled up across the field, in the celestial equivalent of a sharp zoom-in, and discovered himself smack up, not ten inches away from Nechama's face. He thought by now he ought to be used to these harsh changes in distance, which took place entirely without his intention or consent.

THE CABALIST'S HANDBOOK OF PRACTICAL MESSIANIC REDEMPTION teaches that real movement is impossible in the higher realms. This is because everything above the World of Action is rooted in ideas alone, and ideas do not move, nor, for that matter, can they coexist at the same spot. THE HANDBOOK explains:

> *Think about a sea voyage, then try to think at the same time about a walk through the garden of a great mansion. You'll discover that you cannot devote your full attention to both ideas at once. Once you start thinking, you are traveling outside the World of Action.*
>
> *The same is true for more abstract notions, such as Good and Evil. They cannot coexist as ideas, but they can be compromised down in the World of Action. Motion was the very first invention of the Creator, who made it possible in His wisdom through the advent of space.*
>
> *But sometimes mortals can travel through the Worlds of Ideas, provided some higher being moves them about. In those instances, their motion is very much*

unlike ambulation on earth. One moves without moving, walks without lifting one's legs. It's a funny place up there.

"Would you feel differently about me if you knew for sure I was a clone?" Nechama asked.

This was a unique moment in The Girl's young life. It was the very first time it really mattered what another human being felt about her. Not that she had been oblivious to praise or rebuke before, but she tended to associate those with the needs of the speaker, rather than with her own.

But when it came to this young man's opinion of her, she felt consumed with a brand-new kind of interest. She needed to hear compliments from Jonah Simpson.

"Look, you're extraordinary in so many different ways, I doubt a small thing like a test tube conception could add much to the weirdness."

"Now, *there's* something you may want to avoid saying on a date," she said.

"Nechama, I'll accept anything you might tell me next about yourself. Say you're an alien from outer space? I'll believe you. Say you've been asleep in a cave for two millennia? No problem."

"How's if, for now, I tell you that I'm your friend?"

Jonah melted. His face turned red, his body temperature climbed unreasonably, his hands were trembling, his eyes welled up with tears.

"Works for you?" The Girl asked.

"Uh," he answered.

"Now I have to teach you how to get out of your prison cell," said The Girl.

And Jonah listened. He wasn't completely clear on many of the details. They involved thinking of himself as a collection of molecules, and developing a similar perception of the walls around him. But with The Girl to guide him, the process was relatively painless and not at all confusing.

His molecules floated through the spaces between the wall molecules, then dispersed through the air in the corridor outside his cell, then further out into the military camp surrounding the facility. He then collected his molecules in the pilot seat of a single-engine Cessna 172 seaplane which was bobbing at the pier leading away from the prison encampment.

He did all this molecular traveling with his eyes closed, but was perfectly free of disorientation when he opened his eyes. That was a good thing, because he was spotted immediately upon materializing inside the cabin.

The armed guards on the pier started shooting, but Jonah ignored the bullets and switched on the engine. Then he hung his upper body out the window to pull loose the rope that tethered the plane. Gliding across the water, he picked up speed and lifted off.

He looked around the small cabin for a weapon and discovered a hunting knife under the pilot's seat. He stuck it in his unlaced boot.

They had taken away his belt and laces. DHS crap.

81.

Here's how Victoria Martin ended up standing wrapped in a silly yellow rain poncho alone at five in the morning, on the edge of the posh Twenty-third Street East River Marina. She and Lionel Abulafia had deduced that this was the spot where Simpson would finally touch down.

They expected that he would break out of his confinement, this much was obvious. Or, put another way, if he was unable to break free, he would not be of much use to them anyway.

His route was not clearly mapped as he came in from the north-east, flying a Cessna seaplane by the seat of his beltless pants. Lionel Abulafia tried to enter his subconscious mind numerous times. Simpson's mind had never been easy for the old man to penetrate. Now the landscape of his brain had shifted to the point where every avenue that had once been open and familiar was now gone, or changed beyond recognition. Here and there bits of images could be glimpsed: The view from the Brooklyn Navy Yards, Atlantic Avenue, the evenly lit ceiling of a windowless cell—but no maps, or names that could be matched against real records.

"Our boy is growing," Abulafia reported. He was delighted with the difficulties Simpson's mind was beginning to present. The world needed complicated minds.

Victoria saw the tiny seaplane in the dark sky that was just turning faint blue. It curved around the north-eastern stretch of Manhattan Island. Its single searchlight cut through the dark water below until the pilot discovered the marina signal and nosed down to a landing.

The tall African woman in her glistening yellow poncho suddenly entered Simpson's field of vision as he set foot on the floating pier. It was as if she had materialized out of the drizzle. Simpson was stunned. He almost lost his balance and would have fallen off the wooden pier, had not the huge woman grabbed his arm and pulled him against her.

"I'm a friend," she whispered.

"That's nice," he whispered, already springing into action. Unexpected welcoming committees always spelled trouble. His free hand grabbed the blade in his boot, and raised it at just the right angle to be inserted into— thin air.

The big woman simply was no longer at the spot where he had expected her to be. How could she possibly hold on to his arm and disappear at the same time?

Simpson now knew that his was an extraordinary adversary. He pulled away only to back into the woman's belly as her hands landed on his muscular shoulders.

"Will you settle down for a minute? I'm not going to hurt you."

The soldier realized that she could have already hurt him many different ways had she so wished. He relaxed, remaining alert.

Now that he trusted her a bit, he was beginning to like this mysterious woman. He recognized in her the warrior traits of her blood ancestors, who had fought in the service of the kings of Ghana. She was honest to a fault, completely reliable and at the same time capable of remorseless cruelty. He suspected she was also completely loyal to whomever had sent her.

"I work for Lionel Abulafia," she said.

Jonah smiled, not in the least surprised. "Can you arrange for me to see him?"

"Immediately."

They walked briskly in the perpetual sprinkle up to Second Avenue and hailed a taxi. Simpson tried to stretch his legs, but a New York City cab is the wrong place for that sort of sport.

82.

DHS Agent Evelyn Jackson joined the force straight out of law school down in Atlanta. She'd grown up dreaming about catching church arsonists and mob thugs. But in her entire decade with the FBI she never got to lay her hands on a single Klansman. It was all Arabs and the unfortunate folks who resembled them.

Now she'd been sent to pick up a rabbi.

She sometimes recalled MLK's immortal line, "*We have to live together— black and white, Easterner and Westerner, Gentile and Jew, Catholic and Protestant, Muslim and Hindu.*" What would the great preacher think to see her today, a woman of color rounding up Muslims and Jews in the pursuit of National Security?

She had no doubt of the answer. Still, she went ahead and knocked on the door of the brownstone building on Kingston Avenue in Crown Heights, Brooklyn.

She resolved quietly to meditate less about matters of right and wrong and to relieve future stress through medication.

It was two in the morning, shortly after the THRUST team had botched their raid in the lower Manhattan park. The target was still at large. Jackson's two partners stood behind her with their guns drawn.

A rotund, seventy-five-year-old rabbi with a large black skullcap, white shirt, nice black tie and black suspenders answered the knock. He did not look very threatening, but they cuffed him anyway and took him in.

Rabbi Meir Kholodni seemed more amused than upset about the violation of his civil rights. His fortitude had to do with the centuries of conditioning his movement had endured, which taught its members that no government was ever going to become so free and democratic that it wouldn't some day decide to send its goons to arrest Cosmic Wisdomniks in their homes.

Rabbi Meir Kholodni was the head of the office of emissaries which supported the logistics of more than five thousand different movement institutions worldwide, from the tiniest Cosmic Wisdom House to the movement's great rabbinical college in New Jersey. He had a good idea of what the United States government wanted from him. He was well aware of Nechama Goutkind's year-long journey across the country, from emissary reports that arrived daily in his office. Now the government would demand access to the same information.

Kholodni's interrogation took place Monday at 5 a.m. The three agents who picked him up were also in charge of his questioning.

He was led into the large hall. The walls were marble, the ceiling was very high. These offices used to belong to the City of New York, which built them in the late 19th century and gave them to the federal government after the 2001 attack on the World Trade Center.

Kholodni turned to his chief interrogator and joked: "This is the first time I'm meeting government officials and it's not to ask for money."

"Do you know why you are here?" Evelyn Jackson asked.

"Let me answer that with a story," Kholodni said. "After the Nazis captured the small village of Klausenburg, in Transylvania, they ordered the local Jews to form a circle in the village square. Then the Nazis paraded the cabalist master Reb Yehoshua Yehuda Mandlebaum into the circle.

"The soldiers tugged on his beard and earlocks and pushed and kicked him like a living football from one to the other. The people stood in silence. What could they do?

"Finally, the Nazi commander asked the question that occupied everybody's mind, Jews and Nazis alike, on that day. 'Be honest, Rabbi,' the officer said and caught the old man by the neck, making him kneel on the ice. 'Are you really the Chosen People?'

"The soldiers started laughing. The Jews did not laugh, so the Nazis beat them up until they joined the general merriment.

"The master at that point was just a bloody heap of bones and clothes on the ground, but the bloody heap cried out in a clear, high pitched voice, 'Absolutely, yes! We *are* the chosen people!'

"So the officer kicked him a few more times and lifted his rag doll body to stare into his half-closed eyes, and screamed, 'Are you *kidding* me? Look at yourself, you call this *Chosen*? You think God would allow me to do *this* to His people?' And he threw the old man down so that the back of his head hit the ground, and his followers were sure that he was dead.

"They were sorry, because he was a fabulous master, but what really made them sad was the fact that they, too, would have very much liked to know what their master had to say about the chosen people thing.

"To their delight, for both reasons, the master was still alive. He rose up to a sitting position, and the officer permitted the Jews to lift him up to a standing position.

"'We *are* the chosen,' the master said, and shook a bony finger in front of the Nazi's face. 'See how you choose us!'"

Kholodni concluded: "Of course, the Nazi shot him on the spot, but the point was made for eternity. So, do I know why I'm here? I'm chosen."

Several hours had passed. Kholodni admitted he had met Nechama Gutkind a few times, being a close friend of her family, but would not say more.

"We can keep you here for weeks if we want to, a man your age, why should you suffer?" one interrogator finally asked.

"In that case, I would appreciate it if you let me have back my prayer shawl and phylacteries. I brought them with me, but the man at the desk took them away."

"Let's hope he's careful," said another interrogator. "Those sacred things, they're irreplaceable..."

"I hope you get a good price," said Kholodni.

"You'll get your possessions when you answer our questions," said Jackson. She was close to giving up, which meant the old rabbi would be undergoing a less benign interrogation next.

"We've been talking for many hours and you refuse to help," Jackson tried one last time. "Now, you and your movement are all good Americans. We have nothing against you, we don't even mind that you maintain so many centers in Israel, a country with which we've been having a... troubled relationship this year. But we must apprehend this young woman. She is a threat to national security."

Kholodni looked up. "You can't be serious. What terrible thing has she done?"

"You want the truth?" Jackson admitted, "Even *I* don't know. But she's done enough, apparently, to scare Washington half to death. When the DHS wants somebody caught this bad, they end up caught, trust me, and she'll be better off if she's picked up by *us*. We're FBI, we don't run gulags, she won't turn up in a prison cell on the dark side of the moon."

"This is mad," said Kholodni. "She's innocent, she never hurt anyone in her life."

"All the more reason for you to do your best to protect her and hand her over to us," said the other interragator.

"I don't know where she is."

"Yes, you do," said Jackson. "You run a network of religious facilities around the world and you know whenever she checks into one of them for shelter. We're not fools."

"I still can't help you."

Their faces hardened, and Agent Jackson began citing the various punitive measures the Cosmic Wisdom movement was going to endure if he failed to cooperate:

"You will be added to the terror list. Your travel papers will be revoked. Contributions to your cause will become illegal. Your facilities will come under scrutiny for any imaginable violation of any imaginable ordinance. Your members will be picked up for questioning daily, starting this morning. Not once, not twice, but as many times as it will take, until one of you gives her up. We'll hurt your organization so badly, it'll take you fifty years to recover.

"You have enemies, Rabbi?" she continued. "Everybody has enemies, and I suspect your group has its share. What do you think your enemies will do once you come under such a massive attack? And for what? All we want is access to this young woman—for her own good."

"No," said Kholodni. "All you want is to kill her."

Having concluded that the rabbi was not going to cooperate, Jackson and her two underlings proceeded with a conditioning program that was not so much intended to break him as to deliver a stern message to his comrades at the Cosmic Wisdom leadership.

Kholodni was stripped naked—Agent Jackson showed no inclination to leave the room, despite his loud pleas—and strapped to an inclined board, with his feet raised and his head lowered. His three interrogators taped his wrists and ankles together, to completely immobilize him, and covered his head with a black hood. A piece of cloth was stuck in his mouth.

His interrogators then repeatedly poured bucket after bucket of water on the rabbi's face. They heard his muffled screams. They knew he was experiencing the terror of drowning without actually being in severe danger—unless his heart gave out.

They were not interested in his information any longer, so they missed his animal cry, after fifteen buckets, give or take: "I'll talk! Let me out! I'll give her to you!" When the torrents of water continued, he realized they were attempting to frighten his entire movement through this exercise, and this realization renewed his resolve. He was deeply ashamed of himself for breaking down, but only he and God knew...

The water never entered his mouth or nose, but Kholodni certainly experienced a thousand drownings. His gag reflex kicked in again and again, he choked on imagined water, but the longer his ordeal lasted, the stronger he became.

Kholodni returned home at 9 a.m., Monday, a complete wreck. His wife and youngest daughter carried him from the police car to the house.

The first thing he did was put on his prayer shawl and phylacteries and recite an abridged prayer.

Then, while chewing on a slice of cheese, he got on the phone to confer with his colleagues.

Evelyn Jackson sat down before her comm/link screens, to report to all her different bosses. Kate Collinwood was pleased with what she had to say. "You did well, Evelyn," she complimented her. "He'll carry the messages to his colleagues, and they will be very rational about it."

"He's a tough old man," said Jackson.

"He has a movement to run, payrolls to meet, bills to pay, licenses to apply for. He'll come around, as will his buddies."

"Now we move on to the next old man?" Jackson inquired.

"You bet," said Collinwood. "Go pick up Lionel Abulafia."

83.

Rabbi Mordechai Gutkind got off a sixty-minute conference call with the inner circle of the Cosmic Wisdom movement, which was led by the recovering Rabbi Meir Kholodni. He'd been up and working for 18 hours. He was ready to drop into bed when the phone rang. He heard Leah answering the call quietly downstairs, then the yellow light appeared on his nightstand phone. It was important. Everything was important these days—he was secretly longing for a triviality here and there…

"Motte'le, it's Lionel."

"And Victoria." She had joined them by mind link from the cab in which she sat with Jonah.

"The complete set," Gutkind said and his heart sank. It was bad news and it involved Nechama'le.

"How's Kholodni?" Abulafia inquired. He liked the old man, who was made in the old mold—tough, smart, and sweet.

"They tortured him," said Gutkind. "I'm probably next."

"Not likely," said Abulafia.

"They're ready to destroy us, Lionel, you know how they work. In one month they can bulldoze over us, it'll be like we never existed."

"Makes you wonder how much your little kid is really frightening them."

"Yes, it does, doesn't it."

"So, you've been doing the math, Motke?"

Gutkind felt as if he'd been kicked right in the solar plexus—Abulafia's question was cruel and came out of a deep knowledge of the nature of leadership. "It's my job," he said, finally.

What could he say? That weighing lives against one another was what a leader did? The ancient mystic knew all about it. So what did he want?

"You came up with a bottom line?" Abulafia inquired quietly.

"I could use your help," Gutkind said.

"What's your inclination, Mottel?"

"Honestly?"

"No, lie to me..."

"Honestly, I'm inclined to turn her in. I have one daughter and five thousand institutions. I know no one will ever tell me I should do it, but I think I should."

"But you haven't. Why not?"

"Because I'll wake up tomorrow morning in bed and my wife will look at me with her loving eyes and she'll ask, 'What's happening with Nechama'le,' and I don't know how I will live through that."

"You'll live."

"I suppose..."

"Do it, Motke," said Lionel Abulafia. "Turn her in. It's what you're supposed to do."

Rabbi Mordechai Gutkind was stunned. Coming so somberly and un-flinchingly from the oldest man on Earth, the command sounded almost as if it was God Himself who pronounced it.

"You're giving me permission or ordering me?" Gutkind asked.

"I'm saying it's what you should do, you don't have a choice, she was born to die just this way, she's *Moshiach ben Yoseph*."

The *Cabalist's Guide to Practical Messianic Redemption* is cagey, to say the least, about the origin and identity of the vanguard messiah, an offspring of Ephraim, son of Joseph, whose role is to prepare the world for redemption. It's a warm-up comic spot; get the people thinking nice thoughts, help the wheels of state slow down a little, perform a bunch of miracles, get on the wrong side of the powers that be and get crucified—so that when the real messiah, son of David, appears in his full glory, the major networks will send a guy.

The *Guide* is not enamored of the concept which is born from a conviction that everybody deserves to be redeemed—*except* the messiah son of Joseph....

"You don't have a problem with this?" Gutkind pressed.

"This is not about my problems, it's about doing what must be done."

"They'll kill her...."

"Possibly."

"Lionel... It's too much."

"You know, Mottel, how every man has his special commandment, that only he can perform in a certain way?"

"So this is *my* special commandment? Kill my daughter?"

"Take your daughter, your only daughter, whom you love, Nechama, and bring her to one of the mountains which I will show you..."

"Why is Victoria on the line?" Gutkind was suddenly inspired to ask, hoping the old man's right hand held a different opinion about Nechama's fate.

"To help you cry," said the big woman.

"I'm not crying," said Gutkind.

"You're going to."

Rabbi Mordechai Gutkind's spot on the Spiritual Continuum of Everything was between Mongol emperor Kublai Khan (1215-1294)—who expanded the empire his grandfather Jenghiz Khan had founded by defeating the Sung dynasty of China and launching relentless campaigns against Japan, Myanmar, Vietnam, and Indonesia—and Dr. Ferdinand Porsche (1875-1951), creator of the Volkswagen beetle.

84.

The popes, every last one of them, dreaded their meetings with Samael, the darkest archangel. He was a truly frightening creature, with an enormous red lion's mane, sparking yellow eyes—and the claws; some popes were simply transfixed by those claws, which could tear a person in half with a single, decisive motion.

Then there was the ease with which the evil archangel plumbed the depths of a man's soul; he tested, twisted, teased and tweaked it. One couldn't lie to Samael. In that sense he was the most honest celestial being, unerringly highlighting every iniquity.

As an archangel, Samael was peerless. Al Qaedar's humble origins in the empty wilderness of Arabia helped him retain a sense of healthy realism about his true place in the scheme of things. Olaf, the archangel of the Norse people, started *his* career as a six-breasted troll and as a result destined his nation to an everlasting state of sexual confusion. Samael was a living, breathing extension of God Himself, or rather, the aspects of which even God Himself was a little ashamed. However, since those aspects of Himself were the very reason God had bothered with the making of the world—from one point of view—Samael was the reason for Creation.

For some time, God has sought the execution of Samael. Until that cosmic event occurs, however, the old Dragon will continue to enjoy powers comparable to those of his Heavenly Master.

THE CABALIST'S HANDBOOK OF PRACTICAL MESSIANIC REDEMPTION gives some idea of this creature's power:

God invested a tremendous amount of resources in the Exodus from Egypt. It was to be the greatest educational project since the toppling of the Tower of Babylon, a theatrical piece involving all the forces of nature, utilizing pathos and humor, drama and adventure. The liberation of the Israelites was expected to mark the first time in Human history that slaves were freed from their masters; and the fact that the masters had been ruling a hefty chunk of the world for a millennium only served to make the show that much more spectacular. Blood flowed, frogs hopped about, smoke rose, pestilence oozed, millions perished, until at last the house of the Pharaoh collapsed before the children of Jacob.

Just then, as the Israelites stood on the shore of the Sea of Reeds, Egyptian chariots rushed them from the back. This was Pharaoh's last-ditch effort to retrieve his slaves (and keep that page of history from turning). And Samael was there.

He was magnificent, as usual, eyes burning, mane flying. His hoofed foot bore firmly into the sand and his beautiful dragon's head touched the sky. He announced his purpose there: He was an advocate for his client, the archangel Ra, celestial patron of the Egyptians. Ra petitioned the heavenly court to place an injunction on the Exodus, citing a variety of reasons, chief among them being that the Israelites were just as rotten, morally speaking, as their Egyptian oppressors.

Moses, the great liberator, was speechless. The man had never been great in the speech department to begin with, which is why he regularly enlisted the help of his more relaxed brother, Aaron. But this time Aaron wasn't invited. Samael was not about to play fair, despite his reputation for honesty. The Dragon knew well it was now or never. Let the Jews out of Egypt, you might as well kiss the rest of history good bye.

In the beginning, God created fifty gates of wretchedness, each one a little lower and narrower than the one before. The idea was to permit Samael to lead folks down the path of self destruction, and make it a little harder each time for them to work their way back out. Starting at the first gate, some poor zhlub would cheat on his resume, and would end up many gates down the road having sex with the corpse of his murdered neighbor's wife.

It was commonly accepted up in heaven that once a man crossed the threshold of the fiftieth gate of debasement, there would be no turning back.

"If it please the court," began Samael, winking at Ra, "I'd like to present this affidavit from a reputable celestial statistician, showing the Israelites have

all entered through forty-nine gates of corruption. I'll name it Court Exhibit A, with Your permission."

God allowed this submission of evidence and the Court examined the contents of the written testimony.

"Now, with the court's permission, Exhibit B, showing clearly only 75 percent of all Egyptians have entered through the fiftieth gate, establishing that a full quarter of them are morally equal to the Israelites. My question is, are we going to destroy Egypt, by eliminating its chief source of energy, slave labor, over such a marginal moral discrepancy?"

It was a brilliant argument, it was cosmic lawyering of the highest magnitude, and, had the court followed Samael's logical conclusion, the Egyptian regulars and their chariot cavalry would have been permitted to circle the runaway slaves and herd them back to their shacks downriver.

Not that day. Never mind that Samael had been fiddling with the stats—he included the Hebrews in the aggregate Egyptian population, so that the twenty-five percent of Egyptians who hadn't yet crossed the fiftieth gate were Israelites. God just wasn't going to nickel and dime His evil aspect on this day, which was designated to be the culmination of His year-long, ten-plague Egyptian tour de force.

So God leaned across His bench and asked Samael, "Hast thou considered My servant Job, that there is none like him in the earth, a perfect and an upright man, one that feareth God, and escheweth evil?"

Talk about coming from left field. Talk about an unfair diversion. What the Lord, blessed be He, in His wisdom, did here was what any producer of a major extravaganza does when, at the last minute, the cops show up at his door with a warrant to arrest his top star on charges of statutory rape: He sets them loose on his other star, the one not scheduled to open at the Winter Garden that night.

Samael, who knew all there was to know about coming from left field, nevertheless swallowed the bait. Job had been in his sights for some time, and he couldn't trifle with a chance to bring the self-righteous, phony bastard down.

So Samael answered the Lord, off the cuff, "Oh, yeah? Doth Job fear God for naught? Hast not Thou made an hedge about him, and about his house, and about all that he hath on every side? Thou hast blessed the work of his hands, and his substance is increased in the land.

"But put forth Thine hand now, and touch all that he hath, and he will curse Thee to Thy face."

And the Lord, concealing a con artist's smile under His celestial mustache, said unto Samael, "Behold, all that he hath is in thy power; only upon himself put not forth thine hand."

So Samael accepted the bet, dropped Ra and his Jewish defamation case like last night's singles-bar pickup, and went forth from the presence of the Lord to *keep up with the Jobses.*

Right away God turned to Moses with a huge smile and Moses, a more deft warrior than a talker, raised his sword and slashed the Egyptian Ra right where it counted. The poor fellow collapsed in pain on the beach, grasping his bleeding privates. Then the great liberator whacked the celestial oppressor across the neck and his pretty bald head rolled lifelessly into the water. Then came the parting of the sea and the Exodus final act.

Eventually, God got around to intervening on Job's behalf, to save him in the nick of time from Samael's malignancy, but not before every last Israelite had crossed the sea on dry land, and every last Egyptian soldier had drowned.

Samael never forgot the way God had tricked him that night in Egypt.

The popes knew better than to say anything nice about the Jews during Samael's visits. By now, nearly six millennia after Samael's emanation from God's backside, the archangel was more than a little crazy when it came to Jacob's children. What would it take for the army of millions of the pope's supposed believers to go do something decisive against them, already?

"You know, sometimes I ask myself why I bother," Samael ranted at Innocent XV. "I spend two thousand years investing in you people, and what do I get in return? Ecumenical freaking resolutions? Regrets over the pogroms? Apologies for the Holocaust? What are you, a bunch of sissies?"

The pope knew better than to talk back. Samael was very clear and direct in his methods of inducting new popes as they took office. He'd appear in their chamber on the night of their inauguration and show them what it felt like when an archangel cuts open their face with his claws. After he restored them, not too many popes had dared defy him (with the noted exception of brave, old John XXIII, but that's a story for another time).

"Look at the Muslims, for Chrissake, look at them going after the Jews with such relish; they know how to make it fun. Why can't you people be more like them? Where's your murderous joy? I remember the crusades...."
The archangel was about to trail off nostalgically, but was halted by the obvious discomfort that registered on the pope's face.

"Yes, I know, I know, those were different times," Samael grunted. "Anyway, I'm disappointed in you, *Doge*, and you know what happens when Samael is pissed at a mortal."

"There's no need to threaten, I'm well aware of the problem at hand," Innocent XV responded with refreshing firmness. "Look, I alerted the Americans, they're out there, looking for the messianic pretender."

233

"Are you the one who brought Al Qaedar into this?" Samael asked sharply.

The pope remained silent.

The Dragon stuck his face an inch from his host's aged face. "I'll ask one last time, *Doge*, did you ask that Arab bastard to get involved, yes or no?"

"Not directly, I didn't," said the pope. "But I must say I'm glad he's in with the Americans."

"You would be," Samael spat. "That son of a camel driver has more moles inside the US government than you have freckles on your white Irish ass. And worst of all, you, *Doge*, don't understand what you're doing to me—and to yourself, you old, old fool. If you're not careful, he'll build a minaret right here, on top of St. Peter's."

"I understand the dangers involved," the pope muttered quietly.

"No you don't, stupid," said Samael. "Here's what I want you to do: Tonight, you, me and the Arab, right here, strategy meeting. We can't have the Arabs taking over this freaking Armageddon, you hear me? You get the three of us together tonight or, so help me, I'll get the Libyans to drop the big one on Rome."

After the archangel evaporated from the chamber, Pope Innocent XV sat back motionlessly for twenty whole minutes, laboring to regain his composure. When, at last, he was once again in possession of all his faculties, he called his secretary, the young Jesuit Brother Marcello, and asked to be connected to Sheik Yasmin in Gaza City. Marcello, tall and quick in his ankle-length brown cassock, bowed out and went to embark on the familiar struggle with the overseas phone lines.

85.

The archangel Al Qaedar recognized the river Tiber as he flew across the city of Rome. How many of his people had been brought here in chains over the years? How many times had his warriors attempted to press onward, to take this seat of European dominion? But then, in the latter half of the last century, how many Roman lips had been puckered to kiss rich Arab asses flatulent with oil fumes?

Al Qaedar descended into the Vatican compound and landed on the pope's balcony, high above St. Peter's Square. He knocked on the tall glass door and Innocent XV rushed to let him inside.

"You've redecorated?" the archangel asked. "My compliments, I like the Arabesque motif. Is this part of your exit strategy?" and he let out a dry laugh. Humor wasn't his strong suit. Besides, hadn't the Koran said jokes were the tools of the evildoer?

"The room was redone by Paul VI, your eminence," said the pope. "You haven't visited here in quite some time, I dare say."

"And if it were up to me he'd never again set foot here," roared an enormous, fiery creature that materialized suddenly at the center of the spacious chambers. The archangel Samael couldn't resist a dramatic entrance.

"As the red one is here already, maybe we can start," said the archangel of Arabs everywhere.

"Not before you beg for my forgiveness," said Samael.

"This is bad," Pope Innocent XV whispered aside to his secretary, Brother Marcello.

"Your forgiveness? Indeed," Al Qaedar snapped. "I owe you nothing, big boy. And if you've asked me here to try and intimidate me, you'd better think again. I advise you to choose your language very carefully when next you speak."

Samael's golden body shimmered, his eyes sparked some more and for a moment it looked as if he was going to pounce on the smaller, darker archangel. But he didn't. Instead, he said, in the coldest tone imaginable, "Where *were* you when I needed you?"

Al Qaedar's voice turned just as cold. "You're still stuck on something that occurred more than three thousand years ago?"

"I'm not stuck, I'm questioning your loyalty. I needed you, and you left me hanging in the wind."

THE CABALIST'S HANDBOOK OF PRACTICAL MESSIANIC REDEMPTION tells this version of the story:

When Grandfather Jacob was returning home to Canaan from Padan-Aram, on the edge of the Syrian desert, he was afraid that his brother Esau would try to murder him. The brothers were twins, you see, and Grandfather Jacob bought from Uncle Esau the right of the firstborn, which meant that it was Jacob, not Esau, who would inherit from their father the role of the family priest, in charge of making sacrifices to God and, in general, being extra connected to the loftier realms.

Now, even though Grandfather Jacob bought from Esau the right of the first-

235

born, fair and square—he served him a heaping bowl of red lentils in exchange— Uncle Esau was unhappy about the deal and swore revenge. Things got worse and worse between them, until Jacob had to flee.

Fast-forward 21 years later: Grandfather Jacob decides to return to Canaan with his wives and children and all his great possessions, ready to start a new life but still frightened of his brother's anger.

Uncle Esau was nearly as big in the heavenly realms as Grandfather Jacob. He had his own archangel. The worst and most powerful archangel, he was imbued with so much of God's power, he could walk in and out where God was sitting, and not wait for an invitation. This was Samael, the bastard who assassinated our great master, Rabbi Abraham Abulafia, outside the gates of Rome. And this Samael decided he would kill Grandfather Jacob, and thus change the course of history. No Jacob: no messiah; no redemption; just everlasting Human Condition with no hope of reprieve.

So the night Grandfather Jacob came back, Samael ambushed him, on the eastern bank of the Ford Jabbok.

Now, to begin with, Samael was a little worried that Grandfather Jacob would be surrounded by his sons, tough boys, especially Levi and Simeon. Those two, if they got mad, could annihilate an entire city with their bare hands; which, by the way, they eventually did—but that's a different story altogether.

So Samael made a deal with Uncle Ishmael's archangel to come help him kill Jacob. But, when the chips were down, Ishmael's archangel didn't show. This was a blow, because if Jacob had faced his two most powerful enemies at one time, Heaven alone knows if he could have stood up to them.

Finally Samael lost his patience and decided to attack alone. He jumped on Grandfather Jacob from above, falling on him like a screaming hawk falls on a day-old lamb out in the field. Samael expected our pious and scholarly Grandfather Jacob to collapse, but Jacob was made of sterner stuff. Jacob had been a shepherd for twenty-one years. He sired twenty-four children from four wives. One time, to impress his future bride, beautiful Rachel, he lifted up a rock from the mouth of a well that usually took a whole gang of shepherds to lift. Plus, Grandfather Jacob was the most perfect man who ever lived: When God said, "Let Us make man in My image," He was referring to Jacob. So Grandfather Jacob gave the archangel Samael a run for his money, or, more aptly, a fight.

They wrestled in the open dark field for hours. Truth be told, Grandfather Jacob had an advantage, because while Samael had to fight to win, all Jacob needed was a draw. Since all the angels must return to heaven at dawn, to sing God's praise, if Jacob survived that long, his life would be spared.

They wrestled in silence, each met the other's challenge, each knew well in advance where the other would move, each blocked the other's attack and launched his own, relentlessly. This was the fight for the messiah: This was the fight that would decide the fate of the world. If Jacob lived, the world would be redeemed, but if Jacob died—there would be no redeemer.

The archangel was no fool, so he understood Grandfather Jacob's strategy was to fight for a draw until dawn. Samael activated plan B: When he saw that he would not prevail against Jacob, he twisted the hollow of Jacob's thigh permanently out of joint. If he couldn't kill Jacob, he wanted at least to maim him.

The logic went like this: You, Jacob, swindled Esau out of the right of the firstborn? Well, guess what, I'll deprive you of the benefits of this right; everybody knows a priest making sacrifices to God has to be unblemished in body and mind—I'll make you lame, you will limp on one leg for the rest of your life, and say good bye to your special connections in the higher realms.

This, too, could have signaled the death of our aspirations; Grandfather Jacob's strategy could have backfired and a draw would have proven insufficient. The end of the world could have gone to Esau.

"Not so fast," said Grandfather Jacob, who had the face of God—which should have been a dead giveaway to Samael, come to think of it. Our grandfather Jacob changed the rules on Samael. "I ask from the heavenly court that from this day forward, the children of Israel eat not of the shrunken sinew which is upon the hollow of the thigh of a lamb, a goat or a cow." And they do not do so 'til this day.

This meant that the very definition of a blemish was suddenly changed; if that piece of an animal is not kosher, then that piece is out of the game, it isn't considered part of the animal at all. And Grandfather Jacob was still considered perfect as before, even though he did limp for the rest of his life.

Poor Samael thought he could ambush Grandfather Jacob, and all along it was he being ambushed by God and all His Hosts, who seemed at the moment to be eating out of Jacob's hand.

And then God went ahead and changed His own name, the scary seventy-two-letter-long name that can be used to make floods and blow up mountains and split seas. God transformed the last three letters in His name to the sounds M–OOO–M: MUM: which means "blemish" in Hebrew. In this way, God made imperfection part of His perfection.

Poor Samael realized too late that it was he who was out of his league. He also realized he might be able to push back the arrival of the messiah, but he'd never be able to stop it altogether. It was there, on the bank of the Jabbok, at a minute before dawn, that Samael had to admit defeat.

With oily, golden tears in his eyes he begged Grandfather Jacob to let him go. But Jacob was too smart to send him away without an official note of surrender. And by surrender he meant the eternal kind, the kind that can't be taken back.

So Samael bowed down before our Grandfather Jacob and declared: "Your *name shall be no more Jacob, but Israel, meaning The Master of God. (Can you imagine?) For as a prince hast thou power with God and with men, and hast prevailed over me too, My Lord."*

And from that day on, Samael has been blaming Ishmael's archangel, Al Qaedar, for his humiliation, because, had the Arab SOB shown up like he had promised, the dark angel might have had a fighting chance against our grandfather. And the animosity between the white-skinned, light-haired people and the olive-skinned, dark-haired people now appears to be eternal.

"Where were you hiding that night, you sniveling coward?" Samael roared, back in Pope Innocent XV's chambers.

And more than 3600 years after the event, Al Qaedar told Samael what had happened.

"Jacob's father, Isaac, invited Ishmael and me to dinner. They were half brothers, you'll recall, Isaac and Ishmael, but not on the greatest of terms. So when Ishmael got the invitation he was extremely flattered. Isaac, you must understand," the archangel turned to the pope and explained, "was the chintziest, most ungiving man that ever lived. Isaac never, ever, gave anybody anything. He just sat at home, in the dark, wouldn't even spend a penny on a candle. So, obviously, to be asked in by the most private human being on the planet was something special*.

"We came early, figuring we'd knock off early, then go meet you by the side of the brook at midnight, like we agreed.

"But the old fox, Isaac, he had us good. He took us into his dining room, which was inside another room, which was inside another room, seven rooms around. Then we heard a succession of clicking sounds, and all the locks on all the doors were shut around us. This blind little guy, Isaac, this tiny man who you'd think couldn't defend himself against a flea—he had both of us locked up until dawn.

"This is why you were on your own, brother. We didn't betray you, we fell for the same plot you did. We were outsmarted by our cousins."

Samael remained quiet for several minutes. This was brand new information which God Himself had kept from him. Which meant History was

---

* Abraham was a living depiction of the cosmic quality of unconditional generosity. His house was always open, in all directions, to everybody. You didn't have to be good to be fed by Abraham. You didn't even have to be hungry, come to think of it. All you needed was to show up and take. His son, Isaac, was the complete opposite. When his father died, he nailed shut all the doors and built walls inside walls and sat there, blind and silent. Not a people person.

not the way he had imagined it these past thirty-six hundred years.

He smiled and waved his terrifying red mane. "This little bit of adversity might prove most beneficial, brother. You and I may still have a chance to win this thing together."

"Why do you think I'm here?" Al Qaedar said, "To feed the pigeons?"

86.

"Here's an idea you may want to consider," Pope Innocent XV suggested to his two very dangerous guests, the archangel of all Arabs and the prince of darkness. They both turned towards him.

"Obviously, neither one of you supernatural dignitaries has been able to capture or kill The Girl using direct means," said the pope. "This leaves us with a few logical conclusions. Brother Marcello, will you do the math for us, please?"

The pope's able secretary recited in a well modulated voice, in fluent Latin: "One: there is no mystery girl, and you've been chasing the wind. Two: there *is* such a woman, but she's protected by God Himself. Three: this woman is not protected by anyone or anything, you've simply failed to discover her weak point."

"Thank you, Brother Marcello, very well put," said the pope. "Now, personally, speaking from the limitations of my own mortality, I cannot find answers to options One and Two. But I may be able to offer a direction regarding option Three. In other words, if she can be had, I know a way."

"We're listening," said Samael. Al Qaedar, too, sat down in one of the plush, green armchairs, ready to be enlightened.

"The oil of anointment," said the pope. "We've got a small jar of it, among the treasures from *you know where.* As soon as I was installed in office, I asked a biologist friend of mine, a Jesuit (wouldn't you know it?), to take a look at that jar. According to him, there were a few molecules that he could work with. Well, he fooled around with it for a month or so, and one day he called me asking for immediate audience.

"I invited him right away, naturally, and he told me this: The ointment is a living thing."

"What?" Both archangels roared in disbelief.

"It's a culture that grows on its own, provided it receives the right stimulation. My biologist friend wasn't quite sure what would be required to

239

get it to start growing again. According to him, even a simple ray of light falling at the correct angle could do it. Or perhaps the trigger has to do with timing, maybe the substance was designed to remain dormant for a prescribed period and then come back to life. When all is said and done, we've got ourselves some bona fide oil of anointment, a liter of it. This was the ointment used by the prophets to anoint Jewish kings."

"Congratulations," said Samael. "It sounds like you'll get a nice position in the Jewish palace once we lose everything."

"With all due respect, Milord, we could offer it to the other side as a show of good faith."

"Why?" Al Qaedar probed.

"Because there's only one living Jewish person who can safely touch that sacred ointment and not be killed on the spot. I'm convinced it's The Girl."

"So we put it out there as bait," mused Al Qaedar. "It's worth trying. Call Lionel Abulafia."

"*You* call him," said Samael, "I don't feel comfortable in his vicinity. Even the sound of his voice makes my mane go flat."

Only Brother Marcello reacted in surprise to the archangel's open admission of timidity, and in front of mortal witnesses, no less. But the pope and Al Qaedar both knew that it was precisely Samael's unlimited honesty which made him so powerful.

"I can't come out to him," said Al Qaedar. "He'll recognize me immediately and use my own fury at the Jews to destroy me."

"Then it must be you, Marcello," said the pope. "Get your things packed, we'll send you to New York this morning. Meanwhile, get on the phone with that Jewish master."

"You don't think he'll see right through me?" The young secretary worried.

"You're mortal," said Samael, "how many secrets can you possibly know?"

87.

Nechama Gutkind woke up in a dark and musty closet. Her wrists were bound with duct tape and secured against the metal clothesline overhead. Her ankles and mouth were taped, as well. She recalled an ancient *New*

Yorker cartoon: Two prisoners hanging by their chained arms and legs, way up high on the stone wall of a torture chamber; and one of them says to the other: "I have an idea!"

She smiled, her lips pulling at the tape.

She tried to conjure up her last moment of pure happiness and her mind rested on the kiss she shared with Jonah. With all her heart, she hoped that she lived long enough to replicate the experience. Inspired, she knew she had to find a way out of her predicament.

The universe was being mean to her. She'd gotten used to the frequent chases. What was there to do about those but to run? This time, though, she could hardly move at all.

She took in the odors of her tiny jail cell, hoping to gain some information about her captor this way. Her nostrils were the only part of her body still enjoying freedom for the moment....

Ben Markowitz's NYU dorm closet reeked of rage. Rage drenched the patient love in the bag of clean laundry his mom had washed for him; rage obscured the bursts of sudden compassion by which young Ben would be overcome now and again; rage reigned here, and this was just the boy's closet.

Nechama could imagine the kind of putrid stuff she'd encounter once the closet door opened and the source of all these molecules of rage would make his first grab at her.

For the moment, she couldn't move right or left, forward or back, so she opted to go up.

The Girl shut her eyes and flew through the blue mist. The tiny dots of drizzle water pockmarked her tortured skin with a net of coolness; an unseen sun rose somewhere beneath her feet and sent a wave of orange glow to warm her bare feet; the blue canvas of her flight path turned gray, then white, then contracted back to a range of browns until she landed on an endless, coppery, muddy plateau that was eternally lit by the beams of a silver moon.

She saw the old master in his pool of tears. She'd seen him before, but never came close. Now she would. She noted the demon birds on the branches of the weeping willow. But demons were not a challenge to her.

"I eat demons for breakfast," she said in the meanest tone she could muster. The birds observed her in bemused curiosity. Nice girl, they thought, and how much she's going to learn in such a short time...

The master noticed her, too, and looked up. Something magnificent happened just then.

He stopped crying.

A smile spread across his face, the feline-shaped face with huge blue eyes, eyes that bore right through a person's soul.

You wouldn't believe how fast word spread all over heaven that the cabalist master had stopped crying. You wouldn't believe the size of the celestial crowd that gathered around the pool of tears, the willow, the master and little Nechama Gutkind. One moment she was alone on an endless plateau, and the next she was in the middle of Yankee stadium, late October, bottom of the ninth.

The pool of tears receded. The crowd ooh'ed and ah'ed, but neither the master nor The Girl paid them, or the disappearing tears any heed.

"How beautiful," the master finally said. They were the first words he had uttered in so many years, so it was only appropriate that they be an expression of awe at the lovely things God just goes on producing in His cosmos.

The Girl came to stand just inside the master's reach, but he kept his hands down alongside his body. "It's not time yet, dear," he said. And she understood. When the man who's been teaching with all his heart, for so many years, that it's time already, tells you it's not time yet, you listen.

"You're telling me," The Girl said. "I'm strung up like a chicken down below, in some boy's closet..."

The master smiled for the second time since the late twentieth Century. "I hear wonderful things about your ingenuity. I'm very proud. You'll find a way out, I'm sure," he said.

"But what then?" The Girl asked.

"I can't tell you," the master said and nodded at the tens of thousands of witnesses to their meeting. The Girl understood.

"I'll figure something out," The Girl agreed.

The master's smile broadened. "I think I want to sit down now," he told the sea of demonic and angelic faces around them. He was certainly due for a nice sit-down. An armchair was furnished instantaneously.

Then an angel came, the one who had so often in the past twenty-one years been trying to coax the master into heaven. "Are you ready, at last?" the angel asked and his whole being haloed, washing the entire plateau in bright light reminiscent of a nuclear explosion.

"I want you to go back to the Ruler of the World and tell Him, Blessed be His Name, that the master from Brooklyn has stopped crying."

"That's it?" the angel asked in confusion. "Why don't you come tell Him yourself?"

"That's the next message I want you to deliver," said the master. "Tell Him, Exalted be His Name, that the master from Brooklyn will not go into heaven as long as He in His Mercy does not bring our redeemer."

The enormous crowd burst out in the kind of all-over-the-place laughter the cosmos hadn't heard since the big-bang. They couldn't help themselves. Even Nechama Gutkind giggled, all the way down and back to her circumscribed spot inside Ben Markowitz's closet.

The closet door was open now, and the angry teenager was viewing her body as his heated mind was trying to dream up the most vile thing he could do to this helpless female.

88.

Monday morning found Lionel Abulafia pacing back and forth on the sidewalk in front of his building. More than anything, he wanted a smoke and a cup of tea. But first he had to meet his guest, Jonah Simpson.

The yellow cab stopped near the corner and Victoria Martin ushered the handsome, burly man out. She herded the two men up the stoop and into Abulafia's small apartment. As the two men seated themselves, Victoria excused herself and came back with a silver tray, a shiny teapot, two china cups and a plate with an assortment of sugar cookies.

Victoria Martin's cookies were so incredibly, mouth-wateringly delicious, she was once kidnapped by an Afghani warlord who forced her at gunpoint to bake, bake, bake her incredible sugar cookies just for him. Victoria was finally set free when Najibullah Zaid, her captor, keeled over from a heart attack, the result of her generous use of a secret mix of coconut oil and yak butter. Najibullah Zaid's last words were: "Just another little one, please..." Then he shut his eyes forever. For several more minutes his jaws still made faint chewing motions.

The talented Ms. Martin served Lionel Abulafia and Jonah Simpson each a cup of hot, sweet Earl Gray tea and a saucer with three sugar cookies.

"That's nice," said the old man. "I trust you've recovered from the travails of the last twenty hours, Mr. Simpson?"

"He slept in the cab," said Victoria, before Jonah had a chance to open his mouth. "He could use a good shower."

"Yes, I could," agreed the young man.

At that moment, the world shifted so completely, that the very idea of anyone ever having a leisurely tea and cookies again seemed heart-wrenchingly improbable. Three THRUST vehicles stopped in the street below, and twenty men and women in black fatigues streamed out, headed for Abulafia's front door.

The sage and his housekeeper exchanged fast and furious messages:

"I'll block," she offered.

"We'll fly," he said.

"Foolishness!" Victoria countered.

"Oh, puh-lease!" Abulafia pleaded.

"Careful." Victoria relented.

"And you."

Then the large woman went to greet the nation's finest at the door.

"Are you sufficiently awake?" the old man inquired somewhat urgently of Jonah. "I was hoping to spend some time today practicing my levitation."

"You mean when you flew me out of the McSorley fire you were trying out something *new*?" Jonah was aghast.

"There didn't seem to be another choice," said Abulafia. "And there isn't one now. Your friends are here to pick me up, and they'll be happy, I'm sure, to take you in, too."

Lionel Abulafia motioned for Simpson follow him. They hurried to the second floor panorama window and opened the sliding panels. Lionel folded his arms together, closed his eyes and slowed down his breathing.

"You're not seriously expecting me to jump out the window with you?" Simpson peeked outside and considered the two-story drop with great reluctance.

"How else would we get up high?" Preparing for flight, Abulafia could not safely indulge in a sharper response.

"I've been up high with you, thank you very much." The younger man cavilled.

"Yes, but at the time we were surrounded by smoke and fire and debris— this will be different, trust me. Come, give me your right hand."

As Jonah reluctantly gave him his hand, Abulafia tucked it inside the fold of his own arms. "Safe enough," he assured his guest and closed his eyes once more.

244

At the front entrance above the stoop, Victoria Martin blocked the path of twenty fully-armed soldiers with the fierceness of her gaze alone. She stood at the half-open door, her very large arms folded below her very large bosom, and stared into the hearts of all these fledgling men and women. She didn't say a word. Neither did they.

The magic was broken by the voice of Agent Evelyn Jackson crackling loudly in twenty earpieces. "What's going on over there? Did you pick up the rabbi?"

The man in charge was a youth from Chicago with a long list of citations for bravery in action. He found himself responding with a surprising measure of hesitation: "No, Chief, we haven't gained access yet."

"Why the heck not?"

The boy from the windy city lifted his eyes at Victoria. "We're looking for—" he turned to his comrades for help; the suspect's name had completely slipped his mind. What was going on?

"Lionel Abulafia!" Evelyn Jackson yelled in his ear.

"Lionel Abulafia," he repeated, not at all certain this was the name. He was uncertain about everything at that moment. Victoria Martin could short-circuit a person's mind like that for hours.

89.

Over on his windowsill, Abulafia muttered, "I need a good verse to get me started. Let me see: *As an eagle stirs up her nest, flutters over her young, spreads abroad her wings, takes them, bears them on her wings, so God alone did lead him.** Nah, I want to levitate, not flutter my eagle wings."

He stepped up on the windowsill, then stepped onto the fire escape, his eyes closed. Although still hesitant, Simpson followed suit. "I think I've got one," the holy man decided. *"And he rode upon a cherub, and did fly, yes, he did fly upon the wings of the wind."***

As the words left his lips, Lionel Abulafia began to feel the blast of cool wind that suddenly materialized at his behest. Simpson understood intuitively that he, too, had to close his eyes.

"Now I'll need a good tune, something cheerful," Lionel Abulafia murmured. "Let me see, I really want to soar this time, don't I, impress my

---

* Deuteronomy 32:11
** Psalms 18:10

245

guest and all. How about… How about *Take Me Out to the Ball Game?* No, too corny. *Row, row, row your boat?* Too silly. I know! I'll just rap it and see what happens!"

And with that the ancient man began to gyrate his body in increasing ecstasy—he would have clapped his hands if they weren't folded, with Jonah's own hand tucked under one of them—and he went rapping the biblical verse about riding the cherub and flying on the wings of the wind, twenty or thirty times, until, imperceptibly, his ancient feet left the windowsill and there he was, framed in the center of the window, like a hummingbird, but without the crazy fluttering.

Simpson realized, with some trepidation, that his feet, too, had left their sound mooring and that he rested, strange as it seemed, on nothing at all. His instincts once again were good enough to suggest to him that opening his eyes right then and there would be dangerous. Better to keep his eyes closed and his mouth shut.

It was crucial at this stage of the levitation not to get too excited, the ancient man knew, because, until their bodies picked up some inertia (a term that means that a body in motion likes to stay in motion), the only fuel for the levitation was the spiritual energy pouring out of the song he was rapping. So, if Lionel Abulafia were to have a thought like "Whoopee! Look at me, I'm flying!" he and Jonah would most likely end up sprawled on their backs down by the curb, with all the neighborhood dogs curiously sniffing their calves.

So Abulafia rapped on without cease for several minutes, mindless stuff mixed with meaningful bits, philosophy and poetry, quotes from the morning stock exchange, telephone numbers in the 212 area code, the various views of Jewish law on the danger of consuming fish and meat together, the proper way to store quality red wine, the dispute between Rabbi Akiba and Rabbi Ishmael over the methodology of delineating oral law from biblical verses, and the best way to make plum sherbet.

Like piloting an airplane, the risky part of levitation is at takeoff and landing. So, Lionel Abulafia wouldn't let even the tiniest stray thought of immediate consequence into his mind. He just rapped his lines, gyrated his body, and never let go of Simpson's hand in the fold of his arms. Then, in a sudden burst, they were no longer hovering outside the window, but soaring up, up and away, above the roof, and further up, borne higher and higher by the swift winds, until they reached the woolly cloud ceiling that was floating peacefully above the city.

246

Now Lionel Abulafia permitted himself to stop rapping. The levitation would take care of itself, pretty much, from then on. His body and spirit shifted their cognitive gears to consider the open air as supportive as the ground and the ground below as open as air. It's a thing that happens a lot to flying fish (of the specie *Exocoetidae*, which use wing-like fins in brief, gliding flight), when they switch back and forth from air to water. But with them this happens mostly because their memory is so short, so their thoughts go: "I'm a fish. No, I'm bird. No, no, look at that, I'm a fish. Forget it, see for yourself, I'm really a bird," and so on and so on until sunset, or until something else mercifully eats them.

"You can open your eyes, we're safe," the old man told his companion.

Jonah Simpson opened his eyes and observed the city beneath his feet. Before him lay the Lower East Side of Manhattan, the place where his kin had come to find shelter from persecution more than a hundred years ago. Then, fifty years later, other refugees came, escaping hunger.

Lionel Abulafia leaned back and let the current of air float under him to lift his body up like a nice easy-chair. "See what I'm doing, Jonah?" he said, and let go of his passenger's hand. "Go ahead, sit back, you're safe with me. Can you sing?"

Simpson didn't think his musical talents were of much consequence, and said so.

"How about humming, then, can you hum?" The old man began to murmur a tune softly. Simpson saw how the calm, pretty melody caused Abulafia to gain altitude gradually.

The ex-DHS man hummed a Beatle tune (Abulafia heard it as *Honey Pie*, but Jonah claims it was something more apropos, like *Help*). They rose above the clouds, their heads popping out of the chilly whiteness. The city below was obscured from their view. Simpson couldn't see the East River, couldn't see Grand Street or Delancey.

The old man prepared to do some quiet reflection, undisturbed. But Jonah was only now discovering flight in earnest. He let out a high note and was immediately pushed upward, several feet above Lionel Abulafia's head. This caused him some anxiety, which swiftly brought him down again, until he was able to chase the dark stuff out of his mind and start a merry tune again. He rode the wind with growing competence. He rolled like a child, flipped, somersaulted and giggled in great delight.

He hadn't felt this happy since before puberty.

Convinced that his companion could now take care of himself, Lionel

Abulafia dove into deep contemplation. It had been a full year since he'd begun to sense the great moment. He wasn't clear what it was, but whatever it was just wouldn't let go of his soul. It wasn't just the fact that his beautiful protégé had emerged into the world a year ago, carrying her father's genes into the battlefield of the culture. There was more.

Somebody, actually more like a whole bunch of beings, had been gearing up to bury the status quo, once and for all. For no apparent reason, this yearning for a change had materialized all of a sudden and now burgeoned and spread and Lionel Abulafia knew this thing had God's capricious desire written all over it.

He wished he were a few decades younger, so he could better enjoy the battle which now appeared imminent. He wished he had next to him some of the greats who had left and would not be back until much later. He wished he could do something to protect Nechama. How his heart had filled with glee when he glimpsed her from a distance last night.

Then he recalled his phone conversation with the young woman's father and his heart sank. He dove fast below the clouds, unaware for the longest time of what the dark thoughts were doing to him. At last he snapped out of them and forged a happy rap to go back above the clouds.

Can't let that happen again...

He hadn't slept for more than five or ten minutes at a time these past twenty or so years, since the passing of the master cabalist. These two decades had given poor Lionel Abulafia bad gas.

The beast appeared from the south-western corner of Manhattan Island, rising behind the cluster of mid-height office buildings that had taken the place of what years earlier had been the twin towers of the World Trade Center. He swam across the sky so effortlessly, he put Abulafia's feeble experimentation with levitation to shame.

When he reached the spot where Abulafia and Simpson were floating, he towered above them both. "What the hell is *he* doing here with *you?*" Samael roared in fury, pointing at the young warrior.

"He's my guest," said Abulafia, who labored to regain his composure. At age 130, he was no longer afraid to die, but falling down to the pavement due to loss of concentration in front of the Dragon would be tantamount to soiling his pants.

"No, he's *mine!*" Samael bellowed and whipped his enormous tail in the air, starting a local typhoon. Bursts of flame blew out of his nostrils. Sparks flew out of his huge, red eyes.

248

"Not any more," said Lionel Abulafia sweetly, steeling himself against the pyrotechnics of the Angel of Doom like he hadn't had to steel himself in quite some time.

Simpson, who had been so delighted to frolic in midair, only now noticed the Dragon. He immediately lost his inertia and began to sink. The old man shot after him, using intense psalmology, reciting everything he remembered by heart from Scripture.

Samael blew a violent stream of the foulest smelling air at them, driving both mortals upward at eardrum shattering speed, until they reached the edge of the earth's atmosphere. So many miles above the blue planet, breathing suddenly became enormously difficult. The sky was black in the middle of the day and the galaxy shone bright and clear all around them.

"I have no quarrel with you, Master, I don't want to start anything," screamed Samael. "I only want back what's mine." The air up there was so thin, you had to scream or your sound wouldn't carry.

"You know better than that," cried Lionel Abulafia. "You don't own anybody. This man has free will, and right now he chooses to be my guest."

"He's a professional assassin," argued Samael and pounced his fisted paws against one another in rage. "So don't give me this crap about choosing. His soul is drenched with the blood of his victims, he's *mine*."

"No way," said the holy man. "He's a soldier. He killed for his country. You don't have a claim on him."

Jonah Simpson had rarely, if ever, felt as helpless as he did just then, hung between heaven and earth while two mysterious creatures debated his legal status. In the past, the idea of being helpless would have terrified him. But forty miles above Manhattan Island, his helplessness was actually quite comforting. Until those two resolved their differences he had no decisions to make. So he relaxed and listened, which did wonders for his buoyancy.

"If he's a soldier, then let him go back to killing for his country," Samael victoriously dropped his trump card on the table. "Ahhh, but he's AWOL, isn't he? So he ain't no soldier, and he's mine!"

Although Samael was considered the brightest among all the angels, even he was no match for humans. Daniel Webster knew this when he took the case of Jabez Stone Vs. the Devil up at Cross Corners, New Hampshire. And Lionel Abulafia knew it, too.

"He may not be a soldier any longer, but he isn't an assassin now either, so he isn't yours," he shot back. "Forget it, Samael, put us down and go away, or so help me, I'll clip your wings."

"You're bluffing," said Samael, exposing the biggest, sharpest set of fangs in the universe.

Lionel Abulafia closed his eyes and mumbled something. Immediately the dark angel felt a painful cramp in his right shoulder. This alarmed him a great deal and he decided retreat was the better part of valor.

"Fine, old man, I'll let you two go this time," he growled. "But the day of reckoning is at hand and I won't forget this little interaction."

The sudden flight downward was as ear-shattering as the leap up had been, but not so rough that Lionel Abulafia was unable to correct their course. He stopped at cloud level and turned to receive his young companion with open arms—a clear necessity under the circumstances.

"My God, that was the Devil!" exclaimed Simpson when they were back at cloud level where they floated once again in the cool sunlight.

"Samael himself, my boy," confirmed Lionel Abulafia.

"And you were going to tear off the Devil's wings?" Simpson said admiringly.

"Not really," said Lionel Abulafia and giggled. "Victoria taught me this hex which inflicts pain on a person's right shoulder. It comes in handy whenever a gun is pointed at you. Now, we have a new use for it."

If people only knew how stupid Evil is, they wouldn't fear it nearly as much as they do, contends THE CABALIST'S HANDBOOK OF PRACTICAL MESSIANIC REDEMPTION:

> *Evil can be thrown off by the simplest of tricks. For instance, when the Jews prepare to appear before the heavenly court on the Jewish new year, they blow a shofar (ram's horn) every single morning for an entire month before Rosh Hashanah (New Year's Day). But on the last day of that month, on the eve of Rosh Hashanah, they don't blow the horn at all. It messes up Samael's head and he loses count of when he's supposed to show up to prosecute the Jews before God the Judge.*
>
> *Hasidim pull a similar trick every day. Throughout the morning service Samael is present in every synagogue. He shoots down the most heartfelt prayers and points out everybody's shortcomings. When the service is concluded, the devotees take out a bottle of schnapps and a tray of cake. At that point the accuser figures his job is done and he takes off to do damage someplace else. Then the worshippers eat and drink and wish each other good luck and a healthy, long life, and those blessings go up uninterrupted, directly to the Throne.*
>
> *And when Jews finish their Sabbath meal, they know Samael is going to*

complain about them upstairs, that they're so hoity-toity all of a sudden, too good to invite him to their table, even though they're guilty of so much crap. So they bring in the final course, which is a bowl and a small jug of water, and they make a big deal over washing the tips of their fingers into the bowl, and this, the little bit of fat that comes off their hands at the end of the meal, they serve to the old doomster, and proceed to say the grace after the meal. So Samael, being a spiritual entity, is convinced he was fed the choicest course, because of all the lengthy blessings that follow, and forgets to go upstairs to badmouth the folks around the table.

Mind you, these tricks work precisely because they're so simple. It is human beings who decide, through their actions, how smart or stupid Evil will become. The intelligence and sophistication of Evil draws nourishment from the ever-more complex ways people invent to ward off Evil.

Victoria Martin tapped gently against the outer layer of Lionel Abulafia's consciousness. The last thing she wanted was to startle him with her telepathic message and cause him to fall from the clouds.

"Yes?" Abulafia answered.

"Soldiers gone," she transmitted.

"Tricky lady," he praised her.

"Not for long," she answered.

"I know," he answered.

"Guest arriving," she told him.

"Friend?" he asked.

"You bet."

"Give cookies," he advised.

"Fine. When you back?"

"Five minutes."

"Two."

"Fine, two."

As always, their telepathic waves were short but fierce. Their communication was so strong, they often influenced other beings in the area. Right then, a flock of geese flying over the New Jersey Meadowlands became filled with a sudden urge to eat cookies in two minutes.

It couldn't be helped.

Lionel Abulafia motioned for Simpson to stop his carefree play in mid-air and come give him his hand again. He then emitted a slow, sad tune, beautiful and haunting. He sang of loss and disappointment, longing and despair. Each verse of the song brought the two of them a little further down, until the wind, gently but decisively, blew them through the open window and into their chairs.

Lionel Abulafia's housekeeper observed him disapprovingly. "You look like you've been through a typhoon," she said.

"What makes you think I haven't?" he teased her. "Come on, Vic, no sadness. Life's too short."

"Even yours?" Victoria Martin said and turned to the door. "Prepare. He'll be here in minutes."

"Sure, sure," Abulafia said in an expansive kind of tone, and added quickly, "Oh, before I forget, Victoria, do you have Sheila Markowitz's number?"

"Do I ever." his housekeeper muttered.

"Do me a great favor, call her up and tell her in my name that she must drop everything she's doing and hurry to see her son, Ben. Tell her he's up to his ears in trouble."

"Right away. Anything else?"

"My tea's cold," the old man muttered and picked up a cookie. "You, Mr. Simpson?"

"I'm fine, thanks," said the ex-THRUST man. He was astonishingly happy. All he wanted to do was go out and fly some more.

90.

The sniper returned to Lionel Abulafia's rooftop in the morning, after the elimination of the government surveillance team. Sooner or later somebody would conduct an investigation of the crime scene, and the coyote wanted to be there, if only to do some more trimming of the herd.

Mid morning, a red and white chopper landed in the street right outside Lionel Abulafia's building. This piqued the sniper's interest. The chopper was private, not government issue. A rich guy visiting his guru?

It would be nice to send a warning to these folks, to keep them on their toes. The coyote had discovered long ago that a good wounding was often more satisfying than a kill. And you could always finish them off later.

The tall cabalist master with the big fur hat offered a nice target. Lazily, almost reluctantly, the sniper lifted the already assembled rifle and trapped Shimmele Amsterdam in the cross hairs. No, not the head, too brutal. How about his prominent behind? That would interject comic relief into a very tense morning.

Amsterdam screamed so loud, the shooter let out a burst of staccato laughter. Looking down, the sniper saw the big Jew grab his hindquarters and fall to his knees. This was too rich not to comment on once more. Another squeeze of the trigger sent the big fur hat flying.

Now everybody down below looked up, scanning for the coyote. Time to retreat, and fast. The shooter disassembled the rifle expertly, slammed the briefcase shut and rushed to the stairwell. The shooter heard footsteps, young footsteps, rushing up the fire escape. Danger. The confidence of those footsteps transmitted a serious threat.

Looking back, the shooter saw only one way out: Jump over to the next roof, then slide down the fire escape over there, run down Henry Street to the waiting Jaguar and flee the scene. It took courage, but the coyote was in excellent shape and had done this kind of jumping before. It was now or never.

Jonah Simpson leaped out to the fire escape an instant after he heard the first shot. But when he reached the rooftop, it was deserted. He hurried to the railing and scanned the street below, but saw no trace of the shooter.

A minute later, as the Jaguar squeezed out of its parking space and headed for the FDR Drive and freedom, the car phone rang. Damn, who had this number? Only one man.

Back on East Broadway, Victoria inspected Shimmele Amsterdam's wound.

"Please don't send me to a hospital," Amsterdam begged the large African woman, as Jonah Simpson came down from the roof. "I don't wanna' miss... any... o' this...."

That is when Amsterdam passed out.

The injured area was nicely padded and contained no vital organs, but a metal-piercing bullet is very painful even down in the most cushioned regions.

Five whole minutes later, Lionel Abulafia still couldn't remove the wide and utterly satisfied smile from his ancient face. When Jonah asked him what was so funny about a man catching a sniper's bullet, Abulafia said, "Not just any man, my boy. The clown heir of the cabalist master just took one in the *tuches*... Can't you feel the flapping ends of the fabric of history unraveling?"

Jonah Simpson couldn't honestly say that he felt any flapping, but recent experience had taught him to expect that a lot of the old man's ramblings would not turn out to be complete lunacy.

"I stopped the bleeding," Victoria Martin announced. "I believe he will live."

Amsterdam, awake again, sighed sadly. "Now that we've all been cheered up by the misfortune of a colleague, how can I be of further assistance?"

Lionel Abulafia set his foot on the floor of the red and white chopper. "Tell your pilot to fly us out to Queens, pronto." And he sat down, ready for takeoff.

91.

Ben grabbed the duct tape's end and pulled it harshly off Nechama's lips.

"Talk to me!" Ben demanded.

The Girl spent a moment *not* talking to him, as any self respecting person would have done.

He dragged a dining chair over and placed it backwards, than leaned on the back support with his thighs spread wide, warrior fashion.

"Why did you kidnap me?" Nehama Gutkind asked.

"I didn't kidnap you, I saved you," Ben said. "Half the government is after you. They want you dead. Why? Who are you really?"

"I'm hope," The Girl said.

Ben asked, "What kind of stupid answer is that?"

"It's what I am."

"Hope? Hope for what?"

"What do you need?"

"What do *you* care what I need? I got you tied up in my closet, that's what you should care about."

"Why? You're not going to hurt me. You wouldn't hurt a fly."

"Oh yeah? I got you good with the beer bottle back in the car."

"Yes, but you could have killed me."

"I'm not done with you yet," Ben sneered.

"Oh yeah? What have you got planned?" she challenged him. In under a minute, the taped up woman was pushing her captor against the wall.

He pushed back: "You want it in alphabetical order?"

"Sure, what's the 'A?' " she couldn't back off now, neither could he. She knew she couldn't for a moment appear weak in his eyes. He felt contempt for weak people, being one of the weakest souls that ever existed. He had to admire her if she wanted to come out of there alive.

"Already done that, Abduction!" Ben cried triumphantly.

"So, what's 'B' stand for? Berating? Belittling? Begrudging? Let me guess, you were a spelling bee champ when you were little. Your mommy probably dragged you…"

"Leave my mother out of this!" he yelled.

"Ooh, wittle boy kidnapper afwaid of mommy?"

He slapped her so hard, her eyes smarted and her ears rang. She saw black for a full minute. He slapped her again and she came to. But it was worth it. She now knew everything about him.

"Turns out 'B' is for beating up a helpless woman," Nechama said. She tasted blood in her mouth. It was coppery and salty. *I need water, fast…*

"I'm not a woman beater and you're not helpless," Ben answered. "I really did worry about you. I hit you with the bottle because…" He couldn't continue. Too much shame.

"You ran out of courage?" The Girl guessed. This time her tone was not taunting. Instead, it was an invitation to intimacy.

"I ran out of words," he admitted.

"And right now you're deeply ashamed of what you've done, and you'd give anything to erase last night from history."

"It can't be done."

"Sure it can. It's called fixing. That's what I do. I'm hope, I teach fixing. Do you trust me?"

"No."

"Do you trust your mother?"

"Leave my mother out of this, I told you!"

"It's not up to me. She's on her way over as we speak, you know. She knows you're in some kind of trouble."

"Why? Who told her?"

The Girl wouldn't answer. She wasn't even clear how she'd become convinced that Ben's mother was on her way, but in the past year she'd learned to trust those sudden, unexplained notions.

A funny thing, though, when the thought of Ben's mother coming over was formed in her mind, it didn't have the traditional motherhood and apple pie feeling to it. Instead, it felt like death.

"Who told my mother?" Ben's panic mushroomed into an hysterical episode.

"Why are you so afraid of your mother?" Nechama inquired. This was getting awfully interesting.

"Shut up! Shut up about my mother!" Ben hollered.

Unfortunately, the other tenants in the dorm building had a live-and-let-live policy, and nothing short of a bomb would have stirred them into action—certainly not loud screaming from Ben Markowitz's apartment.

"I wanted to marry you," he suddenly discovered the strength to confess. He was sure she would use his vulnerability to further mock him, but instead she smiled.

"You don't even know me," she said pleasantly.

Ben was so touched by her kindness, by the potential for intimacy, he became eager to explain, to be understood, at last. "I was given your poster by the DHS people," he told her.

"They put me on a poster?"

"No, I actually enlarged the picture they gave me... You're more beautiful than Snow White...."

She held back all obvious comebacks; her life was on the line.

"What's your name?" Nechama asked quietly.

"Ben Markowitz. I'm sixteen," he volunteered.

She smiled again. "Ben, in the Snow White story there's a mother...."

He examined the idea. It seemed credible enough. "You think I used the metaphor because my mother is a murderous witch?"

"Makes sense to you?"

"It's what both my shrinks say."

She moved forward: "Are you really so afraid of your mother?"

"You would be too, believe me," Ben said. Most of all, he wished to regain control of the situation. But each time he and his beloved engaged in conversation, she took over.

He wanted to marry this lovely creature, but was that the relationship *she* wanted?

She pushed harder: "If you untie me, I'll have a fighting chance."

Ben looked at Nechama longingly once again. Would he want his mother to find her here, tied up and helpless?

He was honest enough with himself to realize that once his mother determined to eliminate his betrothed, there was nothing he could do to stop her.

It was getting too late for all this internal confusion. Downstairs the sleepy Bowery was awakened rudely by the gunning of an incredibly powerful engine. A dark-green Jaguar rolled in and double-parked in front of

Ben's building, and his mother, Sheila Markowitz, tall and thin in her tight black running suit, hopped out, carrying her elongated briefcase.

92.

What did it mean for a soul like the Hebron massacre doctor to be reincarnated in the body of a gifted boy, forever pushed around by his relentless, single Jewish mother? It meant both a punishment and a healing, though, admittedly, no small measure of torment.

This was not, by any stretch, only the second time Ben's soul visited our earth. Back in the 1300's b.c.e., this soul was among the warriors felled in Hormah.

The Hormah disaster is well documented by THE CABALIST'S HANDBOOK OF PRACTICAL MESSIANIC REDEMPTION:

> God had just punished a squad of top Israelite agents who had returned from a surveillance mission to the Promised Land. The agents reported the country was fantastic. They even brought a humongous cluster of grapes that took eight of them to carry, to demonstrate just how luscious the land was. But if the fruits were gigantic, so were the people. The spies reported that looking up at the local inhabitants made them feel like ants.
>
> So, naturally, the people hearing this report became very upset and decided to depose their leader, Moses, and head back to Egypt. They had been treated shabbily there, for 210 years, they argued: their male children had been drowned in the Nile, the Pharaoh had bathed in the blood of their babies, but at least no giant had stepped on them as if they were ants. Apparently this ant thing had an extreme cultural significance for those decrepit runaways.
>
> Is it any wonder God was pissed? There He is, laboring to show His chosen nation how incredibly omnipotent He is, and there they go again, doubting that He could protect them from a bunch of invalids with advanced symptoms of gigantism. So God decreed that the entire generation who cried in fear of the Canaanite gentiles would live out their remaining days in the wilderness. The redemption would be resumed only thirty-eight years later, when all the runaway slaves were dead. Their children, born in freedom, would continue on into the Promised Land.
>
> But a bunch of Israelites decided to make a run for it and take over the Promised Land right then and there, to remove in one fell swoop the shame of the spies. They rose up early in the morning and got up to the top of the nearest mountain, saying, "If we're doomed to die, let's go out in a magnificent blast."
>
> Moses warned them that this was no way to please God. Moses claimed they

were trying to satisfy their injured egos; and what the heck kind of business was it for a Jew to do war when God hadn't decreed it? But did they listen? Of course not. And they presumed to go up unto the mountaintop, but looking back they saw that the ark of the covenant and Moses stayed put.

Then they saw giants, nothing but Amalekite and Canaanite giants wherever they looked. The giants chased the poor bastards and smote them, and discomfited them, all the way up to Hormah.

One of those kamikaze warriors was the soul who, many years later, decided to celebrate Purim by single-handedly killing as many Arabs in Hebron as possible. This was in keeping with the way that this soul had conducted itself for centuries; always going out with an enormous flash, often involving blood and fire.

Being reincarnated as Ben Markowitz was this soul's first opportunity to strike a balance. The scales of Heavenly justice would be satisfied if he would learn to metabolize his anger; if, for this incarnation, he could become a silent, submissive victim.

"I don't want to live vicariously through my child," Sheila Markowitz once told *The Jewish Week*, which ran a quarterly special on Jewish education in America. "But you know, when you have your child later in life, you appreciate more all the different stages they go through. Then you discover you can't help wishing for them to succeed at everything you missed out on."

In many ways, Sheila Markowitz was a New York Jewish success story. Her latest collection of short fiction, *Dancing to Brooklyn*, was a best seller. She wrote with knowledge and confidence about religious life, in a way that seemed authentic to her readers. The fact that all her traditional Jewish families engaged in corporal punishment, emotional cruelty and incest made her writings all the more popular.

Sheila herself had grown up in an Orthodox home which, although demanding, featured none of the brutality which was later depicted in her stories. But young Sheila yearned for a different world, the world of free-spirited adventure that lay beyond the walls of her old Brooklyn community. Her parents agreed to let her spend a summer in Israel.

The summer stretched into ten years. During that time, Sheila lived in Israel's largest and most vivacious city, Tel Aviv, which at the time combined all the disadvantages of a major metropolitan center—traffic congestion, no parking anywhere and smog—with few cultural advantages. Sheila discovered soon enough the one thing many Israelis cherished about their country: It was a great place to get laid.

The terrible duress of terrorism everywhere drove the normally licentious Israelis to a grander kind of sexual adventurousness. They all did it all the time, with their neighbors, their storekeepers, their gardeners and street cleaners; everybody got some. This passionate manifestation of a people desperately clinging to life was felt everywhere, including the country's more religious segments. Sexual scandals dominated the public air every week. Sex crime increased. Drugs and alcohol sky-rocketed.

Finally, Sheila decided it was time to get involved directly in the country's struggle for survival. This, incidentally, coincided with Sheila's dwindling resources. Her parents, busy marrying off Sheila's younger siblings, were no longer in a position to pay her bills. At that time, Jewish settlements in the disputed territories west of the River Jordan offered cheap housing and healthy stipends to individuals who would join them. The money came from government coffers. According to many, this was counter to the wishes of most Israelis. When governments changed and became hostile to Jewish towns in the "territories," funds continued to be provided instead by an elderly Jewish millionaire who ran a bingo hall in Southern California. After all, how could the race for God's affection be lost over a few lousy million dollars?

Nobody could figure out what most Israelis really wanted. In concurrent public opinion polls, a vast majority of Israelis would register agreement with the generally aggressive security policy, enthusiastic support for establishing everlasting peace with the Arabs, and rejection of any further givebacks to the other side.

This was in perfect keeping with the Palestinian side, where a majority favored peace, reliable agreements with the state of Israel and the complete annihilation of all living Jews.

Sheila joined a settlement outside the city of Hebron, where getting shot at by a sniper in broad daylight was an everyday occurrence; people scarcely stopped their normal walking to and fro under the barrage of bullets, unless one of them actually fell to the ground bleeding.

The locals were considerably more aggressive than their brothers and sisters in Israel's cities, and instead of investing their mounting angst in boundless copulation, they were into the arguably saner option of hitting the enemy back.

Sharpshooting had developed into the sport of choice in Goren Atad, a settlement that overlooked the Arab village of Atada. If the Arabs could shoot into Jewish streets, why couldn't Jews shoot back? Before long, Sheila became an excellent marksman with many confirmed kills. She was as good at killing as she later became at writing. It was all a function of focus, of eliminating the outside world, save for herself and the subjects of her observation. She understood that if you removed enough obstructions, eventually there was nothing left to stop you.

When she became pregnant with Ben (she never considered the father to be of consequence, so he was never told), Sheila's life changed completely. She decided to extract herself from the constant threat of death and to raise her newborn baby as the best possible child who ever lived.

When the child disappointed her in almost every way, she repressed her hostility and sought spiritual help. Someone sent her to Lionel Abulafia, who impressed her with his deep grasp of life and its tribulations. But she could not open herself up to his teachings. Her soul wasn't in it. Instead she became committed to excellence, her son's.

So, was her statement to *The Jewish Week* reliable? Was she living vicariously through her son? Not entirely. It was the zeal of complete concentration which she sought to cultivate in Ben. The fact that he possessed so very little of that quality drove Sheila nuts.

Driven by a dark and bitter sense of disappointment in her child, Sheila felt a need to seek excellence where she knew it would not betray her. She took baby Ben along on her rooftop missions and taught him everything she knew. Blindfolded, Ben could assemble a rifle in under a minute.

But when it came to the actual kill, Ben was an utter failure. The older he got, the worse his reactions to mom's murder sprees became. When she made Ben come along with her at age eight, the boy threw up every time Mommy squeezed the trigger. It wasn't just appalling, it could be dangerous, especially at those stressful times when Sheila needed to clear out in a hurry.

Sheila's decision to send Ben to NYU at age sixteen was a way to keep him distant, to force Ben to struggle to comply with the only academic program that was difficult enough for his superior intelligence. It was also a way of inflicting some punishment on her kid. If the randomness of Sheila's lifestyle wasn't good enough for Ben, let him be ravaged by the randomness of academia gone berserk.

Her only fear was that Ben would one day kill himself, providing a Shakespearean tragedy kind of ending to his predicament. Sheila never anticipated a Greek tragedy.

93.

Sheila Markowitz found the door to her son's apartment ajar, but kicked it in anyway, to release some aggression. She recognized immediately the telltale signs of interrupted captivity: Torn strips of duct tape strewn about the rug near the closet. They had just been here, she knew. Her next notion was to rush up to the rooftop and scan the territory below. Snipers usually end up thinking like birds of prey, no matter how much they liken themselves to coyotes.

Sheila reached the edge of the roof in seconds flat and looked down. There was her son and some young bag lady, hurrying into his yellow sports car. What to do next? Stop them? Shoot the tires?

Who was the girl? Was she good or bad? Why did Lionel Abulafia have his grotesquely obese housekeeper call her so early in the morning with the warning about Ben? Was her child stepping into some cosmic danger? Was the woman part of it? She had to be, otherwise, why the warning?

Take out the woman. Sheila assembled her rifle with her habitual patience, brought the cross hairs to bear on the moving car and sought the bag lady. It was hard to catch a good fix on her at such speed and distance, but Sheila had handled harder targets. There was her mark, golden-red hair shimmering in the morning sun. Check the distance. She was only going to get one shot at the speed Ben was driving. Silently, Sheila figured the timing and squeezed the trigger.

She watched as the blue and silver MTA bus crossed the four-lane street and cut into her son's path on the right. This forced Ben to slam the breaks and swerve right. The bullet had already been loosed in the direction of his companion. When Ben swerved, his precious head moved into the bullet's path. Sheila watched her son continue to drive several yards onto the sidewalk, well after the bullet had drilled through his brain and come out on the other side, spitting blood and fatty tissue on the windshield. Ben actually brought the car to a full stop with his dead body, following the traffic rules well after his spirit had gone from this world.

Then The Girl turned around and saw her. Sheila knew she'd been spotted. An active American sniper since it had become fashionable in the first decade of the century—she'd been identified for the first time by a live witness. Unfortunately, for the moment, the witness kept out of rifle range.

For an instant, Sheila considered turning her gun on herself, but found the thought intolerable. She needed to hold her son's body right now, and damn the consequences.

The Girl pulled Ben's body out of the car and leaned it against a tree on the sidewalk. She knew the sniper would be all over her in another minute. She had to take the car. She had never before in her life taken anything that didn't belong to her. But truth be told, the car at this point didn't really belong to anyone.

Nechama drove off at great speed. She was sad and frightened and knew those two emotions could kill her. So she decided to come in from the cold.

Sheila Markowitz arranged her rifle in its case in under one minute and rushed downstairs to the street. Her boy's restless soul had found its fixing at last, and Sheila had been destined to usher it out of this realm.

"Why did you have to kill me?" her son's spirit asked inside Sheila's head. The answer was the very last thing that soul needed to hear in order to be completely prepared to take its place at God's feet.

"Because I wanted to protect you," answered Ben's mother and realized, like so many mortal mothers before her, how utterly ridiculous it sounded.

Silently, Sheila Markowitz stood up and strolled back to her car. She paid no heed to the things that had to be done next, like a funeral, a burial, a week of mourning. In her heated brain there was room for only a single purpose: Revenge.

94.

Brother Marcello did not have a good feeling about the whole thing from the start. First, there was the flight with the relic in his leather backpack. The poor young man was so nervous about the special powers of the sacred object, he could barely eat or drink. It's true that the reason he had sought his post with the holy father himself was to taste high level politics and international intrigue; but handling the very ancient oil used to anoint God's kings scared him. What would he do if God, in His righteous ire at the gentile defiling His sacred ointment, decided to skewer his Alitalia jet with a lightning bolt and send it smoking into the ocean?

Then there was the close relationship His Eminence enjoyed with the red fellow, who came mighty close to what Marcello knew to be the classical descriptions of Satan. How could God's messenger on earth be so chummy with God's chief enemy?

His boss elaborated a few times on the distinctions between Satan—a mythical being and as such an ideological necessity—and the Archangel Samael, who was very real.

Satan was a rebel against God, an almost equal of the Almighty, who would only succumb to Divine Retribution in the end of days; whereas Samael was a servant of God, doing only His bidding, if at times with a little added gusto.

According to Innocent XV, the reason all these heavenly beings were knocking on the Vatican door so frequently these days had to do with the approaching Armageddon. Everybody was lining up their spiritual ducks in preparation for the big one, so the place was getting a little crowded.

But how could Samael be in cahoots with the Catholic Church? Brother Marcello was not satisfied with the answers he received. He regarded his entourage, twenty Jesuits who were sent along to see to every facet of his crucial trip. All he had to do was set up the trap for The Girl. These boys would get him there and back and buy him dinner, too. They were the Church power incarnate. Did *they* know about their boss's tête-à-têtes with the Devil?

One other thing bothered Brother Marcello: Wasn't The Girl, in essence, a classic Catholic saint? Why, several parishes across America had already erected monuments extolling her miracles. Wasn't she *precisely* the kind of virtuous young woman who ended up being beatified by the Church after her passing? They required *three* miracles? She had performed *hundreds* of them, for the most part well documented, according to countless eyewitness accounts. So why was the Church scheming to destroy her?

His negotiations over the phone with the old Jew in New York City went fine. Brother Marcello had always enjoyed his contacts with Jews in Rome. He liked them. This rabbi came across as particularly likeable. The rabbi immediately understood the magnitude of the Church's generous offer as a unilateral, voluntary show of friendship between the two sister faiths. Here, a priceless relic found among hidden treasures was to be graciously returned.

Whether the old man bought his story was irrelevant. He was diplomatic enough to accept the returned relic without any qeustion as to why it had taken the sister faith nearly two thousand years to cough it up.

When Brother Marcello suggested, as Samael had instructed, that the precious jar be left behind the headstone of the late master, the old rabbi didn't flinch—at least Marcello sensed no flinching over the phone.

"Sure, put it there," the rabbi said. "We'll send someone to pick it up."

The Jesuit couldn't help inquiring whether the rabbi knew how volatile the substance was, and the damage that would result if the wrong person tried to take it. But the rabbi wasn't impressed.

"Aren't you handling it right now?" He asked.

"Yes, but I'm a gentile," the Jesuit displayed his considerable familiarity with Jewish tradition. "And I never dare touch it directly, only through a protective cloth. If an unqualified Jew touches it, he will surely die."

"Who's a qualified Jew?" Lionel Abulafia asked, obviously smiling.

"In my humble view it would have to be a prophet, which presents a difficulty, as properly sanctioned prophecy is thought by many authorities to be possible only in Palestine. However, if a king or queen about to be anointed were to pick it up, they, too, would not be hurt."

"I'll take your very scholarly recommendations under advisement," the old Jew promised. He added, "If you're in town for a couple of days, why don't you drop by my nightly class? I'm sure you would enjoy it."

At the exit of the arrivals terminal, several Cosmic Wisdomnik youths were handing out pamphlets regarding the messianic plans of their master, upon his return from his state of suspended animation. Occasionally, individual Jews would stop and catch a short discussion, discovering soon enough they couldn't get a word in edge-wise. Considering the fact that the youths in black suits and wide black fedoras had not even been born at the time the master had changed his physical consistency, the fortitude of their faith was impressive. They also came across a lot kookier than they really were, of course, because they were in a group. Individually each one would sound remarkably saner.

One young man in a large, black skullcap approached Brother Marcello with a leaflet. He looked somehow a little less traditional than his brethren: He was beardless, for one thing, and the fedora on his head didn't look like it belonged there. Marcello was about to refuse the handout politely, when the young man forced the pamphlet into his hand whispering, "Brother Marcello, I'm Jonah Simpson. Take the pamphlet and pretend to ask me some questions."

There was no mistaking the man's businesslike tone, so Marcello acquiesced. "Tell me about this master cabalist of yours," he requested, looking to the left and right in suspicion. Had the mission been botched before it began?

"Brother, you know in the depth of your soul who's on the side of the angels here," Simpson replied. "I know you want to do the right thing."

"You know nothing," Marcello whispered back.

"Are you a Friend of Shem?"

That bit was a surprise. Since leaving the seminary, the Jesuit had not heard that phrase from anyone, certainly not in public. If you were a Friend of Shem, you kept silent about it, read the texts in privacy, and waited.

He looked up at the young man and frowned. "Get out of my way," he ordered, and pushed through.

A black limousine rolled in to pick up Marcello. His multitude of companions remained behind as he was driven to the cemetery, going up Springfield Boulevard.

When they stopped at a light, the chauffeur's partition came down, and the young Jesuit was treated to a broad and friendly smile from a fellow very properly dressed in a dark, well-fitting business suit and a black homburg. The only strange thing about him was his red hair, which was sticking every which way from underneath the tight squeeze of the hat.

"You seem worried," the funny-looking man said. His voice sounded hauntingly familiar. Then, as if waking from a dream, Brother Marcello remembered the meeting at the Holy Father's chambers.

"I didn't recognize you in this getup," he said with a tiny smile.

"Tell me what you're worried about," Samael ignored the small talk.

Brother Marcello embraced the backpack on his lap. Then he discovered in himself the rare courage to say: "I don't understand why we're doing business with you. And I don't understand why we're setting a trap for this girl, who appears to be Goodness incarnate."

The archangel in the homburg hat smiled seductively, absorbing nearly all the pope's secretary's doubts with his sweet demeanor. "This is the tough part about faith," he said. "Sometimes you have to accept things that don't make sense. This is why the Jews are so successful. You think they're smarter than anyone else? Baloney. They just believe everything God tells them."

"You're not serious," said Brother Marcello.

"I'm not, eh?" The archangel spat. "They're in perpetual exile, always just five minutes ahead of the next pogrom—yet they say every day, 'I believe with a complete faith that God will send the messiah soon.' God murders them by the millions, and they say, 'Oh, God, how we've sinned.' For crying out loud, a little over fifty years ago we gassed one third of them—can you imagine? Can you imagine if I were to destroy one hundred million Americans in four years, how many would keep their faith in the Big Man Upstairs? And yet, look at these Jews. Incredible. I hate them so much."

Then Samael reached his hand over the front seat partition and grabbed Brother Marcello by the arm. The young monk felt as if his arm had been dipped in a vat of acid. The Archangel's breath stank of sulfur and excrement when he spoke; his greasy face was so close to Marcello's, the monk thought he would pass out from the stench. "I do nothing on my own, all I do is what He tells me to. And you will do as I tell *you*, for mine is the word of God Himself."

The sudden switch to a heavy German accent was not lost on Brother Marcello: "God wants more dead Jews—I deliver. I'm only following orders."

Then the Archangel let go of the Jesuit's arm and closed his mouth, and Marcello was more grateful for the latter than the former.

"Now go hide the blasted thing behind the grave and fly back to Rome, boy."

"Yes, sir."

"And work on your doubts, they are not becoming to one of such high office."

"You are absolutely right, sir."

"Good boy."

But Brother Marcello had no intention of flying back to Rome so quickly. He was going to follow this story to its conclusion if it killed him.

95.

Some of the Jews around him were there to visit departed blood-relatives. But many others had come to pay their respects, talk to, pray to, and read psalms before the grave of the late master. A large visitors' center had been built outside the cemetery wall, and regular prayer services, study sessions, meals, and even sleeping accommodations were made available by the Cosmic Wisdom movement seven days a week.

The master's grave stood alongside the grave of his father-in-law, the sixth grand master.

Special Agent Evelyn Jackson had been scanning the cemetery since the

Jesuit Marcello reported his successful interchange with Lionel Abulafia. Jackson saw only one possible explanation to the fact that the old sage was going along with the obvious trap: He had a trump card up his sleeve. These Jews always did. The entire secret service was still smarting from the switch the old man had pulled on them in the park. Everybody was convinced The Girl was done for, especially after the bosses sent in the irregulars—everybody saw the blade cutting her throat. How could they have been swindled so masterfully?

Jackson had heard the entire THRUST team was retired on account of that flop. She hadn't seen them since. She rather liked their chief, Hammonton. She'd have to buy him a drink some day and get the full story. For all she knew, he was already pitching his autobiography around town.

Still, if you had to lead the clone of a dead miracle worker into a trap, where better to set it up than next to the headstone of her "father?"

But Evelyn Jackson wasn't going to just sit there and wait. When the funny little Roman priest informed her that the artifact the Jews were after would be stashed near the grave, she posted a large army of lookout teams in many places around town, including the dead master's famous old house in Brooklyn, many small and large synagogues, soup kitchens, police stations, libraries, Internet cafés and, of course, Jewish cemeteries.

Altogether, some 1,800 operatives were taking part in this quest, all of them prepared to jump into action and switch from surveillance to shock troops. With this size force at her command, she could not lose.

The anticipated alert call finally came from a team at the intersection of Springfield Boulevard and the Belt Parkway service road. The caller, agent Shaheeda Kayam, the daughter of Palestinian-Lebanese immigrants, saw the red-haired young woman entering through the tall gates, hidden in a crowd of pious school girls. Kayam's team mobilized immediately and followed The Girl. Evelyn Jackson cautioned them not to attack until they received word from her. DHS knew by now that a direct confrontation with The Girl wouldn't work. Evelyn trusted the Jesuit trap better.

The archangel Al Qaedar was not far from there, in THRUST fatigues, outside the International Arrivals terminal at JFK. He asked one member of the special government team there for her handheld satellite navigation screen and traced the Springfield Boulevard route. "Good girl," he said over the comm/link to Shaheeda Kayam, who was one of his moles in DHS. He used a frequency known only to his people inside the US government. "She'll be getting off soon, don't lose sight of her."

Al Qaedar and five of his personal warriors got into their black THRUST van and rushed at a blatantly illegal velocity to the airport exit. Out there they raised the rotors and lifted the vehicle ten feet or so in the air, to cut diagonally across roads, sidewalks, private yards and gas stations, until they reached the cemetery. They parked by the administration building and proceeded on foot among the gravestones. Agent Kayam was already waiting outside the two masters' enclosed mausoleum. Al Qaedar grabbed her shoulders from behind.

"Good work, my child," he hissed. "I'm very pleased. Is she inside?"

"Yes," she said, "right over there."

There was The Girl, outside the mausoleum. She wore a plain cotton dress and thin windbreaker, her beautiful, wavy, golden-red hair falling over her shoulders. There was no sign of the old rabbi around this time. The archangel sniffed the air suspiciously. Older men who managed to remain pure of heart at Lionel Abulafia's advanced age had a special aroma, once your olfactories had dug through the tobacco and booze and halitosis: It was reminiscent of a mix of vanilla extract and hot starch.

Finally, Al Qaedar was forced to accept that The Girl had come alone. All he had to do now was grab the little bitch and slash her throat, and make sure it was really she who went down; the rest would be history, nothing but history, without end.

The promise tasted like boiling blood in his mouth. He knew the taste, which demons fed on openly whenever they could, while angels like himself pretended they didn't care for it so much. But in secret he craved it. This, and a few other elements of his profile, attested forever to his humble beginnings in the Arabian peninsula, when both angels and demons had so few living people at their disposal, gnawing on a bleeding carcass in the burning sun made for a really exciting day.

The target walked into the mausoleum. The archangel stepped carefully over the boundary marker around the graves and entered the dark, covered hallway, adjoining the mausoleum structure. He opened the simple wooden door and peeked inside. Small groups of Jewish men and women stood reading psalms. Al Qaedar spotted the girl near the head of the master's grave. The archangel gauged her distance and pulled out a short, curved *shabariya*.

The girl held on to the master's tombstone and closed her eyes. She seemed to search for the sacred jar with her mind's eye. This was very good. She would be blind to his approach, and the few Jews in there would not comprehend what had taken place until he was gone and her soul had been liberated from the confines of its corporeal prison.

He'd leap over the graves, one step on the small hill of earth covered by semi-burned pieces of papers, the remnants of request notes from the thousands who had visited here recently. A second step should bring him down on the golden-haired creature like a panther landing on a gazelle.

Al Qaedar crouched and leaped forward, knife drawn in right hand. Then things got a little complicated. A very large black woman stopped him cold in mid-flight, and a tall, muscular young man in a black skullcap grabbed his right wrist and released the curved sword from his hold.

The archangel struggled and spat fierce profanities at his attackers, all the while focusing four millennia's worth of envy on the young woman he had sworn to kill. Jonah and Victoria fought back, but they were no match for the mythical spirit of the desert, who finally released himself from their grip and lashed at the girl, causing her to drop the jar, which cracked over the gravestone. Its contents oozed onto the raised earth just below.

The world froze for an instant, as several pairs of astonished eyes followed the disappearance of the sacred ointment into the soil. A shard of the jar rolled down the mound of soil until it hit the low cement protrusion that surrounded the grave. For an entire moment, it appeared the cosmos was taking a pause from itself.

Oh, you couldn't tell if you didn't know where to look, but deep under the layers of soil, something was stirring. A body was returning to life, sending out distress signals to the spirit: Come and get me! The first calls were low-key, even shy. Soon there was some thrashing—and even a cry of panic and frustration.

Al Qaedar was stunned, and for that entire moment he traveled back and forth, multiple times, to that steamy meeting with the Creator, to his first encounter with Hagar, to her wildman of a son. It was a moment too late, but, at last, he understood.

"The bitch," he uttered hoarsely. "Slave girl was in on it from the start... She and Sarah ...." Then he had to follow through to the only logical conclusion, "...and God. Does *anyone* play fair in this wretched universe?"

At that moment of dreadful comprehension, old Lionel Abulafia, covered in a plastic poncho that blocked his clean scent from spreading through the air, got up from behind the tombstones and wrapped his fringed garment around the archangel's bulk.

"You're busted," he told the archangel.

Al Qaedar was immobilized.

Brother Marcello removed the golden red wig and straightened his well-starched white skirt. Moving freely in a skirt presented no problem for him, of course, what with his regular cassock garb.

Special Agent Evelyn Jackson and her multiple teams arrived on the scene less than a minute later, but by then the Jews and their celestial captive had boarded their chopper and flown the coop.

"Damn it," Jackson blurted and leaned back against the mausoleum's stone wall. "She was just here. I'm getting tired of this."

Her assistant asked, "What now?"

"I suppose we go back to the city and arrest the lot of them," said Jackson. "Let's just hope they are there when we arrive."

Strangely, despite her rage at losing her target yet again, Evelyn Jackson experienced a sense of relief. A pall of restriction seemed lifted from the surface of her brain. She felt so light on her feet all of a sudden, she almost broke into a dance. Then she spotted the platoons of black clad irregulars rising from behind the gravestones all across the cemetery and rushing to the exit gates. "We better haul ass," she said, "or there might be no one left for us to arrest."

The earth over the cement-framed grave now showed the first serious crack and looked to be parting to either side, each grain of soil frantically pushing its neighbor to get the heck out of the way. This was some potent ointment the Pope had sent over...

96.

"Anyone want to know what happens next?" asked Lionel Abulafia from the far end of his study hall, as he lit a cigarette. He was still in his tattered, black coat and black hat. He was in great need of a good bath with lots of soap.

Upstairs, Victoria Martin guarded the archangel Al Qaedar. The question on everybody's mind was how long could she, or anyone for that matter, continue to keep an archangel imprisoned.

Rabbi Mordechai Gutkind had been to some of Lionel Abulafia's late night classes, so the group in the small hall did not strike him as exceptional.

His colleagues, Meirke Kholodni, Movement Spokesman Benzion Keel, Keel's special aid, Ziama Levinsky, Gutkind's own son, Berel, and Avremel Dickstein, who ran the Cosmic Wisdom institutions in the state of Connecticut, were awed by their legendary surroundings. But as born and bred Cosmic Wisdomniks, they knew better than to reveal their reactions.

They also knew about the special relationship between their late master and Lionel Abulafia. But unlike the late master, Abulafia had no patience at all for followers and could barely tolerate the few students who paid his rent. Seeing him now, after so many years of estrangement, was a jarring experience for the Wisdomniks. The thing they noticed immediately was his certainty and economy of motion. They noted that Lionel Abulafia never said or did anything except in the most efficient manner. Much like their own master, he had no time for trivialities.

"You have the archangel of the Arabs tied up in your bedroom?" Motke Gutkind wasn't necessarily surprised at the fact that Abulafia and Victoria Martin had been able to outsmart Al Qaedar, but he knew the implications were enormous.

"Don't be so nervous," said Lionel Abulafia and shut the study hall door behind him. "Haven't you read those stories about genies spending hundreds of years locked inside a bottle?"

"This is no genie you've got up there," said Jonah Simpson, who was now dressed in a comfortable tan sports jacket and blue jeans, both gifts from Victoria Martin. "And when it decides to break loose, I suspect we won't be able to kill it or even hold it back."

"You're right, of course," said Abulafia. "We're at the stage of the game where it's all for keeps, and there's nothing any of us mortals can do."

"So, what happens next?" Jonah Simpson asked eagerly. He already decided he would like Lionel Abulafia a lot better if he weren't always so damned pleased with himself. Abulafia's habit of complete submission to the will of the cosmos could get on a person's nerves.

"Next I suspect we get arrested, of course," said Lionel Abulafia. "Even as we speak, federal teams are converging on this place, to take us to quiet little interrogation cells they've set up on Worth Street."

"Why do we sit and wait, then?" Lilith Lydia Hoffschteter, who had just come out of intensive care that morning, was impatient. She was dressed in her tight, black, elastic training suit and was sporting a major bandage around her pretty neck. "If we know they're coming, I say, let's take a powder."

"No, this is when we need to give up," said the ancient scholar. "It's the next phase in the redemption game, and in this phase the trick is to do nothing. We were taught, *The Lord shall fight for you, and you shall hold your peace.** It's not an easy feat for humans: Don't just do something, stand there!"

Considerable doubt spread across the faces of all his listeners. But Lionel Abulafia was resolute, so they all waited to be arrested.

The nice thing about the unearthed figure that emerged from the master's open grave was that it wasn't as dusty and chalky as one might expect. Talmudic scholars have debated whether the dry bones which the Prophet Ezekiel resurrected** were reincorporated naked or dressed. The master's reawakening from his twenty-one-year slumber should put this age-old debate to rest: He was dressed impeccably in a knee-length, black silk coat, shiny black shoes, a bright white shirt with a wide, black tie, and his wide-brimmed fedora.

He still looked about ninety, and needed help stepping out of his grave. Those men and women who had not run away screaming now gathered around him with tears in their eyes. He smiled and asked if anyone there had a car. He needed a lift to the city.

"I'll take you," said a chubby woman in a long, blue dress, and pointed to her jeep that stood waiting on the cemetery lane. "Rita will drive us."

The prophetess Danielle Herzog and the master cabalist sat in the back seat, their faces somber. The master wasn't expecting the woman next to him to say anything. He knew she would speak when there was speaking to be done.

But then something pretty unusual took place, although it probably paled in comparison with a man coming out of his grave impeccably attired after twenty-one years : To the few observers who had stuck around, not so overwhelmed by their awe and devotion to abandon their practical inclination to dig out video cameras and cell phones to record one of the last events in history, to those hardy souls it appeared that the moving jeep with the master and the woman had no driver.

Danielle was very proud of her little friend's accomplishment. Most times, the cars Rita drove hardly ever moved at all.

---

*   Exodus 14:22
**   Ezekiel 37

Upstairs, in Lionel Abulafia's bedroom, still wrapped in the ancient mystic's prayer shawl, Al Qaedar sat, gloomy and almost disturbingly quiet. Victoria Martin had smuggled him under her raincoat right through several rows of special government agents, who stormed the Jewish cemetery suspecting foul play. In their frustration they caused heavy damage to the stones, and dozens of them were arrested by the NYPD. Special Agent Jackson had had her hands full trying to gain their release.

"How long do you think you can keep me here?" Al Qaedar growled at his captor. "As soon as my absence is noticed up above, I'm out of here. I have a contract from God, you lowly mortal, I'm a freaking archangel!"

"Most lowly mortals would have gotten themselves out of those fringes by now," Victoria commented in unabashed mockery. Lionel Abulafia's fringed prayer shawl proved to be an excellent restraint for this desert deity.

"Very funny. You think if I'm spiritually delicate I still can't kill all of you with one slash of my fingernails?"

"Ooh, I'm shaking, I'm scared, I'm—wait, maybe I should get you a fresh fringed garment, something special for the spiritually delicate."

"You will live to regret every single one of your insults, mortal woman," the archangel warned, "and then you'll die."

"Hey, buster," she retorted, having more fun than she'd had in quite some time, "nobody gets out of this world alive."

Some time passed. Victoria Martin poured herself a cup of tea. She didn't offer the bound archangel any. She wanted to avoid further discussion about the removal of his shackles—even temporarily. She knew archangels could be exceptionally, deviously persuasive. Best not to go near the subject.

Al Qaedar sensed that minuscule degree of apprehension inside her. "Your punishment, when I'm finally released, will be much harsher than the rest of them," he promised calmly. "At least they are fighting for their own side. But you are a traitor to your people."

"Really?" Victoria said and settled herself into her chair.

"The Blacks and the Arabs are the same nation, you must be well aware of that," Al Qaedar persisted. "They're all my people, I love them equally."

"That's so nice of you," Victoria said, in between sips of her tea. "Is that why my brothers the Muslim merchants sold my great-grandparents as slaves to the French governor of Haiti? Out of a sense of loyalty and equality?"

"Everybody bought and sold slaves back then, the Jews did, too," the archangel argued, losing some of his heat.

"My master comes from a long line of Spanish Jews, and not one of them has traded in black slaves for at least a thousand years."

"Then why do you call him My Master, pray tell?"

"It's a long story, I was in a huge jam with three different mob families out to fit me into cement shoes." Victoria answered. "Lionel got me out of the East River and revived me. He refused to take anything from me as payment, so I offered myself as his servant. He really digs my cooking, by the way. Anyway, he's my master now because I owe him my life."

"*Again* with the life business. You owe him your life, he saved your life, to life, to life, *L'Chayim*. The problem with the Jews is they love life too much," said the archangel Al Qaedar with unabashed contempt. "Give us life, thank You for the life, sanctity of life, save one life and you saved the whole world."

"Is there something wrong with loving life?" asked Victoria Martin.

"You're no better than the slugs in the dirt, who squirm and wiggle to reach water; or a herd of gazelles in a mad stampede to flee their predator; or mice scrambling away from the cat," Al Qaedar spat in contempt. "My people would rather die than live in shame. My people don't beg for their lives. This is why Allah loves them more than He does the Jews. Remember, black woman, in the end, those who sanctify life at all costs will inherit death; but those who embrace death will merit eternal life."

"Spoken like a true immortal," said Victoria and poured herself another cup of tea. "One more unmarried marriage counselor. I'd like to see you die just once. Which, incidentally, could be arranged."

Al Qaedar cut her with the venom in his perfectly black eyes. "Go for it, sister," he challenged her. "I'm always open to learning new things."

A minute later, Lionel Abulafia, followed by Jonah Simpson, burst into the bedroom upstairs. They saw no trace of the Archangel Al Qaedar anywhere, only Victoria standing in the middle of the room, holding her silver teapot.

"What happened?" Lionel Abulafia demanded.

"He challenged me to try and kill him," said Victoria, lowering her gaze.

"Foolish child, did you fall for that? What have I told you?" her master cried out, more out of concern for the woman than for what might befall them now.

"I didn't exactly fall for it," Victoria said. "I merely asked him, if he was so powerful, could he make himself fit inside a very small space, like, say, my tea pot?"

"And...?"

"He couldn't resist." Victoria said and roared in laughter. "They never do. Shame about my best teapot, though...."

97.

It was late Monday afternoon by the time Evelyn Jackson and her team arrived at the Lower East Side of Manhattan. The area was blockaded from every direction by police cars, FBI vans and Bradley fighting vehicles. Jackson could easily imagine the Bradleys punching holes in the brick walls of the corner building and choppers hovering overhead as the building burned. All she, or any of her peers had to do was give the word. But there was a cost to overt brutality.

Already rumors were spreading about the massive manhunt the government was conducting. The people were holding vigils in thousands of churches, mosques, synagogues and street corners. And because access was blocked to the major networks, phone pictures were making the rounds online. Blogs dedicated to The Girl were riling up folks, and even though no one could offer any straightforward information regarding where she was—they never really did— the level of speculation was reaching an incredible pitch.

One question the special agent had regarding the operation that day was why military personnel, equipment and munitions were mobilized to such an overwhelming extent. She also wondered about the involvement of the Third World irregulars, groups generally considered extra-legal. What were several hundred of "known terrorists," as they were once called, doing on East Broadway? And who was giving them their marching orders? And who would be able to stop them, once they decided to storm the building in search of The Girl?

Some of the security services brass were also on hand, including, Jackson discovered, local THRUST boss Amelia Lopes. There she was, in black fatigues, sipping tea from Styrofoam cups with the NSA liaison, Kate Collinwood.

Suddenly, Lopes was in Evelyn Jackson's comm/link. "What took you so long?" Lopes asked curtly.

"I beg your pardon?" Jackson responded, a bit confused. "I don't believe

I report to you, Chief Lopes."

"Haven't you heard?" Lopes updated her. "We're at war with Israel. All codes are red and I'm the highest ranking officer in the immediate region."

"The invasion started?" Jackson had been glued to her comm/link throughout the ride from the Queens cemetery, but there was no mention of the war moving into its next stage.

"They were going to nuke us!" Lopes said.

All at once, the comm/link, the screens in Jackson's command van, and every television screen on the planet, burst out with belligerent news chatter about the assault on Jerusalem. A barrage of long and short-range missiles combined to deliver a debilitating attack on the Jewish capitol, a blast so ferocious, it was hoped, the Jews would be too overwhelmed to retaliate. With a population of nearly one million in and around the city, the prospect for carnage was terrifying.

Lopes was all business now, and Jackson knew she had already initiated the file on her failure to capture The Girl in Queens. If that bird flew the coop yet again, she, Evelyn Jackson, would be the obvious choice for designated sacrificial goat.

The looming end of her career would be the perfect conclusion to what had been the most disastrous day of her experience in national security.

Captain Frank Bolls from the Bradley platoon approached Colonel Lopes to suggest his unit was in possession of M651 CS incendiary cartridges available to set fire to the building. "If we take them out now, there's no way anyone comes out of there alive."

"I'm amazed, Captain," Lopes said bitterly. "It's like you haven't been here this past couple of days. Get it into your head: We cannot defeat her using brute force."

"Then what are you planning to do, Colonel?"

"Watch and learn…"

"Who's in there with The Girl?" Jackson asked into her mouthpiece.

"We understand that her adoptive father has joined her, came all the way down from Scranton, Pennsylvania," said Jackson's assistant, who was in a makeshift control room on the twentieth floor of the apartment building across the street, scanning the screens.

"The old rabbi is there, of course, and his lady housekeeper. Those two are a permanent feature in the neighborhood. Then there's Jonah Simpson, he's AWOL from Hammonton's THRUST team, which, by the way, is also AWOL. A few other rabbis came in by car earlier. I estimate ten individuals altogether, most likely unarmed and not dangerous."

"I would hold back on the 'not dangerous' part," advised Lopes. "I also recommend that we re-classify Hammonton's team as MIA."

"You know something I don't?" Collinwood inquired.

"Or the other way around," Lopes spat bitterly.

"What's stopping me from walking inside and picking up these elderly rabbis?" Jackson challenged the highest ranking officer.

"These don't resemble your run-of-the-mill geriatric clergy," said Collinwood. "I have a report here that states one of your elderly rabbis and our friend Simpson were spotted levitating together earlier."

"You're joking," said Evelyn Jackson.

"I'm reading from the reports. They floated out of the second floor window, hovered a little, soared above the clouds for a while and returned a little later, through the same window."

"Are the stakeout units boozing again?" Jackson demanded angrily.

"No, Ma'am," was the reply. "Levitation has been shown to be possible for—"

"Never mind," Jackson interrupted the NSA official. "If we want to storm the place, I doubt very much they'd shoot at us. It's not their style. What about Simpson?"

"I doubt he's the Simpson we knew and loved," said Lopes. "I'll bet he's been brainwashed. The stress he was under must have made him a prime target for these people. They're all skilled cabalists." She sighed, suspecting she was about to order yet another losing attack. "Alert the troops, please, I want this over with already."

"Attention all units," Jackson told the entire comm/link system, "we're moving in. Our instructions are to arrest the woman known as Nechama Gutkind, a.k.a. The Girl, for subversive and terrorist activities. We'll also pick up everybody else in there as co-conspirators. We go inside in five, four, three—"

Then Amelia Lopes' voice interrupted on the comm/link, "God damn, who ordered those irregulars to move in? This is THRUST Section Chief Amelia Lopes, ordering all US security forces to move in. Do not let those irregulars get to the suspects, understood? We want the suspects alive."

A swarm of attackers in many varieties of black uniforms spread about the stoop leading up to Lionel Abulafia's study hall and apartment. They banged violently on the front door, cracking many windows; for a minute the tinge of shattering glass played gleefully above the heavy bass sounds of the advancing boots.

A much larger confrontation erupted some six thousand miles away, as UN Coalition forces landed on Israeli shores, complemented by regional military and irregular forces from Palestine, Egypt, Saudi Arabia, Jordan, Iraq, Iran, Syria and Lebanon. Altogether, the uniformed Coalition forces outnumbered the defenders three to one, but the numeric gap widened when several thousand terrorist squads converged on the Jewish state's vulnerable midsection from the east.

Estimates put the expected number of civilian Jewish dead in the tens of thousands, following the first massive missile attack on Jerusalem. Bombing raids on Tel Aviv were set to topple the most thriving population center on the Mediterranean shore. A myriad special forces were on their way to the country's various nuclear facilities, to disable the Jews' ability to launch a suicide doomsday counterattack. The end seemed very near.

A yellow sports car arrived at the siege zone outside Abulafia's building, with no hope of getting through the barricades. The driver abandoned the car and walked right into the thick of the security forces.

Nechama did not allow herself to become discouraged by the fact that several hundred security troops were trying to break into the same place she was planning to visit. The Girl hunched forward and charged in.

"I just freaking saw her!" Jackson's man screamed from the twentieth floor, across the street.

"Her?" Jackson questioned.

"Yes, yes, her, she's right there with you, red hair, about twenty-one-years-old—you can't see her?"

No one at eye level could spot her. She moved too fast and made no gesture whatsoever that would have attracted attention to her progress from down in the street up the stoop. Before long, she was at the massive front door, and then she wasn't.

"Has anybody seen Jonah Simpson?" Lionel Abulafia inquired inside the first floor study hall. He felt responsible for the lad, and became suddenly aware of his absence.

"Didn't you put him in charge of guarding me?" Nechama asked with a very large smile. "Then that must be what he's doing."

"Interesting speculation," said the ancient man and laughed in great relief.

"I usually work alone, though," Nechama added.

The master and his disciple grew silent for a moment.

"So, we're coming to the final stage of the game, when all the plotting and scheming and speculating is over, and everybody's forced to play out their hands," said The Girl cheerfully.

"Well, this one is *your* hand, *maideleh*," said Lionel Abulafia. He placed in her palm a handkerchief with the broken pieces of the ointment jar he had retrieved from the cemetery. She accepted.

"Nechama'leh," cried Rabbi Mordechai Gutkind, who had heard his daughter's voice and rushed downstairs. Just seeing this creature of beauty revived his soul. He felt the tears of relief in his throat. It had been a long year.

"Daddy," said Nechama and went up to embrace him, careful to keep the broken jar away from his person. They both cried.

"How's Mom?" Nechama noted that he was not ready to let go.

"She misses you terribly."

"I'm planning to come home soon," she said. He looked up at her in surprise.

"That's not what I've been hearing," he said. "I hear you've become a regular revolutionary."

"I learned from the best," she said. "But there's nothing left for me to do."

Gutkind tightened his embrace. Then, in a swift motion, he pulled a pair of handcuffs from his coat pocket across his daughter's hands which still held the holy jar pieces. "It's better this way," he whispered. "I must turn you in."

"Daddy, what the hell are you doing?" Mordechai's son, Berel, cried.

"Stay away," the Wisdomnik warned him, tightening his grip on his adopted daughter's body. "Not another of you should be stained by this act," he begged, "but I must. Look outside, for crying out loud, we're outnumbered here, we're outnumbered on this cursed planet. If our nation loses us now, a long, dark night will follow. Forgive me, Nechama'leh, but you must come with me."

An emotional man, despite his reputation for strength and cruelty, Rabbi Gutkind burst into tears. "I have to do this, my sweet child," he said to the pale young woman in his arms. "You understand."

"I love you, Daddy," she whispered, and this made the old man bawl so loudly, his voice for a moment drowned out the sound of the front door crashing in. But all the while he was crying, he never let go of her.

"Good bye, my sweet child, I'm so very sorry," he uttered and pushed her towards the front door, offering her to the bloodthirsty mob in various black fatigues and Ninja suits.

When the door swung open, the hundreds of war-crazed faces froze in awe. There she was for the world to behold, no longer sneaking, shifting, hiding. Many hundreds of soldiers at the scene, and those following the events on the comm/link feeds, could see her smile for the first time. There was so much joy in the smile; it was the kind of smile you could borrow and keep using for a long time: In dreams, fantasies, art classes.

It just wasn't a very good body armor.

Across the street, the sniper had trapped The Girl in her cross hairs and squeezed the trigger. The high power missile left the barrel and sank in Nechama's chest at practically the same moment. She collapsed in her father's arms and he, in turn, collapsed to the vestibule floor.

98.

The small body was dragged into the apartment and the door was shut again. The multitudes in the street remained frozen in their tracks for some time.

"Motke, don't be an idiot," a hauntingly familiar voice cried.

Mordechai Gutkind's head rose. He began to shake.

"Master?" Gutkind asked as he stood and turned around.

Everyone else in the small hall turned around to see the old man in the black coat and the wide-brimmed fedora; his elegant, white beard split halfway down his chest with not a hair out of place. His eyes were as blue and as quiet as they'd ever been.

For a time, the room was silent. The master cabalist allowed his gaze to linger for a moment on everyone in the room, until it rested on Nechama. Time stretched. Onlookers later claimed that the two figures were bathed in an otherworldly glow. There was no mistaking the love and trust that flowed back and forth between them.

Oh, and Nechama wasn't lying down on the floor, she was standing right before her genetic father, same height, same face, except hers bore the freshness of youth and his the beauty of old age.

Abulafia rushed to the door to help the lilith up. "You okay?" he asked.

Lydia smiled, and even with her pointy fangs were exposed, his heart leapt. "It's definitely easier the second time around," she reported.

Nechama Gutkind felt a surge of relief. For the first time since becoming the emotional lightning rod of the universe, she was calm. She could still feel the pull of pain and want, but now she also felt a supreme feeling of confidence and love. And for the first time since her birthday, her leg felt fine.

The master broke the silence, "Bring me the ointment," he ordered.

Nechama handed him the handkerchief clutched in her hand.

"There's ointment inside," she said, "I can smell it."

"The ointment is not essential, legally speaking," said the impossible man with the impossible voice who was aglow in the back of the study hall. "But it's nice to have, anyway."

"Master," Gutkind repeated, and his jaw dropped. Alongside him the entire Cosmic Wisdomnik mission stood, all with dropped jaws.

The master examined the broken jar pieces, raising them so sunlight from the window shone through. He smiled in satisfaction and looked at Nechama. "Good job," he said.

"Thank you. And thank you for coming back," she said, smiling.

"*Nu*, you think the world is ready?" he asked no one and everyone.

"Are you *kidding*?" Lionel Abulafia couldn't hold back his excitement. "Jerusalem is under attack, we here are under siege, the Jewish nation is fresh out of tricks, finished, done for. If ever there was time for Divine intervention, this is *it*."

"Fine," said the cabalist master and stuck two fingers in the ointment. He dabbed the cream on his own forehead. "Let's go liberate the human race, *kinderlach*."

99.

When it became clear that the archangel Al Qaedar had been trapped and imprisoned by the Jews, and that Abulafia was hiding in his apartment from the government forces outside, the next thing Samael did was to pay a visit to the master. He had been waiting a long time for this moment. He thought he would rather enjoy it.

Samael landed with an elegant bounce on the muddy plane, one hundred feet from the willow, under the eternal silvery moon. He looked with deep hatred at the old man who was, apparently, crying again—despite recent reports to the contrary. Samael smirked and exposed a frightening set of steely claws. It was time to rip some elderly Jewish flesh.

The two or three demons perched on the bent and flowing tree branches clapped their hands in uninhibited delight. Word spread like wildfire in the netherworlds, and in a few minutes the second largest crowd ever assembled outside God's own choir was there, ready to witness a cosmic-level execution.

Samael grabbed the old man by the back of his coat and turned him around with a quick, contemptuous motion. What he saw next stunned even him, and he was a very experienced evil archangel.

"What the bloody hell are *you* doing here?" he shrieked, tightening his claws' grip on the coat.

"Minding my own business," said Jonah Simpson. "Would you mind terribly letting go of my coat?"

The next day, Lionel Abulafia received a phone call in his living room. He put down his tea and said, "Oh, hello, Marcello. I trust you're well."

"As well as can be expected," replied the Jesuit. "I've never seen Rome in such a state of panic. Everyone around here is running for cover. It's quite frightening."

"Has the city been attacked?"

"No one knows anything. There are explosions and power failures everywhere."

"How's Jonah doing?"

"He's much better trained for such occasions. The man is made of steel."

Lionel Abulafia chuckled. "May I speak to him?"

A moment later, Jonah Simpson said, "Rabbi, Marcello says we're near the target. What do we do next?"

"Yank the old man out of bed, both of you, and tell him to take you downstairs to his special room. Tell him the Jews want all their stuff back."

"He will understand?"

"Absolutely. And if he doesn't, you have my permission to help him remember."

"What is this stuff, anyway?"

"We're rebuilding the Temple in Jerusalem, Jonah—the war will be over in a day, two days at most. Then you and Marcello will bring home the holy furnishings from the Temple. The gold menorah, the golden altar—there should be a good size storage room packed with ancient Jewish treasures. Marcello will help you pack."

"What do we do with the Pope himself?"

"I don't know. I guess if you *really* want to punish him for our two thousand years of misery, let him sit and watch."

Lionel Abulafia hung up and looked at the tiny creature that was perched across the room, on his windowsill.

"Feeling better, Lydia?" he inquired with a fatherly smile.

"Yes, Master. Took off the bandage myself this morning," said the lilith.

"You folks heal so fast, it's amazing."

"We were designed for intense use," she said.

"So, are you ready to go have fun with an old Jewish man?"

"Wouldn't be the first time."

They both laughed. Then he approached the window and took Lydia's hand.

"Let's fly," he said, his ancient feet already hopping above the windowsill and up, up, into the bright day.

There are conflicting opinions regarding what happened next. One: The fliers were surprised by a confused flock of geese that separated forever the old man and his tiny companion. Two: A sudden gust of northern wind tore Abulafia away from Lydia, spiriting him to an unknown destination. Three: The sage kissed the little lilith on the forehead and flew off on his own. New theories will surface with time.

Regardless of what actually happened, no one disputes the fact that Lydia Hoffschteter returned alone to flutter through the second floor living room window on East Broadway.

Victoria Martin waited for her with a heaping tray of sugar cookies and a service of piping hot tea.

When these two females first met they regarded each other with suspicion, if not outright scorn. Yet here they were, ready to spend a pleasant afternoon together, possibly the first of many. It may be concluded that Victoria and Lydia had grown closer and even learned to appreciate each other after the latter had sacrificed her life and the former saved it. But this is not the entire truth.

As their spots on the *Spiritual Continuum of Everything* drew nearer to one another, both women experienced a rare sense of comfort in each other's company, even a kind of elation born from a homogeneity of spirit.

The *Spiritual Continuum of Everything* had been contracting for nearly twelve months now. Soon, when they were finally rid of the curse of the *Continuum*, all things living and inanimate would grow so close, a man could have an agreeable discussion about the weather with his umbrella; and, of course, the obligatory lion and lamb pow-wow could take place.

Between Lydia and Victoria, it had become harder to identify just who was lion and who was lamb.

Each settled into her own armchair and sipped tea companionably until Victoria broke the silence.

"Welcome back," she said.

The lilith replied with a hiss, "More cookies!"

Acknowledgements

HEARTFELT THANKS...

To my daughter Yarden, who taught me so much about fatherhood, mystical and otherwise. To my wife Nancy, who lovingly let me take a year off, all expenses paid, to write. To Lionel Ziprin, with whom I spent many a Shabbat afternoon basking in his beauty and humor. To my many close friends at the Lubavitch movement whose love for their leader inspired my own love and admiration. To Charlie Roth who introduced me to Buber's world. To Chris Kromm, editor of Southern Exposure *magazine, and director of the North Carolina-based Institute for Southern Studies, whose article "The Ghost of Denmark Vesey—Black labor, Southern politics, and the case of the Charleston Five" inspired the longshoremen chapter. To Steve Connor, Science Editor of the* London Independent, *whose 1998 article "Professor plans cloned babies for childless men" inspired the cloning chapter; to Klyna Dunn, whose "Cloning Trevor" in the June 2002 Atlantic Monthly was also an inspiration; and to the Human Fertilization Embryology Authority (HFEA) whose press releases informed some of the pseudo-science in the same chapter. To Anna Bennet, Debby Caplan and Debra Nussbaum-Cohen, who read the first draft and gave it the thumbs up. To Laurie Gwen Shapiro who gave her time generously to add finish and luster. To my editor Eve and her husband, publisher Larry Yudelson of Ben Yehuda Press, who stuck by the work for three years until it became a book. To my friends at the BYP Labor Day picnics and my friends at the Stanton Street Shul for listening to my readings and giving encouraging feedback.*

About the Author

YORI YANOVER is the author of *Dancing and Crying*, a behind-the-scenes look at the Lubavitch Hasidic movement, published in Hebrew in 1994. He has worked as an entertainer for the Israeli army, a taxi driver, and the first Jewish blogger. He now publishes *The Grand Street News*, a monthly print magazine serving his neighborhood, New York's Lower East Side.

BESSIE SAINER. Bessie's "career" is full of hazards. At the age of twelve, she is exiled to Siberia because of her brothers' anti-czarist activities. At twenty-five, she loses her husband and baby girl to the ravages of civil war in revolutionary Russia.

At forty, she faces down Nazi hoodlums as she tries to disrupt a pro-Hitler rally in Madison Square Garden. At fifty-five, she is driven underground by McCarthyite persecution. At sixty-two, she squares off against racists in the South—and nearly loses the loyalty of her beloved daughter.

At eighty-eight, she is still making trouble and still making jokes.

A profoundly optimistic novel about a remarkable heroine—a rebel, a lover, a mother, a grandmother, a Jew, and an extraordinary human being.

Bessie: A Novel of Love and Revolution by **Lawrence Bush.**

KARIMA AL-TUSTARI. Charming, headstrong Karimah, a young Jewish woman in 11th Century Egypt, follows her heart to live a life of adventure. Although unpredictable, Karimah is guided by her own steadfast ideas of honor and tradition.

Devastated, Karimah's father seeks comfort from Rabbi Nissim of North Africa, who responds with tales from classical rabbinic literature. Karimah, writing home to her brother, quotes not only from traditional Jewish texts, but also from the Arabian Nights.

As events unfold, the storytellers become lost in their own stories which begin to entwine and take on a life of their own. The storytellers learn that their tales are mirrors; the more they are told, the more they reflect the teller.

A Delightful Compendium: A Fabulous Tale of Romance, Adventure & Faith in the Medieval Mediterranean by **Burton Visotzky**

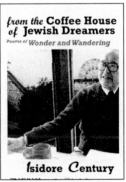

Printed in the United States
204983BV00001B/217-318/P